NOBODY EVER CROSSED
DAG JACOBBSEN—
AND LIVED TO TELL ABOUT IT.

I knew what was coming next. . . . The first thing I saw was Jacobbsen astride a black purebred quarter horse. He was holding a double-barreled shotgun that he rested against one of his thighs, the barrel pointing straight in the air.

"Mr. Williams," he said. "How do you feel now, Mr. Williams? Still high-and-mighty?"

My back was a throbbing mass of pain. "All right, Jacobbsen. Now what?"

There was a thin malicious smile on his face. "A game, my friend. A sport."

"What kind of sport?"

"A hunt!" he announced grandly. "I'll be the hunter and you'll be the hunted. I propose to give you a thirty-minute head start—"

"You're insane."

Jacobbsen shrugged and consulted his watch. "You've already lost a minute. . . ."

Books by Giles Tippette

Bad News

Giles Tippette

J

JOVE BOOKS, NEW YORK

To John Speer,
who isn't. . . .

BAD NEWS

A Jove Book / published by arrangement with
the author

PRINTING HISTORY
Jove edition / August 1989

ISBN: 0-515-10104-4

Jove Books are published by The Berkley Publishing Group,
200 Madison Avenue, New York, New York 10016.
The name "JOVE" and the "J" logo
are trademarks belonging to Jove Publications, Inc.

PRINTED IN THE UNITED STATES OF AMERICA

10 9 8 7 6 5 4 3 2 1

CHAPTER
1

I never knew where they came from. All I knew was that all of a sudden there was a lariat loop around my middle and I was being jerked out of the saddle. I went backward over the rump of my horse and the last thing I remember was flying through the air and then this thunderclap of pain and lightning when my head hit the hard, dusty road.

When I came to, it was a few moments before I could collect what little wits I had left and take stock of my surroundings. At first I thought I was in total darkness, but then, as my head began to clear, I could see little tiny shafts of sunlight streaming through. They weren't enough to illuminate my whereabouts, but they at least let me know up from down. Which, with my head feeling the way it was, was no small relief.

After a while I tried to rise, but the effort was just a little more than I was ready for, so I laid back down, waiting for my body to settle back to itself. My head ached like I'd been poleaxed and my shoulders were sore enough that I could tell I'd been out for some time. I lay there trying to figure out where I was and what was going on, but my head was still complaining to such a degree that I gave it up for a bad job and just decided to rest. Other than the occasional sigh of the wind through the cracks there was not a sound to be heard. I knew I was laying on a dirt floor because I could feel it with my hands, but other than that, I knew nothing about my place of enclosure. I shut my eyes for a time, waiting for my strength to return.

When I felt I could, I slowly rolled over on my belly and got to my hands and knees. This brought an immediate protest from my neck and head, so I just stayed like that, patiently waiting for them to accept this new position. Then, gradually, I got to my feet. At first I swayed and thought I was going to fall, but I put out a hand and encountered a rock wall and steadied myself against that. I waited and gradually my balance returned. Slowly the pain in my head quit demanding so much of my attention that I could give some thought to my predicament. The first thing I wanted to know was where I was. Stooping protectively, I followed the rock wall around three sides, noting the distances by my paces. The room appeared to be about eight feet by ten feet, made of country rock. I straightened up. There was a beamed ceiling overhead, not much higher than my own six feet. The place seemed to be about the size of a root cellar except nobody seemed to be storing any tubers. The only thing I'd run across in my explorations had been a few rocks and a wooden shelf holding several rusty tins of something or other.

Off to my left I could see a pencil-thin beam of light about waist-high. I made my way to it and knelt down. It was the latch hole for a door. I gave it a shove with my hand. There was no give. It was a good, heavy wooden door, and judging from the solid feel of it, it was probably barred with a plank from the other side. Whoever had set out to make me a prisoner had done a damn good job of it.

I bent my eye to the little latch hold and tried to see something, but there was nothing to see, just what appeared to be another room with rock walls. I tried to stick my finger through the latch hole to give it a shake, but it wouldn't quite go through. I felt all over the door on my side, looking for a grip of some kind, but it was completely smooth. Finally I put my lips to the latch hole and yelled out, "Hey!"

There was no answer.

I yelled again. "Hey! You in there! Damn it, answer me!"
There was still no response.

I kept it up until I got tired. Then I sat back against the door
and took stock of my situation. I was mystified—and damn
well worried. I might have been a little scared if I hadn't started
getting angry. Whoever had taken me off my horse had done a
thorough job of it. They'd taken my boots, my hat, my cigars,
my matches, my wallet, my belt, and, naturally, my side arm.
Turning out all my pockets, I found that the only thing they'd
missed had been a couple of 30.06 cartridges I'd absentmindedly stuck in my pocket that morning when I'd been reloading
my saddle gun. But rifle cartridges without a rifle aren't much
good. Nevertheless, I scratched around in the dirt floor and hid
them just in case my abductors planned to make a better search
at some future time. I didn't know what I was going to do with
them—maybe prise the lead out and try to set fire to the door
with the powder. Though how I was going to ignite the powder
was beyond me. There was probably flint in the rock walls, but
to make a spark you needed steel and I didn't have any. Still,
you conserve what resources you've got.

After that I just sat there trying to muddle out my circumstances. But no matter how long I thought on it, it just didn't
make any sense. I'd been riding through, coming up from the
coast through the hard rock country of Texas, heading for San
Antonio on business for my family's ranching interests. Then
the next thing I know, I'm jerked out of the saddle and
imprisoned in somebody's root cellar without a word of
explanation. It was just a muddle. I didn't have any friends or
enemies in that part of the country—hell, I didn't even know a
soul. What did whoever had me want with me? I couldn't have
been trespassing; I'd been on a public road. And I hadn't had
opportunity to give offense because, traveling overland as I'd
been, I hadn't even spoken with anyone in three days, just been
camping out and staying in the saddle. I met a few horsemen
along the way, but we'd just nodded as we'd passed.

It had to be a case of mistaken identity. Though I couldn't
for the life of me get any mileage out of that theory. I
considered robbery, but that didn't make much sense either. I'd
only a little over two hundred dollars on me and, if that was

what they were after, they could have taken my wallet and my horse and guns and lit out. Why bother to bring me to this place and lock me in?

Then a chilling thought struck me. What if whoever "they" were had imagined I'd gotten a glimpse of them before I was knocked out and would be able to identify them later? Maybe they hadn't had the sand to kill me right then and there. Maybe I was in an old line cabin far out on somebody's range and had been left there to die of thirst and hunger? It was spring, and if this was a line cabin, it wouldn't be used again until winter. By then all that would be left of me would be bones.

The very thought made my mouth suddenly go dry and brought on a raging thirst. I made myself quit thinking about it. I'd been in some tight places before and I wasn't no stranger to danger, but it had always been out in the open. An enemy you could see. An enemy you knew. This was a whole new experience for me and, to tell you the truth, I found it more than a little frightening.

To take my mind off it I made my way across my cell to the shelf and took down one of the rusty cans. Then I hunted around on the floor until I found a piece of rock with a halfway sharp pointed end. I set the can on the dirt floor and pounded at the top of the can with the rock. At first it just dented, but I kept on until I felt the top break through a little. Naturally I didn't know what I had, so I raised the can to my lips and took a careful sip. Canned tomatoes! God, the juice tasted wonderful. There were bits of rock around the hole I'd gashed in it, but I didn't care. I sucked off every bit of the juice and then tried to widen the hole to get at the tomatoes. It didn't work. All I succeeded in doing was cutting my finger slightly. I was about to get another can and open it, but then I counted and there were only four cans. I decided, until I knew what was in store for me, to husband what provisions I had.

But at least the tomato juice had taken the raging thirst out of my mind. I hadn't even been thirsty until I'd started thinking about it.

I had no idea what time it was. I knew that it had been coming on for noon when I'd been roped out of the saddle, because I'd been looking out for a nice place to stop and have some lunch. But then, I didn't know how long I'd been out or how much time had passed since I'd come to. I just sat by the door, watching the light get dimmer and dimmer. Finally, when my cell got totally dark, I curled up and slept as best I could. Not that I slept deeply; part of my mind was awake and attuned for the slightest sound.

I heard them the second they came in. I could hear them moving around, hear their muffled voices through the heavy door. I got up as quick as I could, though I was plenty sore, and got over to the latch hole. I yelled through it, "Hey! You out there! Hey! Let me out of here. My name is Justa Williams and I'm from Matagorda County, Texas! Let me out!"

I heard them talking among themselves, though I couldn't make out any distinct words or how many of them there were. I yelled again. Then I put my eye to the latch hole and saw the midsection of a man approaching. I could hear him fumbling with the bar across the door. I tensed my muscles and eased my shoulder against the door. My plan was to burst through and head for freedom the moment the door came open. I didn't feel that these men, whoever they were, had good intentions toward me. But before I could react, the door was suddenly whipped open and two men grabbed me as I rose, jerking me forward and hustling me over to a chair. I was so dazzled by suddenly coming into the light after all those hours in the root cellar that I couldn't see at first. I could barely make out a third man coming toward me. I wanted to fight, but that didn't work out too well. Three against one is not good odds. They hit me in the belly a couple of times to make sure I understood and then slung me in the chair and jerked my hands behind me and bound me to that chair with rawhide thongs. I was sitting in front of a narrow, rough-hewn table. The two men who'd grabbed me were standing behind the chair. I couldn't see them but I could feel them. In a second a big, meaty man in a checkered shirt took the chair across the table from me. By now my eyes had adjusted and I could see he had the kind of shoulders on him that you look for when you want somebody to pick up a heavy load and carry it several miles.

He sat down and just looked across at me. I said, "I don't

know what this is all about, sir, but I believe you have made a mistake. My name is Justa Wil—"

I got no further, for about that time he suddenly swung one of his big, heavy hands and caught me flat across the face. The blow was what you might expect from a hand that was connected to such shoulders. The only reason me and that little cane-bottomed chair I was strapped to didn't go over on the floor was because the two gentlemen behind me caught it and set us upright again. I tasted blood in my mouth. He'd cut the inside of my cheek against my teeth.

"Why'd you do it?" he demanded.

Of course, I didn't have the slightest idea what he was talking about. And I was still under the mistaken impression that an error had been made that could be cleared up. So I said, "Look, I don't know what you're talking about. I haven't done—"

He hit me again. Right across that little table. Not even bothering to rise. Just a wide, swinging, open-handed slap that would have knocked me over again if the boys in back hadn't been holding the chair. As it was, it knocked my head sideways and I felt more blood start in my mouth.

He said, "Listen, saddle tramp, we know you done it. Your best bet is to go ahead and confess. I don't want to beat the truth outer you, but I will."

The man had a broad, heavy face. There was no obvious malice about it, but there was just a little glimmer of something I caught in his eyes. But for all the world to see, he was just a man going about a day's work. Which, in this case, appeared to be to get me to confess to some crime I didn't even know the nature of. It also appeared it was going to be hard to find out, since he seemed disinclined to let me finish a sentence. So I very carefully said, in hopes of identifying myself, "Look, you know I'm not a tramp. You've got my wallet and you know there's better than two hundred dollars in it. And you've got my saddle, not to speak of my horse and guns and—"

He hit me again. When they straightened me back up, he said, "We know where you got the money, boy. You got it offen her. Din't ya? Din't ya?"

I said, "Her who?"

Naturally this was apparently not what he wanted to hear, so he hit me again. This time there was too much blood in my mouth to hold, so I turned my head and expectorated on the floor. He said, and that's when I saw the cruelty that had been lurking behind his eyes come out, "Spit on our floor, will you!"

He hit me really hard this time, so hard that the chair and I crashed over onto the floor before the men behind me could catch it. They grabbed me and set us upright again with me shaking my head, trying to clear the fog and get the ringing out of my ears. I tell you, I was about equal parts scared and angry. Of course, I realized there wasn't much point in getting angry when you're tied to a chair, so I controlled my temper and said, just as reasonably as I could, "Look, my name is Justa Williams and I'm from Matagorda County, Texas, and you can wire the authorities back there and they'll tell you—"

He slapped me again before I could finish, though not quite so hard this time. He said, "Don't smart-mouth me, boy, about any authorities back in some goddamn county nobody ever heard of. You raped her and you robbed her and you killed her, and we know that's about the size of it. Ain't it, boy?"

I said, "First of all, I ain't a boy. I'm twenty-eight years old and I come from a good family and I don't know what the hell you're talking about, but you better quit hitting me."

He slapped me again, filling my mouth with blood. I tried to spit it across the table at him, but my lips were so puffed up that I couldn't spit. All it did was dribble down my chin and fall into my lap. But it did make him flinch. "You told me not to spit it on the floor," I said.

I got it pretty good for that. He hit me front-handed *and* back-handed. On the back-handed blow I thought I felt my nose break. I kept my eyes on him while he was knocking me from side to side. But I don't think Checkered Shirt had been looking into those gray eyes of mine. If he had, I don't think he'd of been quite so happy to slap me if my hands hadn't been bound.

After that he sat there for a while just staring at me. The two behind hadn't said a word. Finally he directed one of them to fetch him a bottle of whiskey. I saw him when he came around from behind me to get it. He was a long drink of water, not uncommon in that part of the country, with a big, half-moon scar on his neck. It looked like the result of a knife fight.

Checkered Shirt didn't offer me a drink, but he did ask me what kind of a name was Justa.

"Hell, you're so damn smart that you drag me in here and cage me up and accuse me of a crime I don't know nothing about. You figure it out."

He was too busy with his whiskey to bother hitting me. "You think you're some smart article, don't you?"

I'd been helping my family make it through some pretty rough times since I'd been fourteen. You can show fear in front of these types, which is what they want, or you can act like you don't give a damn, which just confuses the hell out of them. He'd mentioned some crime of rape and murder that I was supposedly guilty of. That being the case, why hadn't I been hailed up before a proper magistrate and charged? This was 1894, and we had laws in Texas. I wasn't going to give in to this bully. There was something going on that didn't quite meet the eye, but I'd had no indication as to what.

He said, "Where was you two nights ago?"

I thought a moment, watching his hands. They were busy with the glass and the bottle of whiskey. "On the trail. Somewhere this side of Gonzales."

"You got anybody that can witness to that?" he asked.

"Not unless you can get my horse to talk."

I thought that was going to fetch me another lick upside the head, but it seemed to please him and he said, "You mean, ain't nobody seen you two nights ago?"

I was puzzled, but I thought I'd better stick to the truth. "If you'd let me talk a while ago, I would have told you I've been riding cross-country for the last four days, heading for San Antonio. I've got business there."

What could be said to pass for a smile flitted over his face, and I could plainly see the meanness in his eyes. "Oh, I reckon you'll be doing all your business right here for some considerable time to come."

I said slowly, because now I was becoming worried, "Just

what the hell are you talking about? Why are you holding me here? What am I supposed to have done?"

Behind me, one of the men sniggered. Checkered Shirt smiled. He was missing two upper teeth just off the front of his mouth. "Why, boy, you know what you done. You raped and killed a pretty young girl in a house just outside of Bandera."

"That's a damn lie. I don't even know where Bandera is. Or even *what* it is."

He said, "Boy, you soon will know. It's the county seat. About five miles from here. And when you get ready to confess, we'll show it to you. They ought to give you quite a welcome."

I was thunderstruck. So stunned that I didn't even know what to say. I was being set up as a murderer and a rapist. That was why he'd been so pleased that I couldn't prove my whereabouts two nights past. That must have been the time that it occurred. The thongs on my wrist were tight, but not as tight as the sudden fear that constricted my chest. I knew, with time and the proper counsel and a fair trial that I could find some way out of the mess, but if the rest of the citizens were akin to my captors, I might be denied all three.

There was a stove against the far wall with a pot of something cooking on it. I'd been vaguely aware of it and the aroma it was putting off for some time, but Checkered Shirt had kept me so preoccupied with his heavy hand that I hadn't been able to give it my full attention.

"This is all a damn lie and you know it," I said. "You know I haven't killed any girl around here, much less raped her. I've never been to Bandera in my life."

Checkered Shirt said, "Oh, I reckon you have. I reckon there are people who'll say they saw you around there the night she was kilt."

"That's it. They'll *say* they saw me. They'll lie, you mean. Listen, you take me in to the sheriff. We'll see about this."

"When you confess," he said.

"All right, I confess. Now take me to the sheriff or the magistrate."

He shook his head and slashed his face with that malicious smile. "When you write it out. You kin write, can't you?"

"How would you know? You'd have to be able to read to tell."

He slapped me again for that one, but he didn't seem to have his heart in it. It worried me to see how satisfied he was with the way matters were progressing.

About that time Long Drink of Water went over to the stove. He looked in a pot and turned back to Checkered Shirt. He said, "Bull, these beans are about done. Ain't we ought to eat? This is mighty hungry work."

Checkered Shirt said, "All right, Lonnie, if you can't wait no longer. Don't matter. We ain't in no hurry." He nodded at the man behind me. "Hays, you go help him. I don't reckon Mr.—uh, Justa, or whatever, is goin' nowhere."

Checkered Shirt, or Bull, got out the makings and rolled a cigarette and lit it. I was already smelling the beans, and now the smoke from his cigarette nearly completed my misery. He must have read my mind because he gave me another fanged smile. "I don't reckon you smoke."

"No," I said. "Those cigars you took off of me were for a present."

"Well, Lonnie is much obliged. Of course, he didn't know you was bringin' 'em to him, did you, Lonnie?"

"What?" Long Drink of Water had arrived with two plates of beans in his hands. He set one in front of Bull and then put the other at the end of the table and brought up a chair. "What?"

"I was just tellin' our guest here you didn't know he was a-bringin' you them cigars. He said he was carryin' 'em for a present."

"Aw, yeah." Lonnie looked at me and grinned. There was something wrong with his eyes. It was nothing you could pinpoint; there just seemed to be a sort of vacancy behind them, as if their owner wasn't at home. He said, "Them's good cigars."

Hays pulled up a chair at the other end and put a loaf of bread on the table. In an instant Lonnie suddenly had a long, slim dagger in his hands. He sliced the bread quickly and with unnecessary vigor. When he was through, he stabbed the dagger into the wood in front of me so hard that the thin blade quivered for a second. Then he looked at me with that vacant smile.

Bull said, "You'll confess, boy. And you'll write it down. Because if you don't, I'll turn Lonnie loose on you with that frog sticker of his, and you wouldn't like that. See, Lonnie ain't quite right, are you, Lonnie?"

Lonnie had his head down, shoveling beans into his mouth. He said something that sounded like, "Naw."

"See, Lonnie don't know where to stop. Or sometimes he forgets, don't you, Lonnie?" said Bull.

Lonnie made another kind of sound. I glanced at the other one, Hays. He was a smallish man, appearing to be a little younger than me. His eyes weren't kind, but he seemed somewhat removed from the proceedings. He ate slowly and without any great show of enthusiasm. From time to time he glanced my way, but there was nothing to read in his face.

I said, "I've got a mouthful of blood. I've got to spit."

"You better swallow it, boy," Bull said. "You better not spit it on the floor."

I turned my head and spat on the floor. Bull was smoking. He hadn't touched his plate yet. He took the cigarette out of his mouth and said, "Hit him, Hays. Hit him in the stomach."

Hays was eating. He said, "Oh, hell, Bull, I'm busy. Hell, it's just a damn dirt floor. You can't expect a man to swallow his own blood. It'd make him sick. He might throw up, and then what a mess we'd have."

"Aren't ya'll going to feed me?" I asked. "I could use some of those beans."

Bull said, "When you confess."

"I told you, I confess. Now feed me and take me in to the sheriff."

"You got to write it out and sign it."

"At least give me some water."

"I done told you . . . when you write it out and sign it."

I considered. I was going to be in a bad way after a few more days in the cabin. And I had no earthly idea what they planned for me if they couldn't break me down. Having no idea of the sort of law they had in that part of the country, I couldn't be sure they'd ever be called to account for what they'd done to me—or what they might do. It seemed my best chance was to get some food and water in me and then take my chances. I said, "All right."

"All right, what?"

"All right, I'll write out a confession and sign it."

Bull said, "Hays, jump over there to that little bureau and bring back paper and pencil. Then untie this boy so he can write."

When my hands were loose and some feeling had returned to them, I picked up the pencil and looked down at the paper. I said, "Who am I supposed to have raped and killed?"

"A widder girl name of Mary Mae Hawkins."

"A widow girl? How old was she?"

"What the hell's that got to do with it? Just write."

Of course, I was trying to find out all I could about this crime I was supposed to have committed. I said, "I'll have to tell the sheriff something. How old was she?"

Hays replied, "She was a young-un. 'Bout twenty-two or twenty-three. Her husband kilt hisself in a horse accident. 'Bout a year ago."

I wanted some water badly, even more than I wanted food. "Look, you've got to give me some water. I'm swallowing all this blood and it's about to make me sick."

Bull said, "Aw, shit." But he motioned at Hays and the young cowboy fetched a pitcher of water and sat it in front of me. It must have held a quart and a half. I just kept drinking until I'd almost finished it. I would have, except Bull suddenly jerked it out of my hands and slammed it on the table. He said, "Write, goddamn you! Or I'll turn Lonnie loose on yore face and your balls."

"What night am I supposed to have done this?"

Bull's face was getting red. "Fuck all that! Jest write that you raped and kilt Mary Mae Hawkins at her ranch house outside of Bandera. Then sign yore name."

"How am I supposed to have killed her?"

"Goddamn you!" he swore. He reached across the table and slapped me hard.

I could feel the blood start afresh in my mouth. I started to get up, but Hays and Lonnie simultaneously pushed me back in my chair. "Give me something to eat first."

Bull said, "Lonnie . . ."

Lonnie pulled the knife out of the table and stuck the thin, sharp point just inside my nose. He said to Bull, "Kin I do somethin'?"

"You gonna write?"

I didn't see where I had much to lose. I took the pencil and printed out:

> To Whom It May Concern:
> On April 12, I murdered and molested a widow woman named Mary Mae Hawkins in her ranch house near the town of Bandera.

After that I signed my name. I had deliberately gotten the date off by two days, hoping and assuming that none of the three would know what calendar day it had happened. I shoved it across to Bull. He studied it for a moment. "What is this here word? This one here?"

He was pointing at *molested*. I said, "It means the same thing as rape. It just sounds more legal. Now how about something to eat?"

He shoved his plate across to me. He hadn't touched it, yet I still felt like I was eating after him. But I was so hungry, I didn't care. I asked Hays for some more water. He brought back another pitcher.

I ate as fast as I could, shoveling in the beans and the bread. I was plenty hungry. Bull just sat there reading my "confession" over and over and rubbing his jaw. Finally he said, "I don't like this here word. This *molested*. Or whatever you call it. That ain't no word a saddle tramp would know."

All of a sudden it hit me. They were going to take me into the sheriff all right, but it would be belly-down across a saddle with a bullet in my back. Shot while trying to escape. And my confession all neat and ready. They didn't want a live suspect who could talk to turn over to the sheriff, they wanted a dead culprit who couldn't. And the confession would wrap it all up.

I held out my hand. "All right. Let me see it. I'll change it to rape."

My heart was in my mouth while he hesitated. Finally he put the paper on the table in front of me, but he kept one hand on it as if he suspected I might try and tear it up, which, indeed, was what I had in mind. I bit at the insides of my cheeks and then took a tiny sip of water, swishing it around until I could feel my mouth filling up with the bloody flux. I picked up the pencil, stalling as long as I could. When my mouth was full, I suddenly sprayed it all over the "confession," soaking it with blood and water, obliterating the pencil writings.

Then I tried a break for the door. They caught me before I'd gone two steps. Bull was in a rage. While Hays and Lonnie held me, he hit me in the stomach and chest and finally in the jaw. The last blow almost put the lights out. I was barely conscious when they flung me into the root cellar. Bull stood in the door, his chest heaving, cussing me steadily. He said, "All right, smart boy, we'll see. We'll let you rot in here for a time, and then, if you ain't come to yore senses, I'm gonna send Lonnie to work on you. Jest him. Can't none of the rest of us stand to watch. You'll understand once he gets his hands on you."

Then he slammed the door and I heard it being barred. I crawled, as best I could, and got my ear to the latch hole, hoping to hear whatever was said. I could only make out Lonnie, who had a high, carrying voice. I heard him say, "Bull, Mr. Jake says we got to git this done plenty quick. He says cain't too much time pass."

I heard Bull mumble something back, and then they went out the cabin door and were gone. When I could, I eased my back against the door and slowly let my body relax. I'd worked hard all my life and I was a rawhide-tough one hundred and ninety pounds spread over a pretty good frame. If I hadn't been, I wasn't sure I could have withstood the beating I'd taken. Even so, I was sore all over from my waist up. And I knew that more was coming. At least, however, I'd gotten plenty of water out of the ordeal, and none of the blows Bull had given me in the stomach had been sufficient to bring it up.

I sat there reflecting and trying to think. My plight appeared far more serious than I could have imagined. Someone had raped and killed a woman, and they wanted a culprit and apparently didn't much care who it was. At least so long as it was a stranger. I couldn't for the life of me believe that they thought it was me. The tone of Bull's questioning had suggested that. He had never once protested when I'd asked how and who and why. He just wanted a confession and the hell with the truth. Which suggested they might already know who'd done it and were looking for someone to take his place. Could it have been Lonnie? That idiot's cruel, vacant stare certainly fit in with such a criminal act. I wished I'd been able to find out how she'd been killed. Probably stabbed, I thought.

Then they'd referred to Mr. Jake, who wanted it wrapped up quick because too much time was passing.

I shook my head. It was too much for me with as little as I had to go on. And the pain in my body didn't help. All I knew was that I had to get out of that cabin or I was done for.

My thoughts turned toward home. I was the eldest of three brothers. My middle brother was Norris, a quiet, thoughtful man who was slow to anger but, once angered, made a deadly, analytical enemy. He was twenty-six. Our youngest brother, Ben, was twenty-four, and a dandy with girls. He was also hotheaded and one of the best shots with either rifle or pistol that I had ever seen. In a land of expert horsemen he excelled. On top of that he was absolutely fearless. Or "recklessly fearless," as Norris said.

At that moment I missed them desperately. Our mother had passed on some few years back, and that shock, coupled with already failing health, had made a semi-invalid out of our father. It had fallen to me, as the oldest, to take over the family affairs. We held considerable grazing land down on the coast, some twenty thousand acres on which we were running about five thousand cattle. In addition to that we had some interests in the banking business in that part of the country, my father being on the board of directors at several banks in small, surrounding communities. We were no Johnny-come-latelies to that part of the country, since our family had settled there in 1820. So I knew that if I could just get word home, help would be on its way and the whole mess could be straightened out.

But that was the rub. How to get word home. I first had to get out of my prison, and that seemed nigh impossible. But I knew they'd be back the next day, if not sooner, and I didn't know how much more of Bull's work I could take.

For just a moment my mind turned to a beautiful young woman named Nora. She and her family had just moved from Houston to the little town of Blessing, which was right on the edge of our property. In the past, because of my responsibilities to the family business, I had not had much time for the ladies. But in Nora's case I had made an exception. I had been courting her steadily for six months, a situation she seemed receptive to. Prior to my trip to San Antonio I had been seriously thinking of asking her to marry me. I had planned to use the trip, and the distance it would put between us, to assess my feelings and make sure I was certain of what I felt in her presence.

Well, it seemed I'd been given a good deal more to think about than Nora or buying blooded breeding stock in San Antonio.

I resolutely turned my mind from her and from home. Nothing or no one could help me so long as I remained a prisoner in that root cellar. I didn't know if they would be coming back that day or night. All I knew was that I had to find a way out. I was not an unintelligent man, nor was I unresourceful, but I was desperately limited by the tools I had at hand. Not to mention the weakened condition I was in.

I sat and waited, trying to will strength back into my body. The day lengthened and there was no sound of their return. Finally the little shafts of light through the interstices between the walls and roof began to fade. I had formulated a plan, and even though it seemed devoid of hope, it was at least an attempt. I struggled to my feet, feeling the effects of every blow Bull had hit me with. It was an effort, but I made my way across the cell in almost total darkness, fumbling along the walls, until I found the little wooden shelf in the corner. I took the cans off and set them carefully against the wall and then wrenched the little plank loose. My intentions were to use it to try to dig under the rock walls somewhere. I got down on my hands and knees, exploring along the floor, dragging the plank after me, looking for a soft spot. There didn't appear to be any. The floor was hard, packed dirt. I finally settled on a spot near one of the far corners and began to dig.

It was almost hopeless. The ground was too hard, and the plank, which was about four feet long and a foot wide, was too thick. It wouldn't bite into the dirt. But I kept gouging, struggling to scrape away even the top layer. After an hour's work I had only made a hole some two feet across and perhaps an inch deep. I lay back, perspiring and weak, my chest heaving.

It suddenly occurred to me that I should be careful about sweating. I'd be losing water and I didn't know when I was going to get any more. Consequently I was still resting when I heard them come in. As quickly as I could, I replaced the shelf and then made my way over to the latch hole and put my ear against it. Maybe it was because it was night and sound carries better, but I could hear them talking much clearer. Bull said, "All right, get him out of there."

"I don't see how he can take much more, Bull," said Hays.

I heard Checkered Shirt's voice go up: "You jest leave the thinkin' to me, Hays. Mr. Jake wants that confession and pronto. Now you and Lonnie git him!"

It was different than it had been that morning. They didn't bother to strap me to the chair. Lonnie and Hays held my arms while Bull stood in front of me. He asked if I was going to write out and sign a confession. When I said no, he commenced pounding me in the stomach and the ribs. After about every five or six blows he'd ask me again. By then all I could do was shake my head. Finally he fetched me a roundhouse wallop to the jaw with his right fist. For a second I went out, lights dancing in my head. Hays said, "Hey, Bull, you ain't supposed to hit him in the face."

"The hell with the sonofabitch!" Bull said. He hit me again, in the same place, so hard that he knocked me loose from Lonnie and Hays and I crumpled over on the floor. I was stunned but not completely knocked out. I laid there with my eyes closed, hoping this was the end of it. I honestly didn't know how much more I could take. Then, slowly, through the ringing in my ears, I could hear them talking. Hays was saying,

"Mr. Jake said not to hit him in the face. It ain't supposed to look like we beat a confession out of him."

Bull said, "Hell, we'll say he fell off his horse."

Hays sounded doubtful. "He already looks like he's fallen off two or three horses."

"Well, I'm tired of fucking with him. In the morning you bring Lonnie up here and let him work on him awhile. I imagine he'll sing a different song after about fifteen minutes of that."

Hays's voice got adamant. "Not me. I ain't watching that moron with his knife. I draw wages but not for that kind of work."

"Are you back-talking me, Hays?"

"No, I ain't back-talking you. I'm just not going to do it. I ain't paid for that kind of work."

Bull sounded disgusted but he gave in. "Well, all right. But come with him anyway. Just in case Lonnie gets lost. As bad off as this character is, Lonnie ought to be able to handle him."

"I'm staying outside. I ain't having a damn thing to do with it."

"I *said* all right! Goddammit, don't rile me."

Hays said, "Them knife marks will show. How you going to explain them?"

Bull laughed, if it could be called that, then said, "They won't show. He'll go up inside his nose and his mouth and his ears. Maybe even his balls. I once seen a cattle thief that Mr. Jake had brought in beg to be hung before Lonnie got through with him."

He nudged me with a toe. "Throw some water in his face and bring him to. I want him to know what to expect in the morning. Make him sleep better tonight."

I felt the sudden deluge of water hit my face. I slowly opened my eyes but made no attempt to rise. Bull knelt down by my side and jerked my head off the floor by my hair and said, "Time to wake up, sonny boy. School bell's ringin'. Don't want to be late." Then he gave my head a vicious shake. "Now listen, boy, I've tried to be fair with you. But you're just a smart aleck. Well, we'll see how you like what you got coming."

Then he told me almost exactly what he'd said to Hays, about what Lonnie was going to do to me the next morning. He got up, saying, "I jest hope, for yer sake, he don't get excited. If he does, he gits carried away. I jest hate it when he does that."

After that he had them throw me back in the root cellar. The last thing I heard, before they slammed and barred the door, was Hays asking, "Can't I put him some water in there?" and Bull answering, "Hell, no. Fuck the sonofabitch."

Then I was just laying there in all that pain and all that blackness. My ribs were so sore, I could barely breathe. I felt my face. The whole right side was puffy, and it felt as if a couple of my teeth had been loosened. I didn't know if I was going to get out of the mess or not, but I resolved, then and there, that if I did, somebody was going to pay. Whoever was behind all this had made a mistake when they'd roped me out of my saddle. A big mistake. They might kill me, but they'd still have my brothers to contend with, and there was no story they could concoct that Norris wouldn't see through.

But I wanted my own revenge and I cast about in my mind for some way out of the ordeal I knew was coming. Just from what Hays had said about the confession being beat out of me, I was now absolutely certain, if I hadn't been before, that they wanted the corpse of a supposed culprit. So signing a confession wouldn't do me any good. And I wasn't about to let that moron work on me with a knife, even if it meant running straight into a six-gun. Of course, Bull was right: I was in no condition to handle Lonnie. He might, just by himself, be able to overpower me and tie me up. He was as tall as I was, though nowhere near as strong. Or near as strong as I had been.

The longer I thought, the closer to dawn it got. I still had no plan. I'd gone and gotten the shelf plank, but it appeared hopeless as a weapon. It was dried out and light and about half rotten on one end. Even if I got the opportunity to deliver a full blow, it would hardly faze a grown man. In desperation I'd crawled all over the floor and found all the rocks I could and piled them up by the door. They weren't much; the biggest was about the size of two of my fists. Anyway, he was going to open that door with a drawn pistol, and what was I going to do with a rock, especially in my condition?

I was so tired and so weak. I'd also regained my thirst, but I didn't feel up to attacking another can of tomatoes. So I just sat by the door, waiting. And thinking. Though there no longer appeared to be much to think about.

Sooner than I'd wanted, the little shafts of early-morning sunshine started coming through the cracks. About an hour later I heard the front door open and somebody come in. I turned my body and put my eye to the latch hole.

CHAPTER
2

It was Lonnie. I saw him pause just inside the door and call back through. "Hey, Hays! Hays! Ain't you comin' in?"

I couldn't hear what Hays said, but Lonnie just shrugged and called back, "Awright, don't blame me iffen you miss all the fun. I'm gonna put on some coffee first."

I lay back against the door, panting, and no mistake, fear and panic rising in me. The sadistic sonofabitch was making coffee. Probably he'd brought his lunch so as to make a good job of it.

Well, he wasn't going to work on me. I'd die first.

My mind was racing feverishly. In a few moments he'd be taking that bar off the door and dragging me out into that other room. I had to do something.

I was sitting, propping myself up on my hands. Almost accidentally the fingers on my right hand began digging into the dirt and I found the two cartridges I'd hidden there. I took one up and looked at it, holding it in front of the little shaft of light that came through the latch hole. An idea began forming. An idea I didn't have the slightest hope would work.

But it was something.

Very carefully I slid the cartridge into the latch hole. It was a tight fit, but by working it carefully I was able to ram it all

21

the way in until it was stopped by the rim of the firing cap. It would fit, but would it fire? I picked up the biggest of the rocks and looked at it doubtfully. I was going to have to hit the firing cap exactly, and I was going to have to do it in the dark, because once the cartridge was in place, I wouldn't have the light from the latch hole. As carefully as I could, I got hold of the end of the cartridge and drew it out. I put my eye to the hole. I couldn't see anything, but I could hear Lonnie whistling some monotonous tune. I heard him say, "Boil, damn you." and I knew the moment wasn't far off. I took up the rock and practiced positioning it in front of the hole so I'd know where it was in the dark. I sat there, tensed and ready.

Outside, I heard him pour coffee in a cup and then take a noisy sip.

I was becoming fearful that Hays might come in. But strangely, I wasn't too worried about him. I felt as if he were a reluctant participant in whatever wrongdoings were being perpetrated. I had even, at one time the night before, heard a sound outside and thought, with wild hope, that it might be him coming to release me. Of course, it had just been a night noise, and I certainly didn't expect him to stop Lonnie from his diabolical work, but I wasn't worried about his interference. I thought he would stay outside.

Then I heard boots clumping across the hard dirt floor and I knew the time had come. I heard Lonnie sing out through the door, "Hey, boy! Hey, you in there! You ready for ol' Lonnie to give you some fun? You just wait. It's a-comin'."

I peered through the latch hole. I could just see his midsection. The timing was going to have to be perfect. I'd have to wait until he unbarred the door and stepped up to swing it open. And I'd have to do it all by sound.

With a shaking hand I shoved home the cartridge in the latch hole. It immediately got black. I put my left hand on the door, holding the rock poised back from where I thought the cartridge cap head was located. Through the door I felt the plank being removed. I heard, and felt, Lonnie set it on the floor. Then I felt him step up to take hold of the handle. He had to be in front of the latch hole. With all the strength I had left,

I smashed the rock toward where the end of the cartridge should be.

In the narrow confines of the rock-walled room it sounded like a cannon had gone off. The rock splintered in my hand and shock waves ran up my arm and through my shoulder. But even through the echo of the shot I could hear a long, drawn-out scream and I knew I'd hit my man. I never paused. I put my shoulder to the door and began shoving. Obviously Lonnie had fallen right down against it and was in the way. But I kept shoving until I could squirm my way through. I knew there would only be a few seconds before Hays would respond to the sound of the shot.

Lonnie was on his back, writhing around, clutching his blood-soaked abdomen. I didn't pause. In one instant I was out, and in the next I'd jerked his side gun out of its holster and was holding it, pointed at the door. I was none too soon. In another second Hays came rushing through, yelling, "Lonnie! Lonnie, what the—"

He hadn't bothered to draw his pistol, obviously thinking that any shooting would have been done by Lonnie. He was a full step into the room before he realized I was holding a gun on him. He stopped. He was smoking a cigarette. He let it fall from his fingers and slowly raised his hands. He said, "I'll be damned."

I motioned with the gun. "Get your hands up higher and get over here."

He did as he was bid, and I told him to turn his back and unbuckle his cartridge belt. I put the barrel of my pistol to the back of his head. "Do it slow and easy. You draw anything but a breath and I'll let a hole in you."

He said, "I ain't no fool."

When his gun and cartridge belt had fallen down around his feet, I directed him to go and stand by the door to the root cellar. He walked over, looking down at Lonnie. Lonnie was still rolling about, moaning. The shot had taken him just below the belt buckle. He and the floor were all over blood. Hays asked, "How'd you get the gun away from that fool?"

"I didn't," I said. The pitcher of water was on the table, and

I reached for it, watching Hays over the rim, while I drank half of it down.

"Then how in the—"

"Never mind. You'll figure it out later. It's my turn to ask questions," I said.

He shrugged. "I can't tell you much."

"You will, or you'll be down there with Lonnie. You boys have made a mistake, a big mistake. You have picked the wrong cowboy to play your little pranks on."

"Look, I ain't liked this from the first. I—"

"Where am I?" I said.

"You're north of Bandera, about six miles. The road is about a mile east of here."

"They got a telegraph in Bandera?"

"Yeah."

"They got law?"

His face twisted into a half smile. "Yeah, but it's not your kind of law."

"What do you mean by that? You know damn good and well I never raped nor murdered any girl."

"You'll see. If I was you, I'd stay the hell away from Bandera. And I'd get out of this country as fast I could."

"What's the nearest town the other way?"

"Little place called Comfort. They ain't got no marshal, but they ain't got no telegraph neither. It's about twelve, fifteen mile."

"San Antonio?"

"A hard three days' ride south. But you got to go through Bandera. You could cut around it, but that's mighty rough country. And the shape you're in . . ." He let his voice trail off.

"Where are my boots?" I asked.

He nodded his head. "Over there in the corner."

"And my horse and the rest of my gear?"

"Probably up at ranch headquarters." He shrugged.

"What ranch headquarters?"

He shook his head slowly. "No, sir. I don't think so. I don't mind helping you get away because I ain't been holding with any of this, but I ain't going to get myself in any more trouble than I already am in."

"Was there a girl raped and murdered?"

He nodded. "Yeah. Three nights ago, just about. Maybe four."

"Who did it?"

His eyes went blank for a second and sort of flickered off to one side. But he shook his head and said, "I don't know."

Lonnie made an especially loud moan just then, and Hays glanced down at him. "He's gonna die," he said.

"You think I care?"

He shook his head. "No, I don't reckon I would if I was you. You got used a mite hard."

"Why were ya'll trying to pin this on me?"

"*I* wasn't trying to pin nothing on nobody. I was just drawing wages."

"That's a hell of a reason," I said. "Then who was trying to pin it on me?"

He just shook his head.

"Who is this Mr. Jake I heard ya'll taking about?"

He shook his head again. "No, sir. I don't believe so."

I had been sitting on the edge of the little table and now I eased off it and straightened up and cocked the revolver, aiming it straight at his chest. "Do I have to ask you again?"

He shrugged. "Works out the same either way. You shoot me now, I'm dead. I tell you too much, I'm dead. I will tell you this, though. You ain't got all the time in the world. Bull will be over here pretty shortly. He might have help with him. If I was you, I wouldn't lollygag around here asking me questions I'm not going to answer. They got fifty riders on that ranch they can set out after you. Was I you, I'd get on one of them horses out there and get to kicking. You better get out of this country if you don't want to swing."

I considered for a moment and then I told him to take everything out of Lonnie's pockets and his own and put the contents on the table.

He gave me a startled look. "You'd rob a dying man?"

"Ya'll robbed me," I said. "I haven't got a penny."

I backed up to keep him in a clear field of fire while he did as I'd told him. What ended up on the table was a sack of tobacco and some matches and papers and twenty-six dollars in gold and silver coins. I put it all in my pockets, using just one hand. "All right," I said. "Now get Lonnie by the boots and drag him back into that cell."

"He'll die before help comes."

I didn't say anything, so he took the tall cowboy by the scuffed boots and dragged him into the cellar. He came back out glancing at the latch hole on the door. The wood was scorched and burned. "What the hell happened to that door?"

I picked up the pitcher of water and handed it to him. He took it. I said, "Now get back in there. Back way away from the door. And don't try to rush it when I go to bar it or I'll shoot you. The only reason I haven't so far is because I do believe your heart wasn't in all this business. But don't think I ain't plenty angry and looking to get my own licks in."

He moved back until he was out of sight in the gloom. I swung the door almost to and picked up the plank to bar it. Just before I dropped it in place, I said through the little crack that was left, "Tell Bull I'm going to kill him. And soon."

He didn't say anything, and I barred the door and then went over and scooped up my boots and eased my feet into them. My hat was there, crumpled up in the corner. I straightened the crown and jammed it on my head. Next I went over to the hand pump by the washbasin and got a stream of water going and washed my face and drank until I thought I'd bust. I didn't think I was ever going to get my fill of water. There was a half a loaf of bread laying on a sideboard. It was stale and a little moldy, but I didn't care. I grabbed it up and went to tearing off mouthfuls as I hurried for the door. A sudden sense of urgency had come over me. I knew that Hays hadn't been lying when he'd said Bull would be along directly. If I'd known he was coming alone, I would have waited for him, but I couldn't be sure and I was in no condition to fight several men. I hurried out the door.

The fresh air hit me like a tonic. I'd forgotten it could smell anything but musty and dank. All around me was the hard rock country of south central Texas. It was rough country; low-rising hills crowned with rock and sand and cactus. All over

were scattered thick copses of mesquite and cedar and stunted
post oak. What grass there was was liberally salted with a good
helping of brush and briars of all kinds. It was poor cattle
country, and I figured a man would need at least twenty acres
to keep one cow. Still, I knew I was in the roughest part, that
it fell away to good grazing land to the south and east.

There were two horses tied up out front. One was a
good-looking bay gelding with, judging from the power and
the size of his rump and hindquarters, a lot of quarter horse in
him. I stuck Lonnie's gun in one of the saddlebags and then
buckled Hays's gun belt around my waist. There was such a
difference in our sizes that I had to use the very last hole to get
it to fit. Then I gathered up the reins of the gelding. Both
horses wore the same brand, a sort of T with the wings of the
T hanging down at a forty-five-degree angle. Like an arrow. Or
like the way the branches on one of those spruce trees shape
down from the top. I figured the animals belonged to the ranch
the three of them worked for, the one obviously owned by the
mysterious Mr. Jake.

The horse was turning and I was having trouble mounting,
as sore as my belly and ribs were. I had one foot in the stirrup and
was hopping up and down trying to swing my other leg over
when I caught sight of two riders off in the distance. They were
headed my way. Through the shimmering heat I studied them
over the top of the saddle. They appeared to be about a quarter
of a mile away, maybe a little more, and were coming at a slow
canter. I stood stock still, not knowing what to do, patting the
gelding on the neck to soothe him. I could run, but I didn't
know how fast the gelding was and I didn't know how fast their
horses were. Besides, they most probably knew the country
and I didn't.

I kept watching. They were definitely making for the cabin.
I had one advantage: the sun was in their eyes and I was in the
shade thrown by the porch roof. And I had the gelding between
me and them. I bit at my lip, trying to decide. They could be
honest citizens who might help me. Hell, everyone in that
country couldn't be as crazy as Bull and that Lonnie. I decided
the only safe way was to check them out. At the point of a gun.

I ducked low and scrambled back into the cabin. With my

revolver at the ready, I unbarred the door and opened it and called out to Hays. He came into the light, his hands half up, blinking. I motioned with the revolver. "Get over there to that front window. Two riders are coming. I want to know who they are."

I followed him over to the narrow little window, the end of the gun stuck in his back. He put out his hands and leaned against the wall and peered through the slit of a window. After a minute he said, "Can't tell yet."

"Keep looking."

After a minute he said, "I think . . ." He paused for another span of seconds, then he said, "Yeah, the one on the off side, on the roan, that's Cully."

"Who's Cully?"

He turned his head halfway around to me. "Nobody you want to go into business with. He runs a close second to Bull for mean. He's the other ramrod of the gun hands."

"Gun hands?"

"Yeah, we got two breeds at that place, gun hands and them that thought they was hirin' on to work cattle."

"Who's the other one?"

Hays peered. "I think it's one of the new ones. But if he's with Cully, he's bad news. They maybe sent him along to see a sample of Lonnie's work. They like to break the new hands in kind of sudden."

"Why do you suppose they're coming here?"

Hays shrugged, as well as he could with both arms against the wall. "Probably to see if the work got done. See if Lonnie went too far. They don't trust me all that much."

I said, "Will they hello the cabin or just come straight in?"

"They'll call out. They're careful boys."

"All right," I said. I stepped aside and motioned with the revolver. "Just back across the room and stand in the door of that root cellar."

He did as he was bid and I followed him. The door was partly swung into the room. I eased just the slightest bit behind it and shifted the revolver to my left hand. I said, "Now, when they call out, you answer back. And you say the right thing. The right thing. You understand me?"

"Oh, I understand you all right, Mr. Williams. I ain't got no doubt that if I say the wrong thing I'm gonna be the first one that gets shot."

"You must have done good in school," I said. "You are a quick learner."

"I'm trying to be."

"Soon as you answer, you step back into that root cellar. And you do it smartly because I'm going to slam this door shut and bar it and I'm not going to have a whole lot of time."

"Look, I don't know what your plans are, but if you're planning on having a conversation with them two, you're gonna be wasting your breath. Was I you and you me, I'd shoot the both of them the second they come through the door."

I said, "Well, you're not me."

He agreed. "That's true. But then you ain't me and you don't know Cully like I do."

"Yes," I said, "and you could be lying. That could be two innocent strangers or two ranchers and I'd have killed the wrong men and then really be in trouble."

Around the edge of the door I could see him nod slightly. He said, "That's true. Except I know it's Cully and another mean one and I know you're hurt some and I know if you give them anything like a chance they gonna be all over you like hair on a dog."

"You just do what I told you."

"Oh," he said, "don't worry about that. I know my part."

"I mean well back in that root cellar. Back in the dark so they can't see you when they come through the door."

"Like you say."

I cocked the pistol. I could hear the sound of the two horses and the low murmur of two men talking. Then I heard the creak of leather. They were dismounting. After another second, one of them called out, "Hays? Lonnie?"

Hays yelled back. "Cully?"

"Yeah. Ever'thang all right?"

"Coffee's on."

"Lonnie done?"

"He's going too far. Come help me hold him back."

I heard them laugh. Then the same voice said, "Shit, Hays, you got a weak stomach."

I hissed at Hays to get back and then I slid behind the door. I knew it would take their eyes a second to adjust from the sunlight outside. I wanted them all the way in and away from the door. I didn't want one of them cutting and running. I wanted them together.

I heard their feet on the hard-packed dirt floor. One of them dropped a bundle he was carrying. It sounded like saddlebags. He said, "Hays? Where the hell are you?"

At that instant I shoved the cellar door closed and leveled my revolver at the two men. The one to my right was so startled at my sudden appearance that his hand made the start of a motion toward his holster. But then he saw it was a fool's play and relaxed. The other, younger, just stared at me, his lower jaw a little slack. They were just average-looking men, a little unkempt; both could have used a shave and were a little day-worn and travel-stained. Except they didn't wear their revolvers the way a working cowboy does. A working cowboy generally has his in a bigger than necessary holster so that it won't fall out as he goes about his duties. He also wears it high up on his belt to keep it out of his way because he doesn't figure to have much use for it other than to waste cartridges missing jackrabbits and rattlesnakes and maybe to fire it into the air to run some reluctant steer out of a clump of brush he's holed up in.

But these two were wearing their guns low and they were wearing cutaway holsters. I would have bet that the trigger pull on either of their guns would be just as light as they could make it.

The older one, the one to my right, said, "What's all this? A holdup or something? We ain't carryin' no money."

I figured him to be the one Hays had called Cully, but it was the younger one, the kid, that was worrying me. He kept moistening his lips and shifting his weight from one boot to another. He looked awful nervous. He also looked like the kind to make a grandstand play to impress the boss. If that was what Cully was.

I said, "Hold the palaver. Get those hands up. Now!"

They did as they were told, slowly and reluctantly.

The older one said, again, "You ain't gonna tell us what this is all about? Boy, we just a couple of working hands, me and this kid here. Just hired on. Supposed to bring some grub up to this line cabin." He kicked at the saddlebags.

"Shut up. Don't make me tell you again." I wanted their guns on the floor, but I wanted them better positioned first. I said, "Now just ease on around to your left. Away from the door."

The older one said, "Sure, fella. Whatever you say. Just don't get itchy. Around toward the stove?"

He moved, but they were getting too far apart; the young one wasn't moving as fast as the other. I said to him, "Move! Move, dammit! Get away from the door!"

I stepped toward them. The kid was in front of the window, the other was beside the stove. "Now unbuckle your gun belts and let them drop. Use your left hands. And I'd be real careful."

I had pressure on the trigger, my aim more toward the kid. He looked the most likely to do something foolish. But nothing happened, and in a few seconds both belts were on the floor. I didn't actually know what I was going to do with them. If they were, indeed, who Hays had said they were, my best bet was to lock them in the root cellar. I didn't suppose they'd be willing to tell me any more than Hays had and, from the looks of them, probably less. My only interest was in getting away. The sudden appearance of these two had just delayed that. But getting them into the cellar, with Hays already there, might prove to be a tricky piece of business. I needed to render them as harmless as I could. Besides that, I thought I might try a stab at finding out what I could. I said, "All right, who are you two?"

The older one said, "Shit, names don't mean nothin'. We're ridin' the range lookin' for strays with our brand. Work for an outfit about twenty mile from here."

"And you just happened to know there was a man named Hays in here?"

"Works for the same outfit."

"How about Lonnie? Didn't I hear you asking after him?"

"Look here, could we put our hands down? My arms is gettin' tired. An' the kid's been sick." He jerked his head. "Stummick's been botherin' him."

I'd heard all I needed. This, indeed, was Cully. I said to the kid, "Now I want you to reach down and take hold of your gun belt. Then I want you to pitch it out the window behind you. Remember I said the belt. You go near that gun and *I'm* gonna give you some stomach trouble. Do it slow."

He was watching me, his tongue flicking out like a lizard's, wetting his lips. He looked awful nervous. Without taking his eyes off me, he bent down and reached for the belt, which was just at his feet. I'd brought my pistol to bear on him. His hand got to the belt, started to grasp it, and then moved swiftly toward the handle of his gun. In that instant I dimly heard the older man say, "Mind if I have some coffee?"

My brain was trying to register the two disconnected incidents at once. The kid was moving incredibly fast. He had the gun half out of its holster and was diving forward when I shot him in the chest. I didn't see the slug slam him up against the cabin wall because I was already whirling on Cully, expecting to find him bent over, reaching over for his revolver. Instead I found a sheet of brown liquid flying toward me. He'd thrown the coffeepot. I fired wildly, blindly, through the curtain of coffee, firing where I'd last seen him.

Then he came crashing through the wet mess, catching me in the chest with his shoulder. My revolver went flying and my back hit the floor with a thump. He was on top of me, flailing away with rights and lefts. Some of the coffee had gotten into my eyes and I was about half blinded. I held my arms up fending off his blows as best I could. A solid shot got through my defense and caught me on my sore jaw. Little lights danced in my head. I reached up and grabbed him around the neck and tried to roll him off me. But he had his knees braced wide for leverage and I couldn't move him. I was the bigger man, but he was strong, strong with an almost maniacal kind of strength.

I let go of my bear hug around his neck and went for his face with my fingers. Now that I wasn't covering my face, he was pounding me with powerful blows from both fists. Then I got a thumb into his eye and he yelled and jerked back. It was the break I had been waiting for. I heaved with my middle body and shoved him under the chin with both hands. He went backward, with me clawing my way to get on top of him.

But he caught me with a foot in the belly and shoved, and I went sprawling. I scrambled up as fast as I could, but he still was able to catch me with a hard kick in the stomach. I staggered backward. We were both up and he was advancing with his fists up. A little blood was trickling out of the eye I'd gouged. It had swollen shut. My breath was coming in gasps and I knew the additional pounding I'd just taken had weakened me even more. I couldn't last much longer. I backed away as he came on, frantically looking for something to use as a weapon. The kid lay dead to my right, stretched along the wall, but his gun had skittered further toward the end of the cabin. I had no idea were mine was. The closest was Cully's, right at the base of the stove. I could reach it in two steps, jerk it up, and fire.

He saw me glance at the gun and he saw what was in my mind. As I took the first step toward the gun belt he charged. He caught me in the ribs, smashing me against the heavy iron stove. The pain in my ribs was so intense, I almost cried out. He had me in a hug, squeezing me tighter and tighter against the stove. I couldn't get a breath. I pounded on his hard back and the back of his neck. It was useless. Then I groped behind me on top of the stove. My left hand found the handle of the skillet, the heavy cast-iron skillet they'd been cooking beans in. He'd lost his hat in the melee and, with all the strength I had left, I brought it smashing down on the top of his head.

For an instant nothing happened. I hit him again.

I felt his grip loosen, felt the pressure lessen. He staggered back half a step. Using both hands, I brought the skillet smashing down on him again. He made a kind of half groan and then sunk to his knees. I leaned up against the stove gasping for breath, the heavy skillet dangling from my right hand.

For a second we stayed like that. Then I took a staggering half step forward and to my left. I had to pause for a breath, and then I drew back and hit him flush in the face with the side of the skillet. It was a roundhouse swing with my whole upper body behind it. I heard the crunch of bones and teeth as the skillet hit him. He went over backward without a sound and just lay there, his arms outflung. His face was a bloody mask.

I leaned over, panting, gasping, and then I staggered over to a chair and sat down and leaned forward, trying to get air in my lungs, trying to handle the pain in my chest.

I don't know how long I sat like that, but I slowly became aware of a rustling sound. In dread and fear I thought Cully had somehow managed to get back up. Or that the kid wasn't dead. I hated to look, but I slowly raised my eyes. It was Hays. He was kneeling by the saddlebag Cully had brought, going through its contents. I looked slowly toward the root cellar door. It was standing open. I had forgotten to bar it. And now the mistake was going to finish me off. It didn't matter how much smaller Hays was. He'd come out of that saddlebag with a gun or he'd get one from someplace around the room. And I was too weak to stop him. He straightened up and came toward me. But it wasn't a gun he was carrying, it was a bottle of whiskey. He pulled the cork and held it out. "Here," he said, "I reckon you can use some of this."

All I could do was stare at him. I said, still gasping, "What?"

"Whiskey, Mr. Williams. I never seen a man take as bad a beating as you have here lately. Drink some of this down. You got to be hurtin'. This oughter deaden the pain some."

I reached out with a heavy arm and took the bottle. My breathing was easing some but the pain in my ribs was still there. It took a moment before I could raise the bottle to my mouth and take a long pull. It burned like the raw whiskey it was, especially with the fresh cuts in my mouth. But then it got to my stomach and began doing its work. I handed the bottle to Hays. He had a polite swallow and then handed it back. I straightened up and looked around. The cabin looked like a saloon after a bad Saturday night. I had another pull at the whiskey. Hays turned and sauntered over to where Cully lay. At the same time I spied a revolver laying just a few feet away. I eased out of my chair, retrieved it, stuck it in the holster at my side, and then sat back down. I knew Hays had seen me out of the corner of his eye, but he didn't say anything. He said, "Boy, you sure beat the shit outen Cully."

"He didn't do such a bad job on me."

He went over to look at the kid. He was on his chest and Hays leaned down and turned him over. He said, "Dead smack center. Dead before he hit the floor. I wonder what his name was. I never did get it. We had a lot of hard cases like him. They came and went. Depending on Mr. Jake."

I pulled at the whiskey as he came back over and said, "Yeah, yore face is lumped up some more. Funny, I never think of Cully with fists. Just with a gun. I think you busted some of his teeth. Good day's work."

I looked up at him. "Why, Hays? You could have come out of that cellar and knocked me over with your hat."

He shrugged and looked away. "I tol' you, I don't hold with all that bunch does."

"But you were with them at first. You helped hold me while Bull tried to knock my head off."

"I might not have had all the choice you think I did."

"Meaning what?"

He looked away, then said, "Wal', I don't know about most people, but if it comes to seein' a stranger git beat up and gettin' beat up yourself, I'd druther it was the stranger."

"They'd have beaten you up if you hadn't taken part?"

He shrugged. "I dunno. I know Bull don't like me. And I know he knows that I don't like the shit they was doin' to you. So naturally, out of all the hands they got back there at ranch headquarters, he made me come. He thinks that's funny."

"And he'd of beat you if you hadn't?"

He shrugged again. "That or worse. I've seen that bunch get up to some pretty bad business. The boss wants somethin', he wants it awful bad. That's why they sent Cully down here to check up. Make sure the job got done."

I had another swallow of the whiskey and offered him the bottle. He shook his head. I was feeling better. "Why don't you quit?"

"I been goin' to," he said. "But I was tryin' to make it to the end of the month so I could draw all my wages." He looked around. "Until all this foolishness come up. I hadn't counted on that."

"And you won't tell me who the boss is? This Mr. Jake? The one who is behind all this?"

He shook his head. "Oh, you'll find out. If you stick around here, you will. But I'd as soon you didn't hear it from me. I wouldn't want that to get around."

I stood up. "Well, I won't press you. Is Cully dead?"

"Naw. Worse luck."

"I need you to drag him into that root cellar. If you wouldn't mind."

He looked hesitant. "Couldn't I just tie him up? I don't want to be in there with him. Not when he comes to. I don't want him to get any ideas. That sonofabitch would just as soon strangle a body as look at them."

I was curious about something and I thought I might never get another chance to ask it. I said, "Hays, why didn't you take a hand? The door was open."

He gave me a wry smile. "Take a hand on which side, Mr. Williams? Cully's? I wouldn't have had much stomach for that. I wouldn't help Cully fight a rattlesnake, much less an innocent man like you. Take yore side? I coulda done that. Fact of the business is I almost did when he had you up against that stove and was squeezin' the life outen you. But if I had, I'da had to killed him. You can see that, cain't you?"

I nodded slowly.

"And I ain't never kilt nobody before. Ever. Not even in hot blood. But if I hadn't, or you hadn't, then my life wouldn't'a been worth a plugged nickel."

"Rock and a hard place," I said. I tried to heave a breath, but it was still too painful. "Nevertheless, I appreciate what you done."

He was still standing and I was still sitting. He studied me. "Who are you, Mr. Williams? If you don't mind my asking. In spite of the circumstances that you got coffee an' dirt all over you, I can see you dress like a gent. An' you talk like one. But you're about as tough as rawhide an' you fight like you been in more than your share."

I half smiled, even as painful as it was. "Let's just say I'm a working gent. Hays, I'm what I said I am. I'm a rancher from down on the coast. I was just passing through on my way to San Antonio. Until I ran into this mess."

He looked over at Cully. The gunman was still in repose.

Hays said, "I think you better get to passing on through jest fast as you can. Damn, I wish you'd kilt Cully. I'd hate to be in that cellar with him. It ain't too bad now that Lonnie's dead and has quit gurgling, but Cully? Shit."

I said hesitantly, "I was thinking of not putting you back in there. Hell, I keep forgetting to bar the door, anyway."

He said quickly, "Oh, no, you got to put me in there. You can see what they'd think if I was loose. Hell, you might as well kill me."

"Yeah," I said. "I see your point. Tie Cully up. Good and tight."

I waited while he did that and then put him in the cellar with the bottle of whiskey. "I'll turn all the horses loose. They'll head for the barn and somebody will come looking for you." I barred the door. "Take it easy."

His voice came muffled through the heavy door. "You better get kicking."

I rode east and, just as Hays had said, came to the road within a mile. It was the very same road I'd been traveling when I'd been ambushed. At its edge I paused, deliberating about what I should do. I could turn northwest and head for Comfort and thence to Kerrville, which was about twenty-five miles away and get word to my brothers and lay up there until help arrived. Or I could turn southeast for San Antonio, sixty miles distant. I couldn't go overland, not without provisions and water and not without the map that had been in my saddlebags. I sat there deliberating. Hays had said they had fifty riders. They'd split them and send half one way and half the other. And they'd catch me, in the condition I was in, and then it would be all to go through again. Only this time they might just dispense with the formalities and use a rope. I didn't know what nature of men I was dealing with, but if the ones I'd met so far were any sort of indication, I didn't much think I wanted to meet the rest. Not hurt and alone.

Hays had said, with a kind of twisted smile, that there was law in Bandera, but not for me. I wasn't exactly sure what he meant by that, but I had a fair idea. Well, it was the closest and they had a telegraph office. I could at least wire for help, and no matter how crooked the sheriff, he'd have to put me in jail and hold me for safekeeping until some sort of trial. And I really didn't want to leave the country. I was plenty good and angry, and every time I moved and hurt, I got just a little more angry. Accordingly, I turned the horse and started him up the road to Bandera at a lope. I wanted to be damn sure I got there before I got overtook and detained again.

Bandera was a little one-street Western town. Most of the buildings were built of native rock and there was no shortage of dust in the road or in the air. There were a couple of saloons, a bank, a couple of cafés, a church and a school at one end, a few dry-goods and mercantile stores, and a hotel. I kept my eyes skinned for the telegraph office. It was in with a freight outfit. Naturally, the train didn't come to Bandera. Nobody was going to build a rail bed through that kind of country if they could help it.

I reined my horse around at the telegraph office and dismounted stiffly and went in. The freighting company took up most of the room, but there was a telegraph operator sitting over behind a little railing in one corner. He looked up as I approached, a little shock coming over his face. I hadn't seen myself, but I reckoned I was a sight. I just said, "Fell down a cliff. Need to send a telegram."

"You ought to send for a doctor."

He was a little dried-up old man with elastic arm bands and a green eyeshade.

"You got one in town?" I meant it seriously because I was pretty sure my nose was broken and that I had a couple of cracked ribs.

He shook his head. "Naw. We got a dentist, but no doc. One comes down from San Antonio ever' two weeks, but he was just here."

"Give me a blank."

He handed me a telegraph blank and I wrote:

Am in Bandera, Texas. Am in serious trouble. Come
Immediately. Bring Ben. Bring several thousand in
cash. Bring letter of credit made out to Bandera Cattleman's Bank. Wire San Antonio for a good lawyer to
arrive here posthaste. Will be either at the hotel or in
jail.

I sent it to Norris, care of the Blessing National Bank. I knew they would get it out to him immediately. I handed the wire to the operator and watched his face while he read it. He went through it twice and then glanced up at me, a little suspicious fright in his face. He looked uncertain.

I said, "Send it."

He hesitated. "Well, I can't right now. I think the lines are busy."

"Hit your key and let me listen. I was in the Signal Corps in the Army and I'll know." I moved my hand and touched the butt of my gun.

He swallowed, making his Adam's apple bob, and put out a tentative finger and tapped his key. It was clear. He looked up at me.

"Send it. I'll be standing here listening. Don't get a dot or a dash out of place."

"Look here. If you've done something against the law, I ain't supposed to send this. That would be aiding and abetting or something like that."

"Do outlaws send for letters of credit and for relatives and lawyers? Now send the sonofabitch or I'll come back there and do it myself."

Reluctantly he put his finger to the key, holding my message with his other hand, and began sending my wire. I listened carefully. I hadn't been in the Signal Corps in the Army, but the wire operator at the train station in Blessing had taught Norris and I how to operate the key and how to look up in the book for the code that would access the different parts of the country. I was a little rusty on my Morse code, but it sounded all right. When he was through, I said, "How much do I owe you?"

He counted up the words and the wire came to $3.20. I paid him and then gave him a long look. "I know you're going to run right down to the sheriff as quick as I leave. I ain't going to try and stop you. But you might consider I ain't guilty of anything. I'm going to the hotel. I haven't had anything to eat in two days. I want time to have a steak and take a bath. Maybe have a drink of whiskey. Then you do what you think you need to do."

He looked at me, fairly astonished, and didn't say anything. I turned around, went out, mounted my horse, and rode down to the hotel. There was nobody in the lobby except the clerk. I could see they had a café and a saloon in conjunction with the hotel. I signed for a room, paid for one night, and then told the clerk I wanted a steak and a bottle of whiskey sent up to my room. "And I'll want a bath if I have time."

He, too, was looking at my face. I was in no big hurry to have a glance in a mirror. He just said, "Yes, sir."

"And make it pronto on that steak. I am plumb famished. And my horse is out front. The one with the arrowhead brand."

He looked puzzled. "Arrowhead?"

"Yeah, the one looks like a lazy T with the arms falling down."

"You mean Treetops?"

"Yeah."

He gave me a strange look but said he'd get my horse seen to and get the steak and the whiskey to me. I went up the stairs to my room on the second floor.

I managed to get the steak eaten, along with some potatoes and canned peaches, and get a few drinks of whiskey in me, before the sheriff arrived. I'd even had time to have some cigars sent up, and I was sitting there puffing on one and sipping on a glass of whiskey when the hard knock came on the door. I was grateful to the telegraph operator for giving me the time, though I still hadn't managed to get the bath. I yelled, "Come in!"

A voice said, "This is the sheriff."

"All right. Come in, anyway. It ain't locked."

There was a pause and then the voice said, "No. You come open it. How do I know you ain't settin' there with a drawn revolver?"

"Oh, hell!" I said. But I got up and opened the door, swung it wide, and stepped back. A plump, middle-aged man with gray sideburns was standing there with a leveled six-gun in his hand. Behind him I could see Bull and another cowboy that I hadn't seen before. I just turned around and walked back to the table and picked up my cigar and whiskey and stared at them.

The sheriff took a cautious step into the room. Behind him,

Bull was pointing over his shoulder at me. "That's him, Sheriff, that's the murderin' sonofabitch!"

"Shut up, Bull, I'll handle this." To me the sheriff said, "What's your name?"

I took the cigar out of my mouth. "Justa Williams. As you damn well know."

He cleared his throat. For a man in authority he seemed mighty uncertain of himself. "You are under arrest for murder and rape and horse theft."

"And you are about to make the biggest mistake of your life." I pointed at Bull. "I bring charges against this man for assault and battery and attempted murder *and* horse theft. Take a look at my face. You reckon I got this mess from falling off a horse?"

"That's what he says. Now stand up and unbuckle your gun belt. And no funny business."

He looked too nervous to fool with. Also, I didn't know what his role was in this little charade we'd been playing. For all I knew, he was just looking for a chance to shoot me. So I did as he bid, standing up and carefully, with one hand, undoing the buckle of Hays's gun belt and letting it fall to the floor. "Sheriff, I don't know what's going on here, but I advise you to proceed with caution. In other words, don't let that gun go off by accident. I'm from a good family with connections, and I've already gotten a wire off for help."

He looked uncertain. "I know about that," he said. "You even admitted in the telegram you was in serious trouble."

"But I didn't say I was guilty of anything, just in trouble. There's all kinds of trouble, which you are likely to find out about very soon. Those two behind you are guilty. They're not in trouble—yet."

"You're coming to jail with me."

"Think it over, Sheriff. If I was guilty of anything, would I have ridden into town and put up right here at the hotel? You ought to be able to see that."

"You get them hands up and march," he persisted.

"All right. But I warn you, nothing had better happen to me on the way to that jail—or in that jail. And what are these two men doing here?"

My questions made him uncomfortable. I had the feeling he wasn't as sure of his authority as he'd like to have been. He said, "Just you never mind. Now get them hands up and march. And no funny business."

"The only funny business is what's going on here." But I did as I was told. As I passed Bull he barely gave me room and whispered, "I hear tell you is gonna kill me. We might jest see about that one, won't we."

It was only a block to the jail, but you'd have thought it was the Fourth of July parade the way people lined the side of the street and gawked at the sheriff marching me along in front of his pistol. Inside, there was a big office with a barred door in the back wall. Through that was another room containing three barred cells. The sheriff held a gun on me while Bull unlocked the middle one. I walked in, helped along by a little shove from him, and then turned to look back. The sheriff was clanging the door shut and turning the key. I was a prisoner again. "I want to repeat that you are holding me without evidence," I said. "And nothing had better happen to me. I've got two brothers on the way, and one of them is capable of figuring out how to blow this whole town up and the other one is capable of doing it." I nodded at Bull. "Is he a deputy?"

The sheriff looked disturbed. "Well, not exactly."

"Then get him exactly the hell out of here."

The sheriff swelled a little at that. He blustered, "Listen, boy, don't try and tell me how to run my jail."

Bull said, "I told you he was a smart mouth. Oh, he kilt her, all right. I got plenty men will swear to that."

I looked at him. There was nothing to say. I went over and sat on a bunk. They left.

I sat there on the bunk carefully feeling the left side of my face. It was good and swollen and sore, so sore that I'd had to chew the steak on the other side of my mouth. But I didn't think any teeth had been loosened. I felt my nose. It, too, was swollen, but I moved it around a little and nothing grated, so I figured maybe it wasn't broken. I'm sure I was a sight of yellow and black and blue bruises and black eyes, but it was my ribs that mainly hurt. They were all right just sitting still, but I daren't take a deep breath or cough, and I believe a sneeze would have killed me.

They left me alone for the balance of the day, giving me plenty of time to think. But not having much ammunition to think on, I was pretty well reduced to simple worry. I knew it would be several days before my brothers could arrive, but I was hopeful they would have gotten the name of a good lawyer in San Antonio and sped him on his way with a telegram. I didn't feel quite as vulnerable in the jail cell as I had in the root cellar, but I didn't feel a whole lot more secure either. This Bandera and what few of its citizens I'd met so far seemed about the locoest bunch I'd ever run across in my considerable travels. I just hoped the sheriff had sense enough to know that if he let anything happen to me while I was in his care, my brothers would tear him and the town into small pieces and to hell with the consequences.

Evening came, and with it my supper. It was brought by a tense-faced young man of some twenty-odd years wearing suspenders to hold his britches up. He wasn't wearing a gun, but he had a badge on. When he'd slid my tray through the little opening in the door, I asked him if he was a deputy.

"Part-time," he said. "I tend to the jail when we got prisoners, which ain't very often. Mostly I work at my daddy's mercantile."

He started to go, but I asked him to wait. "Look here, I'm most curious about a number of things. Maybe you could put me in the know."

He looked down at the floor. "I ain't supposed to talk to you."

"Hell, an accused man has got a right to defend himself. I'm gonna know things sooner or later. That brand on that horse I borrowed, for instance, Treetops. Is that the name of a ranch around here?"

He was still looking down. Finally he said, "Well, I guess that can't hurt. Yeah, that's the Treetops ranch. Belongs to Mr. Dag Jacobbsen."

"Jacobbsen. Do they call him Mr. Jake?"

"Some do," he said. "I don't."

"Is he the big wind around here?"

"I reckon I ought not to talk about Mr. Jacobbsen."

I didn't want to push him. "All right. Who is this Bull?"

He glanced up at me, just the slightest bit of distaste showing in his face. "His name is Wilton Purdy. They just call him Bull. I guess on account of his size and strength." Then he added, almost under his breath, "Unless it's short for 'bully.'"

"Is he the foreman at Treetops?"

He looked grimly amused. "Mr. Jacobbsen appears to have several foremen. Yeah, I guess you could call Wilton Purdy a foreman, though he don't work no cows."

"I see," I said. "What's your name, if you don't mind my asking."

"Name's Davis. Alvin Davis." He glanced at my face. "Wilton do that to you?"

I touched my ribs gingerly. "That and a few other things. He had some help."

"Lonnie Kritz?"

"I didn't get his last name, but, yeah, his first name was Lonnie. He and a few others. One named Cully and one whose name I didn't get a chance to catch and one named Hays."

"Ray Hays? Doesn't sound like him."

"He wasn't as enthusiastic as the rest."

"The others are godless heathens," he said. He said it sternly, with righteous judgment, his face set. "Jehovah will smite those who walk in the paths of the Devil. His hand has long been lifted against Lonnie Kritz. And the other one."

"Whose name I never got." I picked up my tray and took off the napkin that covered the food. I said, "Well, not to worry about ol' Lonnie. Where he's headed, there'll be plenty of knives for him to play with."

But the strange young man was gone, leaving me to wonder if God hadn't gotten confused in his smiting. Seemed like I'd taken more than my fair share. But, one thing for sure, it was lucky I'd gotten away as fast as I had. As fast as the sheriff had come to collect me with Bull in town, it couldn't have been much more than a half an hour when he'd come to the line cabin after I'd left.

The sun finally went down, but even though I was dead tired

and weary in every muscle and bone, it didn't bring sleep. Worry about my predicament and the pain in my ribs made it hard to get comfortable. The dawn finally came, and a little later Alvin brought my breakfast. I tried to get him talking again, but he just shook his head quickly and vanished the same way he had the day before. I stared thoughtfully after him. He was a strange one, all right. Something about him made me think of a rope with too much strain on it.

The sheriff came in just as I was finishing my breakfast. He spent a little time studying me, being careful, it seemed, to stay well back from the bars. "Ain't never seen a hardened criminal before, Sheriff?" I asked.

"Don't go to smart-mouthin' me, boy," he snapped.

"What the hell is your name anyway? I want to get it straight for when I sue you."

He kind of got red in the face at that, but he said, "My name is Rose. Sheriff Rose."

"Sheriff, huh? That's a funny first name."

He got even redder. "You won't sing such a smart tune when we stretch your neck with a rope."

"Oh, bullshit. Now, are you going to take my complaints against Wilton Purdy and the others or not?"

"What? Who are you talking about?"

"You know damn good and well who I'm talking about. The men who abducted me off a public road, stole my horse and other belongings, including about two hundred in cash and a valuable rifle and handgun, and who held me against my will with the intentions of murdering me. Now, are you going to take my charges?"

"What I'm taking is you. Up before the judge this afternoon to bring the rightful charges against you that have been lodged. Triple murder and rape and horse theft."

I had been sitting with one boot propped up on the bunk. I dropped it to the floor and sat up straight. "You ain't taking me before any judge, not until my lawyer gets here."

I told him I had a lawyer coming from San Antonio.

He said, "We got lawyers here."

"Shit!" I spit on the floor. "I wouldn't trust anybody in this town as far as I could throw a hay barn. Especially a lawyer.

I warn you, you had better not fuck with my due process of law. I've read the Constitution, and even though you think it may not apply here, you'll be surprised to find it does."

He was just a flabby faced, overweight, middle-aged man trying to act self-important. I felt if I'd yell "Boo!" at him loud enough, he'd of jumped backward. But he swelled himself up and said, "Morton, down at the telegraph office, tells me you know how to work a key, know all the codes and all. Now you're telling me about the law. I reckon you think you're pretty smart, don'tcha?"

"In this place that wouldn't be anything to brag on. What do ya'll do here, take turns being the village idiot?"

He got so angry, he almost shook. "We'll just see about you, boy. I'm half a mind to come in that cell and break your head."

"You better listen to the other half," I said.

He turned around and stalked out and I laughed—the first time, it seemed, in several days. My daddy could have told him about breaking my head. When he'd finally get so put out with my stubbornness that he'd just throw his hands in the air, he'd always say I never had to worry about my future, that I could always get work as a battering ram if everything else played out.

But while baiting the sheriff was good fun and a way of getting back, it wasn't doing me any good. He was the one with the key to the jail cell. And he could make it hard or easy on me.

I still couldn't believe, however, that he hadn't even bothered to ask me my side of the story. It seemed as if his mind was already made up and anything I'd have to say would be just a waste of breath. All I could do was sit and worry and hope for the best.

I awoke from a nap in the late afternoon to the sound of voices coming from the office part of the jail. They were easy to hear through the barred opening in the separating door. I recognized one, Sheriff Rose's, and thought I could figure out the other one. Sheriff Rose was saying, as I got up and moved up to the bars to be closer, "An' I say you can't see him, not without no order from Judge Hummil, an' he ain't in town."

"I have anticipated you. I have an order from the district

court in San Antonio ordering you to make the prisoner, Justa Val Williams, available to me for legal counsel."

"Don't care. Don't know nothin' about no district court in San Antonio. Judge Hummil is the only judge we recognize around here."

"Goddammit, Sheriff, a district court judge is superior to a circuit court judge. Even in this backwater hick town you ought to know that."

"Listen, that don't cut no ice around here."

"Goddammit, am I going to have to get a United States marshal down here to teach you the law?"

"Don't you yell at me in my own office, lawyer boy!"

"All right, all right. All I want to do is see my client, and you are not entitled to stop me. If I have to, I'll wire a United States Marshal in San Antonio that you are holding the district court's order in contempt. I think that'll get you a quick trip to San Antonio."

I was smiling. I apparently wasn't alone anymore, and it looked as if my brothers had picked a real wildcat for an attorney. I could just see Sheriff Rose backing down as he said, "Now, hold on, hold on. Let's don't go to talking about contempt of no courts. I ain't holding no courts in contempt— in San Antonio or otherwise. I was just makin' sure ever'thin' was in order."

"Then let me in to see my client!"

The door opened and Sheriff Rose led the way. Behind him came a man in a white linen suit with a collar and a tie, carrying a briefcase. He appeared older than he'd sounded, looking to be about forty. Sheriff Rose told me to step back, and then he unlocked the door and let the lawyer in. He looked doubtfully at the briefcase. "I probably ought to search thet."

"Be careful, Sheriff Rose," I said. "There's dangerous material in that case. Books. You open one, you might hurt your eyes."

He gave me a look but didn't say anything, just slammed and locked the cell door. He said, to the lawyer, "Call me when you're through."

We shook hands. "I'm Tom Hudspeth," the lawyer said. "I got here as fast as I could after I got the wire from your brother yesterday. I did delay to get that district court order because I know about this place and I figured, correctly, I'd need it. I took the overnight stage. Got in about an hour ago. What the hell happened to your face?"

With relief I said, "I am mighty glad to see you. I appreciate you rushing down here. Believe me, it appears I need all the help I can get."

We sat down on the opposing bunks and he said, "I've been by Judge Hummil's office. He's conveniently out of town, but I got the list of charges from his clerk and read them. How much of it is true?"

"Oh, I killed that Lonnie fellow and the other. And would have killed Wilton Purdy if I could have. I believe, though, it might be regarded as self-defense anyplace else in the world." Then I started at the beginning and told him everything that had happened and just how it had happened. I also told him what little I knew and what little I was guessing at.

When I was through, he nodded. "Well, Mr. Williams, it is obvious this is going to take some time to get sorted out. I will say, not trying to make you feel any better, you understand, that you couldn't have picked a worse place to get yourself in trouble. I have never had any firsthand dealings around here, but I've heard of it. Bandera is notorious and is avoided like the plague, except for the ignorant, the greedy and the wicked."

"What the hell is the matter with this place?" I asked.

"A man named Dag Jacobbsen."

"Who the hell is he and what's he got against me?"

"I don't know about the last. I think you were just handy. Why, I don't know. I'll tell you what I've heard about Jacobbsen. He's originally from Chicago. Apparently has a pretty fair education and is reported to be an intelligent and cultured man. I've heard he's second-generation Scandinavian. Either a Swede or a Norwegian. I never can tell them apart. Apparently, when he was a young man, he went out to the Alaskan gold fields and made a modest stake. He apparently took that and went into the timber business in Oregon and northern California and made a fortune. Then he came here. Word is he was looking for cheap land to build an empire. I understand he owns a quarter of a million acres."

"An empire?"

Mr. Hudspeth shrugged. "That's what I hear. Apparently the man is some sort of megalomaniac. He's got all the money you could spend in two lifetimes, and now he apparently craves power. Hence, Bandera. He controls everything here, including the law. Judge Hummil is a circuit court judge, but he has a very small circuit. He headquarters here in Bandera and, I think, answers only to Dag Jacobbsen. You've already seen the sheriff in action."

My heart sank. All I could think of was that I should have taken Hays's advice and tried to quit the country as fast as I could. But would I have made it before they caught me? I said, "Has he got any weaknesses? Any way we can get at him?"

Hudspeth shook his head slowly. "Not that I know of. He's got a son, Torrey, who's about twenty or twenty-one. The old man is around fifty, by the way. The son is supposed to be a slight disappointment to Jacobbsen. He sent him down to the new university in Austin, planning on later sending him to a college back East, but the boy failed in his work in Austin and had to come home. They say he reads a great deal and drinks even more. He's supposedly not interested in much of anything."

"Jacobbsen is disappointed because the boy is not going to follow him in business?"

"Not necessarily. I don't think Jacobbsen cares about that. I just think he'd like to see the boy take some interest in something. He's got a daughter that's quite a different kettle of fish. Her name is Marriah. She's beautiful and she's supposedly strong-willed and hot-tempered. I don't know about her personality, but I saw her one day in San Antonio and I can testify that she is certainly beautiful."

"What about the girl, the girl that was molested and murdered?"

Hudspeth shrugged. "Nothing. She was. I stopped in at the hotel saloon and asked a few questions, but it didn't come to anything. She was a pretty, young lady in her early twenties. Widowed, as you know. Apparently she was one of the few people about that Jacobbsen had any affection for. I was told she was often a guest up at his ranch headquarters."

"Wait a minute," I said. "Was Torrey up her dress?"

"I wondered about that, but it won't wash. She didn't seem to pay that much attention to him. Besides, his father wouldn't have considered her a suitable match for the crown prince."

"You were talking in the saloon. Who do most people think did it?"

The lawyer glanced up at me. "Why, you, of course."

"Great." I smiled slightly. "Doesn't sound like I'm going to get a very fair trial around here. What about if we take this Torrey and hold him for a swap? If his daddy controls the law, he can let me go."

Hudspeth shook his head. "First, that's hardly a matter to ask your lawyer. But second, it would be nearly impossible. Jacobbsen has got a huge rock mansion about ten miles out of town. He sits up there like a feudal lord. He's damn near got more men than he has cattle. Don't ask me why. Vanity, I suppose, but I wouldn't call him a rancher so much as an army commander. I'm telling you, Mr. Williams, I'm worried about this situation. We obviously cannot win a trial here. Our only hope will be to file an appeal as quickly as we can."

"What if they try me one day and hang me the next?"

He didn't say anything, just looked out the cell window. "Do you want me to arrange for a doctor?"

I shook my head. "There's nothing a doctor can do now. If I've got cracked ribs, they're already healing and all a doctor would do would be to hurt me, and I've had all that I can handle. You might see if the sheriff would let me have a bottle of whiskey."

He opened his briefcase and pulled out a bottle of sour-mash Kentucky bourbon. "I already thought about that."

I had to smile. "You're a very good lawyer, Mr. Hudspeth." I put the whiskey under the little pillow they'd provided me with. "What about bail?"

He sighed. "I don't know. Hummil will be back tomorrow and I'm going to try. By the way, your brothers should be here tomorrow, and I'm going to try and head them off before they present that letter of credit to the bank here."

"Why?"

He stood up. "I've got an idea. Look, there's nothing much

more to talk about today. I'm going to go out and nose around tonight and see what else I can find out. I'll see you tomorrow."

"Be careful," I said. "Else you're liable to find yourself in here with me."

CHAPTER
3

Judge Hummil had the unsightly habit of spitting on the floor in his own courtroom. And this in spite of the fact that he had a spittoon placed at each end of the little table he chose to call his "bench." He was a vicious-looking, dried-up old man in a black suit and a string tie. I appeared before him that next morning, in company with my lawyer and the sheriff, to answer to the charges that had been brought against me. The courtroom was just a large, square rock building with wooden floors and few windows. There were about six long, backless benches for the spectators and they were empty except for Bull and Hays and a couple of other cowhands I didn't recognize. No evidence was asked for nor given, and I pleaded not guilty to all charges. The judge ordered me bound over to stand trial some thirty days hence. The sheriff took hold of my arm and said, "Let's go."

"Wait a minute," I said, then turned and pointed toward Bull and, to the judge, said, "I'd like to lay some charges of my own against that man. Wilton Purdy."

Judge Hummil banged his gavel and said, "Out of order."

"When has it come to be out of order in a courtroom to lay charges?"

The judge took time to spit on the floor, and then he banged his gavel again. "Ten bucks. Contempt of court."

Tom Hudspeth was pushing me toward the door. "Go along, Mr. Williams. Just go now and leave this to me."

"Just wait a damn minute," I said. "If all it costs is ten bucks to show contempt for this court, I know a bargain when I see one. I ain't begun to show my contempt for this whole damn county, let alone this court."

But now Tom was pleading with me, and the sheriff was pulling on my arm. Tom said, "Please, Mr. Williams, don't make trouble. You're just making my job harder. Go along with the sheriff. I've got business with the judge."

Once more I got to be the object of attention as the sheriff paraded me down the street in handcuffs. He had drawn his pistol and kept it leveled at my back. When he put me in the cell, he said, with some satisfaction, "That smart mouth of yours is gonna make you plenty of trouble around here."

I sat down on the thin mattress. "You're planning on hanging me, aren't you?"

He said, "If I have my way."

"So how much more trouble can I get in?" I asked.

He just gave me a look and left.

I kept expecting my lawyer to show up, but the time dragged on and he didn't show. Around noon Alvin brought me my lunch. I asked if he'd seen Hudspeth. He just shook his head. Then I asked if he'd seen my brothers. He said, "I wouldn't know your brothers."

I said, "Well, they wouldn't know you either. But they *would* come to the jail and announce themselves as my brothers. I just want to know if the sheriff is keeping them from seeing me."

He shook his head. "I just been here off and on."

Then he left and all I could do was sit and fret and nibble at the bottle of whiskey and wonder where my lawyer was. I'm not a good hand at waiting, and I'm not a good hand at letting others tend to my business. I have always been a man who likes to be in control. Even when I was no more than a kid I was that way. My father made me foreman of our ranch, the Half-Moon, when I was just eighteen, putting me in authority over men much older than myself. And that when my mother was still alive and he was in full and robust health. I guess he figured it was easier than arguing with me on an almost constant basis. He complained that I would be the ruin of his stomach because I always caught him at suppertime to bring up the most complex and pressing problems. But it wasn't his stomach that harmed his health; it was arthritis and a weak heart.

And now I was completely lacking control. And had been for several days, caged up as I'd been. Dependent upon the skills of a lawyer I didn't know. Unable, because of the bars, to walk around and learn on my own the best way to protect my life. In the dark as to the truth. Unable even to see my real enemy, who I figured was no doubt this Dag Jacobbsen.

So I sat and fretted. It was mid-afternoon before the sheriff brought Tom Hudspeth through the intervening door back to the cell area. He surprised me by unlocking the door, leaving it open, and then stalking away. Hudspeth sat down across from me. I said, "What the hell's going on?"

"You're free on bail. But sit down for a minute. I want to talk to you."

Well, I was that amazed. I had no idea I'd be granted bail. "Praise the Lord!" I blurted.

Tom said, "Praise ignorance too."

I was vastly excited. "How'd you do it?"

"They still think you're some sort of saddle tramp or something. They hadn't caught on, when I was asking for bail, that you come from a substantial family. At first Hummil was going to deny bail altogether, but I told him I could go to the district court in San Antonio and get it set and probably a lot lower than he'd set it. The stupid sonofabitch didn't know enough law to know I couldn't have done any such of a thing. So he set it so high, he thought you could never raise it. He even cackled when he told me."

"How much?"

"Thirty-five thousand."

I laughed. It was a considerable sum, but well within our means.

Tom said, "Then I had to wait around for your brothers to

arrive with that letter of credit and get it over to the bank
and—"

I sat forward. "Are they here?"

He put up a hand. "Just wait. I want to get all the satisfaction
out of this I can. So I got a cashier's check and took it to the
judge and I wish you could have seen his face. He like to have
swallowed that goddamm plug of tobacco he sucks on all day
long."

"Good for you!" I smiled. "Let's get the hell out of here. I
want a bath and a shave."

"Wait a minute. There are some restrictions. You can't leave
Bandera Country, which isn't very big. And you've got to
report to the sheriff every morning."

"I'm not going anywhere. They may *wish*, before I'm
through, that I had, but I'm not. I came to Bandera on purpose.
Now let's get out of here."

There was no one in the office as we left. I guess the sheriff
wasn't fond enough of me to stick around and wish me luck.
We stepped out in the street and it was a mighty good feeling.
Tom said, "Your brothers are waiting at the hotel. We're going
to double up. Ben will be in with you and I'll room with
Norris."

He didn't say it, but it was clear the arrangements had been
worked out for safety, not economy. I said, "How are they?"

"Mad as hell. I assume you have some authority over your
younger brother, Ben?"

"Not so you'd notice. He's pretty wild."

"Well, he's going to have to be restrained. He could make
trouble for us. I think he expects to solve this whole business
with a gun and his fists."

"That's Ben."

People were staring at us as we walked along. I felt like
stopping and selling tickets for a good look. Tom said, "By the
way, this fellow Hays wants to come see you at the hotel this
evening."

I was so surprised, I stopped dead on the boardwalk. "What?
What for?"

Tom half smiled. "He asked that he be allowed to tell you

himself. I think you'll be pleased. I just advise you to handle him carefully. He could help us, perhaps, if he would."

We were at the hotel, so I didn't say anything. Tom led the way to a room on the second floor and there were my brothers. Naturally there had to be some joking around and backslapping and remarks like, "We can't trust you out of our sight" and "You can get in more trouble than most men can manage in a lifetime."

But it wasn't long until we all sobered up and got sat down at a round table that was in the middle of the room. Ben was like a vibrating wire or the fuse of a stick of dynamite—set to go. Ben was dark and handsome. He was built like me, only on a smaller scale. He was an extremely good man with horses, and that was his job at the ranch. We'd started a breeding program at the ranch between Morgans and quarter horses, breeding for speed with staying power, and Ben was in charge of that.

Norris, at twenty-six, had gone almost prematurely gray. He had the long, somber face of our father and his quiet, analytical common sense. He was taller than me and lanky, but without my shoulders or muscles. He mostly tended to our banking interests and kept the books and records for the ranch. He had very little to do with the workaday chores and raising of the cattle. Not that he wasn't capable, and not that he wasn't a good man in a fight; his interests just ran to a different bent.

There were glasses and a bottle of whiskey on the table and we poured out all around, toasted to "luck," and then knocked them back. Ben couldn't stop looking at my face. They'd both been apprised by lawyer Hudspeth of all that had transpired with me. Ben put his glass down and suddenly exploded, "I'm going to kill that fucking Bull before this week is a day older!"

I said quickly, "No, you're not! You leave him the hell alone. You see him on the street, you cross over. You hear me? He belongs to me."

"You're my brother. Ain't no sonofabitch gonna—"

I put an edge in my voice. "Ben!"

He subsided. "Well, all right. I guess you got the right. But you ought to see your face. Them sonsabitches!"

Norris put in quietly, "Justa, that was some slick trick you pulled with the 30.06 cartridge. How'd that come about?"

It sent a chill through me to relive that moment. If it hadn't worked . . . Well, it had. "Luck and desperation. If I hadn't taken too many cartridges out of the box when I loaded my saddle gun that morning, I'd of never had them two in my pocket. Then they overlooked them. Then if that latch hole hadn't been there. And if that cartridge hadn't fitted it almost exactly. And if there hadn't been a rock there. And if I hadn't hit the firing cap in the dark. And if that Lonnie hadn't been standing in the right place." I shook my head and shivered again.

"I hope the sonofabitch took all day and night to die," Ben snarled.

"He was gut-shot," I said. "I doubt he went painlessly."

Tom Hudspeth cleared his throat. "We've only got thirty days. We should start formulating some sort of plan."

"I want a bath and a shave first," I said. "And some money. Norris, did you bring some cash?"

He said, "How much do you want?"

"Give me three or four hundred."

He got out his wallet and counted me out three hundred dollars. That was Norris. If I'd said, "Give me five or six hundred," he'd of given me five.

They'd come up on the train to San Antonio, that being the fastest way, and then bought good horses from a trader there. They'd bought two extra so they could travel fast, switching off as they rode. They'd made the sixty miles in under twenty hours, which is flying. I asked Ben if he'd gotten me a good horse.

"Yeah, and we brought your spare saddle from home as well as our own. We'll have to get one for Mr. Hudspeth."

The lawyer said hastily, "Oh, I don't expect to do much riding. I'll headquarter here and assimilate information as it develops."

"You going to stay the whole way?"

"As long as you need me," he said simply. "I may have to go back to San Antonio from time to time for some other matters, but your case is paramount on my calendar."

That made me feel better.

I said, "Let me get cleaned up. I'll feel better, and be better able to think." I'd had the same clothes on for what seemed like a week. Of course, my others were in my saddlebags, wherever they were. I turned to Ben. "Little brother, I don't want to go out on the street just yet. Will you go to the mercantile and buy me some clothes? Jeans and shirts and socks. I'm about a size larger than you are. And buy me a good Colt .42-.40. If you can't find one, just get me a straight .42. You know I like a light trigger pull, so look for that, and if you can't find one, buy a file so we can fix it. And get me a saddle gun. Please?"

He got up. "I'll tend to it."

"And on your way, stop at the desk and tell them to send a bathtub up and tell them to send a boy to the barbershop and have a barber come up here. I don't want to get a shave with a bunch of gawkers hanging around. And get me a tooth-brush."

When he'd gone, I took off my shirt. Tom Hudspeth said, "Oooh." I looked down. My whole rib cage was a mass of bruises, some of them yellow turning to blue, some of them already a deep blue-black. Bull had done an outstanding job on me. Surprisingly, my stomach wasn't bruised as badly, prob-ably because of the heavy layer of muscle I had there, built up from years of hard work. I just said, "God, I smell like a wet saddle blanket."

Norris said softly, "Justa, this should never have happened. And we're going to get it straightened out. The responsible parties are going to be very regretful for this."

Words like that from Norris, knowing him as I did, sounded more deadly than Ben with a gun in his hand.

Hudspeth got up. "We'll have a conference this evening. Now I think I'll walk around town and scent the atmosphere."

Norris said, "Hold your nose."

When he was gone, I asked how things were at the ranch. Norris said they were fine. "We've lost very few spring calves. And it looks as if the market is going to hold up fine, at least through the summer. We're a little long on mama cows right now, and I think we should sell some for beef. Especially the five- and six-year-olds."

"How's Dad?"

"He's all right. He was getting around a little better just before we left. The weather's been warmer."

"How much does he know?"

"Not all of it. We just told him you were in some trouble up here that required our presence." He stopped for a moment. "I don't think he wanted to know too much. I don't think he wanted to put us under the obligation of lying to him."

There was a knock on the door. Norris drew his revolver, but it was only three Mexican boys with the galvanized bathtub and buckets of hot water. I said to Norris, "This place will do it to you."

"Yeah," he said. He put away his pistol.

I took off the rest of my clothes and got in the bathtub while the boys poured in the hot water. I sent them for more. The hot water was like a balm to my bruised body. I sunk as low in the tub as I could get, immersing my chest. I intended to soak as much of the soreness out of me as I could.

Norris said, "I've got better things to do than watch you take a bath. I'm going out."

"When you coming back?"

I'm not the only one in my family with a smart tongue. My brother Norris has a very dry turn of mind. He said, "I'll be back simultaneous with my return." He took off his gun belt and dropped it down beside the bathtub. He didn't say anything; he didn't have to. He gave me a little salute and went out.

I kept those Mexican boys running, bailing out the water as it cooled and replacing it with hot. The barber came and shaved me and clipped my hair while I stayed in the bathtub. He said it was the first time he'd ever cut a man's hair while he was taking a bath, so I gave him five dollars for his trouble. He hesitated at the door before he left. He said, "Bad talk about you on the street. But you don't seem like such a bad feller."

"Maybe I'm not," I replied.

He juggled the five-dollar gold piece in his hand and looked at me appraisingly. "Lot of things go on around here," he said, "that don't ever'body agree with. If you know what I mean. Some of us was here when this was a good place to live."

"How long has Jacobbsen been here?"

"Ten long years. At first he looked like a godsend. Was gonna do this, do that. Bring a lot of money into the county. Make for a lot more jobs. Some of it was true. He did bring a good sight more money into the place. But . . ." He let it trail off.

I finished it for him. "But you're not so sure it's been worth it?"

"I never said that." He put the coin in his pocket. "Well, if you need anything else, Mr. Williams . . . I got some salve might draw some of the color outer yore bruises. You want me to send it up? Be glad to."

I shook my head. "Thank you. But they'll go away soon enough. Meanwhile they serve as a reminder."

Ben came back and I reluctantly got out of the bath and dried off and put on the clothes he'd fetched. I gave the Mexican boys two dollars apiece, and they scooted off with the tub and the buckets. I sat down at the table and examined the handgun Ben had bought. He'd managed to find a .42-.40. That's a gun chambered for a .40-caliber bullet but built on a .42-caliber frame. It makes a nice combination. The bigger frame gives a solid feeling in the hand with less barrel deflection when you fire, and a .40-caliber slug is plenty big enough to provide all the stopping power you need. Ben had bought a box of cartridges and I opened them and began loading the gun. "The trigger pull seems a little stiff," I noted, "but I'll use it this way awhile."

Ben was sitting in the corner with a bottle of Neat's foot oil and my holster, working to soften and slick it up. "I could fix it easy enough," he offered. "I got the file."

"It'll loosen up. I'll go out in the morning and bust a few caps and see how it is then. What'd you do with the saddle gun?"

He jerked his head. "In the corner. Box of cartridges beside it."

The clothes fit well enough. He'd brought me two pair of jeans and a pair of corduroy saddle pants and three shirts, two light blue and one khaki-colored.

Ben said, "When we going out to that ranch and blow those suckers to hell?"

I said, "Lot of options to think about. We don't want to get hasty."

"Seems like they got a little hasty with you. Hell, we got a ranch to run. Let's settle these fuckers' hash and get home."

"Listen, Ben, I don't want no rashness out of you. Right now Jacobbsen is holding all the cards. We don't do nothing until we find a way to even up the odds. You keep that in mind. One of us under charges is plenty."

We ate dinner in that evening. Neither Norris nor Tom thought it was time yet for me to be too free about the streets. Tom said, "Let's don't look for trouble. You're just out of jail, and some hothead might take it upon himself to start trouble. That judge is looking for any reason to revoke your bail."

I had to agree with his thinking, especially in view of what I had just told young Ben. Nevertheless, I seemed to be just exchanging one cell for another, though, I had to admit, the accommodations were steadily improving.

Norris said, "Give it another day, Justa. There's no point in nosing around until we know what we're looking for."

So we had steaks sent up. When we were through eating, we poured out some whiskey, lit cigars, and mentally put our feet up on the table. Norris started off, "First thing we ought to realize is that they, and I guess I mean Jacobbsen by that, is now going to know he's not dealing with some tramp off the road like they originally figured. Not since we paid that bail."

"How much was that letter of credit you brought for?" I asked.

"A hundred thousand. We didn't know what to expect, so we came prepared."

"You can bet Jacobbsen either owns or controls that bank," Tom added. "So he already knows that he's dealing with substantial people."

"What the hell's that got to do with it? I'm already charged. What difference does it make how much money we got?"

Tom said, "Makes a lot. *My* theory is that Jacobbsen sent his men out to find a patsy that they could pin it on and get rid of quick. Money buys time, and Jacobbsen will know that. I think he's hiding something. Didn't you figure yourself that if they'd got that confession written up and signed that you'd never have seen the light of another day?"

"Yes," I agreed.

"Well, what if you had been a less resolute man, less resourceful, less intelligent? You'd have signed that confession, wouldn't you?"

"I damn near did anyway."

"Then all this would have been over and some innocent soul would now be resting in the cemetery."

Norris said, "It's difficult to ask questions around here about the Jacobbsens, but I can't believe he's not involved in some way. He's too eager for a quick resolution. I don't believe he's spurred on by outraged justice."

"They do say he was fond of the girl, this Mary Mae Hawkins."

"Then he'd want her rightful killer found. Not just shotgun justice."

Ben joined in. "I like this boy Torrey. From what I've heard about him, he'd be just the kind would murder a woman."

"But they say he never paid her the slightest bit of attention."

"What'd she think of him?"

"Nobody seems to know. At least they're not saying. I've been trying to find out if she was having any kind of money troubles where she might be playing up to the Jacobbsens. But I'm not doing much good on that line. They won't talk over at the bank."

"What about the old man himself? I've heard his wife not only acts like a cow, she's about the size of one."

"Don't you reckon he's a little old?"

"I don't know about that. He's not much more than fifty, and I hear he's a vigorous, energetic fifty. I couldn't quite get up next to it, but I heard faint rumors that he might have dallied with a few of the ladies around here before this."

"Can't we *buy* some information?" I asked.

Norris said, "What the hell you think Tom and I have been trying to do? The problem is that most of these folks are more scared of Jacobbsen than they want money."

"No, the problem is we can't get to the people that know," I said. "And the people that know are all on that Treetop ranch. That's what we've got to get an entry into."

"How?" Ben said.

I shook my head. "I don't know yet. But I'll figure out something."

Norris got up. "We're beating a dead horse. Let's walk around town a little."

Tom said, "Justa, where did you get that name? It's unusual."

Norris laughed and Ben said, "He was named after a hymn. Our mother's favorite hymn."

I said, "That is a damn lie, and you both know it."

"No, it ain't," Ben insisted. "Not according to our daddy. You ever heard the hymn 'Just a Closer Walk with Thee'? Just a . . . Justa."

"Don't tell the man that."

"That's what Daddy says."

"Only when he's trying to get my goat."

They started out, but Tom stopped at the door and looked back. "I don't want to alarm you, Justa, but you should be mighty careful. I don't think Mr. Jacobbsen wants a trial. Don't have anything to go on, it's just a hunch."

I said dryly, "For some reason I tend to agree with you. Wonder why?"

They left, and I settled down with the bottle of whiskey and a passable cigar. I had my revolver laying on the table in front of me. I'd drawn the window shade and I was facing the door.

After about a half an hour there came a knock. From the table I called, "Come in. It's open."

At the same time I picked up the revolver, cocked it, and pointed it toward the door. It swung half open and Ray Hays sort of eased into the room. As soon as he saw the revolver, he stopped and put his hands half up and got a kind of scared look on his face. He said, "You won't be needin' that. Not with me. Leastways, I hope you won't. You remember you done had the chance and you didn't take it."

"How do you know I haven't changed my mind? How do you know I haven't given it a lot of thought and seen the error of my ways?" I was only kidding him, but he wasn't quite sure.

He thought about what I'd said and then said, "Gen'lly a man's first hunch is the right one."

I laughed and put the revolver down and waved him into the room. "Come have a seat."

He took a step into the room, but he shook his head about the chair. "Thank you much, but I wadn't counting on stayin' but a minute. I just come by to tell you the straight of a few things. You seen me in that courtroom. I want you to know that wasn't my idea. I pretty much done it with a gun at my head."

"I sort of thought that."

"An' you kin forget that horse-theft charge. After I got shut of Bull and them other'ns, I hunted up yore lawyer and signed a paper he wrote up saying I had loaned you that horse and that I was co–co–co somethin'."

"Coerced."

"Yeah. That. Into bringing charges against you."

I said, "Mr. Jacobbsen is not going to like that."

"He ain't my boss no more. The sonofabitch. I drug up. Quit. I'm on my way out of town now. That's why I don't want to tarry. I just been hanging around until I could see you an' tell you I was almighty sorry about my part in that shameful business. If I'd of knowed what I was really gettin' into, I'd of shucked out first thing."

I leaned toward him. "Then how about giving testimony about how I got roped off that road, what went on in that line cabin, and how Lonnie and that other man came to be killed."

He looked at me a moment and then slowly shook his head. "I'm sorry, Mr. Williams, I can't do that. I'm takin' a risk right now, hanging around town as long as I am. See, I'm just one man. I can't fight Treetops. You've got your brothers and it's said you've got money. I'm just one man, and a poor cowhand at that. Soon as word gets back that I give evidence about the horse theft, they gonna figure I'll talk more and my life won't be worth a plugged nickel. I don't reckon you understand what them folks is capable of."

"I don't?" I asked dryly.

That brought a wry smile to his face. "Well, yeah, I reckon

you do. Look here, I better get along now. I just wanted to tell you what I had to say."

He started to move to the door. I said, "Wait a minute. At least have a drink." I pushed the bottle and a glass toward his side of the table. He looked at the whiskey and wet his lips. He said, "Well, one wouldn't hurt, would it? Them roads are mighty dusty."

I watched him pour himself out a full tumbler and waited until he'd downed it before I asked what had happened after I'd left. His eyes got big and he said, "Damn good job you left when you did. We wadn't in that cellar no time. Bull and another hand come up within fifteen minutes. And, boy, was he mad! Lord, he even took a swing at me, but I dodged."

"Did you come under any kind of suspicion? Have another drink."

He picked up the bottle, poured himself out another tumblerful, and said, "Yes, sir, kind of. Bull taken the position that me and Lonnie ought to have been able to handle you. That if I hadn't had such a weak stomach, I'd of been in there when you done for Lonnie and could have shot you. Say, we finally figured out what you done through that latch hole. That was a pretty good little trick, Mr. Williams." He took a healthy swallow of his whiskey. "Anyway, Bull wadn't a damn bit happy with me. Then we went straight into town, and that's why I never had no chance to get out of givin' evidence against you."

"What about Cully?"

He shook his head slowly. "I tell you, you done some job on him. The hand that come with Bull had to help him back to the ranch. An' pack that young one you kilt. I reckon Jacobbsen ain't real happy right now."

"What will you do now?"

He shrugged. "I don't know. Ride until I'm clear of this country. Look for work."

"You any good with cattle?"

He made a wry face. "That's what I thought I hired on at Treetops for. It's what I done all my life. I should have knowed they was a catch."

"A catch?"

"The kind of wages they was payin'. Ain't nobody pays that kind of money for working cattle. I just never thought I'd be hired to hold somebody whilst they got the hell beat out of them."

I thought a bit. "You want a job on our ranch? Strictly working cattle? But it pays better wages than most. Sixty dollars a month and found. If you do, I'll make out a note to our foreman down there. It's in Matagorda County. Six days' ride from here."

The strangest expression came over his face. He looked at me and blinked. "You'd do that for me? You'd hire me, after all what . . ."

"Yes," I said. "I figure I owe you. If you hadn't been the man you are . . ." I let it go at that. There was no point in embarrassing him.

He swallowed. "You'd hire me? Even after what I helped them do to you?"

"I don't think your heart was in it."

He said softly, "Well, I'll be damned." Then, before I could say a word, he'd slipped through the door, closing it behind him, and disappeared. I poured myself a drink and sat there. Hudspeth had told me to handle him carefully. Apparently, I hadn't done a very good job. When the others came back, I told them about it. Nobody said much of anything or had anything to report. We went to bed.

It was early the next morning when the tap came at the door. I was at a table against the back wall washing my face in the basin. Ben was sitting on his bed yawning. I yelled, "Come in." I knew it wasn't Norris on Tom Hudspeth because our rooms had a connecting door. There was a mirror on the wall and I glanced up and saw Hays sidling in. I turned around. Ben had pulled up a revolver and was holding it, leveled at the door. "Hays, this is my brother Ben," I said. "Ben, this is Ray Hays. Put the gun down." I dried my face. "Sit down, Hays. We've sent for coffee. You look like you could use some. It ought to be up in a minute. Ben, go tell Norris and lawyer Hudspeth to get in here."

Ben got up, but he was looking at Hays.

"Go along, Ben, like you were told," I said. "Don't worry about Hays. He's a friend." When Ben was gone, I sat down at the round table and Hays gingerly took a seat opposite. "You look mighty grubby, like you slept in your clothes."

"I did," he said. "I laid up in the brush out of town. Spent most of the night thinking. You wasn't joshing about that job?"

I shook my head. "No."

"Why would you give me a job?"

I shrugged. "We can always use good hands. You look like a cowman to me."

That same strange expression came over his face again. It seemed to be equal parts disbelief and gratitude. He sat there a moment, considering. Finally, he kind of sighed. "Like I told you, I spent most of the night thinking. I believe I will take that job. But I'd like to start here. What's the name of the outfit again?"

"The Half-Moon."

"Then I'd like to start working for the Half-Moon right here. I believe I can be of some help. That is, if it's all right with you. I take it you're the boss."

"I am," I said. "But I ought to tell you that the work around here might be a little dangerous."

He said dryly, "I probably know that better'n you do. I thought on it. I ain't got an extra amount of grit, but I got a little sand. I don't know if I got enough to have done what you did. If it had been me, I'd of cut and run as soon as I got out of that line cabin. But I'll stick. If I go to losing my nerve, I'll tell you."

"Fair enough."

"One thing . . ." He looked down at the table.

"What?"

"Wonder if I could draw a few dollars on my wages. You taken the last four dollars I had."

I laughed and dug in my pocket and gave him two tens. "You'll sleep up here with us. From now on we all stay together. Nobody goes out by themselves."

"That sounds mighty good to me," he said.

The others came in and we had coffee and then breakfast and then, when that was cleared away, we set a bottle of whiskey in the middle of the table and began to talk. Tom Hudspeth did the majority of it, questioning Hays in a gentle, subtle way. It seemed to me that Hays answered as truthfully as he could. The upshot of it was that he laid it out pretty much as we'd had it figured. The only part he didn't know about was my being roped off my horse. He said, "Naw, I didn't have no hand in that. That was Bull and Lonnie's work. They stored you in that line camp and went back to report to Mr. Jacobbsen. I just happened to be around ranch headquarters and they took me along for extra help. All Bull told me was that they'd caught the man who'd killed Mrs. Hawkins and our orders were to get a confession out of him."

"If Bull had got a confession, would I have been taken into the sheriff alive?" I asked. "Or would Bull have taken me out to the road and put a bullet in my back?"

He looked down. "I can't say for sure, but that was the way I was reading it." He smiled slightly. "That was a pretty good trick, you spittin' blood all over that paper. Lord, that made Bull mad."

"What happened after ya'll left that first time?"

Hays said, "We went in to report to Mr. Jacobbsen. Seen him on the porch of the ranch house. He likes to call it the mansion, though. Bull told him what had happened and he got angry and cut Bull across the neck with his quirt. He said we was to go back and get that confession or else to turn Lonnie loose on you."

Norris said, "Why would he keep somebody like this Lonnie around? He was obviously a sadistic moron."

"I don't know what that one word means, but he was a moron, all right. A mean moron. See, you got to understand about Mr. Jacobbsen. He ain't no moron, but I figure him to be meaner than Lonnie."

"How so?"

"The dogs, for one thing. He keeps a bunch of fighting dogs and he matches 'em every once in a while. Just for his own pleasure. I mean his own. Nobody else gets to watch. Not that I would want to. He's got one hand out there whose only job is to feed and train them fightin' dogs. Then there's a standing reward for anybody that can capture a bear alive. When he gets one in, if it's a good enough size, he puts it in this little enclosure with a bull and lets 'em fight it out. An' he's the only one that watches." Hays suddenly stopped. "Naw, I shouldn't say that. That's wrong. Sometimes he makes Torrey watch. That and the dogfighting both. I forgot about that."

Norris said, "He *makes* him watch?"

"Well, I'm not altogether sure about how it works. Torrey goes, but whether he goes willin', I couldn't say. See, he's always got this sulled-up look on his face. Never smiles, never laughs. Looks the same all the time. Ain't no way to know what that boy is thinking."

"Anything else?"

Hays hesitated. "I kind of hate to tell this," he said. "It never happened to me, but I seen it."

"Seen what?"

"Sometimes he whips the men."

"What? You mean with a whip?"

"Yes, sir. Shirt off, hands tied to a snubbing post. He gives 'em however many licks he thinks they got comin' for whatever it was they done."

We all stared at each other. Finally Ben burst out with "Why would a man stand for it?"

"Because of the money. Mr. Jacobbsen pays double and triple wages, depending on your job. Some of the men just figure it's worth it. You don't got to take it. You can quit. But you got to take it if you want to stay on the payroll."

Ben leaned back in his chair. "Shit!"

We talked some more, and finally, lawyer Hudspeth sighed, sat back, and said, "Well, with Hays's testimony we can get you out of the killing of Lonnie on self-defense. I don't know how much good his testimony about what went on in the line cabin will help. Certainly on appeal, but not in the first trial. And I don't know what he can do to help with the real danger: the charges of rape and murder."

Hays shook his head. "No, sir, I can't do you much good there. You can bet that they'll be three of four hands that will get up in court and swear that they seen Mr. Williams around Mrs. Hawkins's place. And Bull is gonna swear he caught him running from there and chased him and caught him. That'll be the size of it."

"Yes," Hudspeth said. "I'm afraid it is."

Ben said, "I still like that Torrey for the rape. It sounds like him. But everybody says he never went near the woman."

"Who says that?" asked Hayes.

Ben looked at him. "Everybody we've talked to. Says he wasn't interested and neither was she."

"Damn if that's so," Hays said. "I've seen him ride down there of a night half a dozen times. And when I'd be out working night pasture or coming back from town, I've seen him leaving before dawn."

We all looked at him.

He said, "An' that ain't all. I've seen the old man do the same."

"Dag Jacobbsen?"

"The very same."

"They were both fuckin' her?"

"Well, I don't know what they was doin' in there, but whatever they was at, they took a considerable time doing it."

We looked at each other. Norris said slowly, "Well, that more or less explains why they were in such a hurry to set somebody up. Stop any looking around. A dead culprit." He looked over at me. "You're more of a threat to them now than ever."

I turned to Hays. "But why me? You got any idea?"

He shook his head. "Just what Bull said. I think it was because you was the first stranger along the road. I knowed after that first beating you took that you wasn't the kind would have done no rape and murder. And I reckon Bull knowed too. Except he didn't care. Mr. Williams, I tried to get out of going back that night. I even tried to get him to quit hitting you in the face."

"I heard you," I said.

"And for what it's worth, and I don't reckon you'll believe this, I wasn't going to let Lonnie go too far. I'd of stopped him."

I believed that, too, though I didn't say so. Instead I said,

"So, by now Jacobbsen knows he's got the wrong man. What do you think that'll make him do?"

Hays said simply, "Try all the harder to pin it on you. He's got to pin it on somebody, and I don't reckon he'll want to start all over again."

"That's just dandy," Norris said bitterly.

Tom Hudspeth got up from the table and walked to the window and looked out. "It's hard to believe a thing like this can happen in this day and age. I have got to think of a way to bring a federal marshal into this."

Ben said, "What we've got to think of is a way to get on that ranch and get our hands on the old man or the son."

"What about the daughter, this Marriah?" I asked Hays.

He cocked his head. "Damnedest-looking woman you ever saw. Ain't a hand on that ranch wouldn't give a year's pay to get a sniff of her."

"That's not what I mean. What's she like?"

"Oh." He thought a moment. "Naturally, I don't know much about her. She kind of holds herself aloof. But I reckon, just from what little I've seen, that she's the best of the bunch. I don't think she holds with a lot that goes on at that ranch. I think she hates Jacobbsen."

"What makes you think that?"

He shrugged. "Nothing much. I just overheard her yelling at him a few times. The way I've seen her look at him. Heard her call him a coward one time. Little things."

At the window Hudspeth said, "Justa."

"What?"

"If you want to get a look at the lady in question, here she is. Standing in front of the mercantile."

I crossed the room. While Tom held the curtain aside I looked down into the street. She was standing on the board-walk beside an ornate carriage, obviously waiting for someone. That she was beautiful there could be no doubt. She was wearing a simple, light, lemon-colored frock that went well with the wild yellow of her hair. Even from the distance I could see the lightly tanned evenness of her features and the near perfection of her figure. But, more than her looks, there was a certain distinction about her that I put down to pride or arrogance. I could see people passing, the men lifting their hats, the women speaking. She gave each a barely perceptible nod. "Thinks enough of herself," I said.

Hudspeth said, "Or she might not think so much of her present company."

About that time a man, obviously a ranch hand, came out of the mercantile with a load of packages. He put them in the carriage, helped Marriah in, then got on the driver's seat and gathered in the reins. I watched until they'd disappeared out of town. When I turned back into the room, I said, "Well, at least I've seen the enemy. Part of it anyway."

"Maybe she won't turn out to be the enemy, Justa," Tom said.

I just gave him a look, thinking my own thoughts.

CHAPTER
4

Hays was readily accepted by the others, with only Ben seeming to have any reservations. But that was just Ben; in a tight place he never really trusted anyone outside of the family. I told him, "Look, you'd have to have been in that cabin with me to understand what Hays did. I know it don't sound like much telling it in a hotel room, but he took some chances. I know for a fact that the last time Bull hit me in the face, he let me go so I could ride with the blow. Otherwise it would have been much worse."

Consequently, when I decided to make my first venture on the street, it was Hays, along with Ben, that I took to back me. This was nothing against Norris. I have said he was a good man in a fight. But Hays knew the town and knew the people and would be better prepared to warn me of any impending conflict.

We set out in the early evening, just when a crowd would be collecting, and went in the first of the three saloons in town. Hays asked, almost deferentially, what I had in mind. I answered him truthfully, "I don't know, Ray. I'm just testing the waters. Likely I will meet some of my future jurors. I want to get a look at them."

We were walking down the line of men at the bar. Heads

turned as we passed, but no one said a word. My face had
improved some, but it still bore the ravages of Bull's work.
Anyway, there'd be little doubt that I'd be recognized, not after
all the parades the sheriff had led me on through the town.

When we were seated at a table in the back, Ben said,
"Justa, you're not seriously ever going to let them get you in
their damn courtroom, are you?"

"Not if I can help it," I said.

We sat there and then Hays said, hesitantly, "I reckon I
better go to the bar and get us a bottle. I don't reckon
anybody's going to come serve us." He started to rise, but Ben
put out a hand and stopped him.

"Ben, take it easy. We don't want to start any trouble." I
could see his eyes getting that certain look.

"The bastards will come to this table. I'll see to that."

I put my hand on his arm. "Look, you're not out on bail.
Now set." Out of the corner of my eye I could see that Hays
had half risen. He was giving me a questioning look. I nodded.

Ben watched him go to the bar. He said, "I'll take it this one
time. I'm telling you, big brother, this place is starting to piss
me off."

We had a few drinks, just looking around and listening. We
got some looks, but nothing more than that happened. Not that
I was expecting it to. I didn't figure Jacobbsen thought me fool
enough that I could be provoked right there in town in a public
place.

But I was proven wrong. As we were leaving the second
saloon, the very last man at the bar muttered something about
". . . murderin' swine runnin' loose on the streets." Hays
was leading the way, Ben was last, and I was in the middle. I
turned, but too late. Ben had already whirled and hit the man
with a hard, overhead right. It had dropped him to his knees by
the brass rail, amid the spilled beer and the tobacco spit. Then
Ben kicked him in the face. The man went over backward. I
immediately drew my revolver. To my right I could see Hays
doing the same. The saloon had gotten very quiet. Men were
stopped in mid-action as if by the powder flash of a photog-
rapher's camera. Some with drinks halfway to their mouths,
some in the midst of speaking to their neighbor, some with a

hand of cards half arranged. We faced them. Ben said, "Any of you other bastards want some of the same?"

I could see the back of his neck. Even under the deep tan I could see the anger. He, too, had drawn his pistol.

I said, "Who is this man? Who does he work for?"

The bartender came to our end. "Look here, you clear out. I don't want any trouble in here. Just clear out and stay out. Or I'm calling the law."

I pointed my question at him. "You tell me who this man works for and we'll go."

But it wasn't the bartender who answered, it was the man next in line. He was tall and heavy and his gun was not set up like that of a range cowboy. It was the rig of a man who knew how, and who often used a handgun. Something a working cowboy was seldom called upon to do. He stared me in the eye. He said, "He works for Treetops." Then he jerked his head back along the bar. "Jest like most of the men here. What about it?"

"Tell your boss I want to meet him, and soon."

The man laughed, but without much joy in it. "Oh, I think you'll be seeing Bull first. He said if I saw you to remind you that ya'll ought to have a meeting."

"Tell him to come in to town."

The man glanced to my side and said, "Well, Hays, I see you've fixed yourself good. I hope they give you to me. I never did much like your ass anyway. There was always a little bit of the girl in you. I bet you crawl real easy."

Hays said, "Shut your mouth, Taggert. You come near me and I'll send you home across your saddle."

"Shut up, Ray. Let's get out of here," I said. I glanced down at the man on the floor. He was starting to come around. We backed for the door. Nobody moved and nobody said a word.

Outside, I put away my revolver and said, "This ain't going to get us nowhere. It'll be the same every time. I've got to get at Jacobbsen. That's the only way."

"What about this Bull fellow?" asked Ben.

I shrugged. "Situation I'm in, I can't go after him. He's got to come for me, so it's a clear case of self-defense."

"Boss, he knows that. Or Jacobbsen does. So he's not going

to do it. He might waylay you on the road somewhere, but he's not going to come into town and start a fight."

"I know," I said.

For two days I did nothing except sit and think, drink a little whiskey, eat, smoke some cigars, and do more thinking. Hays mostly stayed with me while my brothers and lawyer Hudspeth scouted the town for any information they could get. Tom said what we all already knew: "Look, we're going to have to find out who actually killed that girl. That's the only way I feel we can be absolutely sure of getting you off."

But Norris said, "The problem is that more than likely it was one of the Jacobbsens. That's the obvious reason for their unseemly haste in choosing Justa. But defining the problem brings us no nearer to solving it."

At that point I said, "Look, I think everybody in this room had better get it straight what my intentions are. Of course I want off those charges. But that ain't my main direction. I am compelled to go after Jacobbsen. I intend to smash him. I figure, in the doing, that we'll turn up the real culprit, but my plan is to bust Jacobbsen's ass. You can call me vindictive if you like, but either way, that man is going to wish he'd never, ever fucked with me. I'm going to finish him off, and that Bull and anybody else that gets in the way."

Nobody said anything for a moment after I finished. Finally, Tom Hudspeth sighed. "Justa, I suppose I can understand how you feel even though I didn't go through what you did. But as your lawyer, I've got to advise you that taking that attitude is not going to help your case. We've only got three weeks to your trial and we've got to concentrate on exonerating you."

"I don't blame him," Ben said. "I think we ought to get up in those hills around the ranch house and pick off anything that moves with rifles."

Hays said, "It could be done. I know ways to get us on the ranch."

But Norris said, "Let's not talk foolish. Justa is angry, but he's been angry before. He'll get over it and begin thinking like himself."

I gave him a look. "Norris, I *am* thinking. And I'm not

angry. I'm just determined. Don't start talking like a banker. There'll be no compromises on this matter. Now, let's all get to bed."

Next day, I wandered over to the mercantile. I took Hays along with me and left him stationed at the door. Alvin seemed to be one of the few people in town who would talk with me and I wanted a quiet word with him about Marriah Jacobbsen's comings and goings. She'd been in my mind a good deal lately; not because of her beauty, though I was not unaware of that, but because I'd come to the half-baked idea that she might provide me with some sort of entry to her father.

I found Alvin in the back sacking dried beans in ten-pound lots. He didn't look up from his work as I came to him and said hello. He just said, "I'm busy back here. My father's up front if you've come to buy."

"No, I just wanted to pass a few words with you."

Still without looking up, he said, "Ain't got no words to pass with you, Mr. Williams. I'm partly an officer of the law here, an' I ain't supposed to talk to you even if I wanted to, which I don't."

"That's where you got it wrong," I said. "It's because you're an officer of the law that you *have* to talk to me. You've got to make every bit of evidence that the law holds available to me. If you won't take my word for it, I'll get my lawyer to bring a writ against you. But I'd rather do it in a friendly manner, seeing as you're one of the few hereabouts that have treated me civilly and I bear you no ill will."

He put a sack of beans on the scale, studied the pointer, and then added a slow stream from a scoop until the needle came to rest exactly on ten pounds. Then he tied the bag off with string and set it aside with the others he'd already finished. It was hot in the back and his hair was down over his forehead in a damp cluster.

I said, "I can see by the way you sack beans that you're a fair man."

He looked around at me. "I ain't got nothing to tell you, Mr. Williams. Just leave me be."

He spoke so sharply and nervously that it took me up short. He acted almost afraid of me. I thought it was because he assumed I was a murderer, so I said, "Now don't tell me you believe I killed that woman. Or raped her. You know better than that. You know Jacobbsen has his hand in this, clean up to his elbow."

"Jacobbsen!" he said. He almost spit the word out. And even after he'd said it, the muscles at the corner of his jaw continued to work.

Again the intensity of his voice had taken me by surprise. I had noticed, when he'd come to me in my cell, that there had been a certain tenseness about him, an unnatural, closely held emotion of some kind. Of course, when you're viewing people from the wrong side of a set of jail bars, you tend to view them in regard to your own predicament. But I wasn't in jail now. "Which Jacobbsen? The son or the old man?"

"Never mind," he said. He bent to his barrel of beans again.

"All right, you don't want to talk about Jacobbsen. I can't blame you. Neither does anybody else in this town. Obviously everybody is scared of him. But what about that poor woman, that Mary Mae Hawkins. Wouldn't you like to see her real abuser and killer caught? They might hang me, but they won't have the man that done the work. Think of that poor, innocent woman. Justice should out."

All of a sudden he raised up and stared at me with a burning fever that passed his previous intensity. "Poor, innocent woman!" He snarled. "She was a harlot, a common, cheap harlot. A disgrace to the very name of womankind. Spreading her legs for—" He stopped suddenly. For a second he continued to stare into my eyes and then he dropped them to the forgotten scoop in his hand. Without another word he went back to his work.

I was so startled that for a second I was taken aback. By the time I could start in on him about what he'd said, all he would do was shake his head. I couldn't get another word out of him on the subject. Giving it up as a bad job, I let him settle down and then was able to get the information out of him I'd originally come for. Marriah had no set schedule, but she usually came into town at least once a week, sometimes twice, and she always stopped at the Davis Mercantile. They brought in special fabrics for her as well as mineral water and delicacies that they wouldn't ordinarily sell.

I said, "Sounds a bit spoiled, don't she?"

He gave me a cold look. "If she can afford to pay for it, what business is it of yours?"

"None, Alvin. Just passing the time."

I went back to the hotel in a very thoughtful mood. Ben was at the table cleaning his gun. Hays and I sat down and poured ourselves out a drink. I was turning things over in my mind. Finally I said, "Ben, I want you to put your lady-killing talents to work."

He glanced up. "My what?"

"Now don't play modest on me, little brother. I've been expecting a paternity suit to be brought against you ever since you've been sixteen. I want you to scout around among the local belles and find out what you can about Alvin Davis. That's the young man who works at the mercantile across the street for his father. Find out who he's walking out with and what they have to say about him."

"Why?"

I rubbed my face. "I don't quite know. There's something gnawing on that boy, something that don't quite meet the eye. I think he knows something he's not telling. He may have seen something. But I can't seem to get close to him. Maybe if I could get something on him where he'd have to talk to me. Some little breath of scandal with one of the local girls. He appears to come from a mighty straitlaced family. Respectable and intending to stay that way. I figure if you put on your best manners and what little charm you've got, you might get further than I would asking on the street. But don't push."

Ben looked amused. He finished loading his gun and holstered it. "So," he said, "you've finally come to recognize who's the best-looking in the family. Taken you long enough."

I said dryly, "I don't believe I said that. What I believe I said was that you were more nearly the right age to approach some giddy eighteen- or nineteen-year-old flibbertigibbet. At least you'd speak the same language. But try and keep your mind on business. You're looking to find out what they've got between their ears, not between their legs."

Hays laughed and Ben gave both of us a sour look and stood up and put on his hat. "You really know how to send a feller off on a job with a rush of enthusiasm, don't you, big brother?"

"Where girls are concerned, I've always found that dampening your enthusiasm was the most practical approach. And stay out of trouble."

When he was gone, Hays and I poured out another drink and then sat there, sipping meditatively. After a time Hays said, "I envy you that, brother. An' the other'n too. Ya'll are a family."

"Never had a family?"

He shook his head. "Naw, not to speak of. The consumption taken my ma when I was twelve, an' then my daddy jest kind of lost all interest in anything and followed her pretty quick. My two sisters went to aunts and uncles, and I sort of took out, finding cow work wherever I could. Been at it ever since."

"Where was this at?"

"We was homesteadin' up in Oklahoma. Boomers. I don't know if we'd of made a go of it anyway." He looked down in his glass and then up at me. "I want to say I'm mighty grateful for this chance you're giving me. I won't let you down."

"That's why I hired you," I said.

Not much happened the next couple of days. Tom Hudspeth had to go back to San Antonio to tend to some pressing business. He promised to be back as quickly as he could. He left me with the admonition to be wary and not to worry. That night we decided to eat at a café down the street rather than going to the hotel dining room. Not being quite ready, I sent the others on ahead and then set out a few minutes behind them. Just as I was stepping up on the boardwalk after crossing the street, I was confronted by three men walking abreast, leaving me no room to pass. I stopped. It was either that or step off into the street, which I had no intention of doing. I'd known the little dustup in the saloon would not be the last confrontation, so I'd been halfway expecting this one. We stood there staring at each other. I didn't recognize any of the men; they were just ordinary. They didn't, except for one, look especially like they might work for Jacobbsen. One of them said, "Get off the walk, pigshit. This is for decent folks."

It didn't make me mad. All it made me was determined that

word should get around town that I was growing tired of this game and wasn't going to play at it anymore. I said, "Let me pass."

The biggest of the three, at the end toward the street side, said, "Onliest place you are goin' to pass to is the great beyond. Now crawl around us."

"You're looking for trouble. Well, you have applied to the right man."

The big man said, "Would you listen to—"

Without warning, I kicked him as hard in the crotch as I could drive my booted foot. Air came out his mouth like a deflated gas balloon. He doubled over, clutching himself. Before either of the other two could react, I whipped out my pistol and cracked the second in line over the head. He toppled to the side, stumbled over the man I'd kicked, who was slowly going to his knees, and fell into the street. The third man was clawing at his side gun. I put the barrel of my pistol between his eyes and backed him against the face of a building. I didn't say anything, just looked at him. Fright had come across his face. He was trying to stammer out something. I didn't let him finish. I said, "Who started this?"

"I—I—"

I pushed harder and cocked the hammer of my revolver. It made a deathly *clitch-clack* sound in the night quiet. "I'll ask you again. Who started this?"

"I—" he said.

"No."

His eyes darted around. Then they seemed to cross as he tried to focus both of them on the barrel of my revolver. He licked his lips. "This ain't—"

"No. Give the right answer. Now."

He swallowed. "I, uh, I, uh . . . I reckon we did."

"Louder."

"We did."

"On whose orders?"

"Uh, nobody's."

"Sure?"

"Yes."

"Not Jacobbsen's? Not the sheriff's? Not Judge Hummil's?"

His eyes darted around again.

"Don't look for help. This thing has got a hair trigger, and I don't think I can miss from this range."

"No. No. It was, uh, our own idea. We done it."

I slowly uncocked my revolver and removed it from his head. Then I stepped back a couple of paces. We'd drawn a small crowd. I looked around. There were a few women in the crowd, but it was mostly made up of men. I said, almost as if I were talking aloud to myself, "I am getting thoroughly tired of this foolishness. The smart ones will realize my patience is wearing thin and will leave me the hell alone."

Then I started up the walk toward the café. I hadn't taken two steps before I saw Ben. He was leaning against the side of a storefront, his revolver held almost nonchalantly in his hand, covering the crowd and the two men in the dust of the street. I stopped and asked him what the hell he was doing there.

He said, "Oh, I thought I'd backtrack on you. I pretty much figured something like this would happen if you come along by yourself." He raised his voice so the little crowd could hear. "Don't fergit, I know this breed of shitless chicken-fuckers and how brave they are when it's about ten to one in their favor." He spit on the ground. "Of course that's ten to one when you got your back turned to 'em. That's when they really get brave."

I took him by the arm. "Come along," I said. "Don't be agitating these good citizens. Remember, some one of them might just be visiting."

I glanced back as we went along. They were still standing there, staring after us. No one had even made a move to help the two men who were still down in the street. I said, "Some town."

"What?"

"Nothing. Relax. Let's eat."

Next day, I put Hays to watching the mercantile full-time. If Marriah showed up, he was to come and find me posthaste. Tom Hudspeth had not returned and we were anxiously awaiting his arrival. We'd applied to Judge Hummil for permission to examine the Hawkins' ranch house, the site of the crime, but had been refused. In addition to his other business,

Tom was going to secure a writ that would give us that right. It would also, as he had warned Hummil, carry great weight in his probable appeal as another example of Hummil denying me due process of law. None of this seemed to faze Hummil. None of us could figure out if the man was just in his dotage or he actually thought that Jacobbsen could defy the law of the land.

Norris said, "This contraption of a town is beyond the pale of my understanding. Is it so inbred? Is it frightened? Is it so isolated? Stage comes through. The mails arrive. Of course, I can't say that I've ever seen an outside newspaper, and the one they present as such here could hardly be called that. I confess to being baffled."

"It's Jacobbsen. Has to be," I said.

"One man can wield that much power? In this day and age?"

"All he has to do is control certain machinery. The law, the judicial system. The county and city administration. That's not that many people. The rest follow like sheep. Look, before Jacobbsen came, this was a very poor place. Look at the land around here. You'll see more sheep and goats than cattle. Look at the number of relatively new buildings. Money, Norris, money. These people were barely grubbing out a living, and then Jacobbsen came along and began shoveling out the money. It meant new houses, new dresses for the wives, candy and soda pop for the kiddies, new saddles, plenty of food and whiskey. Money to live on. No more sweating from dawn to dusk just to get a roof over your head and a little something to eat. Money for luxuries. New stores. You think that wouldn't make you turn a blind eye? You think that wouldn't naturally make any enemy of Jacobbsen's your enemy?"

"Not mine," Norris said.

"Oh, bullshit."

"Perhaps I have a greater faith in human nature than you, Justa."

"You? You cynical bastard. Don't make me laugh."

Ben came in. He plumped down at the table. He'd been out on his own, pursuing the mission I'd given him. I said, "Well?"

He shook his head. "You're on a wrong one here, big brother. Or as best as I can find out. I've cozied up to about a half a dozen of the local belles, if you can call them that, and all they do is either titter or look dumbfounded when I ask them about Alvin. He doesn't go with any of these girls and never has. Oh, maybe a church social or something like that, but nothing else. It seems to be his choice, since he's about as eligible as any around here, but he just don't seem to take any interest. They say he's a mama's boy. And he works all the time, either for his daddy at the mercantile or at the sheriff's office. And when he ain't doing that, he's in church. They say they can't open the church doors without him showing up. You're chasing rabbits with a bear gun, big brother. I don't think the sap has rose up in old Alvin's tree yet."

I rubbed my jaw. Ben's report came as something of a surprise. It just wasn't consistent with my image of the coiled inner spring I'd seen in the young man. I was still convinced he knew something of the Jacobbsens. If not their involvement in the murder, at least something that might be helpful. The dead woman and the Jacobbsens went together, and both subjects had brought a surprising response from Alvin. There had to be a tie-in. But I said, "Okay, thanks. I know it was a hardship on you to have to handle such a chore."

Ben yawned. "You think you're joshing me, but you didn't see some of the ladies I had to press my attentions on."

Norris said, "The tribulations you press down on this boy's brow."

It was growing past six o'clock when Hays came in. I raised my eyebrows in a question. He just shook his head. "No sign of the lady. A wagon come in from Treetops and loaded up three hundred pounds of salt lick and called me a coward and a traitor, but that was all."

"What'd you do?"

"Smoked and looked at 'em. They was two of the few that is actual cowhands. Not some of Jacobbsen's gunnies. They just cussed me 'cause they felt it was expected of them."

Norris said, "Hear anything on the street?"

A little shadow flickered over Hays's face. He glanced at me. "You understand," he said, "that folks don't talk around me like they used to. Still, I heard a few remarks, kind of in the ear-to-the-door style." He looked at me again. "Boss, you have made an impression. I don't reckon none of the ribbon clerks will be takin' you on again. Not unless they is way too drunk to be sensible. But I'm hearin' some wishin' that some of the rougher element of that bunch out at Treetops would come in and do for you."

"Bull?"

Hays hesitated. "I don't know. Bull is what you might call the last card. Jacobbsen don't generally use him 'less he's still bankin' on the court. On them charges. Though I got to say that the way Mr. Jacobbsen thinks is a pure mystery to me. But you will have noticed that we ain't seen no sign of Wilton Purdy, not since your day in court. That's strange for him. He used to come into town two or three nights a week to throw his weight around and get drunk. Been better'n a week now."

I looked over at Norris. He shrugged. "Jacobbsen could be keeping him out of your way. Purdy will be the principal witness against you. He may not want to risk his accidental death. After all, he's supposedly the one who ran you to ground as you fled the murder scene."

I looked at Hays questioningly. He said, "Word will have reached Jacobbsen that you ain't no setup, that you're a handy man with a gun. And will fight. It ain't sayin' much, but he's also already figured you're smarter than Bull. Onliest way he's gonna set Bull on you is if there ain't no other way and if he's holdin' all the high cards."

It was all becoming more and more of a muddle. Dammit, I thought, I had to find a way to get inside Treetops and confront my real enemy. I was becoming so desperate, time passing as it was, that I was even thinking of my early plan to capture Torrey or Marriah and work out some sort of swap. But I didn't want it that way. I wanted to smash Jacobbsen! I wanted to put him in that line cabin and starve him and deprive him of water and beat the hell out of him and let him go through days of agony while he worried what I was going to do with him.

I said to Hays, "But Jacobbsen *has* to come to town sometime!"

He just shook his head slowly. "Not so you'd notice. And when he does, he comes with about twenty riders and never goes anyplace public. He's got a house here, that big house set back from the street on the side of the hill. He stops there overnight sometimes to check on his hired hands here in town. Then he generally goes on into San Antonio. He does all his socializing there or in Houston."

Norris said, "But you told us he went to the murdered woman's house."

"That ranch house is damn near on his property. In fact, his northern fence takes it in. He'd leased all Miz Hawkins's husband's range. Her husband wasn't doin' more than workin' for him. So when he went to her, he was still right at home. Guns all around."

"Shit!" I said.

A little before noon the next day, Hays came tearing into the room. Ben and I were sitting there having a drink of whiskey and worrying about how things were going back home. It was one thing to be trapped on a false criminal charge and have to fight your way free, but it was quite another to have that set of circumstances compounded by the deterioration of your family business back home. I had just finished assuring Ben that Mr. Dag Jacobbsen was going to make up whatever revenue we'd lost by our enforced absence from our work when Hays had come tearing in. I looked around.

"She's down there," Hays said. "She went in the mercantile. I watched her pick out some stuff and then come up here. I don't think she's going to be long."

"Shall I come?" Ben asked.

I shook my head. "Naw, I ain't afraid of her. I bet I can lick her in a fair fight."

Hays said, "You ought to hurry. She didn't look like she was going to tarry."

I put on my hat and went out the door, telling Hays not to follow me too close. "Stay across the street."

She was already out of the store by the time I got out of the hotel. She was standing by her ornate carriage, obviously waiting for something or somebody. Since her driver wasn't around, I figured it was him. I crossed deliberately to her, taking off my hat as I did. When I'd come up to her, I said, "Miss Jacobbsen, my name is Justa Williams. I'm from

Matagorda County, Texas. I wonder if I might have a word with you."

Well, the look she gave me I can only describe as arrogant. But that was all right with me, as I tended to be a little arrogant myself, though I think I was a better hand at disguising it than she was. But she looked at me a touch longer than she needed to if she was going to act uninterested and aloof. I said, "Would you be willing to speak with me?"

For a second I thought she was, because something flickered in her eyes. But then, without a word, she turned and started for the door of her carriage. I said, loud enough for it to carry along the street, "Am I to take it, then, that not only does cruelty and insanity run rampant in your family, but rudeness as well?"

That made her turn. She swung around, her eyes blazing, and stepped toward me. She lifted her hand and swung, intending to slap me in the face. I intended that she should do no such thing. I caught her by the wrist as her hand came forward and held it there. I smiled at her. Her eyes blazed back, but she made no effort to free her wrist. She said, "You . . ."

"Do better than that, Miss Jacobbsen. I know you've had a good education."

At that instant I felt a rough hand on my shoulder. I let myself be pulled around. As I wheeled, I cocked my right fist and hit the man behind me full in the face. It was her driver. He went flat on his back. I jerked him up with both hands, then held him with my right and hit him hard, again, with my left. Blood spurted from his nose. Without letting go of him I dragged his slack weight to the side of the carriage and boosted him into the driver's seat. He just slumped there. Then I went back to Marriah. She hadn't moved. I walked past her and opened the carriage door. She glanced at her driver and then she looked at me. I just stood there silently, holding the door for her. When she didn't move, I said, "Get in. He'll come to in a minute. Tell your daddy I don't like people laying their hands on me. In any way."

I'd left her no choice. People had stopped on the street and were staring. Without a glance left or right, she gathered her long skirt and stepped into the carriage. I said to her, through the window, "You and I are going to have a talk. Bet on it. Maybe not today, maybe not tomorrow, but soon." She was staring straight ahead. I closed the door with a sharp click. "And tell your daddy that he and I are going to have a talk also. And the sooner it is, the better it's going to be for him."

She turned her face, then, and looked at me. But only for a second. I couldn't read what was in her eyes, but there was something, and it wasn't hate or disdain or even arrogance. I tipped my hat to her and walked away.

When I got back to the hotel room, I sat down and looked at the knuckles on my right fist. They were skinned and red. Ben had been watching from the window. He turned and lay down on his bed. He yawned. "Damn good-looking woman. Didn't seem too friendly."

I worked my fist. "That leaves me about two hundred and ninety-eight to go."

"Two hundred and ninety-eight what?"

"Licks. Punches. Blows. I figure I got hit about three hundred times in that line cabin. I'm getting the balance of mine in. Hopefully some of them will be on Jacobbsen."

Ben laughed. "Big brother, you are the cat's whiskers. Here you are facing a murder charge in the most unfriendly town I ever saw, and fifteen minutes ago you was telling me how Jacobbsen was going to remunerate us for our lost time. Now you are figuring the licks you plan to get in to even up the score for the beating you took. You are some hombre. Has it ever occurred to you to be scared?"

I looked over at him. "I was plenty scared in that line cabin. You can bet it will be a long time before I forget that."

There not seeming to be much else we could do for the time being, we settled down to await Tom Hudspeth's return from San Antonio with the court order allowing us to examine the murder site. I still kept Hays on watch for Marriah. I have admitted to arrogance and a certain amount of vanity, and it may well have been those two qualities that caused me to suppose I saw something in her eyes that was very much akin to a spark of interest. And why not? Surely she couldn't have found much diversion among the male species in Bandera, not stacked up against a woman like her. I was not the most handsome, nor the most charming, not the most intelligent man afloat on the prairie, but I was willing to take my chances among the various gentry of my present surroundings. I lay awake that night thinking about her, thinking about her wild, blond hair, about the way her breasts pushed against the material of her dress, about the flash of calf and ankle I'd had as she lifted her skirt to step into the carriage. She was a desirable woman, and no mistake. And I hadn't had my ashes hauled in a considerable time.

It suddenly popped into my mind about that time that I hadn't instructed Ben to check with any whores the town might have about young Mr. Alvin Davis. But I put that thought aside. They might not even have such in a sterling city like Bandera, and if they did, the very churchy Mr. Davis hardly seemed the type to throw patronage their way.

CHAPTER
5

We rode out for the Hawkins place on a windy spring morning.
Tom Hudspeth had returned with authority for our visit from
the superior court in San Antonio, but it had taken his
enthusiastic rejection to keep Sheriff Rose from accompanying
us. The full five of us made the trip. We didn't expect any
trouble, but the Hawkins place was, legally through lease, a
part of the Treetops ranch.

It was near to a five-mile ride, and as we went along I
strained my eyes to the northeast, hoping to catch sight of the
line cabin I'd been imprisoned in. I knew it was somewhere in
the distance, but probably well beyond my line of sight.

We came into the ranch yard and dismounted. Even though
the Widow Hawkins had been dead less than two weeks, the
place had already taken on that look of abandonment and
disuse. We tied our horses and stepped up on the porch. The
door swung open to my touch, showing the front room of a
typical small rancher's home. I said, "Ain't no use us all
clumping in there. We'd just get in each other's way. Ben, you
and Hays go search through the outbuildings."

"What are we supposed to be looking for?"

I shrugged. "I don't even know what we're doing here in the
first place. I guess look for anything out of the ordinary,

anything that looks like it don't belong. Evidence of an uninvited guest."

Ben said, "Well, in view of the fact that we don't know what is supposed to be here in the first place, that sounds like a mighty tall order."

"Just go along," I said to my middle brother. "Norris, for the time being, would you stay out here on the porch and keep watch and see if we are going to draw any company? Let Tom and I have a look around first."

He nodded and the lawyer and I went in. First we took a quick walk through to acquaint ourselves with the place. Besides the sitting room, there was a bedroom, a kitchen, and what we took for a sewing or quilting room. The living room was by far the biggest and accommodated a big table obviously intended for dining. Other than a divan and a few chairs, there was a daybed in the big room, set against the side wall near a window. Tom pointed at the daybed. "That's where they supposedly found her. At least that's the way the sheriff's report reads."

I looked at it. It was just an ordinary daybed, brass-backed, on the wall side with little pillows thrown up against the brass piping so you could sit on it like a divan if you wanted.

I said, "She was supposed to have been strangled to death?"

"That's what the doctor said. He was in town from San Antonio when they found her, so he came out and acted as coroner. I think he is the coroner for this circuit."

"Who found her?"

Tom gave a little snort. "Ironically enough, it was a party of ladies from the church in Bandera, bound out here on a mission of good deed. Seems Mrs. Hawkins had been slipping in her church attendance of late, and the good ladies had come to remonstrate with her. I think they were greeted with a rather unexpected sight. The report says Mrs. Hawkins was laying on the daybed nude from the waist down. Her skirt had been thrown up over her head and her underclothes and stockings torn off and deposited on the floor. Oddly enough, she still had one shoe on her naked foot. Nobody can figure that one out. Almost as if the murderer had come out of his insensibility and tried to redress her. Though why start with a shoe?"

"How long had she been dead?"

Tom shook his head. "Doctor really couldn't say. A day, two days. Rigor mortis had set in, but no decomposition or bloating. But the bruises had formed. One other thing: She had a pretty good-sized knot on the back of her head and a piece of stove wood was found near the bed. But the doctor doesn't think that's what killed her. It looked like she'd put up a struggle, broke free, and was trying to run when the killer fetched her a lick with the stove wood and brought her back to the bed."

I said, "How do they know she was raped? Wasn't she seeing each of the Jacobbsens pretty regularly?"

"Bruises on her thighs, on the inside. And scratches. And her vagina was bruised like the man was having a tough time getting inside her. Like she was putting up a hell of a fight."

I didn't like the sound of that too much. If Jacobbsen had already been up her skirt, why would she fight him? I said slowly, "So we got to figure it was a stranger or somebody she didn't want to have her."

He slowly nodded his head. "I'm afraid so. Of course, she and Jacobbsen—or Torrey for that matter—could have had a falling-out and she'd decided to cut them off and whichever it was wouldn't take no for an answer."

"What about the strangulation? Man just grab her around the neck and squeeze?"

Tom seemed to ponder that for a moment. "No, she wasn't hand-strangled. Some kind of small cord was used. Like a pigging string. Or a sash cord or miller's rope. But nothing like that was found around here. But whoever did it nearly cut her neck in two. Busted her larynx. Doctor said there was still an imprint in her neck deep enough to lay your finger in by the time he got here."

"I guess the house has been pretty well gone over."

"Oh, yes. The sheriff, naturally, and the judge, and that Davis boy who's a deputy. And apparently anybody else that cared to have a look. I don't think we're going to find anything."

"Anybody else visit her besides the Jacobbsens and the

ladies of the church? I mean, did she have any friends that dropped out from town?"

Tom shook his head. "Not that I know of."

"What about supplies?"

Tom said, "Now this is just what I hear, I can't prove it. But it's my understanding, mostly from Hays, that her supplies were bought by the Jacobbsen supply wagon on their regular run into town and dropped off for her. I hear she seldom went into town, which is why the church ladies came out."

There was a small secretary standing against the wall. "What about papers and such?" I asked.

"Judge has got all those. I've seen them. Nothing much. Letters from her family back in Virginia. Lease agreement with Jacobbsen. Sale of her cattle to Jacobbsen. Ranch correspondence and the like. Bankbook."

"How was she fixed?"

"Not bad, but not as good as you'd think. Had about six hundred dollars in the Bandera bank. Of course she could have sent more on to another bank somewhere else."

Something kept catching my eye at the back of the daybed: the corner of a small piece of paper, mostly hidden by the long curtains that fell from the window. Tom had started off toward the sewing room. I stooped and pulled out the paper. It turned out to be a bill from Davis Mercantile. The name at the top, the name to whom the goods had been billed, was neither Hawkins nor Jacobbsen. It was a run-of-the-mill list: canned goods and some yard goods. The last item struck me. It was for fifty pounds of fine-ground cornmeal. Bandera had a corn grist, located on the little river that ran just to the north of town. I couldn't figure out what a bill for goods consigned to some other party would be doing in the Hawkins cabin. It could have been that one of the Jacobbsen men had also picked up an order for these other people and then had dropped the bill while he was delivering Mrs. Hawkins's supplies. I stuck it down in my pocket, but it continued to nag at my mind.

Norris came in. "All quiet," he said. "Where's Tom?"

I sat down at the table, pondering. "In one of those back rooms."

"Ya'll find anything?"

I shook my head. "No. And I didn't expect to. I guess we're just going through the motions for something to do."

He went off to find Tom and I sat there, still thinking. The name on the mercantile bill had been one Amos Grummet. I determined that I would make it my business to investigate this Mr. Grummet and see if he also had been in the habit of visiting the Widow Hawkins. Maybe he'd stopped by on his way home from town for a sociable cup of coffee and an unwilling piece of ass followed by a murder.

It was easy to see how the scrap of paper could have been overlooked even with all the gawkers, both official and unofficial, the ranch house had drawn. It had obviously fluttered out of his pocket when he'd been struggling to get on top of her and had floated down and skittered in behind the curtains. It wasn't the sort of thing, even if it had been noticed, that the investigators would have been looking for. Obviously they would have been looking for something more tangible, like the man's saddle or his boots or maybe his wallet. I surmised that a stray gust of wind had slightly dislodged it as we'd opened the door. Just enough to reveal a corner. I thought of speaking about it to Tom, but I thought I'd keep my own counsel until I did a little checking on Amos Grummet.

Ben and Hays came back in, Hays with a good deal of straw sticking to him. Ben said, "Hays got into the hayloft, but the murderer wasn't hiding up there. Hays would have found him if he had of been. Get right in the midst of his work, did Hays."

"You pushed me off that railing," Hays said. "What if there had been a pitchfork stuck down in that pile?"

"You slipped, Hays. You know you did."

I said, "All right. Enough horseplay. Let's get back to town."

On the ride back into town I ruminated on my last meeting with Marriah. Even though she was only habituated to come into town once or twice a week, she had shown up the day after our first meeting. I'd taken Ben with me and followed her into Davis Mercantile. The place was dark and cool. Alvin was nowhere to be seen, but Mr. Davis had called to me. I'd waved him off and followed Marriah to the back. Her driver had stayed out front and I'd left Ben to keep him company and keep him from interfering. She'd been looking at some fabric when I'd come up to her. I'd taken off my hat. I'd said, "Well, we meet again, Miss Jacobbsen. And quite sooner than I'd expected."

She hadn't looked around, just kept turning over the folds of fabric. I could see at a glance that it was just cheap material, nothing she'd be interested in. It had been my distinct impression that she'd made for this dark recess in the back so that I would follow her. I'd said, "Still plan on remaining silent? You afraid to talk to me?"

That had turned her on me. She'd given me a burning look. "Afraid of you, Mr. Williams? Hardly, I should think. After all, I'm not a defenseless woman in an isolated cabin."

"Oh, that's hogwash and you know it. Now turn around and face me. I've got some questions to put to you."

"Mr. Williams, you are a low cur and a reprehensible criminal. I don't care even to be in the same room with you, much less hold conversation."

"You know I'm none of those things. Look at me. I know better from what I see in your eyes. And I see that you've taken the trouble to remember my name. You don't remember the name of a low cur."

"It's hardly forgettable. You've insured it on everyone's lips."

"Oh, nonsense. And you know it. Look, your father, or your father and your brother, are trying to set me up for something I had no hand in. I don't know why and I don't care why. I just want him to stop. So if you value his health, you'd better advise him either to meet with me or call off the dogs. Otherwise he can consider himself, as well as you and his son, in jeopardy."

She'd looked at me as if I'd taken leave of my senses. "Are you threatening me, Mr. Williams? I'll call the sheriff."

"You call whoever you want. I'm starting to get more than a little angry about this, and when I get angry enough, I generally do something. So if you value your father's well-being . . ."

"You? You harm my father? Don't make me laugh. Besides, I'm not concerned with his welfare."

And with that she'd whirled around and taken her leave. I
hadn't tried to stop her. But her last words had left me
confused. Had she meant that she didn't give a damn for her
father's welfare? Or just that she didn't suppose that I could
pose a serious threat to him?

I had no idea, but on instinct I leaned more toward the first
interpretation than the last.

It was almost as if thought could summon up reality. All of
a sudden, just coming around a bend in the road, I saw
Marriah's coach. Or I assumed it was hers because I'd never
seen anyone else driving it. Hays looked around at me,
recognizing it almost as soon as I had. I told the others I wanted
them to ride on ahead, that Ben and I were going to drop back.
I said, "I'm going to try and have a word with the lady."

"What if it ain't her?" Norris asked.

"Then I won't stop."

Ben and I slowed our horses until quite a gap existed
between us and the others. The coach swept past them and then
came abreast of us. I got a glimpse of golden hair inside and
wheeled my horse, Ben doing likewise. I came up on the right
side of the coach, Ben on the other. He had orders to stop the
driver, so he rode up to the front with a drawn revolver in his
hand.

When the coach was stopped, I pulled my horse up next to
the window. Marriah was sitting elegantly erect, staring
straight ahead. "Morning," I said.

For a moment I thought she wasn't going to speak. Then she
said, "Have you added highway robbery to your list of crimes,
Mr. Williams?"

"So far," I said, "you haven't been robbed of anything
except your pretention of indifference toward me."

That brought her head around. "Pretention of— Why, you
arrogant, low-bred bastard! No woman of any character would
have to *pretend* indifference to you."

"Well, be that as it may. That's not why I stopped you. I
want you to give your father a message. You tell him I insist on
seeing him."

She made a motion with her hand. "Then go and see him.

The gate is no more than a mile from here. The mansion just two miles after that. Ride on if you're so determined."

I gave a short laugh. "No thanks. Not without invitation. I don't want a bullet in my back."

"Which would be no more than you deserve."

I'd had enough. "Oh, bullshit! You little spoiled bitch! For two cents I'd jerk you out of there and tan your ass. Talk about pretentions. You're full of them. I don't know who you think you are, but whoever it is, you're not."

"Keep your filthy talk to yourself!"

"Why? Does it excite you?"

She called to her driver. "Sam! Sam! Drive on!"

I smiled at her. "I think ol' Sam is occupied right now. I think he's got his hands in the air. Hard to drive a team that way."

She said, "You will stop harassing me! I demand it!"

I said, as coolly as I could, "I've only just begun. You tell your daddy that I'm going to make life hell for him and you and anybody else from Treetops until he decides to sit down with me and get this matter resolved."

She said, some of her composure breaking, "Your quarrel is with the law, not with my father."

I favored her with the slightest of smiles. "Now, even you don't believe that. Why bother to say it? Just tell your daddy what I said." After that I backed my horse a pace or two and called for Ben to let the driver go. I tipped my hat as the carriage pulled away. "We'll meet again, Miss Jacobbsen. Hopefully in the company of your father."

On the way back to town I asked Hays if he'd ever heard of an Amos Grummet. He just shook his head. But he said, "Of course, that don't mean nothin'. Lots of home folks around here I don't know. They's even some out to Treetops I can't call the whole names of. Remember, I ain't been here quite a year yet."

I set out on my inquiries about Amos Grummet with a fair amount of excitement. I still hadn't told Tom, first because I knew he'd want to take an oblique, law-oriented approach rather than the frontal confrontation I preferred, and second

because I wanted more to go on before I laid it in front of him.
Naturally, I first applied at Davis Mercantile for information.
Alvin was not there, but Mr. Davis was. With suspicion, and
only grudgingly, would he admit that Grummet was a customer
of his. It took even more pressing to find out where Grummet
lived. I think he assumed I was going to kill the man.

For a while I didn't think he was going to help me. He just
stood there, a thin, disapproving man with the piety pulled up
around his mouth about as tight as the elastic sleeve garters he
wore. I said, "Look, I'm sure I can ask elsewhere. I may have
to ask ten people, but somebody will tell me. Ya'll are the
damnedest set of folks I ever saw."

At last he unloosened his mouth enough to ask what I wanted
with Grummet. I said I had business.

"What kind of business would that be, Mr. Williams?"

"My business!" I snapped. "And none of yours. Listen, my
brothers and I have done considerable business in this store of
yours. Guns, ammunition, clothes. If you want it to continue,
you'll be of some help."

"If you'd just tell me your business—"

"I'm in the cattle business, goddammit! What's it to you?"

He reared back. "Sir, I'll thank you not to take the Lord's
name in vain in my presence."

"That wasn't the Lord. I was saying goddammit to a heathen
god. That all right with you? Now how about those directions?"

It was like milking a dry cow, but he grudgingly directed me
out the south road toward Treetops. He said, "About two mile
out of town you'll hit a little road coming in from your left.
Branch off there. His place is on the right about a mile further
on. It's set off the road about half a mile." He peered at me
from behind his storekeeper's rimless glasses. "You did say
cattle business?"

"Yeah. Why?"

"Because Amos has never raised nothing but mules."

"You need mules in the cattle business. Didn't you know
that, storekeeper?"

I left him staring after me and went outside and mounted up
and rode off down the street. I was going alone and I was doing

it on purpose. I knew that it was slightly chancy, especially as near to Treetops as my route would take me, but I felt it was necessary. I didn't know who this Amos Grummet was, nor anything about him. But it was my instinct that the man who could rape and murder a defenseless woman would have to be a coward and I didn't want to ride up to his door with a force that might scare him off. Of course, if this Grummet was implicated, that left me high and dry so far as the Jacobbsens went concerning the crime. But that was all right. The crime wasn't what I was holding against Jacobbsen. Anyway, for all I knew, this Grummet might have been sent by the king of the Treetops ranch.

The side road came up and I duly turned left as instructed. It was good spring now, and down in my part of the country the trees and the grass and all nature would be greening up. But up here in these hard rock hills everything maintained a steady consistency of brown. Oh, the cedar was green, though not a particularly pleasing shade, and the mesquite was aiming for it though mainly just coming up yellow, but for the rest, sand and umber pretty much held the day. You can get all the rain you can ask for, but it's still nearly impossible to get jagged rock and caliche clay and thorny briars to do much of a job of coming green. I looked at the country thinking it was no place I'd care to be afoot and short on provisions and water. I reckoned there'd been folks who'd hiked through it but I had no desire to be one.

About a mile down the side road I saw wood smoke rising in the air and went to hunting for a turnoff. Within a hundred yards I found a wagon track breaking off to my right and rising up a gentle hill. After a couple of hundred yards I passed through a cedar break and came into a clearing occupied by a stone-and-lumber cabin with a considerable number of corrals in the back. I could see the corrals were full of mules, so I knew I'd come to the right place. I rode right up to the house and halloed. It was a good long wait, but finally the screen door opened and an old man came out, shading his eyes with one hand against the sun. He was hatless and nearly bald, wearing old run-over-at-the-heels boots and a set of bib overalls. It took him a moment to focus on me and then he said, "Yes, sir. What be you wantin'?"

Well, he certainly didn't look like a man given to a crime of passion, but that didn't mean he didn't have a son. I said, "Are you Amos Grummet?"

He was still squinting. "Who's askin'?"

"Name is Williams. I understand you're in the mule business?"

"I be. You lookin' to buy a mule?"

"I don't know. Are you Amos Grummet?"

"I am. Now what about this mule? You be wanting more than one? I got several nice matched pairs."

I took the Davis Mercantile receipt out of my pocket and held it out to him. I said, "Does this belong to you?"

He took it and gave it a squint, turning it this way and that as he tried to make out what it was. Finally he bawled out, "Ma! Ma! Bring me my specs."

It appeared she'd been listening behind the screen door, for it wasn't but a moment before she was out on the porch, a wizened little old woman in a poke bonnet, handing him his reading glasses. He studied the receipt for a moment, then looked at me belligerently. "Hev' you come to collect his? Is Morris Davis sendin' out rowdies to collect his bills? This ain't even due yet. I been doin' business with him for— Well, I'll jest be damned!"

I said, "I'm not here collecting. I'm asking if that's your bill."

"Of course it is. Any damn fool can see it's got my name on it." He peered at me over the top of his spectacles. "But look here . . . how come you with it?"

I said, "When'd you order that lot of goods?"

"I don't know. Ten days, two weeks ago. What business is it of your'n?"

"Did you know Mary Mae Hawkins?"

"Of course I knowed her. Poor girl. I know ever'body in this part of the country. Sold mules to most of 'em. Say, what are you doin' askin' all these questions?"

"You got a son?"

"Look here, you tell me what this is all about!"

His wife spoke up. "We ain't got no son, ner no other man about the place. You reckon if we did, Amos would look so worked down? Got two married daughters. Both of 'em moved off and left us to manage best we could. Nary an ounce of gratitude ner thanks in the pair of 'em."

I said to Amos, "You have any idea how that bill came to be in the house of Mary Mae Hawkins?"

He frowned. "Where?"

I reached out and plucked the bill out of his hand and stuffed it back in my pocket.

"Now jest a minute, mister, that's my propity. You—"

I wheeled my horse around and loped him out of the clearing without another word. Amos Grummet obviously was not going to be much help. Still, the question kept banging around in my head—what was that receipt doing under the curtain by the death bed? If it had been a Treetops rider delivering supplies to Mary Mae, how had he come by it? The answer could have been that it simply had gotten mixed up in his wagonload of goods and fallen out while he was unloading at Mrs. Hawkins's house. It easily could have been simple happenstance with no connection to the crime.

I got back on the main road, still mulling the problem over in my mind. I'd pulled my horse down to a walk and we were just shuffling along, in no particular hurry. Then, suddenly, there came a tremendous thump against the front part of my saddle. An instant later I heard the crack of the rifle. I took the barest second to glance to my right. I saw powder smoke from a crag of rocks at the top of a small hill. I delayed no further but slapped spurs to my horse, leaning low over his neck and riding for dear life. I heard another shot, heard the slug whine over my head, but then, in another half minute, we were out of range.

I pulled up just outside of town, scared and shaken. The bullet had hit the horn of my saddle, just an inch from where I'd been resting my hand. It had not been a warning shot. It had been too close from too far away. No marksman was good enough to come that close on purpose. The man had been shooting at me and he had very nearly succeeded. There is something about a blind ambush that must get at your very nature. It's the helplessness of the thing. You have no defense. One second you're riding down a public road and the next you're shot out of the saddle and laying on the ground with a bullet through you, bleeding your life away. There is no defense.

I was, therefore, in a very grim humor when I walked into the hotel room. It was nearly lunchtime and the whole group was gathered around the table as I came in. They all looked up. Tom Hudspeth said severely, "Where the hell you been? We've been about to start out looking for you."

I poured myself out a drink. I have to confess that my hand was still shaking. The thought of how close that bullet had come to me . . .

They were busy with questions, but I downed my drink before I told them what had happened. Tom and Norris's responses were predictable. They immediately began remonstrating with me for going off on my own. I said, "What difference does that make? If there'd been ten of you around me, how would that have prevented the sniper from having his shot? Shoot one of you?"

"Hell, we could have charged the bastard," Ben said. "Caught him. Made him confess. See who put him up to it."

I just looked at him. "Up a hill? With him forted up in a pile of rocks? How many of us do you think would have got to the top?"

Even Norris had to agree with that. Still he mumbled about the foolhardiness, as he put it, of my going off on some errand by myself.

"Well, it's obvious they must be feeling the heat," Tom Hudspeth said. "If Jacobbsen has taken such a strong step, he must be getting desperate. Maybe, Justa, your pressure on Marriah has had something to do with it." He slammed his hand on the table. "Dammit, I'm getting off a telegram today demanding a U.S. Marshal down here. They're willing, they're just spread so thin."

Hays was sitting to my left, straddling a chair. He rubbed his chin with the point of his thumb. He said, "It's passing strange."

"What is?"

"Several things. That shot, for one thing. I know that stretch of road, and I know that small, low, crowned hill. That wouldn't be a shot of more than seventy or eighty yards. Justa, any good marksman wouldn't have missed you as slow as you were going."

"He damn near didn't."

Hays said, "It wasn't Jacobbsen."

"Aw, bullshit!" Ben exclaimed. "How you figure that?"

Hays looked thoughtful for a moment. "Well, Justa didn't speak to nobody except ol' man Davis. So who else knew?"

"Anybody he told," Ben said impatiently. "Hell, Treetops has men in town damn near every day. Anybody could have seen him ride out. Or they could have had a man just permanently stationed there. Hell, who knows."

But Hays still shook his head. "No. It don't sound like Jacobbsen. I'm telling you, Justa, if he wanted you shot off the road, he's got a dozen out there who wouldn't have missed. It just don't ring true." He got up and put on his hat.

I said, "Where you going?"

"To talk to ol' man Davis. I want to find out who he told."

I looked at Tom Hudspeth. He shrugged. "Let him go. It can't hurt our popularity around here any. I don't think he'll find out anything, but I'm almost inclined to agree with him about Jacobbsen. I think he still expects to let the courts do his dirty work for him."

After Hays had left, I put the receipt from Davis Mercantile on the table and it passed from hand to hand for examination. The consensus was the same as mine; that it had been a simple coincidence, in no way tied to the murder. Tom said, "And don't forget, it could have been dropped after the murder. There were enough people traipsing through that house."

But Norris said, "What about the date? It's almost the same as the day the woman was murdered."

Tom shook his head. "You forget, we don't *know* exactly what date she was murdered. Remember? The doctor couldn't place it any closer than a day or two before she was found."

He got up. "At least I can do one thing. Sending a telegram to the U.S. Marshal's office might not get one down here, but it will at least make Jacobbsen think we might."

Before he went out the door, he said to me, "Justa, don't ride off by yourself anymore. I know you're the boss, so I'm not telling you, but I am making strong recommendation."

Hays was a good long time coming back. He sat down, still with that same thoughtful look on his face. Ben said, "You better quit hanging out in that saloon by yourself. Unless you want a quick trip back to Treetops. They might let you fight those dogs you told us about by yourself."

"Ain't been in the saloon," Hays said.

"Then where you been? You ain't been talking to Davis this long."

Hays shook his head. "He wouldn't talk to me. Said I was trash and to git outer his store. So I took me a little ride. Out the way Justa went."

I glanced at him quickly. "What?"

"I located the place where you was sniped at pretty easy. Then I went up amongst those rocks on the top of the hill. Found where the sniper had laid up." He put his hand in his pocket and came out with two cartridge hulls. "Found these."

Ben looked at them. "Ordinary. Winchester 30.30. So?"

Hays said, "I also found some footprints. Only they wasn't made by boots. They was made by shoes. Regular shoes. Like townspeople wear."

I glanced at Norris. He was thinking the same thing I was. "What does Jacobbsen wear?" he asked.

Hays studied me, then said, "I thought on that. He wears both. Sometimes boots, sometimes shoes." He looked around at me. "But, boss, I'm telling you, if it was Jacobbsen, he wouldn't have missed. He's a damn good shot and he wouldn't have used no ordinary Winchester carbine. He's got a rack full of them European-made guns with them telescopic sights. And would he have ridden out in shoes? And how would he have got the word so fast? You went straight out there and didn't tarry long."

"But who else?" Norris said.

"Yeah," Ben put in. "Who? Somebody from town?"

Hudspeth said, "Somebody from town doesn't make any sense, not unless Jacobbsen has put a quiet bounty on Justa. It has been Jacobbsen all the way. He has been the one so eager to pin this on Justa, even to providing witnesses and coercing the law."

Norris asked quietly, "Justa, did the old man, Grummet, say if he got his supplies?"

I shrugged. I hadn't asked. I'd been so disappointed that the trail had gone cold on my hot idea that all thought of further investigation had gone out of my mind. I said, "I was too busy trying to get away before he sold me a mule."

"Then he didn't indicate if he'd picked up his supplies or if they'd been delivered?" Hudspeth asked.

Again I shook my head.

"How do they tie a fifty-pound sack of cornmeal?"

I looked up. "With a piece of miller's cord. About four or five foot long."

He and I were thinking the same thing, about the way the girl had been strangled. Tom said, "Maybe we ought to make a call on that gristmill."

I said, "Maybe we ought to make another call on Mr. Davis at his mercantile. That place is gettin' a little too coincidental for my taste."

"Alvin?"

Ben said, "Not likely. He couldn't choke a frying chicken, much less a woman. And how would he rape her? From what I've heard, he don't know where a woman keeps it."

It left us more in a muddle than ever. We kept talking it over, examining every aspect and coming up with the same old conclusions. Finally we gave it up for a bad job and sat down to play a few hands of poker to relax our minds. I won forty-five dollars. Ben, as usual, lost, and Norris just about held his own. Tom Hudspeth was the big loser and I told him I hoped he was better in the courtroom than he was at the poker table or else I was a gone gosling.

The surprise was Ray Hays. He played a careful, daring game. On the last hand of the night he bluffed me out with two pair when I was holding three of a kind on a five-dollar bet. It hadn't been the five-dollar bet that had caused me to fold my hand, it had been the fact that it had been his last five dollars. While he was raking in the pot I asked what he'd of done for money if I'd called.

He gave me a cheerful look. "Without, I guess," he said.

The next morning, like a bolt from the blue, there came a knock at my door. We were just having coffee and I got up to answer it. It was one of the Treetops ranch hands with a letter for me. It was from Dag Jacobbsen. I closed the door on the cowhand while I read it. It invited me and whatever associates I cared to bring to call in at his ranch that afternoon at three P.M. to discuss matters of mutual interest. The tone was polite, if terse. The paper was of heavy linen. It asked that a reply be sent via the messenger as to whether this would be convenient.

Ben had been reading over my shoulder. He said, "Well, I'll be damned!"

"So will I," I said. I opened the door. The messenger was waiting in the hall. I said, "Tell Mr. Jacobbsen that we'll be there."

CHAPTER
6

We gathered around the table in my room for the conference. Of course, there was no question of not going. That it might be a trap never even came up. If Jacobbsen wanted to lay a trap for us, there were many less incriminating places to stage it than his own ranch.

I guess the major question on all our minds was what he wanted, or, as Tom Hudspeth put it, "What has driven him to this step."

On that we were all agreed that it was a combination of factors: our own investigations; my insistent encountering of Marriah; our unwillingness to quit; Ray Hays and what he might tell us; and last, but certainly not least, Tom's attempts to involve the federal authorities. They could come in on a case if there was some question about malfeasance by a local court. Then, too, Jacobbsen had certainly discovered that we weren't without resources.

For some time we pondered what sort of proposal Jacobbsen was likely to make. Did he want to assure us he had had no hand in my misfortune? Did he want to propose some sort of truce? Did he want to warn me off his daughter? Did he want to see if I'd plead guilty to some lesser charge? Had he a threat in mind?

We tried to think of all the approaches so we could have an answer ready. In the end Tom Hudspeth said, "There's not but one thing for it—we'll have to go out and see what the man has in mind. Sitting around here guessing is not going to do us any good."

Then we discussed who should go. In the end I decided that it would be Ben and I and Tom Hudspeth. Hays and Norris would wait in town to summon outside authority in case we three came to any grief. Hudspeth gave Norris the name of the U.S. Marshal in San Antonio, as well as the name of the district court judge.

We rode out about two o'clock. As we were clearing town Ben said, "Well, you been pushing for this, big brother. Reckon anything will come of it?"

"I intend on making something come of it," I said grimly.

"What if that Bull is there? You intend on shooting him on sight?"

"My God, I hadn't thought of that." Tom Hudspeth looked uncomfortable, though part of that was his strangeness to a saddle. He said, "How will you handle that, Justa, if it arises?"

I shook my head. It hadn't occurred to me either—until Ben had brought it up. I said, "I don't know. That may be the one option we hadn't thought out. Do you think Jacobbsen will deliberately try to provoke me?"

"He might. But you'll be waging war on his battlefield. I hope you'll keep that in mind."

"I hope my temper will keep it in mind," I replied.

I tried to say it lightly, but it was a troubling thought. The idea of having access to Bull with my hands free and a gun at my side was a prospect I'd relished for hour after hour in that root cellar. My bruises may have disappeared, but my memory hadn't.

Tom said, "It's my advice we keep very still until we've heard him out thoroughly. Justa, I know it will be difficult for you, considering your personal feelings, but I want you to let me lead this meeting. I'm not as emotionally involved as you."

Well, that was true. Jacobbsen hadn't sent Lonnie after him with that stiletto. But he did have a point. Memories of those desperate seconds just as Lonnie was lifting the bar were likely to cloud my judgment.

Four miles out of town there was a turnoff to our left. We took it and, a half mile later, came to an imposing rock archway over the road. Sticking five feet high from the top of the arch was a wrought-iron replica of the Treetops brand. We swept on through the edifice and continued up the road. In the distance we could see a huge building, bigger than our hotel, with an imposing number of outbuildings scattered about. It was sheltered right at the base of the tallest hill about and could be nothing else but the ranch headquarters. I had looked in vain for the line cabin. I figured it was at least a mile farther to the north and hidden by the rolling hills.

We saw riders all about, some of them fairly near, some far-off. Some openly had rifles out, though none were pointed our way. None approached too close, but they all watched us.

The mansion—and it truly appeared to deserve the name— had a wide veranda all the way around. At least on the two sides we could see. We rode up to its edge and waited. In a moment a Mexican appeared. He was wearing a white coat, the kind I'd seen on waiters in big hotels in Dallas and Houston. He said, "The señor is waiting for you een hees beeg office. I will show you."

We dismounted and tied our horses and followed him. He led us in through the double entry doors and down a long, cool hallway. Our spurs jingled musically off the tile floor. The servant stopped beside another set of double doors. He swung them open and then stepped aside. We entered.

It was a big, square room. Obviously an office. Two walls were lined completely with books. The floor was white tile with woven rugs scattered around. Overhead, there was a big chandelier fixed up with kerosene lights.

Jacobbsen was sitting at a massive desk against a wall that looked through a window out into a courtyard. He had his back to us, but he turned as we entered and stood up. He said, "Come in, gentlemen."

He had heavy blond hair, not light and wild like Marriah's but tending more toward brown. Here and there, especially at the temples, it was streaked with gray. He was a big man with good shoulders and long arms. He carried himself like one who'd led an active life and was still fit and able. He came toward us, his hand out. "I'm Dag Jacobbsen."

Tom shook his hand and said his name. Ben and I just looked at it. After a second his hand dropped. He looked at me. "You must be Justa Williams."

I kept my voice as even as I could. "That's right," I said.

He looked at Ben. Tom said, "This is Ben Williams. One of the brothers."

"The other one didn't come?"

"No," Tom said.

Jacobbsen smiled thinly. He looked as if he understood. "Can I offer you something to drink? I'm having brandy."

I shook my head and Tom said, "Mr. Jacobbsen, we don't regard this as a social visit."

Jacobbsen shrugged. "Please yourself." He had no accent, neither Eastern nor Scandinavian nor Texan. Perhaps the different parts had each neutralized the other. But there was in his voice the sound of a man used to being obeyed. He didn't have a particularly deep or powerful voice, but there was a certain command in it, even on the slightest statement.

There was a couch and several chairs behind us. Jacobbsen waved us toward them. Ben and I sat down on the couch and Tom Hudspeth took a chair to our left. Jacobbsen brought his desk chair forward and placed it so that he was facing us. Then he put another chair beside his own and called toward a small door at the back. "Torrey!"

The door opened and a slim, dark-haired young man wearing a white shirt and blue trousers came into the room. He moved slowly, timidly, seeming almost afraid. Jacobbsen waved him forward impatiently and almost put him in the chair alongside him. He said, "This is my son, Torrey." He didn't bother to introduce us, so I figured Torrey wouldn't be doing much talking. I figured he just wanted to give the boy an object lesson in how to handle troublemakers. Watch the old man in action.

Jacobbsen sat down and I noticed that the climate of the country he'd been inhabiting for so many years hadn't done much good on his fair skin. I figured he either stayed inside a

lot during the hot summer or lived with a pretty good case of
sunburn. He was wearing a white ruffled shirt under a kind of
short, Spanish-style jacket. His britches had a little flare to
them at the bottom. He didn't appear to have a gun, not unless
he had a derringer secreted about his person somewhere. I did
not, however, doubt that there was plenty of armed help just
outside any of the three doors that led into the room.

Tom said, "Well, you invited us out for a discussion, Mr.
Jacobbsen. I believe you mentioned something about it per-
taining to our mutual interests."

"Yes," Jacobbsen replied. But he didn't look at Tom. He
had his eyes on me. I stared back. Tom had taken off his hat,
but Ben and I hadn't.

We waited, but it was a long moment before he said anything. Then, "It appears we have fallen upon difficulties here."

"We?" Tom said. "What difficulties have you fallen upon,
Mr. Jacobbsen?"

"Perhaps *difficulties* is the wrong word. I expect I should
have said *misapprehensions* or *misunderstandings*. Still, they
appear to be leading to difficulties."

"How so? In what regard are you speaking?"

"Your client," Jacobbsen said, "seems intent on involving
me and my family in his present plight." He was talking to
Tom, but he steadfastly kept his eyes on me. "For what reason
I don't know."

"How has he done that?"

"He's made certain representations to the townspeople. He's
spent a considerable amount of time asking after me and my
affairs. He's defamed me to the court and the law. But worse,
he's involved my son and my daughter—my daughter to the
point of forcing her to hold a conversation with him. He's also
pistol-whipped and threatened several of my men."

Well, it was all I could do to hold my comments in. I wanted
to lash out at him so bad, it was like a live bomb ticking in my
right hand. I could feel Ben tensing beside me. But I had
promised Tom that I would hold my peace for the time being.

Jacobbsen said, "I see that these two men are wearing side
arms. I don't ordinarily receive visitors who are armed."

That was about all I could take. I had to say, "Then you wouldn't have received us at all. I'd no—"

Tom said sharply, "Justa!"

I subsided.

After a pause Tom said to Jacobbsen, "Well, sir, my client feels that he's been falsely accused and badly mistreated, not only physically but also where his rights within the law are concerned. You can well imagine that a man in that position is going to do everything in his power to put matters to rights. I might point out at this instant that my client has considerable resources in his power, not the least of which is his absolute resolve. He's not a man easily deterred once he thinks he's been wronged."

"So I've heard," Jacobbsen said dryly. "But if he's innocent, what is he so worried about?"

I said, "Try false witness for one."

Jacobbsen just looked at me. He appeared to be faintly amused.

"Is your main false witness about?" I asked. "Mr. Purdy? Wilton Purdy?"

Jacobbsen said, "I wouldn't know. But I have heard you are interested in him. I even hear you've threatened him."

Tom put in hurriedly, "Mr. Jacobbsen, let's get back to the subject. You've made certain remonstrations about my client's actions in regard to yourself and your family. Surely you didn't ask us all the way out here just to get that off your chest. What exactly do you have in mind?"

I was watching Jacobbsen's face carefully. He spoke fine words and wore fine clothes and lived in a mansion. For all the world to see, he was a gentleman. But behind those yellow, catlike eyes of his I could see a sneering cruelty. This man didn't have the slightest concept of morality. It suddenly struck me that I was perhaps looking at the most selfish man I'd ever seen. For a moment he shifted his glance from me to Tom, then he said, "This whole affair is becoming wearisome to me. Your client is causing too much trouble, not only to me but also to the townspeople. They look to me for guidance. Let's just say that what we have here is a case of mistaken identity. I'm willing to have all charges against your client dropped. Let he

and his brothers make their way home"—here he turned his
eyes on me—"and look after affairs on their smallholding. I'm
sure a ranch of even that size needs work."

I didn't rise to that bait. He probably knew that the
Half-Moon, although much smaller than his acreage, was
almost as valuable a property on account of the much better
grazing land.

Tom gave a short bark of laughter, then he said, "Now let
me get this straight, Mr. Jacobbsen. *You* are proposing to drop
the charges against Mr. Williams?"

"That's correct."

Tom said, "Would you mind telling me where you get your
judicial authority, Mr. Jacobbsen?"

Jacobbsen turned those flat, unemotional eyes on him. He
said, "From money, sir. Money and power. What else is the
source of authority?"

Tom's mouth dropped open. But he recovered in time to say,
"Well, you have confirmed what we have suspected all along.
And by the way, what I've tried to inform the U.S. Marshal's
office in San Antonio is that the judiciary is corrupt, as well as
the sheriff's office. That it was indeed you, sir, who were
making the rules. I'm not surprised, only that you'd admit it so
openly."

Jacobbsen didn't even bother to respond to the sally. He just
said, "Well? Are you amenable? Quit the country and the
matter is forgotten."

I said softly, "What about the murder, Mr. Jacobbsen? The
rape and the murder? Or has enough time passed where you
don't really have to worry anymore?"

He said, "What exactly do you mean by that?"

Ben stirred himself. I knew he wouldn't be able to sit quietly
through all that had been said. He pointed his finger at Torrey.
"I reckon you know what he means. Only reason you jumped
Justa was to take the heat off that boy who's sitting in that chair
not saying anything. I think we all know who done the murder.
You ain't doing my brother any favor with all this talk about
dropping charges. The truth of the matter is, you *want* us out
of this country before we come across the truth."

I was watching Torrey. He stirred uneasily at Ben's words

but made no other sign. Most of the meeting he'd been staring down at his hands.

Jacobbsen said coldly, "I advise you to watch your words. That's a serious accusation." He turned back to Tom. "All right, give me your answer. What do you say?"

I stood up. "*I'll* be giving you your answer, Jacobbsen. You can have all the charges dropped that you want. I'm not concerned about that. But me and you and your bully boy have still got some business to settle. And I'm not quitting this country until it's settled—to *my* satisfaction. You made one big mistake, Jacobbsen, when you set your pack of wolves on me. I intend for you to regret it. Mister, I am bad news, and I'll have you. I'll have you good. Then I'll leave." I watched the flush coming over his face. I'd waited a long time for that moment and I was going to savor it. I twisted the knife a little deeper. "And when I do, I might just take your daughter with me. I think she fancies me. But I'll also see the U.S. Marshal's here to put your son in prison for rape and murder."

He was so enraged, he was shaking. His voice was nearly out of control. He said, "Why you low-bred, despicable bastard! Who do you think you're talking to? You'll never leave this place alive." He suddenly yelled, "Cully! Arty!"

Ben and I drew even as the two small doors opened and several men poured into the room holding rifles. I leveled my pistol at Jacobbsen and said, "You better select your next words mighty carefully or else I'm going to let some light through you. Your hired hands may hit me, but this gun is going to fire and take the guts out of you."

"And I'm going to stop the line right here with your pretty boy," Ben said. "That nice white shirt of his is going to get all messed up."

Tom Hudspeth, stuttering said, "Let—let—let me remind you, Mr. Jacobbsen, that we are here at your invitation. People know, including the authorities in San Antonio."

Yet we all stood there in a frozen tableau: me and Ben on our feet, our guns drawn; the men with rifles at the door; Torrey seated; Jacobbsen on his feet, his fists clenched, glaring hatred at me.

Then, into that frozen and desperate silence, the double

doors suddenly opened and Marriah walked in. She looked around coolly. "Why whatever is going on here?"

Almost deliberately she walked straight into the middle of the room, putting herself between me and her father, but also between me and the riflemen. She said, "This is monstrous! I won't have it. Father, send your men away immediately. A gunfight in the house! Disgraceful."

Slowly, bit by bit, Jacobbsen appeared to relax. Marriah apparently had one hell of a say. Without taking his eyes off mine he called, "Cully! Withdraw."

Ben said, "Cully? Justa, ain't that the one you beat the shit out of with a skillet? Lord, he looks it." He laughed.

I shifted my eyes just enough to see my recent adversary. It did my heart good to see his face as lumped up and bruised as mine had been. He had a strip of plaster across his nose, and it appeared, though I couldn't be sure, that his scowl might be a little crooked on account of some missing teeth. I certainly hoped so. I gave him a little smile and he looked back at me with an awful mean gleam in his eyes. He said, "You sonof—"

But he got no further because Marriah stamped her pretty little foot and said, "Out, out! All of you! Stop it right now!"

Ben and I watched them pull back. They did it reluctantly. When they were out of the room, we slowly reholstered our guns. I said, "Miss Jacobbsen, that was an extraordinary thing to do. A little dangerous, but extraordinary."

She tossed her hair. "Mr. Williams, I am not the least interested in your opinion of my actions. Or of me. I am only interested in you leaving this house and this ranch without further ungentlemanly conduct. Pray do so, sir."

I said, "Tom, you got anything further to say?"

He shook his head. "No, not at this time. In view of circumstances, it would seem pointless."

"Ben?"

My younger brother just grinned, but without much humor. He said, "No, not right now. I just wish ol' Dag here would come into town and let me buy him a drink."

I half smiled. "Somehow, Ben, I don't think he's going to take you up on your invitation." Then I gave Jacobbsen one more look. I said, "Remember what I said."

A look of some cruel inner humor passed across his face. He said, almost nonchalantly, "I think you'll have more reason to remember what I said."

Then we were gone out of the house. Outside, we mounted up and rode away. We did not expect pursuit, but we were on our guard nevertheless. A hundred yards away from the ranch house I turned in the saddle and looked back. I could see a solitary golden-haired figure standing on the veranda, watching our departure.

Tom didn't exactly chastise me, but he did say, "Justa, do you think it was particularly good politics to make him angry?"

I didn't answer for a moment. Something else was crowding my mind, something I'd been thinking about from the moment we'd left Jacobbsen. After a little I said, "I don't know, Tom. I don't know if I'm doing any of this the right way. But I don't think it's possible for him to get any meaner just because he's angry."

Ben said, "I'll amen that. God, I'd like to have shot that sonofabitch. Right through his ruffled shirt." Then he looked at me. "Of course I realize that would have been your right. But I'd of liked to have shot the rest of the bastards. Why'd that damn girl have to come in just then?"

Tom said, "Because she was listening at the door. Thank God."

"Aw, Tom, we wouldn't let none of them hurt you." Ben grinned. "Big brother and I would have handled them tramps. You mighta got shot a little bit, but not a whole bunch."

Tom said dryly, "No thank you. I'm perfectly happy to be out of there with no more damage done than was." He shook his head. "I'm very fearful this is going to get worse and worse." He didn't sound happy.

We were approaching town. With about a half mile to go, I pulled my horse up. The others did likewise, looking at me questioningly. "Tom, you ride on into town. Ben, you stay here and watch my back."

Tom looked dismayed. "Oh, Justa, you're not going back out there!"

I got down from my horse. "No." I looked around for a handy rock to sit down on. "No, I'm just going to take a seat and ruminate. Ben, would you watch my back?" I jerked my head. "Maybe up the hill?"

Ben got down, with Tom staring at us both questioningly. Ben took his saddle gun out of the boot and then tied the reins of both our horses together. They began cropping at the sparse grass along the edge of the road.

Tom asked, "What the hell is going on?"

"Justa is going to think a spell," Ben replied.

Tom looked puzzled. "What?"

Ben pointed a finger at his head. "When he's got something gnawing at him, he sits and thinks until he's got it figured out."

"Oh," said Tom.

"You go on back to the hotel. We'll be there before suppertime. Justa, you want him to tell Norris what went on?"

I nodded slowly. "Yeah. Might as well."

After that Tom rode away, shaking his head slightly, and I sat down on the rock I'd selected. While I lit a cigar and got it drawing good, Ben took his rifle and scrambled up the hill behind us to a point high enough where he could command a good view of the road and surrounding territory. He didn't say a word to me other than to mention there was a bottle of whiskey in his saddlebags. Ben knew me pretty well. Our horses had found some good grass and shade under a fair-sized mesquite tree. They were content just to stand and wait. It was me who was troubled. Ben had tied their reins together in such a way that they couldn't get them tangled in their feet; I wished he could have done the same for me and my uncertainty.

CHAPTER
7

I stared off in the distance, smoking and thinking. After the little exchange that had just taken place back at the Treetops, it didn't take a scholar to figure out that me and Jacobbsen were headed at each other like a couple of runaway freight trains on the same track. My words had turned it into a personal vendetta. He'd offered me a way out, offering to drop the charges and have the indictment quashed if I'd quit the country, but I'd thrown it back in his face, vowing to destroy him. Before I'd just been the casual object needed to fill the role of suspect and villain, a convenience to be dealt with in his ordinary harsh manner. But then I'd made it me and him and I'd seen, with no possible mistake, that elated cruelty in his eyes. I had become now a very personal object for his intense wrath and punishment. And, by transference, I'd also involved my brothers and anyone else that was affiliated with me.

And I'd had to wonder, as we rode away from the ranch headquarters, if I had that right. No matter how bad I wanted to destroy Jacobbsen, no matter how much he had it coming, no matter how sure I was that I could do it, did I really have the right to risk the others? And not just the others but myself. Because I was, with our father in such poor health, the bond that not only held the Half-Moon together but the family as well. Norris was good in his area, as was Ben, but neither was as uniquely qualified as I was to oversee all matters, be it business or ranching or family or trouble. My daddy had said as much the day he'd called me in to lay the awful burden on my shoulders. He'd said, "Son, beginning today you're taking over. I want to step down now and give you the job while I'm still around and able to give you advice and counsel."

I made a mild protest, claiming that Norris was better qualified. "Paw, Norris has been to the university and he's better at business than I am. Just because I'm the eldest . . ."

But he shook his head. "It's not just because you're the eldest, it's because you're the best for the job. I grant you that Norris has more book learning and a good head for business, and you'll use that. Norris wouldn't know how to use you. Or Ben. But you will. Business is not just figures and cattle and horses and hiring and firing people. Business is sound judgment and being able to see beyond what you got in your hand. You'll make mistakes and I'm going to let you make mistakes because that's the best way to learn. But when you do, we'll discuss 'em and see if there's not a way for you not to make the same mistake twice. I know I'm asking an awful lot of you at your young age, twenty-four, but I don't have no choice. Since you mother . . ." He looked away for a second. I looked away also, to give him time. When he came back to me, he said, "I just don't have the strength I once did, Justa. It's got to be now. I've got to know that the family will be taken care of. I'd like to hand you the reins gradual like, but there may not be time. That's why I've decided just to thrust them at you."

That had been four years ago. To all outward appearances my father had still seemed to be in good health. His arthritis had only begun, and he hadn't taken the bullet that nicked his lung and sapped his strength. But to those of us close to him there had come a definite change. After our mother died, something seemed to go out of him. Oh, he was still capable of those quick and sometimes humorous outbursts of temper, still possessed of the same wily logic, still a shrewd trader, still able to sit a horse all day long. But he just didn't seem to care that much anymore. Just that little spark of vitality seemed to be gone. At the time he was only a man of sixty-two years, but almost overnight he seemed to have aged. What Indians and the Civil War and carpetbaggers and scalawags and rustlers and crooked bankers and onery cattle and mean broncs hadn't been able to accomplish in all his years, that little mound of fresh dirt had done in less than a minute.

It worried me hearing him talk about me taking over while there was still time. I was afraid he was going to grieve himself to death and said so. He'd laughed and shook his head and said, "No, son, I ain't planning on going nowhere for some time. I'll be around looking over your shoulder until you're going to *wish* I'd go. Now, you've practically been running the ranch for some time and all the hired hands are already used to working for you, so that's no big change. The big change is you'll be sitting in my chair and making *all* the decisions. I've told your brothers already."

I asked their reaction.

My father said, "Norris is in full agreement. He sees the logic of the matter. Norris is a great one for logic."

"What about Ben?"

"Ben said it didn't make any difference to him." Then he got that dry turn of voice in his mouth and said, "Of course, I understand what he means by that. He doesn't figure to listen to you any more than he did to me."

I smiled at that.

But my dad said, "You keep a tight rein on that boy. He'll make a hell of a man someday. If he lives." Then he gave me an understanding look. "Justa, I know I've worked you hard all these years. And I've laid responsibility on you beyond your age. And it was all for this day. In the future you're going to find yourself in some fixes and I might not be around to help you out. So you might as well start learning how to play a solo hand right now. Two men can't break a bronc. Ain't room in the saddle."

Well, he'd been right about that. Both about the fixes I'd get into and about the room in the saddle. But I had my leg over one hell of a bronc right then and sure wished he was around to give me a little advice.

Since that time I had met plenty of problems head-on. As my mind wandered back over the list of potential calamities that

had been thrown my way, one in particular stood out. It had
happened about three years ago, and what brought it so sharply
to mind was that it was another circumstance where my
personal feelings as well as my duty as head of the family had
been involved. To that moment I could not say if I'd let my
personal feelings cloud my judgment.

It had all begun, innocently enough, with an attempt on our
part to upgrade our cattle. We, like everyone else, were
running longhorn stock, which were almost native to the
region, being direct descendants of the cattle the Spanish
conquistadores had brought over when they'd first settled
Mexico and Texas.

Now, the longhorns, while a splendidly self-sufficient animal, is also hell to gather, mean to handle, will wander across
half the state, dangerous to brand or treat, and, in spite of its
size, carries about half the beef that the imported breeds were
producing. Consequently we were getting bottom dollar at
market, and that with cattle prices higher than they'd ever been
in anyone's memory. Of course, the days of the trail drives
were over so you didn't need a big, rangy animal like a
longhorn that could stand the rigors of such a trip. Cattle were
being shipped to market on trains, and most of the ranchers in
the Midwest and the northern states like Wyoming and
Montana were already going in for shorthorns and Hereford
breeds and even some of the Scottish cattle, Angus. They were
taking these Enlish cattle and crossing them with their range
stock and coming up with a breed that was hardy enough to
stand the hard life in the open, yet stocky and blocky enough
to produce a high beef yield. And these were the ranchers that
were leaving the markets with their pockets full of money.

Well, I figured that we had to do the same or get left at the
starting gate. I talked it over with Ben and Norris, and they
couldn't see where we could do ought else. When I talked it
over with our father, he wouldn't comment. He just said,
"Justa, you've got to follow your instincts. Run this ranch, and
don't come to me about every little thing."

It wasn't exactly an "every little thing." Firstly, it meant a
considerable outlay of capital. And secondly, it meant a
rearrangement of a ranching pattern that had been going on for

forty years, and an adjustment on everyone's part to a new direction. Even down to the lowliest cowhand learning how to handle this new breed of cattle. You couldn't cowboy those imported breeds like you could a longhorn. You couldn't kill a longhorn without a rifle, but you could a Hereford.

So it was with some trepidation that I sent Norris off to the Midwest to buy, wherever he could find them, twenty purebred bulls and two hundred mama cows, preferably already bred. That Norris didn't know as much about cattle as me or my foreman didn't make any difference. None of us knew anything about these breeds, so I just told him to use his best judgment and to do the best he could. Buy Whiteface and Herefords and ship them home to Blessing. We'd be waiting.

The main problem in this venture, and one my brothers hadn't even mentioned, I'd already foreseen and thought I had solved. Our ranch was on the broad coastal plains. As a matter of fact, the back part of it ran right to the sandy beach of the Gulf of Mexico. It was deeded at a little over twenty thousand acres, but that was a misleading figure. The coastal plains ran several hundred miles in length and were, at some points, better than a hundred miles wide. Fencing had not come into common use in our part of the country, as it had in others; so it was standard practice, as it had been for a hundred years, just to let your cattle graze as they would. Then, twice a year we'd go out, as would the riders from other ranches, and cut our cattle out that we were going to market or, if it was spring, brand the calves that were following mama cows with our brand. All that had worked fine in the past because we were all running the same kind of cattle, longhorns.

But now I was fixing to come in here with these imported, expensive cattle and I couldn't very well just turn them loose on the range. Some of those bulls I expected to pay as much as two or three thousand dollars apiece for, not to mention what I was going to have to lay out for the mama cows, especially if they were already bred.

Well, I like to help my neighbor; consider it, in fact, my Christian duty. But not to the extent of turning my high-priced imported bulls loose where they can breed his love-starved longhorn cows and let them drop some high-priced crossbred calves. These matters can be carried too far.

So how was I going to upgrade my herd by mixing *my* longhorns and *my* blooded stock while keeping them separated from my neighbor's?

Fencing was out of the question. First, it was expensive as hell. But, more importantly, it would immediately lead to trouble. If I started stringing fence, I'd most certainly cut my neighbor's cattle off from some water hole they'd been watering at for twenty years. That it was on my property made no difference because I would have had cattle watering on his land for twenty years. Not only that, but it would have interfered with cattle drives and roundups and even gotten in the way of some cowboy traveling cross-country to see his girl. Fencing could do nothing but start fights and make enemies.

I had a solution. There was an island that lay just a little over a quarter of a mile off our shoreline. It was an island of some eight or nine thousand acres. True, it was not deeded to us, but then it was not deeded to anyone. Because it was almost on our land, and because, at low tide, you could practically walk out to it if you didn't mind bogging down in the sandy silt, we had long considered it ours. On occasion we'd used it to hold cattle we suspected of being diseased or exposed to Mexican tick fever. On others we'd quartered horses there we were trying to upgrade, separating them from our regular remuda. And, as a family we'd used it for picnics and fishing and overnight camping trips. There was good water there, though the grass was nothing to brag about. But it was wooded and somewhat shaded and I thought it would be ideal to hold my blooded stock and use as a sort of breeding farm. Sometime past we'd built a sort of flatbed barge-ferry that we'd used to transport various horses or cattle that we were either taking to or bringing from the island. I figured we could station our purebreds there and then ferry out the right amount of longhorn mama cows. Then, once they were bred, we'd bring them back and take over another batch. It didn't matter if they dropped their calves on the open range. They'd be crossbred and there'd be no question who they belonged to.

Meanwhile, our purebred cows would be dropping the

calves they were already bred with and it would give the calves
a gentle place to get a little maturity before they got introduced
to longhorn society. Of course, we also planned to mix in a few
longhorn bulls and let them breed to the Hereford and
Whiteface cows and get another mix that way.

It was going to be considerable work, there was no question
about that. Just poling that barge across took the best efforts of
ten men. And none of them much liked it, either. Which is the
nature of cowboys. If they can't do it on horseback, with one
notable exception, they don't want to do it. But, on top of that,
I planned to have another barge constructed. We could swim
the longhorns over and back, but I wasn't going to take a
chance on the purebreds. But the main article we needed the
second barge for was feed. The grass was just too poor for
those high-toned English cattle. The longhorns could eat it and
thrive, but we were going to have to supplement the diet of the
other cattle. That meant hauling an awful lot of corn and oats.
I figured I was going to have some mighty disgusted cowboys
before this whole endeavor was through and I was able to see
a range full of upgraded cattle.

The surprise of the matter was that it went mighty easy at
first. We got the purebreds across, got them settled, and then
began rounding up longhorn cows and swimming them across.
They even seemed to like it, though those English bulls didn't
seem to know what to make of their new girlfriends at first. But
even that got straightened out.

All in all, it took us the better part of four months to get
matters straightened out and the operation running smoothly.
Counting all costs, of which the cattle had been the biggest
part, we had laid out a little over $56,000 on the experiment.
And it was an experiment. A costly one and a hazardous one.
Hurricanes are a constant threat in our part of the country. They
don't enter the Gulf every year, but they come often enough to
suit everyone concerned. And I had, several times in my
lifetime, seen that island so completely underwater that only
the tops of the trees were showing. My daddy asked me if I'd
allowed for that eventuality. I said I had. He asked me what I
was going to do. I said, "First I'm going to pray like hell it
doesn't happen. But if it does, I'm going to get all the cattle off

there that I can in whatever time I have. Then I'm going to count what I got left and go on from there."

"Not going to count your losses?"

I shook my head. "What good does that do?"

He laughed. "You'll break us or make us," he said.

But trouble hadn't come in the form of a hurricane. Looking back, I almost wished that it had. At least the issues and the questions of right and wrong would have been more visible and the decisions more clear-cut. What had come had been a storm, all right, but a storm that was filled with bitterness and hate and greed and death, instead of wind.

About that time I heard a low call from Ben. I came instantly alert, looking quickly up and down the road. It was empty. I looked up at him. He said, "Can you interrupt your reverie long enough for me to fetch that bottle of whiskey? This is mighty warm work protecting you while your wheels turn."

"Yeah, c'mon," I said.

He clambered down the hill and went to his horse while I kept watch up and down the road. After he'd rummaged around in his saddlebags and found the bottle, he came over to me, swinging it from one hand. He pulled the cork and had a swallow and then said, "What the hell are you thinking so hard about?"

I looked up at him. "That night on the island. You and me and Norris, and Dad."

"Oh," he said. He had another pull, looking off in the distance. "Yeah. Long time ago, though, Justa."

"Yeah."

"You figure to be much longer? I'm getting hungry."

"I don't know," I said. "I've got to get something worked through in my mind."

"What does the island have to do with this?"

"Maybe nothing. Listen, go do your job and leave me to do mine. Go think about girls or something."

He handed me the bottle. "Maybe this will speed you up." Then he went back on up the hill, carrying his rifle, starting little miniature landslides with every step.

The trouble had started about a month after we'd gotten the operation running smoothly, and I was starting to congratulate myself for being pretty damned smart. We were keeping two cowhands on the island on rotating shifts just to tend to the feeding and to watch over the new cattle, and just, in general, to see that everything was all right. One morning one that had been on duty the night before, a man named Pete Worth, came spurring his horse up and said, "Boss, I don't know how it happened, but we got a bunch of strange cattle on the island. I kind of halfway recognize the brand, but I ain't real sure. It appears to be from that new outfit, Ficus and Dunn. But it beats hell out of me how them cattle got on the island."

I asked him if they were mixed or mama cows.

"Not a bull in the bunch. All cows and ever' one of 'em is in season."

Now, of course, a bull will go to a cow when she's ready, will jump a fence to do so, or swim a stretch of water, but a cow won't go to a bull. So it was a pretty safe bet that those longhorn cows hadn't just decided to go visiting on their own. Somebody had helped them. I asked Pete when he thought the cows had got on the island. He shrugged. "Could have been anytime after dark. Me and Pancho was camped down at the lower end of the island and we found the biggest part of them strange cows up at the other end when we rode out this morning to have a look around."

It was no secret to anyone in that part of the country about my experiment; in fact, I'd taken plenty of good-natured abuse over it from dyed-in-the-wool longhorn advocates. So I just naturally couldn't imagine any of our near neighbors stooping to such a trick as to drive some of their cattle out to our island to be bred by our bulls. We were friendly with our near neighbors and used to helping each other, turn and turnabout.

But Pete had said the brand looked like Ficus and Dunn. It hadn't given me a good feeling. The Ficuses and the Dunns were two new families from the northern part of the state who'd come in and thrown their resources together and were trying to take advantage of the booming cattle market. A lot of Texas is ideal grazing land, but the coastal plains are the best. If you could lay claim to just a hundred and sixty acres, deeded, you had hundreds and hundreds of thousands of acres you could graze your cattle on. The Dunns and the Ficuses weren't the only ones to have taken advantage of the situation, but they'd quickly made themselves conspicuous by their quarrelsome nature and their questionable habit of branding every calf that came near their ropes. They were an odd lot; the Ficuses were made up of two brothers, Oral and Flynn, and a small sprinkling of cousins. Oral and Flynn were in their early thirties and they'd left their wives back home while they'd come down to try to make a quick profit in beef. The Dunns were more like a family. Joe Dunn was a big man in his mid-forties. He had two sons that appeared to be in their early twenties. They had a few hired hands, but they mainly did the work themselves, operating out of a ramshackle ranch head-quarters some twenty miles up the coast from us. They weren't popular with any of their neighbors. Fortunately, we'd never had occasion to have a run-in with them. Ben called them trash; Norris said they bore watching; and I just said I was glad they were way the hell up the coast.

Only their cattle didn't seem to know they were off their home range.

It had taken us a hard week's work to gather those cattle out of the bushes and the brambles and the high weeds and drive them into the water and swim them back to shore. In the process we'd damn near wore out half a dozen good horses and nearly that many cowboys. And I still hadn't been sure we'd gotten them all. But whether we had or not, I couldn't waste any more time on the matter, nor spare any more cowhands from their regular duties. My breeding experiment was one thing; we still had a very large ranching operation to run.

I had not deliberately gone seeking Ficus and Dunn, but one day, about a week after we'd cleared their brand off the island, I was in the little town of Wadsworth, which happened to be up near their place, and I chanced to see them coming out of the post office. Rather, I chanced to see the two Ficus brothers. I went up to them and, without much preamble, said, "Oral, Flynn, a batch of your cattle got across the water and onto our island where I've got a breeding operation going on. I think you know that. We've cleared them off and put them back on the mainland. But since they're a good ways off their normal range, I thought I'd let you know. I imagine they're drifting back your way."

Of course I'd known they'd swum those cattle out to the island and they'd have had to think me an awful fool to think I didn't know it. But I still put it in such a way so as not to give offense and to let them save what face they could.

But they wouldn't have it that way. Both of them were stocky, wind- and sunburned items of particular social appeal. Oral bristled up and said, "What the hell you mean handling our cattle? You keep your goddamn hands off our stock."

I told them I would so long as their cattle stayed out of my business.

Flynn blustered up and said, "Listen, I'm tired of you goddamn high-and-mighty Williamses and your high-and-mighty ways. That goddamn island don't belong to you. We'll put our cattle on that island any damn time we want to, and you can just fucking lump it."

I heard them out. We tried to be neighbors in our part of the country. Besides, I figured to just let them blow off some steam. It wasn't the first time I'd faced open envy, touched with anger, because I was a Williams. And if I fought every time it happened, I wouldn't have had time for anything else. I just said, "I don't have any intention of discussing this with you here in the middle of the street. That island is twenty miles off your range. I know why you put those cattle on there. I don't blame you. Just don't do it again."

Oral said, "You go to hell, Williams. We'll do as we goddamn well please. Ain't your damn island."

I walked away.

Within a week they were trying again. But we'd been ready for them. Ever since the first incident I'd stationed four men on the island, having them camp at the upper end, the end where the first cattle had been landed. A little after dusk three riders tried swimming about a hundred head onto the island. But my men were ready for them. They fired their guns into the air and the cattle turned away and made for the mainland shore. The herders, trying to stay with a swimming horse and push cattle at the same time, were in a poor position for a fight. Except for a few stray shots they, too, turned for the mainland.

But now I realized something had to be done. We couldn't afford to keep that many men posted indefinitely on the island. I went looking for Joe Dunn, thinking, because he was the eldest, he might be the boss of the outfit and could be reasoned with. After a long ride I found him on the open range working a bunch of his cattle back toward some common pens we all used for branding and castrating and doctoring worms. I hailed him and came up alongside him. He just glanced at me, not even bothering to pull up his horse. He had a couple of hands with him, though I didn't know if they were kin or just hired. As civilly as I could, though it was made more difficult by him shouting instructions to his drovers, I explained the situation to him and our attitude toward it. I said, "Now, anybody with half an eye can see why you are driving your stock so far from your place. I've got a lot of money invested in this project, and we just can't stand to have it interfered with. I hope you can understand that and that this matter doesn't have to go any further."

Then he reined up his horse. He looked at me, a square-faced look that was thrown out of symmetry because of the wad of tobacco in his cheek. He said, "Williams, I don't give a shit what you won't stand for." He said it sneeringly, his eyes gleaming. "And neither does Oral er Flynn. You got them fancy bulls on that island an' iffen you don't want our cattle hobnobbin' with yore fancy cattle, why, get yore goddamn fancy cattle offen that island. It don't belong to you noways."

Well, we had looked into that. Or at least Norris had. We had a claim to that island, and though it was a tenuous one, it was much stronger than any claim anyone else had. By rights the island probably belonged to the state, but since we'd used it all those years, and since, at least at low tide, it was connected to the rest of our property by dry land, it was the same as ours. I said to Dunn, "You're wrong, Mr. Dunn. We have a claim to that island. By prescriptive rights and by the right of adverse possession over a period exceeding ten years. Not to mention common usage and the improvements we've made on it. But you don't have to understand that. All you've got to understand is that you better keep your damn cattle off of it or there's going to be trouble. And I don't think you'll like it."

He'd spit tobacco juice then, some of it getting on the shoulder of my horse. Then he looked at me. "Oh, yeah, sonny boy? You better git home before you git yore britches whupped."

I rode away, not saying another word. They'd been warned.

Only I hadn't counted on the low meanness of their nature. Ben had been right when he'd called them trash. It was only a few days after my encounter with Joe Dunn that one of the hands on the island came hightailing it back to report that they'd caught an unknown man trying to poison the feed bins. They hadn't been able to catch the man, so they didn't know who he was, but they had caught him in the act of trying to pour lime water into one of our big bins of oats we'd so laboriously transported over. If you want to make cattle bloat up and die, just feed them lime-soaked oats. They'll eat it and twenty-four hours later you'll have a lot of suffering stock.

But while they hadn't caught the man, they'd identified him as being from the Ficus and Dunn ranch. When they jumped him, he dodged off through the thick underbrush and eluded them the rest of the night. They theorized he'd swum to shore at some point. But they'd surrounded his horse and kept it, and that horse had a Ficus and Dunn brand on it.

"That's it," I said. "I've had enough." We'd been sitting down to breakfast when the news came. I'd gotten up and put on my gun belt. "I'm going to get this settled."

Ben had gotten up too. "I'm going."

"No, you're not."

Norris said, "Justa, this has got to go to the law. They're plainly in the wrong. We'll ride into Blessing and see the sheriff and—"

"The sheriff is out of the county."

"All right, we'll see our lawyer and get the process started."

"Too long, Norris," I said. "Too long. Listen, these are people who are trying to poison our cattle. We don't have time to go to a courtroom. Have you forgot how much money we've got committed to this?"

He said dryly, "Not likely, since I keep the books."

"Then you must realize that we don't have time for a lengthy court suit. They could try something again tomorrow. Or the day after. Norris, dear brother, get your nice, kind, sensible head out of your ass. We ain't dealing with nice, kind, sensible people here."

"Damn right," Ben said. "Trash."

And all the while Dad was just looking on and listening, not saying a word. I'd already been to him for advice and he wouldn't give me any.

Norris said, "Justa, there has to be a better way. We are trying to be civilized. And this country is never going to be civilized if every dispute is settled by force of arms. Why don't you just go to their place and burn them out if you want to reply in kind. Or shoot their cattle."

"Norris, I know your habit of using the ridiculous to make your point," I said. "Save that for your school friends who fall for it. I hope this won't go to 'force of arms,' as you call it, but I'm damn well going to put a stop to it."

Ben said, "And I'm going. And you ain't stopping me." He wasn't quite twenty-one then.

I looked at Dad. He just looked back, nothing on his face.

Norris spoke up. "At least one of us is going to act sane. While you're on your mission of vengeance, I'm going into town to the lawyer and establish our legal position."

Ben said, "And me and Justa is going and establish them sonsabitches a position on their backs."

I looked at him. "You are going to behave, and you are going to do what I tell you to do."

"Don't I always?"

"I mean it, Ben. You cut up cute and I'm sending you back."

Dad spoke then. "Try to find them off their land. And count the odds before you get too bold."

After that I went outside and instructed our foreman to double the guard on the island, and then Ben and I rode away. By chance we intercepted the Ficus brothers on the Wadsworth road, on their way back from town. Neither one of them had been wearing side guns, but they were both carrying rifles across the pommels of their saddles, almost as if they were looking for trouble.

Ben and I topped a little rise and then they were there. We were on them almost before they knew it. I didn't waste any words. We'd forced them to pull up by riding our horses directly in front of theirs and stopping. Ben was on my off side, but he gradually came around until we were squared up face-to-face with the brothers. I'd told them what I knew and I told them that if anything else happened, I was going to come looking for them, and this time was going to be the last time I'd be talking. Next time it would be serious.

Flynn began answering me back, telling me just how afraid they were and just how careful we better be. While he was talking, Oral shifted his rifle slowly, letting it come to bear on me. As he began to raise it I suddenly drew my revolver and shot him in the shoulder. The impact of the bullet flipped him off his horse. Flynn started to raise his rifle but then thought better of it when Ben stuck a pistol in his face.

We made Flynn drop his rifle and get down, and then Ben threw both guns out into the brush while I had a look at Oral. The bullet hadn't struck bone, just gone under the collarbone and exited out the back. But he was bleeding. There was a doctor in Wadsworth and I told Flynn he better get him there while there was plenty of time. Flynn was cussing, but Oral hadn't been saying much. We helped him on his horse. He was a little white-faced from the shock of the bullet. I gave them one more warning and then Ben and I mounted up. Just as we were about to ride away, Oral said, "Williams!"

I turned back and looked at him.

He said, gasping a little, "The grass on that island is nice and cured. And about a foot high."

It was. It had come October and the grass had cured off and turned the color of wheat. It hadn't been but a few days since I'd told Norris about it and had said we wouldn't have to feed so much of that expensive grain because the grass would be more nutritious now. But that wasn't what Oral was talking about.

He said, "Ought to burn real good." Then he cackled and they turned and rode toward Wadsworth.

I remembered staring after them and saying, "How do these things start?"

And Ben said, "That ain't important. It's important we put a finish to it. Did you mean to shoot him in the shoulder or was you aiming for the chest and missed?"

I looked at him. "What?"

"Never mind. I think I know."

Well, there'd been nothing for it then but to fort up and get ready for trouble. With the island the battleground. Norris was still calling for law and order, but I said, "Norris, the sheriff isn't even here. And if he was, there's nothing he can do. We can't prove a damn thing except I shot Oral Ficus. He'd have to catch them setting fire to the island before he could arrest them. Then what? They'd be in jail and we'd have a $56,000 barbecue."

But I went to Dad and told him my plans. "I know you said you weren't going to give me advice, but there's an awful lot at stake here and I'm still pretty new at the job. I think you ought to counsel with me on this."

He asked me if I thought it was too late to talk, to reason with Ficus and Dunn. I replied that I'd tried every approach with them I could think of. "Paw, they don't want to talk. You've got to understand, these aren't reasonable men. Ben calls them trash and I believe he's right. They mean us mischief, serious mischief."

Then he asked me if I'd done everything I could think of to avert a collision. I told him I thought so. "Blood has been spilled. They've made a threat and I believe they intend to carry it out."

He said, "All right, Justa, if you're sure you're right, then I think you should go ahead."

I thanked him, thinking everything was said. But he stopped me before I could leave the room.

"One thing . . . you know, this upgrading business is kind of your own personal project. And it's that that these men seem bent on interfering with. You're not taking this personal, are you?"

That had kind of startled me. "Well, Dad, are you saying

you don't approve of me buying those blooded cattle and trying
to upgrade?"

"Oh, hell, no. It's a damn good idea, and one somebody
should have thought of before. We've been trying to make a
living off them damn slab-sided longhorns long enough. They
ain't got enough meat on them to make dinner for a family of
four, and they're wild enough to be in a zoo. No, I'm all for
this idea."

He'd had me confused. "Then what is it?"

"Nothing really," he said. "Just as long as you've allowed
for every contingency you can think of. Remember, you're in
charge of our *whole* business, not just that island. That's why
I asked if you were letting this get personal for you."

"Hell, Dad, we only got fifteen riders besides me and Norris
and Ben. I can't guard the whole damn range. I'm looking for
a showdown with these people, and I think they're looking for
one with me. They'll come and they'll try to fire the island
because they'll know we're on it. What else can I do?"

He just shook his head. "Nothing I can think of."

I went away, apprehensive about what was to come, but
gladdened by seeing some of the old fire in our daddy's face.
He looked like he was about ready to strap on a gun himself.

Of course we hadn't known when they'd be coming, so we'd
made our plans for the long haul. Ben and Norris and I were all
going to the island. And stay there until it was over. I wanted
all of us there so there would be a brother awake at all times.
We'd taken five of our hired hands with us and left Dad with
the foreman and ten riders.

We favored the end of the island where they'd made their
sallies before. But we'd taken care not to leave any of our
perimeters unwatched, taking care to scout the whole island
several times by day and night.

We'd brought tents and food and what lesiure items we
favored in the way of whiskey and tobacco or, in Ben's case,
licorice candy. He'd had a taste for it ever since he was a kid,
and it was a constant source of wonder to all of us when he'd
outgrow it. But all he'd done when he'd come of enough age
that Paw would allow him to drink was to soak the damn stuff
in gin and down the horrible concoction like it was palatable.

From the first we were of divided opinions as to what to do. Norris held that we should do nothing; let the Ficus and Dunn bunch do what they would and then salvage what we could and recover the rest in a court of law. I didn't care for that approach, pointing out the delay it would cause in my improvement program. As well as the uncertainty of legal action. But that wasn't the real reason; the real reason was that I was damn good and angry and interested in blowing their fucking heads off and making them damn sorry they'd taken us on.

Ben, naturally, thought the whole business of waiting around on an island for some supposed attack was just plain foolishness. His idea was just to ride into their front yard and blow them to hell and gone, and put a stop to the mischief before it could make a start.

It was what I would have thought four years previously.

Daily, a rider had come from either Dad or the foreman to keep me apprised of affairs back at the ranch. Business seemed to be proceeding as usual, and all we could do was wait. Other than impatience and the feeling that I might be being made a fool of, and a couple of near mutinous brothers, the vigil hadn't been too tiresome. The October breeze off the Gulf waters was pleasant and cool during the day, and cold enough at night to make sleeping easy. And it was satisfying to see my imported cattle roaming about, looking placid and eating grass and feed and growing fat. Already some of the bred Hereford cows were showing, and they'd be calving in early March. Except for the unasked-for and unexpected trouble, I'd have been feeling very content with my work.

They came on our fourth night on the island. We pitched camp a hundred or so yards back in a copse of wind-stunted oaks, but we'd kept constant guard at the brushline, which was some fifty yards from the water's edge. That night, around eleven, one of the riders we'd brought with us had come creeping back to camp and awakened me. He said, "Boss, you'd better come. Something looks fishy."

Ben was on duty, but he'd ridden to the other end of the island to survey matters there. I sent the rider to fetch him, and then Norris and I made our way to the line of trees and hid in the brush and peered out. It was a good moonlit night, the moon very near full, and we could see as clearly as we needed to. Heading our way, and bobbing gently with the swell, had come a sort of bargelike affair. It was like the box of a wagon, only bigger. It appeared to be about five or six feet wide and maybe ten feet long. It looked thick and sturdy.

"What the hell is that, the *Merrimac*?" Norris asked.

"The *Monitor*," I said, watching it.

Obviously it had been launched from a little spit of land a couple of miles up the coast that actually stuck out farther into the Gulf than the island. The tide was coming in and the craft was being carried down on us by the movement of the water. As it got closer I could see rifle ports cut in its sides and I had no doubt that it contained four or five riflemen. Maybe more. And they were no doubt also equipped with kerosene to start a good fire, and maybe even a few sticks of dynamite.

Norris said, "What should we do?"

"Nothing. They're going to run aground quick, and they'll have a hell of a time setting fire to anything from where they'll be. That sand don't burn. And when they get out of that floating fortress, they'll have fifty yards of open beach to run across. And we've got four rifles already here."

So we lay and watched. By then everybody had been up and ready, except for Ben and the rider I'd sent after him. Slowly the barge neared and then, with a grating we could hear in the stillness of the night, began to ground itself. We just watched. Ever so gently the tide had nudged it forward a few feet in sporadic thrusts, but soon it was out of the push of the water and had settled firmly in shallow water a few feet from shore.

There was not a sound, nothing that could be heard. There had not been the sound of breathing, or of talk, or the click of a rifle being cocked.

We waited. They had to get out of their barge to do us any harm.

Then, just as we'd begun to wonder if maybe the barge was empty, a sizzling stick suddenly came flying out of the barge. It had landed on the ground some twenty yards from us and then went off with a great explosion. They had dynamite. Another stick followed. But they were landing too far away to do us any damage, although we could hear the spray of sand hitting the foliage of the trees and bushes. And behind me I detected the restless movement of the cattle, frightened by the noise. More dynamite came, and then I said, "All right, fire through the rifle ports. And fire at anything else you see. But stay low."

We had been in the process of leveling a lively volley of fire on the barge when Ben came riding up almost on top of us. He was yelling and it was a second, because of the rifle fire, before I could make out what he'd been saying. "The ranch! It's on fire! You can see it from the mainland side of the island!"

Norris and I jumped up. I directed our cowboys to stay in place and keep firing at the barge. Then Norris and I ran back to where we had our horses saddled and all three of us cut out for the water and began to swim for the shore.

We could see the night sky aglow, even from as far away as we'd been. My heart had just gone sick in me. They'd pulled a double attack and I hadn't planned for it. It had been a stupid mistake on my part. As we'd spurred our horses cross-country for the ranch, I had visions of our several barns and the ranch house and the bunkhouse all leaping with flames.

But I had worried for nothing. Dad had been ready. We caught one small party trying to escape, and Ben shot one of the Ficus cousins. Three others of the raiders, including Joe Dunn, were pinned down by the crossfire coming from the bunkhouse and the ranch house. When we added our fire to that of the others, they surrendered.

The raiders had only succeeded in firing one old barn that was mostly empty and that we had been planning on tearing down anyway. That and a few broken windows had been the only damage we'd sustained.

Except for Dad. He'd taken a bullet through the left side of his chest, and from the pink blood that was oozing out I could see it had hit his lung. Norris and I didn't even pause. We loaded him in a buckboard, swaddled up in blankets, and, leaving Ben to deal with the captured marauders, took off for town and the doctor as fast as the horses would gallop.

The bullet had just nicked his lung, but the doctor had to chloroform him and then go in and sew up the tiny tear. It was a hard wait for me while the operation was going on. Some trashy sonofabitch had shot Howard Williams, and it had been my fault. I'd been fooled. By a trashy sonofabitch.

Later, when he was better and we had him home, I asked where I'd gone wrong. He said I hadn't. "The only thing you forgot to do was tell me to be sure and fort up the ranch also, but I thought of that. I figured it had just been an oversight on your part and you wouldn't mind if I took it on myself to make sure we were ready in case they came our way."

That made me smile a little. It also made me realize I wasn't near as smart as I thought I was. I said, "That was what you meant when you asked me if I was sure I wasn't taking this personal."

He just shrugged. "Might have been."

It was hard to say which had been the diversion, the barge or the attack on the ranch. Maybe both, maybe neither. There had been four men in the barge, one of whom had been wounded. I later decided that they'd expected us all to ride in relief of the ranch, leaving them free to fire the island.

The Ficus and Dunn outfit had not come out of the affair very well. Three of their men were killed, two of them kin, and three were wounded. Except for Dad, we hadn't taken a bullet.

The crowning blow to them had been that while they were in jail awaiting criminal prosecution, Norris had instigated a civil suit for damages and won a considerable sum.

Dad told me I'd done all the right things, but I still wondered. He'd put me in charge of the whole enterprise and it seemed to me that I'd left part of it unguarded. If it hadn't of been for Dad, more damage might have been done.

So I sat there on that rock, trying to sort out my present predicament. Was I taking it too personal? I picked up a little stick and drew lines in the dust by the side of the road. I just couldn't, for some reason, see it clear. I turned and called up the hill to Ben. "Come down here."

"We going?"

"Just come down here."

When he was standing in front of me, I uncorked the bottle, had a swallow of whiskey, and passed it to him. When he'd drunk, I said, "Ben, you remember that business with Ficus and Dunn?"

He gave me a fretful look. "Hell, you made mention of that awhile ago. Is that what you've been studying on?"

I nodded. "It kind of reminds me of the situation I've got here. I'm not sure I've got the right to put the family in that same kind of danger."

"What same kind of danger?"

"Well, I got so damned involved with those high-bred cattle, just like I'm getting so involved with Jacobbsen, that I left the main part of our business unguarded."

He gave me a funny look. I knew he was not used to me sounding uncertain. I made sure of that in his case. He was a fine hand at exploiting the slightest sign of uncertainty. He said, "Aw, hell, you're talking crazy. You didn't leave anything unguarded. Hell, there was eleven guns back at the ranch. And Dad."

"But I didn't expect an attack on the ranch and Dad got shot. I blame myself for that."

"Well, that's just dumb," he said. "Let me ask you this. How was Dad before that little fight?"

I looked up at him. "He was kind of sinking. Didn't seem to care much."

"And how has he been since?"

The nicked lung had left him short of breath, making it hard for him to get around too vigorously. We called it a weak heart because the doctor had said it would probably weaken his heart, but it really wasn't. And, of course, his arthritis had gotten worse. "Well, he's not getting around too good."

"Aw," he said, "I don't mean that. That was going to happen anyway. Hell, Justa, he's getting old. Nothing you can do about that. I mean in spirit."

I had to admit Ben was right. "Well, he seems to care a lot more now."

"Then what are you spurring yourself for? And what's that got to do with this business?"

I said, "You heard Jacobbsen. Maybe we ought to just forget it and head home."

He was about to take a drink. He lowered the bottle and

looked at me. "The hell you say! And let Jacobbsen get away with what he done to you? You leave if you want to, but I'm not."

"It might be the smart thing to do," I said.

"Listen, Justa, I know I'm not as smart as you. Norris thinks he is, but he's not, with just the few exceptions you can get out of books. But we're both smart enough to know you don't walk away from a mess like this. It might not follow you, but you'd take it with you and be packing it around on your back the rest of your life. You're supposed to be setting an example for me. Is this the kind of example you want me to follow?"

He'd said the last half in jest, but there was still meaning to his words. I said, "I have to protect the family."

"Then protect the family by making it clear it's best to leave us the hell alone if you've got wrong on your mind."

I just looked at him for a second. Sometimes he could surprise me. I got up, saying, "Well, why don't you go on and get the horses? What's the matter with you? Want to stay out here all day? The others are waiting and they'll be worried. I swear, I never saw such a kid."

CHAPTER
8

As we rode into town Ben said, "Justa, where did you pick up that habit of sitting like that and thinking things through? From Paw? Seems like I've seen him do it."

"I don't know. Might have. Just seems I've always done it."

He wouldn't let it drop. "Yeah, but it don't seem right for you. Seems like something Norris would do. More his style."

I said, "Norris does his thinking, you just don't notice it because he's so much smoother about the matter than I am. I got to work at it because I'm thickheaded and slow."

"Aw, that ain't so."

"You just wait. You'll be doing the same, though likely you'll have to get in a bank safe and close the door before you can concentrate."

Once in town I went hunting for the newspaper office. Ben wanted to know what for, but I just told him to wait and see. We found it and went inside. A little man came up to the counter and asked if he could help. He was eyeing us suspiciously. I asked if he printed up handbills. He said he did. I asked him how much for a hundred.

"Regular size, ten inches by twelve?"

"That would do."

"It would come to five dollars if it's just straight printing. If there's a picture, that would be another five for the engraving."

"No picture," I said. "It's a reward poster."

"A reward poster?"

"Yeah. Give me a blank piece of paper and I'll write it out for you. I want it in big letters. All capitals."

He looked uncertain, but he supplied me with what I asked. I leaned over the counter and carefully printed:

REWARD
FIVE THOUSAND DOLLARS
$5,000

FOR ANY INFORMATION PROVING THAT
DAG JACOBBSEN OF THE TREETOP RANCH
HAD A HAND IN THE MURDER OF MARY MAE
HAWKINS. NO QUESTIONS WILL BE ASKED
AND ALL INFORMATION WILL BE TREATED
SECRETLY.

APPLY: JUSTA WILLIAMS, EAGLE HOTEL

REWARD
FIVE THOUSAND DOLLARS
$5,000
DAG JACOBBSEN

Ben had been reading over my shoulder and he burst out laughing. "Oh, that will burn his ass!" he said. "Oh, hell, big brother, that is good!"

But the printer didn't think it was so funny. He took one look and got a horrified expression on his face. He shoved the paper back to me like it was hot. "I can't print that! Mr. Jacobbsen would ruin me."

I said grimly, "I already figured you'd say that. If you don't print it, I'm going to ruin you. I'll burn your goddamn office down and have five witnesses ready to swear that I didn't."

Ben said, "Yeah, and I'll burn your damn house down. Now print it!"

The poor man didn't know what to do. He just stood there

opening and closing his mouth. I finally took pity on him. I took out three twenty-dollar bills and spread them on the counter. "Here's sixty dollars. There's no reason for Jacobbsen to know you did the printing. Don't put your mark on them. Our lawyer has been going into San Antonio. We could easily have had them printed there."

Well, the little man was in a spot and he knew it. Faced with a couple of desperadoes he knew for certain to be killers. Jacobbsen lurking in the background. Visions of his office and home in flames. Maybe his old woman raped and pillaged. And there was that sixty dollars laying on the counter. A lot of incentive for a poor man. Maybe more than a six-gun. His mind was working but his eyes kept straying to the cash. You can buy a lot of courage with money. He finally said, "They could be printed in San Antonio. They's people in this town takes all kinds of work into there when they could get it done here at home and help the local tradespeople. Makes me mad as hell." He put out his hand and took the money. "And you won't mention it to anyone?"

"Not unless you do. How long will it take?"

"Oh . . ." He thought. "Two or three hours. I can't start right away."

"Yes, you can. Ben, I'm going to the hotel. You stay here and help this gentleman and then bring those handbills straight on over. Urge him along all you can."

The printer wanted to say something, but he took a look at the glint in Ben's eye and turned away, carefully storing the sixty dollars in his pocket. "Well, yes, I reckon I can start on this now. It's a rush job. I'll go get set up."

"Good," I said. I started for the door and then turned back. "Ben?"

"What?" He took a step toward me.

"Well . . ." I said. "It's this. I've got to go over to the hotel and do something I ain't looking forward to."

"What?"

I rubbed my jaw. "I've got to talk to Norris. I've got to ask him to do something and he may bow up his back on me."

"Hel!, you're the boss. Tell him."

I grimaced. "It ain't exactly that clear-cut, Ben. It's kind of got to do with all that thinking I was doing back there on that rock."

He was giving me a shrewd look. Ben fooled a lot of people who didn't know how smart he was. Of course, by the time they'd found out, it was too late and he had them sacked up. He said, "You're right, he ain't going to like it."

"But it makes sense."

"Yes," he admitted, "I guess it does."

"So if we're still talking when you get to the hotel, I want you to side in with me. All right?"

He gave me an innocent look. "Why, don't I always?"

"No," I said curtly. "You don't. In fact, it's a red-letter day when you do. But try it this once. It's important, Ben."

"I understand," he said.

I'd sent Tom and Hays into the next room, leaving just me and Norris at the big round table. I poured us out a drink before I began. When we'd both had a swallow, I said, "Norris, I want you to go back to the Half-Moon."

He looked only mildly surprised, not at all the reaction I'd expected. Then I realized he didn't understand me. "What for?" he said. "Are you planning on taking up Jacobbsen on his proposition? Clear up the legal matters and then be gone from this country?"

"Quite the opposite. That's why I want you back at the ranch."

He looked puzzled. "For how long? You mean go back and check matters out and report to Dad? That's a hell of a long trip for a few days."

I shook my head. Now was when I'd run into his coolheaded obstinacy, that streak of stubbornness I knew so well. You could not out-logic Norris, you had to overpower him. I said, "No, I want you to go back there and stay. Take charge. You'll be there until Ben and I get back."

An expression came over his face as he finally understood what I was proposing. It was a mixture of hurt and anger and disappointment. He said, "You're expecting trouble. Not that we don't already have plenty of trouble, but you're expecting bad trouble. And you want me out of the way. You're afraid I'll get hurt or get in the way. Frankly, I resent the hell out of that. Are you suggesting I'd be a liability?"

Of course I knew he was going to argue and balk, but I was counting on his analytical good sense to come to the fore sooner or later. Norris had always been under the mistaken suspicion, probably because he wore town clothes and read books, that Ben and I didn't consider him our equal in a physical fight. That was far from the truth. But, as I'd expected, he was going to take the immediate assumption that that was the reason I was sending him away. I said wearily, "Now, Norris, don't play the fool with me because it just isn't going to work." I had determined that I would tell him exactly the truth, because to do any less would be considered an insult to his intelligence and because he would be more likely to do what was necessary once he realized how really necessary it was. I said, "Yes, I expect matters are going to get a little rough around here. You heard the report about what happened out at Treetops. I guess I more or less slapped Jacobbsen in the face. And spit in his eye on top of it. Maybe it wasn't the most politic thing to do, but I was angry, and in any case, it's too late now. Jacobbsen is rich and powerful and mean and insane. He'll stop at nothing now. And it won't just be me he'll go after. He'll go after all of us. That's why you've got to go back to the ranch."

"Why not Ben?" he said. "He's the youngest. He shouldn't be involved. It's because you don't think I'm as good in a gunfight as Ben. Isn't it?"

I said dryly, "Norris, let's don't kid each other about that. Damn few men are, maybe myself included. But that's not the reason. I'm trying to put everybody where they can do the most good, and we're spread a little thin right now. You know Dad's condition. It's not the best right now. So somebody, the best man for the job, has got to go back there to look after him and after the family interests. Ben can't do that. You know it as well as I do. And it hasn't got a damn thing to do with who's best in a fight. If it came to that, I'd just as soon have you standing beside me as any man in the world. But you're the best businessman of all of us. Norris, I can't risk the whole family. Dad gave me the job of taking care of all of us, and that's what I'm trying to do."

He got, for him, a kind of anguished look on his normally calm face. "Do you realize what you're asking me, Justa? You're asking me to leave my two brothers in mortal danger and run home. How do you think that makes me feel?"

It was going harder than I'd thought. The problem was I could see his position and sympathize with it. If it had been me in his shoes, I'd of felt the same way. I searched my mind for a way to explain it to him so that he could see why it was correct and good and why it was necessary. And that my request to him was a compliment rather than a denigration. Of course, I could order him to go, but I didn't want to do that. It was not a situation where I wanted to give orders, especially to Norris. I said, "Do you know where I've been? Why I was two hours behind Tom?"

"Hudspeth said you got off your horse a mile out of town and sat down on a rock. It has him puzzled. I assume you were doing what you always do."

I nodded. "I was thinking, running all the options through my mind. Trying to look at it as Howard Williams would."

Then I asked him, as I had Ben, if he recalled the Ficus and Dunn affair.

"Of course," he replied. "But what has that got to do with this?"

"A hell of a lot more than you'd think. I made the mistake that time of taking the matter personally, and if it hadn't of been for Dad's foresight, we'd of suffered a great deal more damage than we did."

He said coolly, "You're not taking this personally?"

Naturally he was going to try and attack me with words, knowing he was the best hand at it. I gave him a sour look. "Of course I'm taking this personally. But what I'm talking about is in that Ficus and Dunn affair I put all my eggs on that island and had no thought of the ranch being attacked. Dad let me make that mistake because he knew he could cover it up for me. But he's not here to oversee my mistakes now, and I've got to think this all the way through."

Norris said, "The situation is not the same. They attacked the ranch. The ranch is not under attack now."

Dammit, he could exasperate me. I slammed the palm of my hand down on the table. "Yes it is! It's under attack from lack of management, from hired hands who give the job a lick and a promise if nobody is there to oversee them, from fluctuating cattle prices, from errors made and opportunities missed. You're damn right it's under attack, and you of all people ought to see that. Who the hell is looking after our banking interests right now? Nobody, that's who. Who's looking after Dad? The same nobody. What about that spur line we've been negotiating with the railroad about? Who's handling that? Dammit, Norris, this is not like you."

"Then if there's that much to put in order, don't you think you'd better stop being selfish and go home and tend to it?"

"Aw, shit, Norris!" I said with some disgust. I got up from the table and walked over to the window and looked out on the street. Fucking town, I thought. I wished feverently I'd never seen it. Alvin Davis was standing on the boardwalk in front of his father's store, wiping his hands on his clerk's apron and looking up and down the street as if expecting to spot somebody with sinful thoughts on their mind.

Behind me, Norris said, "Well, why don't you go instead of me? You are, after all, the boss. Haven't we always said, attack one of us attack us all? So your personal presence isn't required."

I turned around. Norris had always been able to get at me just as I'd always been able to get at Ben. I said, "Norris, that's pretty poor. I don't think I'm even going to bother to answer. But you did get one thing right. I am the boss."

He looked at me defiantly. "Do you mean by that that you're considering ordering me to go home?"

"I'm hoping it won't come to that."

"But you're saying it might."

With a sigh I said, "I'm saying what I've been saying. That we have to think of the family and we have to think of the ranch. And Dad. And that you are the logical one to go back."

He suddenly slammed his fist down on the table. A rare display of temper for my usually even-tempered brother. It, if nothing else, clearly illustrated how strongly he felt about the matter. He said, "Why in the hell do you have to think you can whip the world! You've thought so ever since I can remember! I don't want to leave because I don't think you've got any more sense than to charge straight at that whole damn Jacobbsen outfit. Ben is supposed to be the hothead. Well, brother, you'd better take a look in the mirror. You can get your mind set a certain way and you're harder to turn than an iron-mouthed bronc. Justa, I don't trust you here. Tom can't handle you and Ben is worse. I've *got* to stay."

So it was finally coming out. And I was supposed to be the oldest brother. Though I'd always had the sneaking suspicion that Norris really thought he was. Norris just felt like he couldn't trust me off on my own. In a way it was funny. And I would have laughed if it hadn't of been so damn serious. Maybe Norris was the best of us. Certainly he was the most kind, the most thoughtful, the one who applied his every skill to the family business. He'd been engaged to a wonderful girl for nearly a year. It was time they were married, but Norris kept putting it off until he could get this problem settled or resolve this issue or finalize this one last piece of business. His fiancée, Hollylee, had shown admirable restraint while he'd busied himself with matters other than their marriage. Ben had said it was good because, with Norris, she'd need the practice.

I said, "Norris, let's don't get confused here. I admit to a wild streak and to being headstrong. But that has been in the past. Before Dad gave me the job. I know how you feel about going back and I don't blame you, but the argument you just put forth won't wash. And you know it. So let's play fair. This business has already cost us way too much time and money. Right now the ranch is, for all intents and purposes, being run by Bill Harley. Harley is a good cattleman, and if it was just the day-to-day managing of the range, it would be all right. But he's just the foreman and he's not family and he's not a businessman. And all of that is worrying me. I don't need to be worrying about the ranch right now, Norris. I need to be concentrating on this mess I got here. That's why you've got to go back."

He almost shouted at me. He said, "Then take Jacobbsen's proposition and we'll all go home! I know—" He stopped.

Ben had come into the room, his arms full of the posters. He looked at us curiously but took the time to deposit them on a little side table. Norris stayed silent. I think he expected me to send Ben out of the room as I had the others, but instead, I invited him to sit down and poured him out a glass of whiskey. I'd been standing, but now I sat down. We were three brothers in conference. I told Ben what had been said, and what Norris's reaction had been.

Ben looked at him. "Norris, I know you're generally right about most things, but you're wrong this time. Justa needs you back at the ranch, and you ought to quit arguing with him."

"I'll be damned," Norris said. He looked at Ben in some amazement. "Are you trying to fool someone into believing you're using logic? You'd better try that on someone who doesn't know you quite as well as I do."

Ben said, "If you're so damn hot on being sensible, then you ought to quit being insensible and asking Justa to cut and run. He's not going to do it. And if he did, I still wouldn't."

Norris said patiently, "I'm not asking anyone to cut and run. I'm saying we ought to pick a more favorable battleground." He made a motion toward the window. "We're in a foreign country, we're playing against a stacked deck. I say we go to law. I say we hail Jacobbsen into a state circuit court, maybe even a federal one. Neutral ground. I'm almost certain we'll give him the beating of his life. And Tom Hudspeth agrees with me. We'll sue him for real damages and punitive damages. And we'll collect."

I listened to his talk of giving Jacobbsen the beating of his life. In a courtroom. But my mind was on the days and nights in that cabin, on the blows I'd taken from Bull and Cully, on the fear I'd felt with Lonnie unbarring the door to get at me with his knife. I thought of those things, but I didn't mention them. What I'd endured wasn't transferable. You could tell somebody about it, but they couldn't really appreciate it unless they'd felt the pain and the fear themselves.

But Ben said it for me: "Fuck the courtroom and fuck the

lawyers. And fuck those— What kind of damages did you say?"

"Punitive."

"What the hell are they?"

Norris sighed. "Damages a court awards so the defendant will be warned not to do what he's done again. Sometimes they can be triple your actual damages."

Ben said, "Well, fuck them too. Triple or not. The point is, Norris, Jacobbsen didn't attack us in court. If he had, why, I'd be all for your idea. He jumped us with guns and fists and a knife. And that's the way he's going to get paid back. His kind don't understand anything else. You ought to of seen that sonofabitch today, sitting up in his castle like some damn king. Going to let us off easy. Well, we like to have let about half a dozen of them find the easy way out of this world."

I said, "Norris, you won't hurt Jacobbsen in court. If they awarded us every dollar in damages we could dream up, it still wouldn't come to enough to bother Jacobbsen. And we would have run from the real fight."

"We start that, where does it stop?" said Ben. "Pretty soon a lot of people might get the idea we're easy. I told Justa that this might not follow us home, but if we didn't stop it here and now, we'd be packing it around the rest of our lives." He looked at his brother and said, not sounding at all like the wild kid he was most of the time, "Norris, we're supposed to listen to Justa. He's doing what he thinks is right. What would you do if you was in his place?"

He was beginning to look defeated. I felt sorry for him. I knew how desperately he wanted to stay with us. I said, "Norris, I'll make you a deal. Go home and talk this over with Dad. Tell him I said for you to, and that I want his opinion. I know you'll play fair and give him all the details. If he sides with you, then you make sure everything is all right at the ranch and come on back here. But if he sees things my way and understands my reasoning, then you stay at home and tend to business and take that worry off my mind. Is it a deal?"

He sighed. "Aw, hell," he said. "It's not fair. Here's Ben sounding like an adult, and then you making a sensible proposition. All right, I give up."

"Thank God that's over. Now let's have a drink. And don't

look so gloomy, Norris. Ben and I will be all right. We've got Hays and Tom to help."

Late that night I sent Ben and Hays out to paper the town with fifty of the handbills. I wanted the town to wake up to my little offer. Tom Hudspeth had asked me if I'd seriously expected to get any takers. I'd answered him seriously. "I don't know. I might. Five thousand dollars is a lot of money. Of course, I don't know if anybody really knows anything. But I do expect to have any number of people giving me information they think might be worth something. I don't think it's going to be a waste."

"But aren't you really doing it to irritate Jacobbsen?"

"That's why I know it won't be a waste. I'm going to goad him, and goad him as hard as I can."

"I really didn't realize how serious you were or how serious you considered the situation until you decided to send Norris home. By the way, I think that was smart. I wish I could say the same for this business about the handbills."

We went out about mid-morning and had a good laugh at all the gawkers standing around staring at our handiwork. A few were walking around holding handbills in their hands, studying them and glancing furtively toward the hotel. I said, "We may do some business, after all."

"I wouldn't count on 'em being up long," replied Hays.

He was right, of course. Shortly after noon a deputation of Treetops riders came storming into town and immediately went to ripping down our reward offers. We watched from our second-story window.

Ben laughed, but Tom Hudspeth said, "You are embarrassing the man. You know now that there is no hope of making any sort of a deal."

"I had never planned to make a deal. My deal is the same Jacobbsen gave me when I was roped off my horse."

With Norris gone, I moved Hudspeth in with me and Ben and Hays. I kept the other room and we used it for sitting purposes, but at night I wanted us all together. It was a little crowded but nothing we couldn't put up with.

Norris reached San Antonio safely and wired us just before he took the train home. On Hudspeth's instructions he'd gone to the law firm Tom was affiliated with and left a deposition of all that he'd known and been witness to. He'd also called in at the U.S. Marshal's office, just to add additional weight to Tom's efforts.

Hays came to me that night with a question. It was one well worth considering, and I said I wanted to discuss it with Tom Hudspeth and Ben. My trial was now less than two weeks away and I was becoming worried. I knew that Jacobbsen intended on attacking us, but I couldn't be sure when. The not knowing forced us into a reclusive, stay-together form of existence, and that seriously damaged our ability to go out and gather facts and search for information that would clear me. Our first round of handbills had produced no results, other than some strange and strained looks around town. I planned to wait a day and then have Ben and Hays put the second lot of fifty up.

But that still did nothing to alleviate the uncertainty of Jacobbsen's attack. We had to be able to move around more freely and separately. That night, at supper, I explained what Hays had told me. It seemed that earlier that day, two of the Treetops handbill deputation had made hurried and secret overtures to Hays. They both said the same thing, that they'd "been hearing things. That something was afoot," and that they were willing to give advance warning if the price was right.

Tom asked who the men were. Hays said, "Willard Gibson and Dick Wall."

"How long have you known them?"

Hays shrugged. "Gibson was there when I hired on. Wall has been on the payroll about six months."

"Are they gunmen or cowhands?"

Hays got that thoughtful look on his face. "Gibson is an out-and-out gunman. He used to be one of Bull's favorite boys, but they seemed to have had a falling-out a couple of months ago. He even tried to fight Bull. Got his ass kicked. On top of that, he had to take a whipping from Jacobbsen. Wall . . . he's about half and half. He's pretty much a good hand. He's likable, but he'll get liquored up and they's no telling what he'll do. He got drunk one night and pissed in another man's bunk just for the hell of it and then whipped the man when he complained."

Tom looked at me. "Not exactly first-class citizens."

"Informers seldom are. And I don't expect to find too many model members of the community working out at Treetops." I glanced at Hays. "With one exception."

Ben gave me a look. "How about Marriah?"

I had to smile slightly. "Maybe two exceptions."

Ben said, to Hays, "You trust these two fellers?"

Hays shook his head quickly. "Naw, naw, naw. I ain't picking up that load. They just passed the word to me on the sly and double quick. They done it separate too. So I don't reckon the one knows about the other."

Tom said, "Or we don't think they're acting in concert."

Hays said, "What?"

"In cahoots. Following Jacobbsen's orders."

"Oh."

"Where are you supposed to meet them to let them have an answer?"

Hays said that Gibson would be at one of the saloons that very night and that Wall was going to try and get away the next day and come into town to buy some clothes.

"All right," I said. I got out a hundred dollars and gave it to Hays. I said, "Go over and give Gibson fifty dollars. Tell him if he gives us any worthwhile information there's another two hundred where that came from. That is, if we get the information in time. Tell the same thing to Wall tomorrow."

Hays looked doubtful. "How they supposed to get word to me?"

"Tell them to leave word at the desk that Jacobbsen wants to see you. Then they are to meet you in a saloon. On no account let them get you out of town or catch you alone."

"Ben, you go with him, but hang back. Take the handbills with you. As soon as the streets clear, put up the second batch. And watch yourselves. Run from a fight."

Later, after a few after-supper drinks, they went out. Hudspeth looked at me curiously. "I'm surprised you didn't send Ben home also. And now you let him go out. That's inconsistent."

I shook my head. "You've got to understand Ben. I could have ordered him home, but it wouldn't have done any good.

Norris could understand the reasons why I had to send him, but Ben, though he might also have understood the reasons, wouldn't have gone. Oh, he might have acted like he was leaving, but he'd have stuck around on the edge. You can't protect Ben. He won't stand for it. He recognizes me as the boss so far as the family and the business go, but I'm not the boss where he is personally concerned. Plus, I don't think there's any two men in this country who are a match for him. He might seem wild and devil-may-care, but he's cunning and very smart. Nobody is going to back-shoot him."

Tom looked at me curiously. "Something that has struck me from the first. You have such an air of command about you that seems far beyond your years. You remind me of the military. You even seem to think that way. Were you in the army?"

"Never had time to be in the regular army. Too busy with the family business. But I do have the honor of being a member of the state militia."

"What rank?"

"Major."

"Ah." He studied me for a moment. "Well, Major, I'm not certain about your command decision on these two informers Hays has brought forth. I don't see what good it can do. If they've been sent by Jacobbsen, which I privately believe, their offer comes at just too convenient a time. But if they are a Jacobbsen trick, it appears to me that it would put us in an even worse position."

I said, "In the first place, I don't plan to pay the slightest bit of attention to anything either one of them has to say."

"What if they separately give the same information, leading you to believe they're on the level?"

I took a drink of whiskey. "That won't change anything. We are going to stay on the highest level of alertness. Any information they give won't change that."

"Then what's the point?"

"Maybe it will make Jacobbsen think that I've been taken in. I want to keep him as confused as I can. God knows, he's got me confused. I wish he'd do something. Besides, what can it cost?"

Tom laughed. "Well, for one thing, a hundred dollars."

I smiled slightly. "It's not going to cost me. That hundred dollars is going on Jacobbsen's bill."

"You *are* serious about that."

"Never more so."

Ben and Hays were much later returning than I'd expected. I'd been worried to the point of considering going to look for them. But when they came back, half liquored up and laughing, I got angry. "Where the hell have you two been? Goddammit, you should have been back here two hours ago."

Hays instantly sobered up, but Ben poked me playfully in the belly and said something about having a little fun. He said, "You ought to try it, big brother. Take some of that snarl off your face."

They'd visited the three resident ladies of the evening who did business over at one of the saloons. In other circumstances I wouldn't have given a damn, but I didn't consider it a time for them to be flaunting themselves around town. I jerked Ben up by his vest and threw him back against the wall. He hit it and slid down to the floor and just sat there laughing. I looked at him in disgust. "I kept you here because I thought I could depend on you. Now I see I can't. I don't mind you getting drunk any other time, but I thought you'd growed up enough to know this isn't the time. If I can't depend on you, there's no point in keeping you here. Drunk as you are, do you think you could have defended yourself?"

"Now, listen, Justa—"

"No, you listen, you little spoiled brat. They could have taken you and held you hostage and gotten to me through you. Next you're going to tell me you've been holed up in this hotel so long, you deserved a little fun. Well, being holed up in this hotel is the job. We'd all like a little fun, but it ain't to be right now. I don't see any point in keeping you here. You might as well go back to the Half-Moon."

He got up slowly from the floor and walked across the room and washed his face in the basin. He didn't bother drying it before he turned back to me. He said, "All right, I done wrong. I know it and it won't ever happen again. But I ain't going home, Justa. Not until we get this matter settled."

Tom Hudspeth was sitting quietly on his bed. I glanced at

him. He just shrugged as if to say he'd already heard this before. From me. I looked back at Ben. The water was still running down his face. I said, "You'll go home if I tell you."

We stared at each other a long time. I guess it finally worked its way through his head that he wasn't going to be allowed to select the orders he was willing to obey.

Finally he glanced away.

"Well?" I said.

"Whatever you say."

I thought it over. "All right. We'll leave it at this. I don't guess I have to say any more. You're sorry about what you did, and I'm sorry I had to speak to you about it."

Then I turned to Ray Hays. He was carefully examining the floor at the end of his boot tips. He hadn't moved an inch since I'd thrown Ben against the wall. I had little doubt who it was that had led the excursion, and it hadn't been Hays. "Well?"

"Sir?"

"Did you make contact with Gibson?"

"Yes, sir."

"Did he take the money?"

"Yes, sir. But he said he thought he ought to get more than two hundred dollars for the kind of information he was going to have. He said Bull and Cully and a couple of others had been having a right smart lot of talks with Jacobbsen, and something was stirring for sure. He said he'd probably know only at the last minute and that it would probably be dangerous for him to slip off to warn you, and that he ought to get the extra money."

I said, "Fine. Next time you see him, tell him it's a deal."

"Yes, sir."

He glanced up at me, I guess to see if I were through with him. But I wasn't going to let him off that easy. "What did I tell you to do when I sent you out this evening?"

"Deliver a message."

"And?"

Hays looked down at the floor and then glanced over my shoulder at Ben. I realized his dilemma. Ben wanted to go visit the girls, and he was the boss's brother. He looked down at the floor again. "Get right back here, I guess."

"I'm going to fine you ten dollars off your wages for not doing what you were told."

Behind me Ben said, "Aw, now, dammit, Justa, it ain't Hays's fault. I was the one—"

"Shut up, Ben. I know who did the leading. I can't fine you or I would. But your little prank cost a good man a fine and a reading out. You put him in a box, Ben."

From behind me Ben said, "Ray, don't worry. I'll make it up to you."

I said to Hays, "You take a penny from him and I'll fine you a month's wages. If I don't fire you."

Ben said, "That's damn unfair, Justa. And you know it."

"It certainly is, Ben. And, as the one who caused it, I'm glad you can see the wrong of it. Now let this be the end of the matter."

Later, as we were getting ready for bed I heard Hays say to Ben, "Damn, Ben, I think we got off light. Leave it be. Don't stir him up no more. Hell, he's under all kinds of pressure."

Tom Hudspeth had met me in the hall coming back from the bathroom. He'd thrown me a mock salute. "All quiet amongst the troops, Major?"

I didn't bother to reply.

Next morning I wrote out a telegram on a piece of paper and handed it to Tom. "I want you to take this over to the telegraph office and send it straight off."

He read it and then looked up at me. "I can't send this. They won't understand it in San Antonio."

The wire was addressed to the U.S. Marshal's office. It read:

AM IN RECEIPT OF YOUR LETTER.
UNDERSTAND MARSHALS WILL ARRIVE TWO
DAYS HENCE ON OVERLAND STAGE. HAVE
NEW, IMPORTANT INFORMATION ON DAG JA-
COBBSEN. EAGERLY AWAIT YOUR INVESTIGA-
TION.

I said, "Just send it."

"But what for? I haven't gotten any letter from the marshal. Justa, this will just confuse them. What's the purpose?"

"It's less than ten days to my trial. I've got to force Jacobbsen's hand. Make him do something. If he thinks the marshals are coming, it will seem to him that I have information to give them. He can't have that. He's going to have to try and get rid of me. His little glass castle is too fragile to stand much scrutiny."

Tom was still shaking his head. "But it's going to confuse them. They might wire back."

I said, "I told Norris to stop in and warn the marshal that I might send him just such a telegram and that if he didn't get a second one right away, he was to disregard the first."

"But what good is it going to do?"

"Make something happen and happen fast. We can't sit around here like ticking time bombs for another ten days. Look what Ben and Hays did last night. We can't stay holed up here. I can't attack Jacobbsen, he's got to attack me. This is just another goad, a jab, like the handbills."

"All right. I'll do it."

That afternoon I took Hays with me and we went over to the Lantern Saloon. It was the headquarters for the whorehouse. When I told him where we were going, he'd looked sheepish. I'd told him not to worry, that I wasn't trying to embarrass him. I'd left him downstairs, utterly confused, and went up to the second floor. They had a kind of parlor there. There was a madam, a hard-faced woman with a big nose who was wearing way too few clothes for somebody as ugly as she was. I said, "I want to talk to all your girls. And you."

"Honey, we don't deal in talk here. That's for little boys and girls. All my girls are growed up."

I took a twenty-dollar bill out and handed it to her. "Will that buy some answers to some questions?"

There's two places that money talks, and one of them is a bank. You can get as good a screwing in either place. The old bitch took the twenty and immediately began clapping her hands. "Dolly, Roxie . . ."

When I came back down, Hays got up, looking awkward. We left without him saying a word. When we were halfway across the street, I said, "Which one did Ben have?"

"Uh, I don't rightly know, boss."

"How about you?"

He was blushing scarlet. "I, uh, don't believe I got the young lady's name."

"Roxie? Dolly? Trudy?"

"Uh, maybe it was Trudy."

I whistled, long and low. We were at the boardwalk in front of the hotel. "I sure hope your dick don't fall off."

He turned nearly pale, then said, "Boss, you didn't find out something . . . I mean, you didn't— They didn't tell you they was maybe something wrong?"

I had found out something, a very interesting something. But just how it fit, I wasn't quite sure. But it went a long way toward developing a theory that was growing in my mind.

But right then I had something else bothering me. Ben and I hadn't really spoken since the incident of the night before. I'd seen his face when I'd taken Hays with me to the whorehouse rather than him. My conscience was kind of bothering me. But at the same time Ben had to be handled a certain way. He still needed a firm hand every now and then, but sometimes I tended to overdo it. I said, to Hays, "Run up to the room and tell Ben I want to see him down here."

Hays still had his mind on the possible deterioration of his private parts. My little joke had scared him. He said, "You takin' him to the doctor? Is that it? Had I better figure to go?"

"Hays, run up and get Ben. I'll let you know when it's your turn."

While he was gone, I leaned up against a roof post and stared out at the street. It was Saturday and the streets and stores were doing a better-than-average business. Men in their town clothes and women in their best were bustling about, shopping and visiting and taking a break from their week's labors. Here and there a few lucky children who'd managed to escape from the clutches of mama were running around and skylarking and acting like wild Indians just off the reservation. The scene looked like one I'd seen in a hundred other towns. Except this wasn't a hundred other towns. This one had a malignant growth inside it, and the name of that growth was Dag Jacobbsen. Which went to prove that things weren't always what they seemed.

That brought my mind to Ben and something that had happened a little over a year past. I'd sent Ben, along with a couple of drovers, to herd a hundred head of our good crossbred steers down to the coastal town of Port Lavaca. From there they'd be put on board a cattle boat and shipped to Vera Cruz, Mexico. It was kind of a switch, us sending cattle to Mexico. But my upgrading experiment had worked, and we were producing some prime beef with our small, blocky, stocky cattle that had resulted from the unlikely combination of our rangy, rawhide longhorns with the small, gentle English cattle. They foraged well on the open range, they thrived in our changing seasons, and they produced highly eatable beef. And some of those rich caballeros down there in Mexico had grown tired of that stringy leather they cut off their own version of beef cattle and had taken to a taste for ours. They paid top dollar, and they paid in gold. An all-around satisfactory arrangement.

It hadn't been the first time I'd sent Ben on the assignment and I had no reason to believe that he'd have any more trouble than he had had in times past. But then, just as I was beginning to look for his return, word had come that he was in jail, in Port Lavaca, charged with assault. Well, I'd blown my top. We'd all been sitting in a room we used as a mutual office, Dad and Norris and I. When the messenger left, I got up cussing a blue streak and promising to put to an end, once and for all, Ben's hotheaded sashes. I'd started buckling on my gun belt and yelling for our housekeeper to pack me a bag for the hundred-mile trip.

Norris said quietly, "You're not going."

I looked at him. "What?"

"You're not going. I am."

"Like hell you are. I am sick and tired of him thinking he can settle everything with a fight. He's nearly twenty-three years old now and it's time he grew up. I know what he's done. He's gone down there and got up next to some girl that was already spoke for, and when her boyfriend made an objection, Ben beat the hell out of him. Hell, I'm just surprised he didn't shoot him."

Norris said, "That's my very point. You don't know what

happened. Ben might not be in the wrong at all. But you've already got him tried and convicted, and now you're going to go storming down there, raising hell, and probably just create more trouble."

I said, "Sounds like you're doing a little prejudging. Norris, don't give me advice. I know how to handle Ben and I'm going to jerk that wild streak out of him if I have to use pliers."

Dad was sitting and listening to us. He said something I didn't quite catch, so I said, "What?"

In a distinct voice he said, "Sounds like the kettle calling the pot black."

I wanted to say, "Look who's talking," but I didn't. It was generally considered that Ben and I took after Dad, who'd been a bit of a rounder in his day, and that Norris, with his love of books and learning, had favored the finer qualities that our mother had possessed. Not that she couldn't be firm herself when the need arose. More than once she'd taken a peach-tree switch to my bare legs and made me do an Indian dance.

Norris got up, closing the ledger he'd been working on, and said, "Are you willing to be sensible about this, Justa? For just this one time?"

"You can't handle Ben."

"I've never considered him a sack of oats that needed handling."

"Don't word me, Norris."

"All right, I won't. I'll ask you. Let me handle this. If I need help, I'll wire. But let me go down there and see what's what before you sail into Ben. Justa, he worships you, and it nearly kills him when you find fault. He'd rather you hit him with your fist then tongue-lash him the way you do. Just once, try it my way."

I'd given in—mainly, I think, because I could sense that's what Paw wanted me to do. But I was no less angry and no less determined that I was going to give young Ben what-for when I finally got my hands on him. The hell of it, to me, was that he'd always had the makings of such a fine man in him. He'd go along for long stretches of time, acting just as dependable as you could want, and then that wild streak would have to out. If I'd talked to him once about self-control, I'd talked about it a thousand times. His usual answer was "Oh, yeah? What about . . ." And he'd bring up some incident out of my own past. He had that damnable charm the ladies found so appealing, and that sly way of getting around authority. But it was my job to teach him to pull in harness, and I was going to do it if it killed one of us.

I had got lucky that time. Three days after Norris left, they were back. Rather than causing trouble, Ben had been in the right and something of a hero in the bargain. Three rowdies off one of the cattle boats had been causing trouble along the town's main street, annoying women, knocking men's hats off, tripping people; just generally acting drunk and disorderly. Ben had come upon them after they'd accosted a young lady and were frightening her and using unsavory language and even putting their hands on her. Ben had intervened and there'd been a fight. He'd been carrying a heavy cattle whip with a two-foot hardwood handle weighted with lead. In the melee he'd used that. He'd broken one arm, two noses, and cracked a few ribs. The reason he'd been put in jail was because the young woman had fled, and when the law arrived at the scene, the men had sworn that Ben had attacked them. Which had been easy to believe, considering the damage he'd inflicted. His wire for help had gone out before the young woman had heard of the circumstances and come forward to put the matter straight. By the time Norris had arrived, Ben was being released and making plans to start for home.

When he got back, the first thing he said to me was, "Well, I bet when you got that wire, you hit the ceiling. I bet you said, 'Ben has been up to it again and this time I'm gonna teach him a lesson!' Didn't you?"

I didn't say anything. Norris and Dad were there.

He said, "I bet you never give me the first benefit of the doubt." He lowered his voice and looked grim in imitation of me. "Going to take the wildness out of that boy! Learn him once and for all."

I never admitted to it, and I never knew if Norris or Dad had given me away. I just contented myself with avoiding the subject and giving him a little increased responsibility.

But it made me smile, leaning against that post. In truth I

was too hard on him and I knew it. But he did need handling, sack of oats or not, on occasion.

He came out of the hotel then, looking a little grim-faced. I said, "Let's go get a drink."

"Whiskey up in the room."

I put my hand on his shoulder. "Naw, let's go across to the saloon. We can't stay holed up in that room all the time."

He was still being stiff. "Not what you said last night."

We were walking across the dusty street, angling for the nearest saloon. I said, "I wanted to thank you for helping me with Norris. It was a hard thing to do and it was hard for him. What you said helped matters all around."

"I already had your thanks. Last night. Remember?"

He was going to make it hard on me. "Dammit, Ben, cut it out. I know I'm tough on you. But I'm tough on you because I expect so much from you. And I'm tough on you because you can handle it and because you need it sometimes. I'm aware that I might have handled that matter a little differently last night. But I'm kind of on a short fuse right now. Which ain't no excuse but it is kind of an explanation. But you were wrong and you know it. About all I'm going to say on the matter is that I shouldn't have done it in front of anybody else."

That was as close to an apology as he was going to get from me and he knew it. He got a kind of sly grin on his face and punched his elbow into my still somewhat tender ribs. "You better be careful who you're shoving against walls. If I hadn't been drunk, I might have got up and whipped your ass."

I smiled because it was all right. Ben and I were pretty tight. I'd hurt him and it had hurt me to do so. I said, "Shit, have you lost your mind? The day will never come when you can whip your big brother."

"Yeah? You'll break a leg someday and there you'll be, laying up in bed. Then I'm gonna hop your ass and whip the shit out of you."

"You better wait till I break two legs. And maybe an arm."

We went on into the cool dimness of the saloon and took a table against the far wall. I went up to the bar and got a bottle and two glasses while Ben had a chair. The place wasn't too crowded; three or four men at the bar, about the same number scattered amongst the tables. I looked them over carefully. None looked especially dangerous or especially interested in me and Ben. But I was being alert because Norris had told me to be. I guess he'd assumed I'd of never thought of it on my own. Norris worried; there was no other way to put it. I think it came from being so meticulous, about figures and such, and I think he automatically assumed the rest of the world, mostly me, would overlook the obvious if he didn't point it out. But I put up with that from Norris. I'd of put up with a hundred times worse from him because of the kind of man he was. And that didn't include what I felt for him as a brother. I'd been the only one to see him off at the stagecoach. I'd arranged it that way, thinking he might want to have a few private last words with me. I'd been right. He said, smiling, "I'm not going to take you up on your deal. About laying the matter before Dad. Not that I don't think it was a generous offer. It was. But you're the boss and it's for you to decide. But it's not just because you're the boss, it's also because you're right. I just didn't want to see it because I didn't want to leave you and Ben here. I shouldn't have argued."

"Norris, you would have blown up. If you couldn't argue, you'd die. All them words inside you struggling to get out? Be like the boiler on a steamboat when the pressure got too high."

He said, "Well, you handle this Mr. Jacobbsen and I'll tend to the ranch and the other business. At least you won't have to worry about that."

I'd thanked him and we'd shook hands and I'd watched the stagecoach bearing him off to San Antonio and the train. I'd figured it wasn't even out of town before Dag Jacobbsen knew there was one less Williams brother to contend with.

Ben poured out the drinks and we had a toast, and then I told him that Norris had taken his departure very well.

Ben said, "Make you a bet. Bet you that if this business takes much more than a week, Norris will be back here."

"He wouldn't do that."

"Shit, don't tell me that. Norris had always got to be involved. Don't you remember that Mama used to have to clear the house when she was making bread because Norris couldn't keep his hands out of the dough?"

I smiled at that, remembering. That was Norris. "He told me a funny story before he left. At least I think it was a funny story. You know Norris's sense of humor."

Ben made a wry face. "I do when he explains it to me. What was the story?"

I lit a cigar and said, "He told me a couple of our ancestors used to be buffalo hunters. Or at least they were until the government put a bounty on hostile Indians and began paying fifty dollars for every scalp. Norris said they decided to move down into Texas and try the scalp business for a while, see how it went. He said the first day they opened shop, they came across an Indian, popped him off, and took his scalp. Next day same thing."

"Yeah?"

"So Norris said they got to liking the business. Said that one of them remarked that Indians weren't any harder to hunt than buffalo and were a sight easier to skin."

"Yeah?"

"So they kept on, taking a scalp here, a couple there, and generally doing a fair business. Nothing to write home about, but they were covering overhead. Then it seems that one morning one of the partners got up about dawn and went outside their tent. He was standing there stretching and yawning and trying to wake up when he slowly began to realize they were surrounded by thousands and thousands of Indians. Well, he took one more look around to be sure he wasn't dreaming, and then rushed back into the tent and began to shake his partner. He said, 'Jake, for God's sake, wake up! We're millionaires!' "

Ben laughed slightly. "Yes, that is Norris humor. What do you suppose it means? He's generally got a moral lesson included."

"I don't know," I said. "I asked him, but he said it was just a funny story to cheer us up and make the parting easier."

"Bullshit," Ben said.

"Maybe it means, where Jacobbsen is concerned, that we ought not to get so intent on taking scalps that we let ourselves get surrounded."

Ben didn't reply and I became aware that his mind appeared

to be elsewhere. He'd been fiddling with a box of matches, and now he appeared to accidentally drop them on the floor. He bent over to retrieve them, taking his time. When he straightened back up, he said, "Don't make a show of looking around. Just keep on like we was talking amongst ourselves. But about three tables over, with a clear line of fire at us, there's a gent has just put a revolver between his legs. He thinks the tabletops has got it hid, but when I was slouched down in my chair, I got a glimpse. I bent over to make sure."

I laughed like he'd just told a joke and poured us another round of drinks. "Has he got the hammer cocked?"

"Not that I could see. He might have thought we'd of heard it."

I yawned and glanced casually around the room. The man Ben was talking about was sitting by himself at a table some ten yards distant. There was an alley in the intervening tables between him and us, so he did indeed have a clear field of fire. He had both hands under the table and a mug of beer sitting in front of him. I didn't recognize him. He was a smallish man, wearing a flat-crowned hat. His clothes were ordinary. I hadn't the slightest doubt he was one of Jacobbsen's men. Without making it obvious, I slid my chair slightly to the right and put my right leg up on the next empty chair. It brought my revolver, in its holster, to bear on the man. I casually let my right hand drop down on my thigh. I wouldn't even have to draw. Just get my hand on the butt of my gun and pull the trigger. I, too, wore a cutaway holster.

Ben said, "He looks nervous."

"I noticed," I said. "I'm debating about shooting him right now. Except I think he's waiting for something. If he'd meant to shoot us in cold blood, he'd already have fired. Besides that, there is no way he could get both of us from that position under the table. He's got to know that. And he's got to know that the other one of us would kill him before he could run or shoot enough shots to get us both."

Ben said, "He wasn't here when we came in."

"You sure?"

"Yeah. He come in a few minutes ago while you were telling

that story Norris told you. I got to watching him because he was all eyes for us."

We were doing all this in the most conversational way, occasionally chuckling as if the other had said something funny.

I said, "Then he's waiting for something. I can't figure it right now, but I bet we have company before too much longer."

"Then why don't we take him out of the play while we can?" Ben asked.

I shook my head. "It's chancy. I shoot him and I'll bet you that gun of his would disappear before the law got here. Then it would be cold-blooded murder. It's kind of a tight place, but I think we better give it a minute or two more and then maybe kind of slide on out of here. It's a setup, but I don't know which way it's going to fall out."

We waited that minute more and then, just as we started to get up, a familiar face came through the door. It was Cully, still wearing the strip of plaster over his nose though it appeared that most of the swelling had gone down in his face. He had another man with him. I had never seen him before, not this particular one, but I knew who and what he was. He worked for Jacobbsen, but not as a cowhand.

They came straight to our table. I immediately noticed that they came to the side of the table, being careful to not get between us and the gunman with the revolver under the table. Cully said to me, in a low, vicious voice, "Git up, you sonofabitch! I'm fixin' to settle yore fuckin' hash right here and now."

I realized, then, what the play was. I put out my hand to restrain Ben, who might do something sudden. I rose slowly, pulling Ben up with me as I did. Cully and his man took a step backward, obviously clearing room for gunplay. Cully said, "Now draw yore gun, you pig-suckin' motherfucker. I'm gonna—"

But before he could finish his taunt, I had shouldered Ben to his left, neatly placing Cully and his accomplice between us and the man with the gun under the table. It was clear that Cully intended to taunt me into drawing, making it a fair fight for all to see. But when I did, the man at the table would shoot me. Cully would be drawing also and he and the other would finish Ben and I off. The extra gun gave them all the edge they needed.

But now Cully was aware that his man at the table no longer had a clear shot. He tried to move to his right, but a table was blocking his way. He shoved it aside and took a step. His partner followed. So did Ben and I. Ben glanced at me questioningly. I just shook my head. Cully's face was turning red. He tried shouldering his accomplice to the left, once again clearing the firing lane. But I just stepped to my right, pulling Ben with me. I said, "It ain't going to work, Cully. I've already seen the man with the gun under the table. It was supposed to look like a fair fight, wasn't it? Just you and this bozo against me and my brother. And we draw first and you were so much faster, you just kilt us dead. And who'd of believed it? I'll tell you, not many people have ever seen my brother handle a gun."

He was so angry, the welts I'd made with the skillet were standing out on his face. He said, "You sonofabitch."

By now we had the attention of the entire saloon. I called out, "There's got to be a few honest men among you. I call to your attention that man sitting over there in the flat-crowned hat. He's got a hideout gun under the table. These two were planning to bushwhack us with his help. Cully here says he wants a fair fight. I'm going to offer it to him." I caught Cully's eyes with mine. I said, "How about we step out into the street? In front of plenty of witnesses. That'll make for a fair fight. Just me and my brother and you and your lady friend here."

Cully said, "Fuck you."

I said, "That's no way to talk. Now how about it? I'll let you draw first, motherfucker."

He didn't say anything, just stared at me.

Ben said, "Maybe he ain't a motherfucker, Justa. Maybe he likes pigs. Or maybe he eats cowshit."

We stared at them. Cully's hand was twitching, trembling. It would make it very easy for us if he'd go ahead and draw. I said, "Ben, whichever one draws first, you kill him while I lean around and shoot the bastard at the table. Then we'll get the other one."

It was very quiet and very tense in the saloon for a few long seconds. Ben and I just stood there waiting. I said, to Cully, "Well, you want to go outside or not? I'm not carrying a skillet."

Before he could answer, someone called out, "This one over here has put his gun on top of the table. He's got his hands down."

I smiled. Cully did not smile back. I said, "Guess we'll go outside. If you come out, I'll figure you're serious. Ben, let's kind of walk on out, but let's not turn our backs."

We got out to the middle of the street without incident and then turned and waited. After a few minutes it became apparent that no one was coming out. I said, "Well, don't look like we're going to do any business."

Ben said, "Whew! Justa, that was damn close. We'd of been dog meat if you hadn't figured that out."

"Me?" I looked at him. "You were the one saved our lives. If you hadn't seen that gun, I'd of never got on to what they were up to. Hell, boy, if there's any credit coming, it belongs to you. Shit, that was close. It sends chills up my spine thinking how near they were to having us. I got to be more alert."

We went on up to the hotel room. It was empty, Tom and Hays being off somewhere scouting around for God knows what. We sat down at the table and I picked up the bottle of whiskey and poured us out a drink. I saluted Ben before I drank. I said, "Good job, little brother."

There was a deck of cards on the table and he picked them up and said, "If you really want to thank me, you'll cut high card with me. Say five dollars a card?"

I said, "Are you crazy? You can't beat me at cards. You never have and you never will."

"I thought you said I did such a good job spotting that hideout gun."

"You did. I've told you."

"Then cut cards with me."

I had to laugh. "What has come over you?" We just get done with a brush with death and you want to cut cards."

"Just testing my luck."

"Well, it's going to be bad. Ain't you ever heard that old expression, lucky in love, unlucky at cards? All the skirts you get under, you ought never go near a deck of cards."

"Cut."

"If it'll make you happy to lose five bucks." I squared the deck, cut it about a third deep, pulled off the bottom card, and then replaced the pack. I showed Ben the card I'd drawn. "Ten. Odds are way in my favor."

"We'll see," he said. He put his spread-out fingers on the deck, seeming to press down. Then he slowly lifted up, letting cards shift past his thumb and index finger. The cards reached a point where the next card didn't fall down on the pack, and he slowly lifted it up and showed it to me. It was a queen. He said, "You owe me five dollars. Want to get even?"

I said, "Square the deck. Lightning doesn't strike twice."

I cut an eight and he cut a jack. After that I cut a jack and thought sure I had him, except he cut a king. Each time he handled the cards in that unusual way, first seeming to press down on them and then delicately lifting them up, letting them run through his fingers until one card felt right. I said, "Have you shaved those cards, Ben? Is that a crooked deck? Would you cheat your own brother?"

He shook his head. "Nope. It's fair and square. I'm just better at it than you are. Your cut."

We kept at it. Occasionally I won, but almost invariably Ben would cut a color card, a face card. To win I had to cut a higher one than he did. It was a losing proposition. Finally, when I was seventy dollars down, I shoved the deck away and said, "I quit. I don't know how you're doing it, but I'm not about to believe your luck has changed that much. How are you doing it?"

He poured himself out a drink of whiskey. "I'll tell you for a hundred dollars."

"Like hell you will."

He sipped at his drink and looked at me. "Now don't get angry about this. I'll tell you if you won't dock Hays like you told him you was for something I caused. I'd appreciate that, Justa."

I started to tell him I was docking Hays for good and sufficient reasons. But then I didn't. Considering what he'd done that afternoon, and considering he was more or less asking it for a favor. And, besides, I wanted to know how he could so consistently beat me cutting cards. I sighed and said, "All right. But you tell Ray. I don't want the embarrassment."

He smiled. "I'll tell him you seen you were wrong."

"You do and I'll kick your ass. Now show me."

"It's called pressing the paint." He reached out and turned the deck over and spread the cards out. "You can see that picture cards, face cards, have a lot more paint on them. That paint is slick and it won't stick to the back of the next card like the lower denominations will, like say a four or five that doesn't have much paint, just those little pips."

"So what help is that?"

"I'll show you." He turned the cards back over, squared the deck, and then put his fingers down over the pack. He said, "See, you press down on top of the deck with your forefinger just as hard as you can. That makes the lower cards stick onto the back of the card below them. Then you very carefully lift up on the deck with just your thumb and index finger, holding them very loosely and letting them sift down. Finally you'll feel a break, and that'll be a paint card that hasn't stuck to the back of the card ahead of it." For emphasis he suddenly brought half the deck up in front of my face without looking. "What's that? Feels like a king or a queen."

"Queen," I said. "You little crook, where'd you learn that?"

He smiled. "Ray taught me."

"You and Ray had better not try that out in the wrong place. Somebody with a gun and a bad sense of humor might take exception."

"Justa, it ain't cheating. Ray explained it to me. He said it ain't the one with the most luck that wins at card games. It's the one that knows the most. Isn't that why you say you always win?"

"Give me back my seventy dollars."

"Like hell I will. You lost it fair and square."

I sighed. "I not only got a hired hand on the payroll who's a crook, now I got a brother that's one too. You better give me that seventy dollars back."

But it had been a nice relief from the worry of our situation.

Tom and Hays came in after a little while and took chairs at the table. We told them what had happened. Tom looked a little disturbed, but Hays just shrugged as if to say, "Surprised it ain't happened before."

Ben said, "And I reckon I don't have to tell nobody that it wasn't just blind luck that they come upon us in that saloon."

"With an ambush all planned out," I said. "That had been thought out before."

Tom said, "Then it's clear that even Jacobbsen has his limitations. He can't have you gunned down on the street. He's going to have to draw you into what appears to be a fair fight but which is, in reality, a stacked deck."

At the mention of "stacked deck" I gave Ben and Hays a look, but I said, "I think he's afraid of outside law. The U.S. Marshals you might bring in. He could bully the local sheriff into swearing anything, but if federal people get to ferreting around, the truth will out—and he can't have that."

Hays said, "Well, we can just look for more of the same. We've seen the local rat's nest."

They'd spent the afternoon and evening spying on the house that Jacobbsen kept for town use. It was a big two-story stone affair but nowhere near as big as his ranch house.

Tom said, "It's in use. And I can't think of but one reason. And that's to keep an eye on us and try and do the work the law might fail at."

"Bunch of folks going in and out of there," Hays said. "Maybe eight or ten different ones. I bet we seen it when ya'll got set up in the saloon. Some bugger came riding up to the house and pretty soon Cully and two other'uns left out. It was nearly about the time you say it happened."

"You see Bull?"

Hays shook his head. "But that don't mean he ain't there."

I stood up. "Well," I said, "I don't guess I have to warn anybody to be awful careful. Any bait you see is more than likely going to have a hook in it. Let's go to supper."

• • •

Late that night there came a tap at our door, so light that at first I thought I'd imagined it. But we were all sleeping in such a state of readiness that I was already sitting up, gun in hand, when the second tap came. In the moonlight streaming through the windows I could see that Ben and Hays were also alert. They looked at me and I put my finger to my lips, indicating that they should be still and make no noise. I eased out of the bed and across the room to the door. The tap came again, and before the knocker could finish, I suddenly jerked the door open and stood there, my cocked revolver in hand. In the light of the hall I could see our caller was a little Mexican girl, maybe twenty years old. She cringed back in fright at the sight of me. I swiftly looked up and down the hall. It was empty. I said, "What do you want, girl?"

Soundlessly she held out a note. It was folded over. I opened it, but it was too dark to read. I said, low, "Ben."

He was at my side in a second. "Watch this girl while I strike a light," I said.

I went back into the room to a side table and lit a lantern. That roused Tom Hudspeth, who sat up spluttering and coughing and saying, "What? What?"

The note was written on lavender paper in a fine, female hand. It read:

Mr. Justa Williams,
It is very important that I speak with you. I have sent this note with my maid, Juanita. She can lead you to me. I await your coming in my carriage a half mile out of town on the north road. No one else is with me. I assure you of that. I know this note will take you by surprise, but you must trust me. No one else knows I am doing this.

It was signed, simply, "Marriah."

I turned it over and over in my hand, thinking. By now Tom Hudspeth and Hays were up and standing beside me. They read the note, and then I sent Hays to relieve Ben and let him read it also. When they were finished, I said, "Well?"

CHAPTER
9

Tom said, "You wanted to force Jacobbsen into attacking you. It appears you have gotten your way."

"You think it's a trap?"

He said, a little irritably, "Of course I think it's a trap! What else could it be? Why should Marriah want a clandestine meeting with you at midnight on a deserted road? Do you think she's turning against her family in your favor? Do you imagine she's fallen for you?"

Ben said, "He's right, Justa. This is a setup. And a damn stupid one at that."

I stood there thinking, tapping the note with a finger. Then I said, "Hays, bring that girl in here."

She came into the room trembling and staring wide-eyed with fright at the four big men surrounding her. I asked her exactly where her mistress was and what she'd been told to do. Her answer confirmed what was in the note. I said, "Who else is with her?"

She was still afraid, but she could talk some English. "Please, señor, it ees no one. Me *patrona. Todo solo.*"

I said, "Who drove her? Drove the carriage?"

"Ees me." She pointed at herself. *"Si, you es beneno con dos caballos."*

181

I thought about it. There really wasn't any reason for a Mexican girl not to be able to drive a well-mannered team. I looked over her head, thinking. Then I said, "Girl, you understand that if you are lying to me, if there are pistoleros there, I will kill you."

It scared her and she shrank back, but she said, *"Es no pistoleros. Es solo mi patrona. Es especial usted venga."*

Hays said, "Boss, she's too scared to be lying. You put her up on the saddle with you and put a gun to the back of her head. Then you let her know that at first trouble she gets one through the brainpan and she'll let you know right quick if there's an ambush."

But Tom was still against it. He said, "Justa, you are letting your vanity lead you astray! You think this Marriah is attracted to you, that she wants to help you. I tell you, that can't be so."

I looked around at him sharply. "Tom, I am not massaging my vanity. The woman may have other fish to fry. It looks like too good an opportunity to pass up. I'm going. Hays, go saddle our horses and bring them around to the front."

Ben said, "Let me get my boots on."

"You're not going."

"Hell, I'm not."

I gave him a look. "I'm taking Ray. He knows the country better and he's more likely to recognize anyone we happen to see lurking about as being from Treetops. If it's a trap they'll try and close in from behind me as we leave town. Ray will know them. You stay here with Tom."

I got fully dressed and strapped on my gun belt, checking my revolver. Then I took the Mexican girl firmly by the arm and went slowly downstairs, checking every shadow, every creak in the old wood-and-stone hotel. There was no one in the lobby. Hotels in towns like Bandera didn't keep night clerks on duty. Still holding the girl, I stepped out on the porch of the hotel. Overhead, the sloping roof that jutted out over the boardwalk blotted out a good deal of the sky, but there was still plenty of moonlight to see by.

Ray Hays came trotting around the back from the stables, riding his horse and leading mine. I caught the Mexican girl around the middle and boosted her up in the saddle. Then I swung in behind her. She was so tiny, it wasn't even a tight fit. Hays and I stood a moment looking the town over. Nothing was stirring. There didn't seem to be a light on in the place. I figured it to be coming to one o'clock. I took out my pistol and cocked it and put it behind the girl's head and told her what her lot would be if we were ambushed. She shivered but didn't say anything. I said to Hays, "I want you to stay well behind me, at least two hundred yards, until we fetch the carriage in sight. It'll be parked on one side of the road or the other. When I sight it, I'll wave an arm and you take off on that side and you have a scout above it and beyond it. On both sides of the road. If it's clear, you give me a wave and I'll go up to the carriage. I want you to position yourself a hundred yards or so down the road toward Treetops and stay alert to warn me if anyone's coming."

I rode slowly, just letting my horse shuffle along, alert to any movement on either side of the road. The moon was so bright, the sparse mesquite trees were throwing shadows. I was still holding the reins with one hand, my revolver in the other. I was no longer pointing it at the girl's head, just keeping it at the ready.

In less than a mile I saw the carriage. It was difficult to recognize at first because it was parked beneath one of the few big trees in that part of the country, a large, overflowing oak. Its own blackness caused it to melt in the shadow. It had caught my attention early because one of the team was throwing his head around restlessly, making his bit rattle. It was the noise, in the quiet night, that had caught my attention. I stopped and looked back. I could just make Ray out. I pointed off to my right and watched while he wheeled his horse and plunged into the rock and cactus.

I let my horse shamble forward, stopping now and then to listen. Occasionally, I would catch sound of Hays, but he was moving quietly. After a time I saw him cross the road, well above the carriage, and enter the terrain on the other side. I kept creeping forward until the carriage was only some fifty yards away. The team was stamping and pawing restlessly. I could see they'd been tied to the big oak. My heart, to my own chagrin, was thumping. It was one thing to tell Tom Hudspeth that I was not deluded into believing that Marriah had wanted

to see me for my sake; it was quite another to make myself
believe it. I couldn't get the beauty of her face and body out of
my mind. Ben and Hays weren't the only ones who needed
some relief.

I knew positively that I had seen a spark of interest in her
eyes on every occasion we'd met. And she had walked into her
father's office and almost escorted us out of there. True, it
could be argued that she was doing that mostly for her father
and brother's sake, but I chose to think of it otherwise.

I was watching intently down the road when I saw Hays ride
out into the middle and signal, waving his arm. I raised mine,
waving him farther back down the road. Then I rode slowly
toward the carriage, holding the girl in front of me as a shield.
Ten yards away I caught that flash of golden hair. I stopped my
horse alongside the carriage and looked in. Marriah was sitting
there, alone. I said, "Good evening, Marriah."

She turned to face me. Maybe it was the moonlight, maybe
it was my own wish, but her face looked much softer, even
more beautiful. She said, in that controlled voice of hers,
"Hello, Mr. Williams."

"Alone?"

"Quite. Will you join me?"

I let the girl slide to the ground. I said, "Tell your maid to
go up the road toward town and watch. Bring me word if
anyone is coming."

Marriah spoke to her in rapid Spanish and the girl disappeared up the road. I took one more look around and then
dismounted and tied my horse to a strap on the carriage. I
opened the door and stepped inside, taking the seat opposite
Marriah. I took my hat off and laid it beside me, taking a
second to run both my hands through my hair. Then I looked
at her. She wasn't wearing one of those heavy, ankle-length
gowns. Instead she had on a short skirt of some light material
and a thin blouse that buttoned down the front, almost like a
man's shirt. As my eyes became accustomed to the darker
conditions inside the carriage, I could tell she was not wearing
an upper undergarment because I could faintly make out the
ends of her nipples pushing against the cloth of her blouse. It
made my pulse hammer in my ears and my breath come a little

short. Lying on the seat beside her was a robe that I assumed she'd worn out of the house and to the carriage.

She said, "I'm glad you would come. I know you must mistrust all of my family, including me. But I assure you that you're in no danger."

I smiled slightly. "That depends on what kind of danger you're talking about."

"I don't understand you."

"Oh, yes, you do." Then I sat back and folded my arms. "All right. You said you had something important you wanted to talk to me about. You've obviously dressed to get my attention. Well, you've got it."

At my mention of how she was dressed, she shrank back a little and crossed her arms over her breasts. "I had to dress like this. My father knows I take moonlight drives and I dress lightly, usually in a robe. If I'd dressed differently, it would have made him suspicious."

"All right. My mistake. That wasn't very gallant of me."

She almost smiled. "What a word. *Gallant*. And pronounced correctly. My, my. Perhaps you really are what I am hoping you are."

"That would be?"

"A gentleman."

I smiled. "That sounds like a touch of well-directed flattery. I suppose now I'm expected to live up to it. I will warn you, I'm difficult to manipulate, even by one such as yourself."

The half smile had left her lips. She said, "Don't flatter yourself. I wouldn't waste my time attempting to maneuver you. I want to tell you some things, not for your sake but for mine. And my brother's."

"What?"

"I was listening at the door during the discussion you and your friends had with my father. I heard enough to convince me that you are not guilty. Though, to be truthful, I never really thought you were. From our first meeting you had never struck me as the kind of man who could commit such a crime."

"Thanks," I said dryly. "You seem to be the only one here who thinks that."

She ignored me. "I also realized that you and your brothers

are very capable and determined. I know that you've suffered great harm and you intend to pay my family back for that. I can understand. The Jacobbsens make enemies. Or rather my father does."

I shrugged. "It's an unhandy habit, to say the least."

Now her voice became impassioned. "But there is one thing I must make you understand. I overheard you and your brother accuse Torrey of Mary Mae's murder. I tell you, he had nothing to do with it! He couldn't. He's not like that. I know that he hadn't left the ranch for several nights around the time she was killed."

"Or maybe you didn't *see* him leave the ranch," I said. "But the fact is, I can prove he was going to her. You want to deny that?"

She was leaning forward in her enthusiasm to get me to understand. "I know Torrey was going to her, but it wasn't for what you think. It was for comfort, for sympathy. To have someone to talk to him. Mary was a gentle soul and she liked Torrey. She helped him. You must understand that Torrey is just a weak, helpless boy! My father has almost beat him into the ground trying to change him. But Torrey is just a frightened child. He never could do anything like what happened to Mary."

I said, "Oh, I don't know. As crazy as your father is, I figure the son would be capable of anything. Especially if Mrs. Hawkins was resisting him."

She burst out, "But that's just it. Torrey is not even a real Jacobbsen. He was adopted after my mother couldn't give him any more children after she bore me. My father wanted a son and Torrey was a disappointment. And he's taken that disappointment out on Torrey."

Well, that somewhat surprised me, though it did account for the difference in their looks and coloring. "But why tell me all this? I'm not the law."

A long second passed while she looked at me. Then she said, "Because I can tell you are planning something. I think you are perhaps planning to try and kill my father and maybe Torrey."

It got very still in the carriage after she said that. I said carefully, "I kind of thought it was the other way around. Would you know anything about that?"

"Look," she said, "I don't care what you do to my father. I hate him. I hate him for what he's done to everyone he's touched except me. He can't touch me, though he's tried. But he's ruined my mother. You know Torrey went to Mary. Did you know my father did also?"

"Yes," I said.

"It was him that went for the other. He gave her money. Kept her obligated to him. Kept her in virtual bondage. He is the cruelest man I have ever known. He had her husband killed so he could have her. I can't prove it, but I know he did."

I sat back and studied her face. After a moment I said, "And you're telling me all this so I won't harm your brother?"

"Yes . . . no. Not altogether." She started to say something else and then stopped.

I waited. "Well?"

She looked away, out the window. "Maybe I just wanted you to know."

"Why?"

She leaned back in the seat. "I'm not sure."

"You didn't want me to think you were all like your father?"

She looked away again. "That could be it."

"Why should you care? Just so we won't hurt Torrey?"

She put her hand to her hair and didn't say anything. Then her hand dropped to her neck and she looked up at me. "Does it really matter?"

I eased across the carriage and sat down beside her. "You knew I wouldn't hurt Torrey, anyway, didn't you?"

There was the slightest motion of her body as she shrugged. It seemed to bring us closer together. "I—I couldn't be sure. But I thought there were things you needed to know. In—in fairness to you."

I was close enough to her to feel her breathing increase. "Is there anything else you want to tell me?" I asked, leaning toward her, our faces only inches apart.

"Nooo," she said.

I leaned forward then and kissed her, lightly at first and then with increasing pressure. Her lips parted and I felt her arm go

around my shoulders. After a long time I pulled back slightly.
We were both breathing hard. I half whispered, "I think there's
more to this, even more than what we're doing now. Why don't
you tell me?"

She had to slow her breathing before she could speak. "I
think my father believes Torrey did it."

"Why?"

"Because he beat Torrey after your visit the other day.
Torrey came to me in tears. Dag beat him with a riding crop.
It was awful. And then, later that night I heard him screaming
at my mother that her bastard child was going to bring disgrace
and ruin on his name. He always calls Torrey her bastard child.
I don't know why because it's not true."

"He wants to disassociate himself."

"I know he's very worried that your lawyer is trying to bring
in the U.S. Marshals for an outside investigation. Someone
brought him a telegram your lawyer had sent, and he almost
went crazy. I know he believes Torrey did it and I'm afraid of
what he'll do."

I unbuttoned her blouse. Her breasts rose as if seeking my
mouth. I covered her nipples in turn. She was panting and
thrusting against me. I slowly slid my hand between her legs.
She wasn't wearing any undergarments. She suddenly took my
head between her hands and pulled me down and kissed the
inside of my mouth. As best I could, I undid my gun belt and
let it slide off on the floor. But I did put one hand down and
make sure I could locate my revolver in a hurry. Then I raised
up slightly and undid my jeans and, with her help, pushed them
down.

As I went into her I thought that I could not have arranged
to put myself in a much more defenseless position; virtually
unarmed and in enemy territory. I didn't think Tom Hudspeth
would approve. But in another second I didn't care.

It was a long time before the frenzied rush and tumultuous
emotion left my body. When I was spent and limp, I lay there
for a time. Then, as strength came back, I eased myself
carefully off her and flopped down on the opposite seat. She
lay sprawled out on the seat, one leg up along the backrest, one
on the floor, her skirt still up around her hips. Her eyes were

closed and her breathing still fast. I pulled up my jeans and buttoned them and then sat there looking at her. She was perhaps the most perfectly formed female I'd ever seen. I found a cigar in my pocket and lit it. The smell of the smoke seemed to arouse her, though she didn't move or open her eyes. She said, "There's a bottle of brandy. There's a little drawer under my seat."

I leaned down and slid it out. There were two silver cups along with the brandy. I took them out and poured a good measure in each cup. Without a word I held one of the cups out toward her. Her eyes were still closed, but they suddenly came open and she sat up and took the drink. There was not the slightest hint of embarrassment about her. Even sitting up, her skirt was well up on her thighs and her blouse was still open, but she made no move to cover herself. I very much liked that about her. Before she touched the brandy, she leaned across and kissed me lightly on the lips. "Ah, Mr. Williams," she said, "I would never have foreseen this."

I clinked cups with her and said, "Luck."

"Yes."

We drank. It was exceptionally good brandy. I looked at the bottle. "Napoleon. Your father's?"

"Oh, yes. Everything belongs to Dag."

"He controls all the money?"

She frowned. "Mostly. I made him set a sum aside for me. I got tired of having it doled out to me."

"How'd you do that?"

Her eyes flared. "Told him I'd leave. He knew I meant it." She made a grimace. "I'm his showpiece. He likes people in the big cities to see me. He points me out as an example of Nordic breeding." She shivered. "I hate him."

"It sounds to me like you were the adopted one."

She shivered again. "Sometimes I wish I were." She stopped and sipped at her brandy. "But, you know, he wasn't always like he is now. Oh, not that he was ever any sort of a gentle person. No. But it seems as if in the last five or six years he's gone crazy. Sometimes I think he has a brain tumor or something. He's so, so power-crazy. We have three times the men working at the ranch that we need. He just has them so he can boss them around. It's . . . it's difficult to explain."

"What about your mother?"

There was a note of sadness in her voice. "My mother is a beaten woman. She's long ago given up. All she does is eat now. Torrey drinks and my mother eats."

"Why doesn't she leave?"

With the silver cup almost to her lips, she said, "How? She doesn't have any money. All her relatives are in Sweden. She has no friends." She took a sip and then laughed slightly. "The ironic thing is that several of Dag's corporations are in her name. Taxes or something. She can actually sign checks. Of course, only when Dag tells her to."

"Why doesn't she write herself a check and leave?"

She laughed. "My mother? Don't talk nonsense."

"How about you? Because of Torrey?"

"I suppose up to now that's been the reason. But I've been planning to leave for some time now. I'm thinking of going to Chicago or San Francisco. I'm just waiting until I have the money."

"How you going to get that?"

She said, matter-of-factly, "Dag keeps a great amount of gold coin in his safe from time to time. I have been carefully and systematically stealing a little at a time. When I have enough, I'll go. If Torrey survives this business you're involved in, I'll take him with me."

"I'm not going to hurt him. Personally, I think your daddy did it." I didn't really; I just said it to see her reaction.

"Oh, no. That wouldn't be his way. He couldn't torment and torture her anymore if she were dead, could he?"

I reached down and got my gun belt and buckled it on. I said, casually, "Is there anything you can tell me about what your father might have planned for me?"

She shook her head. "No. That's not anything he would tell me. And I haven't overheard anything. All I know is that he's in a rage like I've never seen him. And I think he's frightened. I never thought I'd hear myself say this about any man, but I think he's afraid of you. Afraid of what you can do. All I know is that lately he's been having a great number of conferences with Bull and Cully. And Gibson. I don't know all of them, but I know that those three usually are the ones for the dirty work."

"Gibson?"

"Yes."

"How about one named Wall?"

She shook her head. "Not that I know of. As I say, I know very few of their names. I avoid them."

Just then I heard the unmistakable sound of a shod hoof striking a rock in the road. I drew my revolver and cocked it, motioning for Marriah to get down. Then I heard a soft call. "Boss? Boss? You all right?"

It was Hays. I stuck my head out the window. He'd ridden almost up to the carriage but had stayed clear of the window. I said, "Yeah, I'm fine."

"You been such a long time. I got worried. It's nearly two in the morning."

"You go along back to the hotel. I'll be right behind you," I said.

When he'd ridden off, I put my head back in the carriage and looked at Marriah. "I want to see you again."

"All right."

"Tomorrow night?"

She shook her head. "It would be too soon. I seldom take late drives two nights in a row. Dag could notice."

"The night after? Say around midnight?"

"I can't set an hour, Justa. It's too hard. I have to wait until I think he's in bed asleep. He doesn't keep regular hours. I'll just have to send Juanita in again."

I said, "All right. But just have her tap on the door and take off. I'll hear it and know and will come. But let's not meet on this main road. There's a little turnoff about a mile farther back. Goes to Grummet's place. Do you know it?"

She nodded.

"Pull off in there about a quarter of a mile. I won't make you wait long."

She got out of the carriage to kiss me good-bye. Up the road we could see her maid coming. I kissed her with passion and longing. Forty-eight hours seemed like a long time to wait to reexperience what I'd just had.

They were awake when I got back to the room, sitting around the table drinking whiskey. Ben said severely, "Dammit, we were getting worried. What took you so long?"

I said, "We had considerable to talk about."

Ben gave me a narrow look. "You sure all you did was talk? You look kind of tousled to me."

Tom Hudspeth said, "Well? What did she have to say?"

I shook my head. "I'm beat. I'm going to bed. I'll tell you in the morning."

Tom Hudspeth and I had breakfast alone in the hotel café. I told him most of what had happened and been said with Marriah the night before. I felt constrained, somehow, to leave out the lovemaking. It could be said that it, too, was fundamental and a matter to be considered in a basic plan of defense, but I somehow couldn't bring myself to talk about it. From a strategic point of view I thought of it as incidental to our purposes.

Tom said, "Well, at least we know there's a certain amount of division in the enemy camp. I don't quite know how to take the news that she thinks Jacobbsen is afraid of you."

I was finishing my coffee. I said, "I think it makes him more dangerous."

"And you believe that her main purpose was to persuade you about Torrey?"

I looked him in the eye. "Yes."

He shook his head. "I don't know. Did you believe her? Were you convinced?"

I nodded slowly. "Yes. I was. I've never liked Torrey for the murder, especially after I got a look at him."

"If not Torrey, then who else is Jacobbsen protecting?"

"It doesn't matter. If he still thinks it was Torrey, it's all the same. He still needs a patsy. Though, now, even if the real murderer were caught and convicted, I don't think it would make any difference. It's gone way beyond the murder. It's him and me now."

"From what Marriah says, it sounds as if your little telegram trick hit home. By the way, what was her attitude like?"

I temporized carefully. "Friendly. Convincing. Supplicating."

He cocked his head at me. "The haughty Miss Jacobbsen? Supplicating?"

I used the lighting of a cigar to hide the slight smile on my face. I said, "Well, she's really rather nice when you get to know her. I think we got a good deal more out of that meeting that we could have expected. Gibson, for instance."

Tom pushed his plate away. "This has certainly gotten a great deal more complicated than I'd expected. I'd thought I was defending a client in a murder trial. I had no idea I'd be mixed up in a feud."

I didn't like that. "It's not a feud, Tom. Don't diminish it to that. I'm varmint hunting. And this part is my business. You can just stay out of that."

"With bullets about to fly? Friend, more innocent bystanders get killed in a battle than the actual participants. It is a feud, Justa. Don't kid me." He reached inside his coat pocket. "I want to ask you something. You got a telegram this morning from Norris. You were still sleeping, so I took it for you." He brought it out and unfolded it. "It says, 'Have had to tell Dad all. He is enraged. Is contacting powerful friends in the state capital to bring pressure on the Marshal's office to send legitimate investigators. Ranch is doing fine. Good luck.'"

He handed it across and I read it and then put it in my shirt pocket. "What did you want to ask me?"

"What you're going to do if outside authority does come here. You don't seriously expect federal marshals to stand by while you try and wreak vengeance on Dag Jacobbsen, do you?"

"As long as Jacobbsen has power he can bring false witnesses against me, and all the marshals in the world can't change their testimony. I have said from the first that I have to destroy the man to clear myself. No one has seemed to have listened to me."

Tom looked disgusted. "Have it your own way, Justa. You've got your mind made up." He threw some bills down on the table to pay for the meal. "One thing they don't teach in law school."

"What's that?"

"How to bill your client for danger encountered while trying to advise him and give him legal counsel in the midst of a blood feud. My partners and I will have to give that long and serious thought. My own feeling right now is that you don't have enough money to compensate me fairly. I've been scared from the day I got here."

I got up. "Just look at it as a learning experience, Tom. Nothing more than that."

"Where do I put this experience to use . . . in the after-life?"

I had been wanting to see the doctor and it was my good fortune that he was in town. I went to see him that afternoon. I had expected to have a hard time of it, perhaps having to resort to a heavy bribe to find out what I wanted to know, but that didn't turn out to be the case. He was not of Bandera, but he knew enough about my circumstances to be sympathetic. When I'd explained further, he was willing enough, without going too far beyond patient confidences to tell me about certain matters. He said, "Yes, he thought he had a dose at first and so did I. So much so that I put him on a bismuth preparation. But when I came back, just last visit, his condition had cleared up, so I knew that it must have been a strain. Amazing the similar symptoms between a strain and the real infection. Pain, drips."

"But he would have thought he had a dose at the time?"

"Oh, yes. Though I had a hard time believing where he said he could have caught it because I know that those girls are clean. They come to me themselves. But a man will lie about that, won't he?"

I thanked him, paid his nominal fee, and left. Hays was waiting for me in the lobby of the hotel. He got up quickly when I came in. "Boss, I got some news."

We got sat down and he said, low and conspiratorially, though there wasn't another soul in the lobby except the desk clerk and he was ten yards away. "I just seen Gibson. Over to the saloon. He says it's Sattiday."

"Saturday? What time?"

"He don't know yet, but he's gonna try and find out."

"Did he say how or where?"

Hays shook his head. "He says he just barely run it down at some risk to himself. Says it is mighty warm work, askin' questions without nobody suspectin' what he's after. He says he ain't really in the know. But he says he'll find out, maybe by tomorrow."

I thought. It was Thursday. "Well, that gives us two days to relax, doesn't it?"

Hays said hesitantly, "He's waiting over at the saloon. He thinks he ought to get a little more money for this."

I took out forty dollars and gave it to him. "Tell him there's plenty more where this came from for good information. You haven't heard from the other one, Wall?"

"No, sir. He might be having trouble getting into town."

We got up. I said, "Do that errand and then come straight back to the hotel room. I don't want anyone out by themselves more than they have to be."

He was still hesitating. "Uh, boss . . ."

"What?"

He sort of glanced away, looking uncomfortable. "Uh, what you said the other day . . ."

"What?"

He cleared his throat. "Uh, after me and Ben went to see them, uh, girls. About, uh . . ."

"About your dick falling off?"

He blushed. "Well, uh, yeah. You didn't mean that, did you?"

I fixed him with an eye. "Ray, didn't you see me go up them stairs yesterday afternoon?"

He nodded.

"And didn't you just see me come from the doctor's office?"

He nodded again, beginning to look unhappy.

I shrugged. "What more can I tell you?"

He swallowed. "You reckon I ought to go pay a visit to the doc?"

I shook my head. "It's too late. Twenty-four hours too late. That's what comes of not following orders. Now run your errand and get back to the room." I left him with a strangled look on his face.

We ate supper in the room that night, played poker for three or four hours, and then retired shortly after eleven. I made no special point of warning the others to be especially alert, but Ben seemed to pick up the premonitions from me. He said, "You expecting something tonight, Justa?"

I said, "I don't know. But I got that tingling feeling. Just be ready to act quick. And don't sleep too hard. Nothing I can put my finger on. Just a feeling."

It was early in the morning, perhaps three A.M., when they made their try. I was awakened by cries of *"Fire! Fire! Run for your lives! Fire!"*

I sat up instantly. The cries were coming from the hallway. The moon was still up good, and by its light streaming through the two big windows that faced the street I could see that Ben and Hays were already up, guns in hand.

I said low, "Get ready!"

It was then that Tom Hudspeth came half awake. He staggered out of bed and, in his nightshirt, started toward the door. I yelled, "Hays! Stop him!"

Hays caught him two steps from the hallway door and jerked him back. Tom was still not quite awake and he struggled, though somewhat ineffectually. I paused to take one quick look out the window near my bed. The overhanging roof made it difficult to see the hitch rail, but I thought I could see the rumps of six or seven horses. I wasted no more time but jumped to the middle of the room and overturned the big table, throwing it on its side for a shield. Ben saw what I was about and he grabbed Hudspeth's bed, which was along the wall, and turned it sideways also, dragging it over to join up with the table in a sort of L-shaped fortress.

"Quick, Hays!" I said.

He dragged the still uncomprehending Hudspeth over to join us behind our makeshift fort. The cries were still going up, but they were not quite so insistent.

"Any second now," I said. I cocked my revolver. "Let them get in good."

I heard them break into the room next door. One or two shots were fired and then there was silence for a second. Then, almost simultaneously, they broke through the connecting door and the hallway door to my room. I yelled at Ben and Hays, "Cover right!"

I let several of them pour through the door and then I began firing. By my side, Ben and Hays were firing at figures crowding through the other door. The sound of so many guns, firing one on top of the other, was almost defeaning. In a second the room was so full of smoke, you could barely see. I just kept firing where the door should be until my revolver was empty. I jerked up my saddle gun, which I had laying by my side, and fired a few more times. I had heard a few slugs wham into the table, but none had hit me. By my side, the guns of Ben and Hays had gone silent. Hudspeth was laying on the floor saying, over and over, "What the hell! What the hell!"

"Anybody hurt?"

"Not me," Ben said.

Hays said, "Nope."

The smoke was beginning to clear. I got up cautiously but quickly, and hurried over to the door. Three bodies lay on the floor. None of them were Bull. I had cartridges in my hand and I hurried out into the hall, reloading as I went. It was empty except for one old man standing in his doorway looking bewildered. I heard heavy boots thudding down the stairway. I turned and raced back into the room. The window was partially open and I heaved it the rest of the way up. I stepped through, out on to the sloping porch roof that fronted the hotel. I was just in time to see two men go tearing away up the street. Fortunately I was barefoot, but the steep roof was still treacherous footing. Teetering and slipping, I worked my way down to the edge. Just as I got there I saw Bull come running out of the hotel. He had a pistol in his hand, but he holstered it as he grabbed up the reins of his horse. I let him get one foot in the stirrup before I jumped. I had meant to land square on his shoulders, but his horse was skitting around, and I caught him in the small of the back just as he went to mount. We tumbled to the ground together. I landed on my side and he on his back. He was taken by surprise, and in that second I heaved myself up and smashed him across the face with my revolver barrel. It stunned him, but in that instant of blood-spurting pain, I still saw recognition alight in his eyes as he saw my face. I was drawing back my revolver to hit him again when I heard a pistol blast from close by. I whirled. A man had just come running out of the hotel. He'd tried a quick shot at me but had missed, probably because of the tumbled mass Bull and I made. He turned to run and I shot him in the small of the back before he'd taken two steps. He threw up his hands and pitched forward.

I was still holding Bull with my left arm. I could feel him struggling. The blow I had hit him was wearing off rapidly. I turned, swinging for his face again, but only was able to clip him on the side of the head. He was wiggling to his right, trying to clear that side so he could reach for his revolver. I slashed at his arm, hitting him with all my strength, hoping to break the bone. I was almost insane with anger and rage. I wanted to tear him apart and then beat the pieces to a pulp, but I also wanted him alive. I wanted to force him to tell the truth.

He was howling, the howls intensifying each time I hit him on the wrist. But then he gave over trying to reach for the gun and suddenly used both arms and shoved me away from him. God, the man was strong!

He held me back long enough to reach his knees. We were there, facing each other, both on our knees, blood streaming down his face. I swung my right arm in a cross-handed blow, as hard as I could, and caught him in the mouth with my gun. I felt the crunch of teeth. I hit him again. He should have gone down, but instead he somehow staggered to his feet, shoving me down as he did. I was on my back and he was there, searching for his revolver. It had fallen out of his holster in the struggle, and through the blood he couldn't find it. With my bare foot I kicked it away. He staggered to his horse, trying to reach across the saddle for his carbine. I yelled, "Bull!"

He turned, dragging the carbine out of its scabbard. I shot him in the side. He kept on trying to get the carbine clear. I shot him in the hip. It made him sag down to one knee, but now he had the carbine out. With that beaten and perhaps broken right hand, he tried to lever a cartridge into the chamber. I shot him in the chest and he suddenly sat down. He just sat there, staring at me; the lever half worked, not moving. I got up to my knees, still aiming at his chest. "Remember me, Bull? Remember the line cabin? Remember I warned you, Bull?"

He just stared at me. He wasn't dead, but there were enormously long pauses between the times his eyes would blink. I went over to him and took the carbine out of his hands. He didn't resist. I said, "You shouldn't have fucked with me, Wilton Purdy. I told you it was a big mistake."

Then I stuck my revolver in my waistband, took that carbine by the barrel, wound up, and hit him in the side of the head as hard as I could. The blow broke the stock off the gun. Bull went over on his side, falling under his horse. He lay very still. I threw the broken gun down beside him and turned. There was a crowd of seven or eight men standing on the porch. Ben and Hays and Hudspeth were there. I started up the steps. They parted as I came through. I said, to Ben, "Let's go see how much damage Jacobbsen is going to owe the hotel."

We had killed six in our room, and one had crawled out into the hall and died. One, on Ben and Hays's side had at least six holes in him. Hays knelt down and looked the man over and said, "I swear, I don't believe this ol' boy is going to be able to take anything but coarse food for some time."

Cully was among the dead, as was a man that Hays identified as Gibson. I said, "Search his pockets."

Hays did, coming out with a wad of greenbacks. He handed them to me. I counted off ninety dollars and then told him to put the rest back. Hays said, "Boss, remind me to never get in debt to you. I don't much care for the way you collect your money."

I said, "You don't reckon he earned it, do you?"

Hays said, "I think we ought to fine him the balance he's carrying for lying."

The raiders had been very ineffective. There were two bullet holes in the table and none in the bed that Hays and Ben had sheltered behind. They'd counted on us being stupid enough to pour out in the hall at the cry of *"Fire!"* and, when that hadn't worked, counted on us being caught unawares in our beds. Instead they'd burst into a darkened room and been blinded by the sudden flashes of our guns. They'd gone down one by one with very little hope. The planning of the raid had been misguided, the execution worse. It was interesting to note that Bull must have laid back in the hall, waiting for events to develop before he ventured in. Well, he'd gotten his. Patience had not rewarded him.

Tom said, "Justa, you've dealt Jacobbsen a severe blow. He'll be a long time getting over this. I think it's over. They have to drop the charges now. Only a blind man could fail to see this has been a planned campaign of persecution aimed at you."

I hadn't answered him. My mind was on Jacobbsen and the expression on his face as he got his first reports of the attempted execution of me and my party.

Of course, there was nothing the law could do to us about what had happened, desire as they might. The sheriff came and made an official investigation and generally acted like a pompous ass, but even he would have had a hard time making it out to be anything but self-defense. Tom did play with him a bit on that, though. He'd said, "Now, Sheriff, far be it for me to tell you your job, but I am, after all, a lawyer and an officer of the court, and I have to tell you that these men might have been lured here to their death. Clear case of premeditated murder."

The sheriff looked at him quickly. "You think so?"

Tom said, "Oh, certainly. Any court in the land would look at those busted locks on the doors and all the bullet holes in the walls and see that my clients deliberately set out to ambush these men. What better place than in their own hotel room at four in the morning?"

Then the sheriff had seen that Tom was having him on and he'd gotten a sour look on his face and muttered something about, "Smart-aleck lawyers. Think they know so much."

There was some talk that Bull had been unarmed when I'd used his carbine to kill him with that last blow. But that had come to nothing when the doctor had testified that the shot in his chest had probably caused the fatal damage and I'd just hit a corpse that hadn't quite collapsed yet.

But I didn't want that to be. I wanted Bull to have been conscious right to the last and heard every word I'd said.

CHAPTER
10

Tom said, "I went over to see Judge Hummil this morning to discuss these new developments and see what changes might have been wrought in his attitude. But he's not in and his clerk doesn't know when to expect him. The sheriff is gone also. I guess you needn't report in today."

Of course, I'd never paid any attention to that rigamarole anyway. We were sitting in the Lantern Saloon. I took a sip of my lukewarm beer and said, "Likely they are both out at Treetops getting their new orders."

A man passed our table and nodded at me. It was a wonder what the death of nine killers could do to the perspective of a town. All of a sudden people were speaking to us on the street, we were getting courteous service in the cafés and saloons, and the hotel had even gone so far as to allow they wouldn't hold us responsible for the damage to our rooms. I think they were discovering that it was possible to challenge Jacobbsen without the sky falling in or the earth opening up or some other dire consequence directed from the Power-in-the-Mansion befalling them. In a way I couldn't blame them. They were just ordinary folks trying to go about their business. I'm sure they hadn't been able to see how Jacobbsen's ubiquitous and obsequious tentacles could someday ensnare them. But, on the other hand,

I had nothing but contempt for them, for the greedy, cowardly milksops they'd become. They'd been taken in, but only once they'd realized that there'd been nothing to prevent them from fighting back.

Except their own cowardice. And greed. And sheeplike qualities.

There had been one interesting exception to our new acceptance. That had been Mr. Davis, Morris Davis. I had gone in the afternoon after the raid on our hotel to replenish my stock of cartridges. Mr. Davis had stood behind his counter giving me a severe look from his tight, pinched, narrow face. He said, "Take your trade somewheres else, Mr. Williams. I don't want you in my store."

That took me off-guard. "What's the matter, is my money no good?"

"You're no good, Mr. Williams, for this town. You bring trouble. You cause trouble for Mr. Jacobbsen, who is the best thing for this town. You're bad for business. Go away."

I looked at him for a long moment, then said, "You do just about whatever Jacobbsen tells you, don't you?"

"I've ordered you out of my store."

I said quietly, "I saw you in your wagon a few days ago, Davis. Looked like you were making a delivery. Do a lot of the delivering yourself, do you? Say, to widow women?"

His pinched face had tightened even more. He had his hands on the counter, made into fists. They'd gone white at the knuckles. "Get out!" he shouted. "Get out or I'll send for the sheriff."

I strolled toward the door. "You do that, Mr. Davis. You do whatever you think is best, because that's what I'm going to do. Especially in your case."

No tap had come on my door that night even though I'd lain awake late expecting it. But then, I hadn't been too surprised. I'd figured that things were probably in a turmoil at Treetops and it would be inconvenient and unwise for Marriah to try and slip away.

But I was expecting a summons that night and the rest of the day and evening stretched out like a long, flat road to be traveled at a snail's pace.

I sat there thinking about Jacobbsen, trying to get inside his mind, trying to guess what he'd pull next. He'd sent in eleven men to try and kill us. Only two had returned alive. I hoped he was good enough at arithmetic to figure out he was getting the worst of it.

Tom said, "Justa, I've got business in San Antonio that I've been putting off for just too long, matters I'd like to get out of the way before your trial. If there is to be a trial. I think events around here are going to be on the quiet side for a time. Jacobbsen has been bruised and he's going to have to take time to lick his wounds. Would it be all right with you if I took a quick trip to San Antonio? I could still catch the afternoon stage and be back here inside of three days."

"I think we can muddle along without your services for a few days," I said. "Though God knows the prospect is frightening. What if we were to get in another fun fight? How would we fare without your steady hand and eyes of steel?"

He gave me a grim look. "I suppose you find my conduct during that frightening business cause for amusement. Well, let me remind you that I am a man of books, not guns. A vocation you'll thoroughly approve of if we find ourselves in court. When we get before the bar, we'll see who has the steady hand and steely eye."

I smothered a laugh. "Oh, Tom, I was just joshing you a little. Actually, I thought you did rather well. You didn't wet your pants." I hastily changed my tune when I saw the look on his face. "Tom, Tom. Don't take it so seriously. I'm in a good mood."

"Going to see Marriah again?"

I just smiled and sipped at my beer.

Tom said, "I assume, once again, it will be all business."

"You just run on along to San Antonio and tighten matters up there. And I'm sure you'll pay another visit to the U.S. Marshal's office and urge them to hurry on down." I gave him a crooked smile. "Tell me something on the square, Tom. Do these marshals actually exist? You keep talking about them, but they never seem to materialize. Are you sure you didn't just dream about them sometime?"

He said stiffly, "No, I didn't dream them up. But for your

information they are assigned to the federal district court whose scope of jurisdiction takes in quite a swath of territory. You'd be amazed at what the citizenry can get up to in such a considerable amount of real estate. And there aren't that many marshals. And they don't like to interfere in local jurisdiction unless there's a clear cut case of malfeasance. So far I haven't been able to present them with prima facie evidence that such exists here."

I laughed and said, "Well, you might mention we had nine men killed here the other night while attempting murder. I don't know if that's prima facie enough for them to call it malfeasance, but it's damn sure starting to smell bad enough that they ought to be able to get a whiff even as far off as San Antonio. If I were to croak Judge Hummil and Sheriff Rose, would that bring them down?"

"Not very funny," he said. "Of course I intend to tell them about what happened the other night. They're interested. They're just spread too thin. But I have hopes we'll have someone here before the trial."

"I thought you said 'if there was a trial.' The main false witness, Bull, is not going to testify. Not unless he's got a real loud voice."

Tom said, "If Jacobbsen is determined to have a witness, he'll have one." He stood up. "I'd better hurry if I'm going to make that stage."

I hung around, drinking another beer, and then made my way back to the hotel. Tom had already gone, and only Hays was there, taking a nap on his bed. I thought of waking him up and making him play me some acey-deucey, but the beers had made me sleepy and I shucked off my boots and lay down myself. It was a warm afternoon, but there was a good breeze coming in through the window. I didn't exactly nap, but I dozed off and on and rested pretty good. After a time Hays got to snoring and I threw a boot across the room at him. He come up, snorting and looking wild, saying, "Huh? What? Huh?"

Then he lay back down and went to sleep again. I lay there thinking about Marriah, hoping she'd be able to rendezvous that night. I looked at my pocket watch, which I'd laid out on the nightstand by my bed. It was close on to six. I got up, yawning, and leaned out the window to see what the town was doing. After a few minutes I saw Alvin come out of the mercantile. He paused a moment to say something to his father, who was still inside, and then started up the street. I watched him as he walked, a tall, somewhat gawky young man wearing a celluloid collar and a black patent-leather bow tie. Standard equipment for a mercantile clerk. It looked more at home on him than his deputy's badge had. I watched him passing the rows of stores and saloons. I saw him glance upward as he passed the Lantern. I imagined he had a disapproving look on his face, directed toward the ladies who occupied the upper rooms. Someday, no doubt, he'd try to round them all up and carry them off to church and bring them to the clean life. To the disgust of every cowboy in the vicinity.

I watched him all the way, having to lean a little farther out the window to keep him in sight. The church was near the end of town, and I knew that the Davises lived two houses past that. I noticed the door of the church was open and I half expected him to turn in there. Ben had said he went to church every time they opened the doors, but this time he continued on until he got to his own home and turned in there.

Ben was just coming in when I turned back into the room. I said, "Where the hell you been?"

"Playing a little poker. Listening."

"Win anything?"

"Aw, it was just a small game. Won about twenty and spent that much buying drinks."

"We still popular?"

"Oh, yeah. I believe they're thinking of standing you for mayor. That is, if you live."

"What's the opinion?"

"That Jacobbsen can't *not* kill you. That you're crazy. That Hummil has done a bugger and left the country. And the sheriff. That the army is probably going to be called in. That this whole mess is going to ruin beef prices and that it's all your fault. But the one thing that I can't figure out is what half the town was doing up at four in the morning the other night."

"What are you talking about?"

"At least that many people have told me they personally saw

you club Bull with his rifle. I could have sworn there were only about six or seven of us watching at the time."

It brought my mood down. I said bitterly, "I wish the sonofabitch was still alive so I could do it again."

Hays got up, snuffling and snorting, and joined us at the table. The management still hadn't fixed the bullet holes. "What are ya'll talking about?" he said, and reached out and poured himself a quick shot and downed it.

"About weaning you off the bottle once we get back to the Half-Moon. You understand that when you work for us, you don't drink until Saturday night."

Ben said, "Hays is going to work for me."

"No, he's not," I said.

"He damn sure is. I run the horse operation."

"And I run the whole operation. Which includes the horse breeding. I started it, remember?"

"But I run it now, and I say Hays works for me."

Hays was switching his head back and forth between us. "Wait a minute. Who am I supposed to listen to?"

"Who hired you?"

"You did, boss. But I sure like to work with blooded horse stock."

Ben said, "See? We've already been talking about it."

I leaned back and yawned. "Aw, the hell with both of ya'll." I looked at my watch again. It was just half past six. It was going to take forever to get late.

I don't know why we were all in such a good mood. I think we felt, as Tom had said, that it was all over, that just a few loose ends needed to be tied up. I think we all felt that except for the formality of recovering my bond money, we could ride for Matagorda County and forget the whole sorry episode.

Except my feelings toward Dag Jacobbsen hadn't really changed. Killing Bull might have diluted them somewhat, perhaps even to the degree that I had to keep reminding myself that it was he, Jacobbsen, who was really responsible for what had been done to me. Or maybe it was Marriah and the fact that she was his daughter. It was difficult to hate a man with such passion when you were hoping to possess his daughter as often as you could lay your hands on her.

Or maybe I was just tired. It seemed we'd been in Bandera forever. Ben must have been reading my mind, for he said, "I'll sure be glad to get home. I hate to think of all the poor girls who are suffering from broken hearts at my prolonged absence."

Getting up, I said, "Not to mention all the horses that need breaking. Let's go to supper. I'm getting so damned tired of these four walls, I think I'll sleep outside the rest of my life."

We ate at a café down the street, having our usual steak and beans and potatoes. Hays had two pieces of apple pie, but I contented myself with a cigar.

Ben was watching him eat the pie. He said, "Hays, where did you ever get such a sweet tooth? Every time we eat and there's pie or cake, you always eat two pieces at least."

Hays was busy ladling it into his mouth with a big spoon. "Never did get enough when I was a kid. I ate a whole pie one time when I was about six that my maw had baked for supper, and she give me such a whippin' that I couldn't look at nothin' sweet for years. Then it caught up with me all of a sudden and I been this way ever since."

"Look, there may come a tap at our door tonight, late," I said. "If there is, don't pay any attention. I'll be going out. Ya'll just stay in bed."

They glanced at each other quickly, and then Ben said, "Justa, is that wise?"

"I think so, Ben. If I didn't, I wouldn't do it, now would I?"

But he was frowning. "I wish you wouldn't forget that she is still his daughter. I don't blame you for what you're doing. I wouldn't mind getting into that myself, but don't you think Ray or I ought to trail you?"

"Look," I said, "first of all, what makes you think I'm getting into her? We talk. Second, she'd sooner help the devil than Dag Jacobbsen."

"That may be what she says."

Hays was frowning again. "Boss, let me follow along."

"No. And no is the final answer. I mean it. Now eat up that pie and let's get out of here. This damn place is like an oven."

For a time I read. Tom Hudspeth had wisely brought a stock of books with him, figuring correctly that he'd have a lot of time on his hands. I'd read most of them, but I could always reread Mark Twain, and I dug back into *Innocents Abroad*, feeling like in Bandera, I was one of the characters who'd been transported to a strange and not so wonderful place. Hays and Ben played acey-deucey, squabbling over every point like two grade-school children.

They went to bed about eleven, but I sat up, reading by a shaded light. Every few minutes I'd glance at my watch, but the minutes just seemed to drag by. I tell you, I was gluttonous for that woman's flesh. I could not, for the life of me, remember when I'd been so stirred by amorous contact. And I was far from an inexperienced man, both in quantity and variety. There had been many a lady among my conquests, as well as a fair sprinkling of milkmaids and lowborn, but comely sluts. I teased Ben about his adventures, but the only difference between him and me was that I had a six-year head start and had learned to keep my mouth shut.

Then, a few minutes after midnight, the tap came. It struck once and then again, lightly. I hastily shut my book and blew out the lamp. Hays had raised up, but I motioned him back down. I went out the door, closing it carefully behind me. I was just in time to see the little Mexican girl disappearing down the stairs. I went out of the hotel and around back to the stable. There was no light burning, but I'd saddled most of my horses in the dark and it wasn't but the work of a moment before I was in the stirrups and riding down the main street. I caught up with Juanita about a half mile out of town and paused to swing her up in front of me. Then I put my horse in a lope and held the pace until we reached the turnoff to Grummet's place. I let the girl down with word that she should watch the road and come to warn me if there was the slightest hint of danger.

There was no pretense to our meeting this time. Under her robe she was wearing nothing but the flimsiest of nightgowns. I took the robe off her and then parted the nightgown, laying her back on the seat. For a moment I just looked at her: the erect breasts; the whiteness of her belly mellowing into the blond silken hair as she parted her legs so that I could touch her with my hand; the long, slim legs; her lips, half parted, her eyes closed. I took off my gun belt and my boots and then slid my jeans all the way off. We didn't bother to talk. Not a word was said.

There was no loss in intensity, though we managed to make it last longer. Or at least it seemed that way. But maybe it was too highly charged, too blinding and transporting to have registered any sense of time on my brain. How do you count the seconds when you're in the midst of a thousand dynamite explosions?

When it was over, I made my way to the other seat, as I had before, pulling up my jeans and laying my gun belt on the cushion beside me. The feel of her was still in my veins, in my nerves. The touch of her skin still tingled against mine. I pulled open the little drawer. The flask of brandy was still there, along with the little cups. I was so drained and weak, I could barely pull the stopper, and my hand was shaking so badly that I spilled some of the liquor as I poured us each out a drink. She sat up and took the silver cup from my hand. She was smiling slightly. It was she who said, "Luck," and me who said, "Right."

I downed mine and then poured out another. She took her time, sipping. I just looked at her. She looked back. After such an experience there didn't seem to be much to say.

I lit a cigar and got it drawing. She held out her hand and I handed it across. She took a few tentative puffs and then drew in a good one. She didn't cough. I said, "Do you smoke?"

"Sometimes. But I prefer Mexican tobacco. This is too bland."

That made me laugh softly. "I don't think anyone will ever accuse you of being that, Marriah. Bland."

I sat there looking at her, thinking about her. I asked a question a gentleman ought not to. But there was so much hunger in her, I couldn't imagine it going very long unsatiated. "What do you do for men when your daddy doesn't rope one off the public road for you and have him held in town on charges so you can have your pleasure?"

It didn't even produce the slightest blush or sign of discomfort. "Probably the same thing you do if an interested and accommodating lady is not willing to meet you on a deserted road in the middle of the night."

I took my cigar back from her and drew on it thoughtfully. I said, "Why don't you move to Houston when you leave here? That's not but sixty miles from our ranch, and it's on the railroad."

She said, "Houston's dull."

"I might could liven it up for you. Or you could come visit the ranch."

Shifting her body, she drew her robe around her. It was growing cool. She said, "Justa, I've had enough of ranch life. I want the big cities now. Maybe even Europe. Besides, what makes you so sure you're going to get out of your charges?"

I took the cigar out of my mouth. "Nobody is going to put me in jail. Not on such trumped-up charges."

She cocked her head to one side. "Do you intend to kill my father? You may have to. He's very determined about you."

It was a strange question, considering what we'd just done. It reminded me of what I'd been thinking earlier. I said, "What's come of the raid they tried the other night?"

She sipped at her brandy. "Obviously he is very upset. He was in such a rage last night that I had no hope of getting away. He stayed up all night, drinking and cursing and sending for this man or that. You could hear him all over the mansion. He even used a shotgun on the chandelier in the main drawing room. It was Mother's pride and joy. It had come from New Orleans."

"What'd she say?"

"She just cried. You don't talk to him in the humor he's in. Some of the men are leaving."

"What?"

She sounded almost sorry for him. "That's hit him very hard, but at least eight or ten men have up and quit and left."

"What kind of men?"

"Mostly the ones who actually worked the ranch. Of course, you killed quite a number of what I call his gunmen." She appeared to look closer at me. "You must be a very dangerous man. Dag simply couldn't believe it when only two came back."

"I had help," I said briefly. "Has Judge Hummil been out at Treetops?"

"He was. He left today."

"What'd they talk about?"

She shook her head. "I don't know. Justa, I can't overhear his conversations. And I'm not sure I should tell you if I did."

That sort of worried me. "I think you better figure out whose side you're on. You say you hate your father. Unless I'm badly mistaken, you don't hate me. You know I'm innocent. You know he's got repayment coming."

"Yes, but I'm not sure I should help you hurt him." Suddenly she looked distressed. "Oh, I don't know! I don't even want to think about it. I just want to get away from this hateful place!"

I stared out the window for a second. "Why not come with me when I leave?"

She slapped her knee. It was a curiously frustrated gesture for one so self-possessed. "I've told you. I don't want any more to do with ranch life, and you are a rancher. I don't plan to end up like my mother, some man's docile slave. Why don't we just have what we're having and let it go at that?"

I shrugged. "Suits me. I wasn't asking you to marry me."

"It sounded like it."

"Not to me. I just said come away with me. I didn't say come away and get married and stay. Besides, you'd be trouble. A man couldn't sit you in one place and expect you to be there when he got back."

"No."

"And as I seem to draw trouble naturally I don't plan on carrying any lightning rods around to attract more."

She slipped to her knees and leaned forward and kissed me lightly on the lips. "How much longer do you think we have?"

I shrugged and said I didn't know. "My lawyer is in San Antonio right now. He should return with a U.S. Marshal or two. His thinking is that after an investigation, this matter is going to end up in federal court in San Antonio. If anybody goes to jail, I reckon it's going to be ol' Dag."

"Jail? My father?"

I nodded slowly. Of course I was talking out of school, but I wanted to see how she'd take it. She sat back on her seat, biting her lip. "Jail? I'd rather you killed him. He'd never go to jail."

"He might not have a choice. The town is starting to come around to see my side of things, and those handbills I put out are fetching me in some mighty interesting customers."

She sighed and finished her brandy and held the cup out for me. I poured it half full. She said, "This is such a mess. Damn that woman anyway."

"You're blaming Mrs. Hawkins?"

"If it hadn't been for her, none of this would be happening."

I looked at her in some amazement. "You tell me you think your father had her husband killed so he could put her in bondage to him. Then he has his way with her until somebody—maybe him in spite of what you said—kills her. And you blame her? My God, Marriah, that's absolute nonsense."

"She led him on. She led all the men on. She wasn't quite the lady she was thought to be."

That put what Alvin had said in mind. I said, "But still—"

"Oh, the hell with it!" she said violently. She suddenly threw her cup out the window. The brandy made a splash against the curtain as it passed through.

"That was smart," I said. I opened the door and eased out. Just as I put my foot on the ground, my horse nickered. Instantly I heard an answering nicker from back in the brush. I jumped back into the coach and hurriedly began putting on my boots and strapping on my gun belt. "Could you have been followed?"

"No," she said. "I was very careful. I promise."

I could see from her stricken face that she was telling the truth. But that didn't mean she couldn't have been followed without knowing about it. I couldn't afford to take any chances. I said, "It may just be loose stock or one of Grummet's animals, but I can't be caught afoot."

"When will I see you again?"

"Whenever you send Juanita. Don't get out. I'm going to be in a hurry." I kissed her quickly and then ducked over to my horse, untied him, and mounted him on the run.

I rode low down the little road, leaning over my horse's neck and keeping him in a hard gallop. I saw Juanita crouched by some bushes at the place where I would intersect the main road. She scuttled back even farther when she saw me coming. I pulled up and looked around. I couldn't see any sign of pursuit. Juanita had disappeared. In a low voice I told her to go to her mistress. After that I turned toward town, walking my horse and keeping a careful lookout behind.

When I got to the stable, I took my time unsaddling my horse and giving him a little grain. There was a horse missing and I sat down to wait. Fifteen minutes later Hays rode in. He guided his horse directly into a stall and dismounted. I followed in right behind him. "Hello," I said.

He jumped nearly a foot and then came down gasping and clutching at his throat. "Good God Almighty!" he said. "Boss, you damn near scared the wits out of me!"

"That's impossible. You haven't got any. Where you been?"

He gave me a surprised look. "Me?"

"You see anybody else here?"

"Why, uh, nowhere. Just couldn't sleep. Went for a little ride."

"Hays, did you follow me?"

"Me? Naw, whatever gave you that idea?"

"You are not my bodyguard. What happened the last time you disobeyed orders?"

He looked down, busying himself loosening the cinch on his saddle.

"I believe I got fined."

"You just got fined again. Another ten dollars. I specifically told you and Ben not to trail me. And you did. I heard your horse nicker."

"Damn this horse!" he said. "I took my hand off his nose for one second and the damn fool lets out a snort. Gets wind of your horse and answers when yours lets go. But, boss, I was just looking out for myself."

"How do you figure that?"

He dragged the saddle off his horse's back and slung it astraddle the stall partition. "Do you know how hard it is to get a job for sixty dollars a month? They don't grow on trees. I can't afford to have anything happen to you."

I gave him a sour look. "You have a damn unusual way of thinking, Hays. Damn unusual."

"I hope I didn't interrupt anything."

I went back to the hotel, leaving him with orders to rub the horses down. They didn't need it, but he did.

Next afternoon, I was standing out on the hotel porch watching across the street for Alvin Davis to come out of the mercantile and go home to supper. He was pretty punctual about leaving at six. Probably his mother insisted he be on time for meals.

Sure enough, at two minutes after six by my watch he came out of the store, closing the door behind him, and started up the boardwalk. I crossed the street, angling to intercept him just as we got clear of the business district. He had just taken to the dust of the road when I came alongside him. "Afternoon, Alvin," I said. "Headin' for supper?"

He gave me a startled look and something like fear came into his eyes. "I guess so. What do you want?"

"Why should I want anything, Alvin? Maybe we're just walking the same way. Maybe I'm heading up to the church. You go that way, don't you, Alvin? Right by the church?"

There was suspicion in his eyes. "The church? What would you be wanting with the church?"

"Why, the same thing all us poor sinners want, Alvin. Help. Help with our sins. What does the good book say, 'Seek and ye shall find. The truth shall set you free'?"

He was giving me uneasy looks. "You're an odd one to be quoting from the scriptures. Just what are you up to, Mr. Williams? The blood you've got on your hands . . ."

We were getting closer and closer to the church. I could see the front door was open. I said, "Well, that's just it, Alvin. That's what I wanted to talk to you about. All this blood I've got on my hands. I thought you might could help me with it."

"Look here, you need to talk to the preacher about that. I'm not—"

"Naw, naw, Alvin. The preacher don't know nothing about blood on folks' hands." We'd come opposite the church and I took his arm and stopped him. "Say, one thing—why doesn't your daddy like me?"

"I don't know what you mean."

"He ordered me out of his store the other day. I think you and I ought to go in the church and talk about it." I tried to guide him toward the steps and the open door, but he resisted. "What is this, Alvin? Don't want to go in the church and talk? That don't sound like you. I heard you was a regular bug on going to church. Let's go in and talk about your daddy. Let's even go in and talk about the Lantern Saloon."

He gave me a startled look. "What?"

"I've always thought you knew more about certain matters than you've let on. So let's go talk about them." I tugged on his arm, but he dug his feet in. I said quietly, "You're going to talk to me, Alvin. Sooner or later." I leaned over and whispered something in his ear. He went pale as a ghost and began stammering. "You—you—you've got it wrong. It's not like . . . like that. I mean—"

I guided him to the steps and up them and through the door. "We'll just sit down in here where it's nice and quiet and have a long talk about all these things, Alvin. Then you won't have to be afraid of your daddy anymore. Or even Dag Jacobbsen."

We talked a good long while. Thirty minutes later I walked out of the church in a very thoughtful mood. I had left Alvin sitting in a pew midway down the church, sobbing into his hands.

That, I thought as I walked back to the hotel, was that. The only thing to do now was wait until Tom Hudspeth returned, put the facts before him, and let him handle the whole business. I heaved a sigh. As far as I was concerned, that part was all over. The only question left was what I was going to do about Jacobbsen.

Hays and Ben were in the room when I came in. They glanced up. Ben said, "Had a telegram from Norris. He wants to sell two hundred head of seven-year-old mama cows for beef. Says the market is up and half those cows will never throw another calf. What shall I tell him?"

My mind was still elsewhere. I said absentmindedly, "Tell him to use his own judgment."

Ben said, looking at me strangely, "He could have done that without wiring you. Hell, you're the boss. He wants to know what to do."

I sat down on my bed and stared out the window. "Tell him to sell. He have any other news?"

"He said Dad is doing better and better the warmer it gets. Said he had to talk him out of getting on a horse and having a look around the ranch."

"Tell him to take Dad out on a buckboard. After all, it's the old man's ranch."

"What's the matter with you? I have the feeling you have left town without notice."

"Aw, nothing," I said. "Just thinking." I decided not to tell them what I knew. It wouldn't make any difference. They could hear it when Tom got back. And they couldn't help me with my decision about Jacobbsen. That was something no one could help me with.

I lit a cigar and sat there thinking. He'd hurt me plenty, but I'd hurt him back. Of course, I didn't know how bad I'd hurt him. I'd killed nine of his men, caused the town to doubt him, and created general chaos on his ranch. I had sworn to destroy him, to smash him, but what real good would that do? He was still a powerful and dangerous man, and either Ben or Hays or Tom or myself might get hurt in an attempt.

On the other hand, I could simply put the whole affair behind me and go back home and get on with the business of running the ranch. I was needed there, and every day that Ben and I were away was costing the family money.

To wrap the whole matter up and leave would be the sensible thing to do. Of course, I'd never been particularly noted for doing the sensible thing.

And then there was Marriah. Her attitude toward the end of the evening had troubled me. It had almost seemed as if she were trying to defend her father. Well, in a way, that was to be expected. Still, I wanted to see her again, to urge her to get away from his influence, to see where his kind of thinking led. Hell, I thought, I'm letting a pair of golden thighs influence my thinking. That was very unlike me. I called across to Ben, "Throw me that bottle. I need a drink."

The light tap that night came as a great surprise to me, though not an unwelcome one. Marriah and I had not really finished our talk before Hays's horse had disturbed us. Maybe she felt, as I did, that we had left our meeting on a wrong note. Since I hadn't been expecting the summons, I was not fully dressed. But it took just a moment to pull on my boots, strap on my gun belt, and shrug into a shirt. I glanced at my two roommates. They appeared to be sound asleep. I knew that neither one of them was likely to follow me, not after I'd made my position so excessively clear on that point.

I got out in the hall as quickly as I could, but there was no sign of the little Mexican girl. Well, I would catch her up outside of town, as I'd done before. I walked around the hotel to the livery stable. I noticed all the horses seemed a little restless, stomping their hooves and tossing their heads, but I put it down to my sudden entrance. I made my way to the stall where I had my horse. I was just at the point of taking down my saddle when black shapes suddenly rose up all around me. I felt hands grabbing at me. I whirled, striking out, kicking with my feet. I felt my right fist make solid contact with someone's head. There was an oath. Then something crashed down on my head and lights danced before my eyes. I felt myself sinking into unconsciousness.

I came to in the saddle. My hands were tied to the saddle horn and my boots to the stirrups. There was also a coil of rope around my middle, securing my arms to my sides. My horse was being led and I was in the midst of four or five riders. They had scarves over their faces and I couldn't, for the moment, think what had happened. My head was aching and there was still a dim veil of cobwebs in my brain from the blow I'd been struck. Something was running across my lips. I put out my tongue and tasted it. It was blood. Obviously my nose was bleeding. I shook my head, trying to clear it, but all that accomplished was to send sharp, shooting pains from the base of my skull up through both temples. I looked around. We were going down a small road that seemed to wind in and out of the hills. It was not the main road that led out of town. A sharp, weakening fear suddenly ran through me; I was being taken back to that line camp, to be locked away again, to be starved

and denied water and periodically beaten. My brain was
starting to function now and I was remembering the tap on the
door, getting dressed, going into the livery stable. Then the
dark shapes and the fight. Then the crack over the head.

With more sadness than shock, I realized that Marriah, after
all, couldn't be trusted. She had set me up. Tom and Ben and
Hays had been right. And I had been wrong. So wrong that I'd
refused to allow anyone to shadow me to the rendezvous.
Wherever these riders were taking me, it would be to a place
that neither Hays nor Ben would be able to find. If I'd just let
one of them trail me, they could at least have followed and
known my whereabouts. Found some way to rescue me.

But it was too late for such thought. I had fallen for the
oldest bait in the world, that juicy morsel between a beautiful
woman's legs.

"Where are we going?" I asked.

No one answered. There was one man in front, one on either
side of me, and, judging from the sound, at least two behind.
The moon was finally on the wane, but there was still plenty of
light to see.

I said, "Why you got your faces covered? I know you're
from Treetops. You ashamed of what you're doing?"

All of a sudden I recognized the little road and the country,
even though I'd only been over it once before. We'd come out
of the little crop of hills and hit flatland prairie. It was the road
to Treetops, to the ranch headquarters. I was being taken to see
Jacobbsen himself.

For some reason it was with a feeling of relief that I
perceived this. The thought of another stint in that line cabin
had almost paralyzed me with dread.

I said, to the silent men around me, "Why don't you talk?
I'm to be killed, I suppose, so what difference does it make if
I recognize you?"

The man to my right said in a low voice, "Just shut up, Mr.
Williams. Just shut up."

"Mr., is it? Why so formal? You've just nearly split my skull
and now you've got me trussed up like a hog being carried to
slaughter. Hell, call me Justa."

The man on my left muttered something I couldn't make out.

I said, "What was that? Why don't you take that scarf down so I can hear you?"

Louder so I could hear him, he said, "Don't make it hard on us, Mr. Williams. We're just doing what we're told."

The man in front suddenly wheeled in his saddle and said, "Shut up, the bunch of you. Can't you see he's just trying to get you to talk?"

Something was different here. These men, except for the sharp-voiced one in the lead, didn't have that arrogance about them that gunmen usually had. Could it be that Jacobbsen was reduced to sending ordinary cowhands to do his dirty work? They didn't seem the least happy about it, and except for the crack on the head, I certainly hadn't been beaten very badly. A blow or two in the face, perhaps a kick or two, but that was to be expected in a furious scuffle.

I said, "You men would do well to just turn me loose and forget this night's work. My brothers will know where I'm being taken and will arrive shortly with the marshals and you'll all go to jail." I stopped. "Oh, I see. You know that. That's why you're wearing the scarves over your faces. That's why you jumped me in the dark. Well, I'll identify you, never fear."

The man in front turned again in his saddle. "Shut up, Williams. If you keep talking, I'll gag you."

I didn't want to be gagged, not with my nose full of blood. We rode the rest of the way in silence.

In the moonlight the mansion seemed to loom even larger than when I'd last visited it. I wondered if I were to be taken into the drawing room and received by Jacobbsen under his shot-up chandelier, but that proved not to be the case. The riders led me around to the back, to a long, low rock building that seemed to be made up of several rooms, like a stable for horses. We stopped in front of the first door and they untied my legs from the stirrups and my hands from the saddle horn and then drug me to the ground. I was unsteady at first, so they half pulled, half carried me into a small room and stood me against a wall. It looked like a tack room. There were several saddles and a few bridles and other paraphernalia on the walls. The dirt floor was covered with straw, and there was a heavy table and several substantial wooden chairs. One of the men had lit a lantern and he carried it in and set it on the table. They threw me into the chair and bound me securely to it. Then they filed out, without a word, leaving me there alone. In the quiet that developed, I could hear the sounds of low growls and an occasional bark through the wall to my left. It was dogs, and I wondered if it was Jacobbsen's fighting dogs. Was that to be the game, to set the dogs on me while I was tied to a chair? Or to release me and suddenly turn a half dozen into the room with me and let me fight for my life as best I could?

That would be some chance. An unarmed man against a half dozen slavering, half-wild fighting dogs.

I shuddered. It seemed so very much like something Jacobbsen would do.

How long I sat there I have no idea. It is very difficult to count the passage of time when you are bound hand and foot, your muscles slowly stiffening to the point of dull pain, your brain racing and turning over every eventuality. The lantern sputtered once and I thought it was about to go out, but then it came back into full light. I was glad. I didn't want to sit in the cold dark.

For a time I struggled against my bonds, but it was no use. I was securely and expertly tied. There was no release, at least not by my own hand. Surprisingly, I was not angry. Or at least not so much angry as disappointed—and not at Marriah, either, but at myself. Disappointed that I could have been so stupid, disappointed that I would have taken such a chance when all was won, disappointed that I had let all those down who had worked so hard for me.

But mainly disappointed that I had let Jacobbsen win. That his intentions toward me were deadly serious, I had no doubt. The man had already proven himself capable of murder; one more wouldn't overload his conscience. And there would be no one, thanks to my careful work, who could swear that I had been taken to Treetop. All Jacobbsen would have to do would be to smile a cherubic smile and swear he'd never seen me. Or say that I'd come trespassing and threatening him and he'd acted in self-defense. Ask anyone. Hadn't I, on many occasions, threatened to do for him?

All the U.S. Marshals in the world wouldn't be able to break down that simplistic defense.

But at least the situation had the effect of resurrecting my hatred for Jacobbsen with a consuming roar. Gone completely was the vacillation of the previous two days when I'd thought of calling the game even and clearing out. If I ever got another chance, I thought . . . Well, the shame of that was I probably never would.

The contempt and hate I was feeling for Jacobbsen were at least accomplishing one thing: they were blotting out the fear that threatened to weaken me both mentally and physically. I knew that, if I were to get out of this mess, I would need every resource at my power.

And then the door suddenly opened and Dag Jacobbsen stood there. He paused for a moment, looking at me, a thin smile on his face. He was holding a brandy bottle in one hand and a glass in the other. Then he came forward and set bottle and glass on the table, pulled up another chair from a far wall, and sat down facing me. He said, the satisfaction plain in his voice and face, "Well, Mr. Williams, you have honored us with your presence again."

"Yeah," I said. "I got your invitation."

He peered at my face. "Ah, you have a bloody nose. Perhaps it had gotten too long and you stepped on it. Poking it into other people's business."

"I came to this part of the country minding my own business," I replied. "But it seems as if I was invited into the business."

He gave me a wide grin, showing his very white, nearly perfect teeth. I wondered if they were false. I doubted it. He was still a very powerful, very fit-looking man for his age. He picked up the bottle of brandy and poured himself half a glass. Then he set the bottle down so I could see the label. "A wonderful liquor, don't you agree, Mr. Williams?"

It gave me a little hollow feeling in the pit of my stomach. It was the Napoleon brandy Marriah had had in the carriage. Jacobbsen said, "But you've had it before. Of course it was in more attractive company than present, wouldn't you say, Mr. Williams?"

I stared back at him.

He threw back his head and took a healthy swallow. "Ah, wonderful brandy. Thirty years old, Mr. Williams. Older than you are I would think." He leaned toward me. "And likely to remain so."

If he was going to bait me, he was going to have to do it on his own. I wasn't going to give him anything to work with.

He said, "Come, Mr. Williams, nothing to say? You were so vocal our last meeting. Perhaps you feel restrained?" He seemed to think that a great joke because he threw back his head and laughed hard and long. I could see from the flush on his face that he'd been drinking more than a little.

I continued to sit and stare at him.

He poured himself out another glass. "Tell me," he said after a moment, "are you comfortable? Would you like a drink, perhaps? No? I'm surprised, Mr. Williams. Well, you won't mind if I do." When he put the glass to his mouth and threw it back, a little leaked out the corner of his mouth and ran down his chin. He wiped at it with his hand, but some dripped down on the white silk shirt he was wearing. I could see other stains on it as well. I somehow had the feeling that he had been up for quite some time, drinking and not sleeping. He seemed to me to be a man worked up and drunk.

Now he leaned toward me confidentially. "Mr. Williams, I don't wish to appear rude about this question, but I am after all a father, so it's necessary you understand. I'm given to learn that you have been seeing my daughter. I have to ask you, sir, are your intentions honorable?"

He made a sound that was close to a giggle when he said it. I stared back at him.

"Come, man!" he said, taking another swallow of brandy, "answer the question. It's fairly put."

"Jacobbsen, you better turn me loose. You'll never get away with this. It's known where I am, and the marshals will be in town tomorrow."

He threw his head back. "By God, sir, I won't have a liar for a son-in-law. There, that's put an end to it. You can't have my daughter's hand or any other part of her. A liar is what you are. And you take me for a fool, which is worse! Do you not think we didn't watch your back trail? No one followed. And as for your marshals! Bah!" He snapped his fingers. "I can buy and sell marshals."

He stopped talking and regarded me for a time, taking an occasional long swallow of the brandy. The bottle was half empty. He seemed to be sizing me up for something; what, I couldn't tell. Finally he sighed. "Well, Mr. Williams, it's late, and delightful as your company is, I've got to take myself to bed. Haven't slept lately. And we've got an entertainment planned for you tomorrow. Going to be quite an event. And you, sir, have the privilege of being the principal actor in the affair. I will, of course, assist. In my small way to be sure, but I don't think you'll be disappointed in the intensity of my contribution."

He got up and walked around the table, looking down at me. I'd been amazed he'd kept his fist off me thus far, so I was prepared for it to come now. But he surprised me. He said, "And you'll need your sleep too. I'll just tuck you in." With that he put out a boot and shoved my chair over so that I fell heavily to the dirt floor, landing on my side.

He took the lantern out with him, saying as he shut and locked the door, "Sleep well, Mr. Williams. You'll have a busy day tomorrow."

The room went black and I lay there stiffening up, my hands and feet beginning to go numb from the constriction of the ropes.

CHAPTER
11

They brought me out into the bright sunshine the next morning, blinking and half blind from the sudden light after the night in the black, dark tack room. They'd stripped me except for my jeans. My hands were tied in front of me. Two of Jacobbsen's men were on either side of me, mostly holding me up because I could barely walk from laying tied up all night. I ached in every part of my body and my mouth was so dry, it felt like it was filled with cotton.

They were walking me over hard, rocky ground that hurt my bare feet and caused me to stumble. When I'd lose my balance, the two men would jerk me upright again, though they didn't seem to do it with viciousness.

Little by little my eyes were becoming adjusted to the light and I could see they were leading me toward a small corral. As we got nearer I could make out a number of cowboys standing around. We got to the gate and passed through, and then I saw Jacobbsen. He was standing beside a snubbing post, a stout post that's planted upright in the middle of a bronc corral that you use to snub an unbroken horse while you mount him. It has an iron ring at the top where a horse can be close-tied until the rider is ready. Jacobbsen was standing there with a rawhide whip coiled in his hand. There was a thin, malicious smile on his face. He watched me narrowly as they brought me across the dust of the corral. I was aware of the cowboys standing around and sitting on the top rail of the fence. Most of them seemed to be looking in every direction, except at me. They were silent.

Jacobbsen said, "Well, good morning, Mr. Williams. I trust you slept well. And did you have a good breakfast?"

He was wearing the same clothes he'd had on the night before; the silk shirt with the puffy sleeves, gabardine riding britches, and soft English riding boots. Except for his unshaven face and the condition of his clothes, he would have looked very much the gentleman.

I didn't say anything. I knew what was coming. The men had stopped me just short of the snubbing post and Jacobbsen made an impatient gesture. "Well, get on with it! You know what to do. You want me to lay this on your backs?"

Almost unwillingly, it seemed, the two men led me forward. They raised my bound hands to the top of the post and quickly secured them there by passing a thong through the ring and then back around my wrists. The man to my right tried to press a small piece of leather in my mouth. He whispered, "Here, bite down on this. That way you won't give him the satisfaction of hearin' you holler."

I spit it out and said, "Why don't you men stop him? What you're doing is criminal."

"We can't. We don't know who'd be for us or ag'in' us."

Jacobbsen yelled, "Don't talk to that man! Secure him and get away, you dolts!"

I turned my head so I could see him. "Jacobbsen, you lay that whip on my back and you better beat me to death. Because I'll kill you."

It brought that cruel smile of satisfaction back to his face. "Oh," he said, "I've no intention of beating you to death, Mr. Williams. That would spoil the entertainment. But I doubt you'll have the chance to kill me."

"You had better not lash me, Jacobbsen!" It was difficult to talk because my mouth was so dry from lack of water.

Jacobbsen raised his voice to the men who were standing around watching. "I want every man to look on this! I want you all to see how this coward takes his beating. This was the man you were all becoming afraid of. Well, *I* wasn't afraid of him. He's a cringing bastard! Listen, he's already begging."

Looking under my arm, I saw a slim figure beginning to edge away from the group at the fence and work toward the house. It was Torrey. Obviously Jacobbsen had forced him to come and watch, and now he was trying to slip away. I said, to Jacobbsen, "You killed Mary Mae Hawkins. You murdered her. And I guess she wasn't the first."

The lash struck. The force and the pain of it almost took my breath away. I bit my lip to keep from crying out. I said, in as loud a voice as I could muster, "You men had better stop him. He'll have you all on the gallows."

I heard the swish of the whip, and then its bite, as it slashed into my back. The blow was harder than the first. Even though the morning was cool, sweat popped out on my forehead. "The man is insane!" I yelled. "A murderer. Federal marshals are on the way."

Swish! And then the cutting, powerful lash. It was amazing how hard the whip hit, with what power. Each blow almost knocked my chest into the post.

Jacobbsen said, "Threaten me, will you, Mr. Williams!"

And then another blow.

"What was it you said, Mr. Williams? That you would smash me? Destroy me?"

I could hear him grunt as he put everything he had into the lash.

"You touched my daughter, didn't you, Mr. Williams! You're not even fit to look at her!"

Another blow.

"You challenged me, Mr. Williams. *Me!*"

Then I heard screaming and a woman's voice. I was too weak to turn my head, but from under my arm I caught a flash of skirts rounding the corral and coming through the gate. It was Marriah. She was screaming, "Stop it! Stop it! You inhuman beast, stop it!"

Jacobbsen roared, "Seize her! Get her out of here!"

I could hear a struggle, hear her panting and yelling in frustration. She called, "Justa, I didn't tell him. He beat it out of Juanita. I swear I didn't tell him."

I just hung there, my weight supported against the ring. At that time it didn't matter to me if she'd betrayed me or not. I was just glad for the respite.

But she was still screaming. "Justa, I swear I didn't tell him! He suspected because so much of the brandy was missing. He knows I don't drink. So he went to Juanita. He hurt her terribly."

Jacobbsen yelled, "Get her out of here, dammit! Take her in the mansion and lock her up! Lock her securely! I'll have somebody's head if she gets out again."

I could hear her taken off, still protesting. Then Jacobbsen came back to me. I could hear the anticipation in his voice. "Just a few more, Mr. Williams. I don't want you too weak for the little sport you and I are going to have. Surely a man who can beard the lion in his own den can take just a few more, eh, Mr. Williams?"

I got through it somehow, without crying out. In fact, it seemed as if the pain were decreasing. I don't think he was hitting me any less hard; I think my poor, flayed flesh had simply protested as much as it could and was now mutely taking the bite of the lash without trauma.

Finally I heard Jacobbsen say, "Hand me that bucket."

In an instant I felt something wet strike my back that almost made me swoon with the agony of it. Vinegar fumes rose around me. The pain was so exquisite that a low moan escaped my lips. I could almost see Jacobbsen standing beside me grinning with satisfaction. He said, "Well, you *are* awake, Mr. Williams! For a time I thought you'd been having a nap."

Then he said, to the man beside me, "Cut him down and turn him around."

They had to hold me up. If they'd let go of my arms, I would have fallen. Jacobbsen stood before me, his hands on his hips. "How'd you enjoy that, Mr. Williams? I must say I did."

I could barely whisper it, but I said, "Fuck you, you sonofa-bitch."

"Ah! Still got fight in you, eh? Good. You'll need it to make our game more interesting." He looked at me critically for a moment. "You don't look very well, Mr. Williams. Maybe I overdid it. I can become too enthusiastic sometimes. Very well, I'll give you a little time to recover." He said to the man on my right, "I'm going in the mansion to get ready. I'll wait a half an hour. Take him back in the room and give him some whiskey and a little something to eat." He took out his pocket watch, unsnapped it, and said, "I'll be wanting my breakfast first. I'll be back at nine sharp. Have my horse saddled and Mr. Williams ready."

He turned toward the mansion, and the two men who were holding me began helping me back toward the tack room. The others, the ones long the corral fence, just watched in silence. I didn't see Torrey. I thought it had probably been him who'd gone inside and told Marriah that I was being whipped.

They got me inside and into a chair. All I could do was rest my arms on the table and let my head sag. The bottle of brandy was still there and one of the men poured me out a glassful. He put it in my hand. "Drink this," he said. "You're going to need it."

I was panting heavily, I guess from the exertion of resisting the pain. I said, as best I could, "W-water. Please. Water."

The man holding the brandy said, "Calvin, run to the kitchen and bring him some water. Better get him whatever you can find to eat. And make it pronto. He ain't got much time."

When Calvin had gone, the other man urged the brandy on me again. I got half of it down, almost choking. He pushed the other half on me and then poured me out another glass. "Listen," he said, "I ain't got much time. I'm Dick Wall. The one you gave the fifty dollars to through Ray Hays. Listen close. When Jacobbsen turns you loose in the brush, don't head north. There's nothing but little box canyons up that way and it's real bad country. He gets you hemmed in up there, you're a goner. You got to—"

I was starting to come back to myself. I said, "What are you talking about? When he turns me loose."

"Listen!" he said insistently. "Calvin will be back any minute and I won't be able to say a word. Head west. There's a little creek about a mile from here. You can get in that and maybe hide your tracks. It circles back to the north and you maybe can make it around a row of hills and ridges you'll see from the creek. Try to get up on that high ground."

I drank some more of the brandy. I said, "Look, I'll give you money. A lot of money. Get into Bandera and tell my brother or Hays where I am."

He shook his head. "I can't take the chance. We've all been called in for this. I'd be spotted immediately if I was to try and leave. There's still Arty. He's like Bull or Cully and he's got orders—"

He stopped talking as Calvin came in the door. He was carrying a pitcher and a tin plate. He put them on the table in front of me. I grabbed up the pitcher of water and began drinking greedily. It felt all too familiar.

Calvin had gone around behind me. He said, "Yore back ain't as bad as it prob'ly feels. It ain't cut all that much. Just some damn big welts. He used that big whip on you. 'Bout like gettin' hit with a wagon tongue. But when he wants to cut somebody up and draw blood, he uses a little blacksnake whip. You kin see bone when he's through."

"Listen," I said. "I'll give each of you a thousand dollars if you'll get word to my brother in Bandera."

Wall looked horrified, but Calvin came around shaking his head. "Can't be done, mister, even if we wanted to. And I ain't sayin' we don't want to, but Jacobbsen, he's got us so we don't trust one an' then the other for shucks. Ain't that right, Dick?"

"That's about the size of it. Mr. Williams, you better eat whilst you can. It's goin' on for nine o'clock and you is fixin' to need your strength."

It was beef and beans, and I did the best I could with them in the little time remaining with my hands tied. Then there came a shout from outside, and Dick Wall said, "It's time." He quickly poured out the last of the brandy. I drank it down swiftly and then followed that with as much water as I could drink. Going toward the door, I said, "What's about to happen?"

"You'll find out soon enough," Wall said grimly. "We ain't supposed to know, but we do."

The first thing I saw was Jacobbsen. He was astride a black, purebred quarter horse that looked hell for stout and hell for

staying power. The only change in his dress was that he'd put
on a heavy leather jacket even though the morning was no way
cool enough for such an article. He was holding a double-
barreled shotgun that he rested against one of his thighs, the
barrel pointing straight up in the air. "Mr. Williams," he said.
"How do you feel now, Mr. Williams? Still high-and-mighty?"

After the brandy and food and water I was feeling considerable better, though no way up to top form. My back was a
throbbing mass of pain, but I paid it scant attention out of
suspicion of what was to come next. I said, "All right,
Jacobbsen. Now what?"

"A game, my friend. A sport. Cut his hands loose."

Wall pulled a short-bladed hunting knife and cut the cords
that bound my wrists. I stood there staring at Jacobbsen,
flexing my hands, trying to get feeling back into them. "What
kind of sport, Jacobbsen?"

"A hunt!" he announced grandly. "The hunter and the
hunted. You will be a good chap and give me a little sport,
eh?"

I nodded at the shotgun in his hand. "We both going to be
armed?"

"Oh, yes," he said. "You don't think I'd be so unfair as to
leave you defenseless. Wall, give Mr. Williams that knife."

The man, with an almost embarrassed look on his face,
handed over the stubby little knife. The blade was barely two
inches long. I examined it. "This is my weapon?"

"Oh, yes. At least the size of a bear or lion's claw, wouldn't
you say?"

I said, "Now I understand why you're wearing that heavy
coat. I don't believe you're in much danger, Jacobbsen. I don't
believe this knife will go through your coat." I suddenly made
a lunge for him, but that had been expected. The two men
grabbed me before I could move a foot.

Jacobbsen chuckled. "Not until the sport begins, Williams.
Please." He pulled out his watch and opened it. "I propose to
give you a thirty-minute head start. Beginning—"

"And you with a shotgun?"

"Aaah!" he said, rubbing one hand up the extra-long barrels
of the gun. "This is quite a shot gun. I meant to explain it to

you. It's a rifled shotgun, very unusual. I've got it loaded with buckshot, but I don't intend to shoot you from much closer than seventy-five yards. Just enough to draw blood. As the day wears on, Mr. Williams, I intend to keep on shooting you. Meanwhile you will be on the run with me in pursuit. Your blood will be pumping out the more you run. Every shot will draw more blood. I intend for it to be a very long, very pleasant day. For me. Of course, you can choose to charge me. In which case I'll shoot the legs out from under you and leave you to perish from thirst and the sun."

"Some sport, Jacobbsen."

He looked amused. "Oh, you always have a chance, Williams. You might take me unawares and stab me with that knife of yours."

"Sure, through that thick coat." I waved my arm around at the men standing by. "Are these your beaters? If I go off course, do they drive me back to you?"

"Williams, you misjudge me. This is between you and I. This is a duel. A legal duel. You are a trespasser who's been given specific instructions to stay off my property. These men have orders to stay here at headquarters. It is only I, the owner, who is going out to protect his property." He looked at his watch. "It is now a quarter after nine. You have thirty minutes for a head start. I wouldn't waste any time. The moments will become precious once I start in pursuit."

"What if I choose not to play this sport?"

He shrugged. "You would disappoint me. You'd also take away what slight chance you have. You'd leave me no choice but to drag you back in the bush and leave you tied to a tree until you perished of hunger or thirst or the sun. Or wild animals." He consulted his watch. "You've lost a minute."

I studied his face. He looked no less haggard than he had the night before. I didn't think he had slept very well. I think he'd spent the night drinking and dozing. But, hard-used as he might look, there was still that gleam of satanic glee in his eye. I said, "Jacobbsen, you're insane. You're crazy. I know it's no use appealing to the men you pay, but they'll pay a price as big as you will. Men get hung for what you're going to do to me."

"Two minutes have been wasted, Mr. Williams."

There was no use talking any more. I suddenly wheeled and started out of the ranch yard at a trot. I was deliberately heading north, in discord with what Wall had advised me to do.

I looked back just as I left the smooth ground and started up into the little hills. Jacobbsen had dismounted and was standing by his horse drinking out of a bottle. The one pressing worry in my mind was that Ben and Hays might take it upon themselves to invade the ranch. The lone two of them wouldn't have a chance. And there was nowhere for them to get any help. I could only hope that Hays, knowing the odds they'd run into, would be able to convince Ben it would be suicide and prevail upon him to wait for Tom Hudspeth's return. My job, then, it seemed, was to stay alive as long as I could. If I could find a good, secure hiding place, a cave perhaps, maybe I could avoid Jacobbsen long enough for help to come—in whatever form it might show itself.

A hundred yards into the rough brush I knew what trouble I was in. The ground was sharp all over, cutting stones and rock. The bushes were all thick and wiry and every bramble seemed to be full of thorns. And that was not to mention the small ground cactus that protected themselves with inch-long spikes. It had been years and years since I had gone about barefoot, and my feet were white and tender. But even if they had been as tough as a bear's, I couldn't have avoided injury.

I stepped on a cactus and, gritting my teeth against the pain, sat down to pull the thorn out. The bottom of my foot was covered with blood. I looked at the other. It was the same. Then I looked back along the path I'd trod. My trail was as clear as if I'd left Jacobbsen signposts. I had to do something to keep from leaving a blood spoor.

But what? All I was wearing were my jeans. All I had was the knife. On an inspiration I quickly cut the leg off one side of my jeans just below the knee. With some difficulty I cut strips off the loop of rough denim. Then I stuck my foot inside the sleeve I'd made and tied it with the strips. I did the same with the other. At least now I had something to keep the blood off the ground, at least until it soaked through.

But I'd lost time in the endeavor. Looking through the cedar and mesquite, I could see that the ground did indeed rise toward a crown of hills. It fell away to my left, to the west, just as Wall had said it would. But supposing that was what Jacobbsen had told him to tell me? I'd just be playing into his hand.

That didn't make any sense, though. Jacobbsen didn't need to trick me to his advantage. Hell, he had all the advantage he needed. As it was, the game was probably going to be too easy for him. I decided to trust my instincts that Wall had been telling the truth. If there was a creek, it would give me water and cover my tracks for a distance. I struck off down the sloping ground to my left.

The creek was a long two miles away. So far as the terrain went, it was easier going, but there were no less rocks or stones or cactus or briars. I had traveled as carefully as I could, trying not so much for speed as for lack of sign. When it was possible, I'd hopped from one rock to the next, taking extra care not to disturb any undergrowth or foliage. Fortunately, as the ground fell away from the hills, it had become more open and there was less underbrush to break through. Of course it also made me that much easier to spot, but I was hoping Jacobbsen would be misled by my northerly direction, where I'd left sign enough for a blind man.

The creek was hard-bottomed and shallow. I threw myself down in its waters and drank my fill and then turned over on my back and let the coolness take some of the pain out of the whip marks.

But I could only rest for a moment. I had to put some undetectable distance between myself and Jacobbsen. I started wading upstream. It was well that I had found the creek because my denim foot covering had begun to split and wear and soak through. I'd left blood on the ground my last few steps to the creek, blood that I'd had to take some trouble to eradicate. I could easily see that my feet were going to be the biggest problem.

By the sun I reckoned it to be at least half past ten. That would mean that Jacobbsen had been on my trail almost an hour. I glanced anxiously toward the high ground, posed by the crags and rims of the hills. There was no clear skyline. The copses of cedar and mesquite so obscured the top that a rider wouldn't be clearly visible. He could be there now, moving through the brush, with me clearly in sight. Moving along slowly, enjoying the spectacle of me stumbling down the stony creek bed, biding his time for the exact shot he wanted. But I knew he wouldn't shoot yet. It was at least two hundred yards to the first break of trees, and he wanted a shot of about seventy-five yards so that he could draw blood. And then shoot again and draw more blood. And again and again so that I slowly became weaker and weaker and then finally bled to death.

It was a cruelly insane plan, the plan of a madman. The kind of plan only Dag Jacobbsen would create.

I kept slogging down the creek. By now the underside of the denim foot coverings I had fashioned were nearly worn all the way through. But it didn't matter in the creek; I wasn't leaving blood spoor.

Ahead was the end of a low rise of hills that angled off to the northeast. My plan was to stay with the creek until I could get beyond the first ridge, and then circle beyond the hills and strike east. Somewhere in that maze of arroyos and caves and crevices I had to find a place to hole up. I was already growing tired. I had been considerably weakened by the night of being tied to the chair and by the beating, but the peril of my situation kept pumping new energy into my flagging limbs. Of course I knew this couldn't last. Adrenaline and fear can only carry you so far. After that the spirit begins to fail and the body soon follows.

I glanced to my right and thought I saw movement amongst a cedar brake that was no more than a hundred yards away. I dropped quickly behind a good-sized rock and watched. In a moment one of Jacobbsen's half-wild cows came bursting out of the brush and ran down toward the creek to water. The movement had started my heart beating wildly, and it was a moment before I could bring it under control. It was not the first of the cattle I'd seen. One had had the same effect on me as it had burst out of a bramble as I was making my way down a rocky arroyo off the last hill. They were rangy, crossbred cattle that looked to have plenty of longhorn and some Brahman and some of God knew what else in them. But it was clear from their appearance that Jacobbsen was no serious cattleman.

The creek was becoming narrower and shallower. It made the going harder. Finally I could see that I could make much better time if I took to dry land. It was difficult to tell how far ahead was the end of the low ridge that signaled the beginning of the little run of high hills. I judged it to be a mile or more. I waded out of the water and sat down. It had occurred to me that the tops of my makeshift shoes weren't worn. I sat down on the ground and untied the strips and then made a double thickness out of the cloth for each foot and tied them back in place. Then I had one last good drink of water and set off as rapidly as my strength would allow me. I was well in the open now, but not so far from the trees that Jacobbsen wouldn't have a shot. I felt very vulnerable.

It seemed forever before I reached the low crown of ground. I had trotted almost the last mile or so. Now the ground was very much different. There wasn't as much undergrowth or cactus or cedar, but there was still plenty of rocks. The sandy soil had given way to a kind of caliche clay that was hard and crusty. I rounded the first ridge and, to my dismay, saw other ridges sticking out from the mound of hills like fingers off a giant hand. It would mean working my way around each one, slowly and carefully. To make one big sweep around the bunch would throw me completely in the open for long periods of time. Plus I couldn't tell how far the ridges extended to the east. There could be ten of them; there could be a hundred.

I made my way by rounding the end of one, edging back toward the hill, to shorten the distance, and then rushing across to the protection of the next. At first I tried climbing over their crests, but it was too hard going. Even the ridges were at least a hundred feet off the flatland floor. But, worse, my makeshift footwear was wearing out again, and soon I'd be cut and hobbling. Worse, I'd be slowed. It was safer to stay to the low ground where the going was easier, if longer, and weave my way in and out.

By now the sun was almost directly overhead. It was growing hot and I was sweating. I was already beginning to feel the first symptoms of thirst. I paused in the shadow of an outcrop and hung my head, panting. It was then that I heard the shout. I looked around. There, at just about the distance he had predicted, sat Jacobbsen atop the crest of the last ridge I'd rounded. Even as I started to whirl and run, he fired. In an instant I felt burning pokers strike all over my back and in my right arm. I ran around the end of the rocky ridge. Behind me, I could hear this wild laugh. He shouted, "Take your time, Mr. Williams! I'm in no hurry. There'll be no mistake this time!"

Still, I ran as fast as I could, on to the next outcropping, around it, and then into a low sink that seemed to signal the end of the fingers. Ahead was the base of a hill, shrouded in dense cedar brakes. I ran into their protective foliage and squatted down, peering over my back trail. Gingerly I felt around on my side and my back. He had been right; the pellets had not entered deeply enough to cause real damage. A few I could feel just under the skin. But my hand came away covered with blood. He'd been right about that too. I would bleed. Slowly, to be sure, but blood would leak out of me. I examined the wound in the fleshy part of my right arm. I could almost see the pellet. I squeezed the proud flesh around the entry hole and the slug, smaller than a pea, popped out. But it brought a small gush of blood with it.

I was suddenly and truly afraid. He had followed me with almost unerring instincts, planning his shot in advance and executing it just as he'd said he would. Probably he'd been tracking my passage all the way down the creek, spying on me as I'd so futilely ducked around one ridge after another, preceding me on my obvious path until I'd paused at just the right distance to give him the first trick in the game.

What had me the most frightened was that I could think of no way to outwit him. I was on his land. He knew it, I didn't. He was armed. He was insane. He was protected from any attack I could make. I was growing weaker. My feet were in ruins and would soon be in such shape that I'd be able to do no more than hobble.

I thought feverishly. I knew he was coming on, advancing, even as I raced my mind for some way to fight back. I glanced up through the cedars toward the top of the first hill in the line they made running away to the southeast. I had to get to some high ground. If I could, perhaps there was a chance I could roll a rock down on him, or jump him unawares from a high place. But I had to move. I couldn't take too many more pepperings with that shotgun of his. As weak as I was, I could ill afford the loss of blood. But there was another advantage to going up the mountain. I could see that from where he'd shot me, he'd have to go back up the spine of the mountain he was on and then cross a series of gulches and arroyos to be on the same ridge of crests as I was. If I could get to the top before he did, I might well catch him below me.

I began scrambling up the steep slope, pulling myself along where I could, with the aid of the stunted cedar and mesquite trees. My feet were becoming worse. It seemed as if some giant hand had taken a rasp and sharpened the edges of every rock sticking out of the hard ground.

There was no way of telling how far it was to the top, but within a quarter of a mile of climbing I was panting and weak. I slumped down to both knees. I had to rest. My lungs were bursting and my legs refused to go on. I put my hand to my back. It came away smeared with fresh blood. My wounds were still bleeding. I sagged there, panting. Suddenly there came a noise from directly in front of me. I dropped flat on my belly. For a second it was silent, and then there came another sound, a sort of thrashing. It seemed to come from no more than twenty or thirty yards in front of me. Snaking my way over the rocks and rough ground, I edged forward until there was a little break in the trees. There, in the midst of a jumble of rocks, I saw a half-grown yearling with his leg caught down in a thin crevice in the rocks. Even as I watched, he struggled, making the thrashing sound I'd heard. I looked around carefully. There was tree cover to my right, the direction in which I'd last seen Jacobbsen. I got up and hurried to the calf's side. He'd broken his leg when he'd caught it in the crevice. He was never going anywhere, even if he got out. I grabbed him by the nose to keep him from bawling and then cut his throat with the stubby little knife. The knife was so short that it was hard doing, but I finally got the job done and the blood gushed out, pouring down through the opening in the rocks. When he was dead, I jerked and hauled and pulled and finally got him up and

on his side on a flat rock. I worked feverishly, taking the knife
and cutting a flap of hide loose at his belly and then skinning
him up the side to his backbone. When I was done, I had a
piece of hide a little better than a yard on each side. I cut it
loose and then trimmed out rough soles a little bigger than the
bottom of my feet. After that I cut off some thin thongs and
made ties. I put the foot protectors on, flesh side inward, and
then tied them securely to my feet with the thongs I'd made.
They were not pretty, but they were securely bound to my feet
and I knew they'd protect me from the rocks.

Lastly, I cut a generous hunk of beef off the calf's haunch
and rolled it in the remaining piece of hide. I didn't know how
long I was going to be on that mountain. I didn't have means
to make a fire, but I could eat raw beef if it came to it.

I was now at a place very near the top of the hill. Beyond it
I could see another, rising slightly higher. Off to my left,
another line of hills rode in to join up with mine, making a sort
of Y. I climbed cautiously, veering off to my left, keeping the
top of the hill between me and where I thought Jacobbsen was.
The packet of beef was a hindrance, but I held on to it. I had
to conserve what few resources I had. It had begun to seem that
what I'd considered an ordeal when I'd been imprisoned in the
line cabin was nothing but a mild excursion compared to my
present plight. The packet of beef dripped blood and I was
constantly shifting it, looking for a way to keep it from leaking
a trail. I finally managed to shove it down the waist of my
jeans.

I rounded to the top of the first hill and cautiously began to
ascend the summit of the next. It had occurred to me that I was
generally heading back toward Treetop ranch headquarters and
I speculated on the thought of reaching there under cover of
darkness and slipping in and securing some sort of weapon, a
gun or a rifle. But I knew it was a long ways; perhaps two or
three, maybe even more, miles across those rugged hills. I
wasn't sure that I could make it.

I was halfway to the top of the second hill when I caught
something out of the corner of my right eye. I was very
exposed. In the rocky soil even the cedar trees had given up,
and the only cover was a few boulders or a rocky outcrop. The

glimpse I had was of Jacobbsen. I turned toward him for a brief instant. He was only about sixty yards away, sitting his horse on a shelf of rock that extended out over a gully. Even as I looked, he stood up in his stirrups and aimed. I threw myself to the left just as he fired. I felt a sting in my right calf and one in my buttock, but that was not the real damage.

I had jumped blindly to the left of a large rock I was behind. Even as I was stretched out flat in the air, I saw that the ground suddenly dropped away at a pitched angle. I let out a yell as I hit, very hard, and then tumbled sideways and then end over end down some hundred yards of rock-strewn, cactus-riddled mountainside before I fetched up against a copse of bramble bushes and low cedars.

Laying there, stunned, I could still hear Jacobbsen's maniacal laughter. "A good one, eh, Mr. Williams? Ha, ha! This is sport, man! Sport, I tell you! Compares to nothing else I've ever done! Now who made the big mistake, eh?"

I lay there breathing heavily. I didn't think I could move.

His voice rang out again in the mountain stillness. "I pray I haven't hurt you too bad, Mr. Williams. We can't cut this short. Take your time. Use your wiles. I urge you not to give in. Perhaps I was too close that time. I promise to be more careful with the next shot."

As carefully as I could, I got to all fours. I appeared not to have broken any bones, though I was now skinned on almost all parts of my body. I could see where the pellet had entered my calf. It had penetrated deeper than the others. If it had cut the muscle, it was going to cause me serious trouble. I began crawling down hill, burrowing into the cedar copse as far as I could go. I thought that if it were a big enough brake, I could lay up in there, protected by the underbrush, until I could recover or until the safety of dark.

Disappointingly, the brake was a narrow one. I had only crawled some fifteen yards when the cedar began to thin and I poked my head out. Downhill was the same rocks and boulders and scraggly, isolated trees. I was just about to turn away when something caught my eye. It was just the vaguest incongruity beyond the line of rocks and trees. I crawled out in the open and then stood up and stumbled over to a big boulder and looked down. There, nestled near the base of the hill, was a cabin. But it wasn't just any cabin. I looked at it long and carefully. It was not a place I would easily forget. It was the line cabin I'd been imprisoned in.

CHAPTER
12

I studied it a long time while I slowly formulated a plan in my mind. It was deserted, as all line cabins are except in the winter. It appeared to be four or five hundred yards distant from the bottom of the hill. Unfortunately there was no cover over that quarter of a mile. But it appeared that it was my only hope. I was going to have to risk it. At least I knew there was water in the cabin and my thirst was a raging fire.

I went cautiously down the slope, but making the best speed I could. It was vitally important that I have a good lead on Jacobbsen. I had not lost my piece of beef, and from time to time I would squeeze a little blood out of it, making each succeeding spoor a little bigger to indicate I was rapidly losing blood.

I hid behind the last boulder that would shelter me before that long trek across the flat plain. I took one last apprehensive look up the mountain and then started. I ran crouching over, staggering from one side to the other, occasionally going to my knees, trying, for all the world, to give the impression of a man on his last legs. Every few yards or so I would squeeze more blood out of the chunk of beef. I'd taken off my cowhide foot protectors and thrown them aside so that my own bloody tracks would add to the impression of a dying man. I staggered on toward the cabin, glancing back, glancing back, ever glancing back toward the side of the mountain for any sign of Jacobbsen. I had to reach the cabin before he brought me into sight.

I staggered on. A hundred yards from the cabin I began to fall more and more frequently. At one point I crawled along on my hands and knees, leaving as much blood as I could. The cabin was just ahead. With ten yards to go, I fell flat and practically hauled myself along the ground by my fingers and elbows. I reached the edge of the porch and pulled myself across it to the front door, which was standing half ajar. I left a great stain of blood on the porch and then pitched the beef inside the cabin. I was under the roof that overshadowed the porch. I knew, even if he were looking, that he couldn't see me under there. I slipped along the wall, stepped off the porch, and then went down the side of the cabin so that it was between me and the mountain that Jacobbsen would have to come off of. I got to a back corner and threw myself on the ground and peaked out around the corner. I could see the whole face of the mountain range from where I lay. If he followed me, I'd be able to see him from a considerable distance. Either he was going to follow me, in which case I'd have to devise some stratagem, or he wasn't. And then night would come. I knew it was only a few miles to the road, and I could make that under cover of darkness. It would be six more miles after that into town. I didn't know if I could go the whole distance, but I would try.

I lay watching. It seemed that forever passed, and then I saw a slight movement halfway down the side of the mountain. He was riding down a gently sloping draw, looking to his left and his right. I slammed my fist into the ground in frustration. He wasn't as good a tracker as I'd thought. He was well off the line I'd taken down the mountain. If he didn't cut to his left, he'd never pick up my elaborately laid spoor. But as I watched, he came out of the draw and began to drift across the face of the hill, studying the ground very carefully. I saw him come to something and stop. He peered at the ground for a long time, and then he slowly lifted his gaze, looking across the prairie to the cabin. After a moment he turned his horse and started down the side of the hill. He was riding more alertly now, his shotgun at the ready. Every ten or twenty yards he would stop and study the ground. When I was sure he was taking the bait, I stood up. There was little time to waste, and my hardest job was before me. I could only hope I'd have the strength for it.

There were grooves between the rocks that the cabin had been constructed of; big, deep grooves, big enough for finger- and toeholds. At the back the distance to the top of the roof was only seven or eight feet. Holding desperately to each finger hold I slowly made my way up the wall a few inches at a time. I knew I had to hurry, but my fingers were so slick from blood and my feet the same that it took all my strength just to drag myself up a rock at a time and then hold on until I could gain breath to make another attempt.

After an eternity of agony I was near the top. I almost cried out in frustration. The roof shingles overhung the wall face so that I couldn't go straight up and over. I grabbed hold of one of the shingles, intending to test my weight on it, planning on swinging out in space and then hauling myself up by my arms. The shingle broke off in my hand. It was rotten. As rapidly as I could, holding to the rock face with one hand, I broke off a row even with the edge of the wall and then slowly, laboriously inched my way over the top and hauled my body to rest on the roof. I wanted to lay there for a long, long time. I was completely spent. But I knew I couldn't. I began to inch forward on the gently sloping roof.

It was an ordinary cabin with an ordinary roofline. First there was the porch overhang, then the main roof, a sort of shallow A, that sloped off at the back to cover the last room, the room I had been imprisoned in. I had to get up to the top of the A part to see over toward the mountain. The shingles were slick with age and rot, but I carefully worked my way up until I'd reached the acme of the roofline. I just edged one eye over, took a quick peak, and ducked down again. In that one look I'd seen that Jacobbsen had cleared the bottom of the hill and was now advancing on the cabin, his eyes on the ground. I hoped that my ruse was giving him the image of a helpless, dying man. I waited a few more minutes and then risked another look. He was closer, now only a hundred yards away. But he was coming much more warily, carrying his shotgun at the ready, hardly glancing at the ground, his eyes fixed on the cabin.

I huddled down below the protection of the roof. My plan was to hope that the sign I'd left would lure him inside the cabin. The moment I heard him go in, I was going to slide off the roof, pull the door shut, and hold it at all costs. Then, when I found the chance, I'd mount his horse and ride off. No doubt I'd take a few more pellets, but I'd be mounted and away.

I chanced one more look. I saw him just as he came close enough to the cabin to be cut off from view by the porch overhang. I ducked back down and waited. In the still air and the deadly tension I could hear his horse chomping at its bit. I heard leather creak, but it didn't sound like a man dismounting. I heard the rattle of the bits again as his horse shook his head. Jacobbsen suddenly yelled, "Williams! Williams! Come out of there! Are you going to hide in there like a cur dog?" There was a pause. "Williams! What kind of man do you call yourself? If you've got an ounce of blood left in you—" Here he stopped and laughed at his own joke. "Come! Come out. I'll give you another head start."

There was another pause. When he went on, his voice sounded angry. "Damn you, come out of there or I'll fire the place and roast you alive!"

My heart fair went into my throat when he said that. I was laying a little to the right of center of the cabin roof and I moved, very carefully, even closer to the right edge. If I had to jump and run for it, the nearest cover lay in that direction.

He'd gone silent again. I lay still, listening to my own heart thump. Then I heard his horse move. I could hear the slow, paced steps of his prancing hooves. At first I couldn't figure out what he was doing. Then I realized he was coming down the far side of the cabin. He turned the corner at the back, and I could just see the top of the crown of his hat. Fortunately for me he was riding very close to the wall. Then I suddenly realized, with sinking heart, that he'd see the bloodstains where I'd climbed the wall. Even as the realization registered on my mind I was rising and running down the slope of the roof. I aimed for the spot where I'd broken off the shingles. There was no time to plan, no time for care, only time to react.

I got to the edge and jumped. He was looking straight up at me as I cleared the edge, starting to raise his shotgun. I hurtled at him, feetfirst, and took him around the neck with the *V* of my legs. He came off his horse, his shotgun jolted out of his hand. We hit the ground in a tumble, with me slightly on top. The fall had appeared to stun him for a second. I knew I had to stop him, and stop him quick. I doubted I had strength for more than one good blow. If that didn't take him out, I would be in trouble. I scrambled to my knees just as he started to raise his head and reach for the revolver at his side. With all the strength in my body I hit him in the face as hard as I could. It smashed his head back down against the ground. I hit him again and again and again until I was so weary that all I could do was sag over him on all fours and pant.

When I could, I got his revolver out of his holster and then hit him over the head. He appeared to be unconscious, but I wanted to make sure. Then I scrambled to my feet. Jacobbsen's horse had run off and was standing a few yards away. His reins were hanging down, and like all good cow horses, he should ground rein. I started toward him, but when I got a few feet away, he suddenly flared his nostrils and backed away in alarm. I had to have that horse. I stopped, my chest heaving, trying to figure out what was wrong. With his reins on the ground he should stand still. Then I realized he was smelling the blood on me. I eased around until I was downwind of him and then came up on him and caught him as easy as you please. I led him over to where Jacobbsen lay on the ground. Then I yanked Jacobbsen's lariat loose from the saddle horn, shook out the loop, and got Jacobbsen under the arms. After that I mounted up, took a dally around the saddle horn, and drug Jacobbsen around to the front of the cabin. I had some trouble urging the horse up on the porch and into the cabin, but I knew I was too weak to drag the big man by hand.

It was cool inside, cool and dim. I dismounted. Jacobbsen wasn't quite all the way in, but I drug him the rest of the way and then took the horse back outside and tied him up. I looked, but the landscape was clear.

I went back inside. Jacobbsen was laying sprawled out, still unconscious. I'd stuck his pistol down my waistband. I had work to do, but my thirst was a gnawing reminder. I went to the pump, primed it with a little water that was in the pitcher, got it going, and then drank and bathed my head until I began to feel just the slightest bit better.

There was work to do. I went to Jacobbsen and stripped him bare except for his silk underwear. I even took a heavy gold-and-diamond ring he had on his right hand. It was tight and I had to rip it off, tearing the skin. I didn't care. I planned to do much worse than that. The lariat was too stiff to make good binding for a man, so I hunted around the cabin until I found the very same rawhide thongs that I had been bound with. I went to Jacobbsen and jerked his hands together behind his back and tied them, making the wraps tight and the knots hard. Then I tied his feet the same way. When I was finished with them, I pulled his feet up and tied them to his hands. After that I ran a loop around his neck and pulled his head up and secured the end of that thong to the line running from his hands to his feet. It left him arched upward with his head off the floor. If he struggled, he'd strangle himself. But since he was unconscious, he couldn't know that so I eased off on the neck rope and let his head fall back on the floor. There'd be plenty of time for that later.

I put his boots on, not bothering with his socks. Fortunately they were bigger enough than what I wore so that I was able to get them on my swollen and aching feet. I went out to his horse and looked in his saddlebags. There were cigars and matches and extra shells for the shotgun. There was even a bottle of brandy. I had a drink of brandy and then lit a cigar and walked around to the back of the cabin and located the shotgun. I checked the load. There were two shells in it.

Jacobbsen was still unconscious when I got back in the cabin. That wouldn't do. I had been waiting a long time for this moment and I wanted his full attention while we discussed some differences that had laid between us.

I got the pitcher of water and poured it over his head. He didn't stir, and for a second a flash of alarm ran through me that I might already have killed him. I bent and felt the pulse at his neck. It was going strong. I got another pitcher of water, and about halfway through that one, he began to shake his head and sputter. I let him have the rest of it so that he'd be good and awake when we started our little talk. He turned his face to the side and stared at me. There was insane hate in his eyes. He said, "You bastard!"

I pulled up a chair and sat down, still smoking the cigar. I said, "I've got a lot of your lead in me, Mr. Jacobbsen. I'm going to have to get it seen to, so our visit can't be as long as I'd like it."

"Fuck you!" he said.

"Such language." I took the bottle of brandy and had a drink. Then I held it out to him. "Care for some? Oh! I see you're all tied up. Ha, ha. But I'm sorry. That's your joke." I got up, "Well, Jacobbsen, time for business. Last time I was in the cabin, some people were urging me to confess to the murder of Mary Mae Hawkins. I guess it has come your turn now."

"You go to hell. I never killed that woman."

I paid him no mind, I just took the chair I'd been sitting in and smashed it against the floor until I broke one of the legs loose. It made a good solid club. Without a word I stepped over and, with a full overhead swing, smashed Jacobbsen in the ribs. His body literally rose off the floor and he let out a long, high-pitched scream. I said, "That's just to get your attention." Then I hit him in the same place. I wasn't trying to bruise him, I was trying to break his ribs. He was screaming again and I hit him for the third time, right in the middle of the scream. The blow was so hard that it cut the wind out of him and the scream died off into a whimper.

"Now, then," I said, "confess. You killed the girl."

"I—I didn't," he said.

I hit him again, trying for the same spot. He screamed again.

I said, "Jacobbsen, be a man. You sound like a girl the way you are screaming. Now admit you killed Mary Mae Hawkins." I hit him before he could answer.

I don't know how many times I hit him, maybe four or five more, before he changed his plea. He said, sounding agonized, "Yes! Yes, I killed her. Don't hit me."

I paused to take a drink of brandy. "Hell, Jacobbsen, I don't know whether to believe you or not. First you tell me one story and then another. What am I to think? The only way I know is to beat the truth out of you." The way I had him tied, the soles of his bare feet were facing up. I gave him a hard, bruising lick across one. It must have hurt pretty good judging from the way he jumped. I hit him again in the same place. "Now, which is it?" I said. "Did you kill her?"

"Yes! Yes! Oh, God, I can't breathe. You've broken my ribs."

"Let me see," I said. "Does this feel like they're broken?" I kicked him in the side and then wished I hadn't. My feet were so sore and his boots so soft that it probably hurt me more than it did him.

"God, don't!" he screamed.

"What would a man like you know about God? Though, for your sake, I hope you have your affairs in order where He's concerned. Now did you kill the girl or not?"

"Yes!" His face had gone white and there was a little blood running out of his mouth.

"No, you didn't. I told you not to lie to me." I hit him very hard on the foot then. He just made a little whooping sound. I think it hurt so bad that he couldn't scream. Either that or his broken ribs wouldn't let him get enough breath for the effort.

I figured he'd had about enough. I wandered away to the window and glanced out. Far across the prairie, maybe a half mile, I could see two riders coming. I watched them carefully. It could be Ben and Hays, but I doubted it. Moving quickly, I found a rag and stuffed it in Jacobbsen's mouth. Then I put on his shirt and his heavy leather coat. His hat was around at the back and there was no time to retrieve it. I picked up the shotgun and watched the riders coming on at a lope. When they were a hundred yards away, I knew it wasn't Ben and Hays. I stepped out onto the porch, staying well back in the shadow. I cocked both hammers of the shotgun. When they were twenty yards off, one of them called out, "Mr. Jacobbsen! Are you all right?"

Then they were close enough to see that I wasn't Jacobbsen. The one on my right, the one I recognized as Arty, suddenly reined in his horse and reached for his revolver. I raised the shotgun slightly and shot him out of the saddle. I swung on the other man, but he already had his hands in the air. It was Dick Wall. He was saying, "No, sir, Mr. Williams. No, sir. I don't want no trouble."

"Get off that horse," I said. "And drop your gun belt."

He did as I told him, moving slow and careful, keeping his hands in the air. "Now catch that other horse up and lead both of them up here and tie them."

When that was done, I told him to go back to the other man. "Is he dead?"

He was peering down at Arty. "Appears so, Mr. Williams. He ain't doing a whole lot of breathing."

"Pick up his handgun and sling it over here. Then pick Arty up and carry him into the cabin."

He came by me on the porch, staggering under the load of the gunman. As he got into the cabin he saw Jacobbsen. "Gawd A'mighty!" he said. "It's Mr. Jacobbsen. Is he dead?"

"You just worry about your own skin. Dump Arty in that back room."

After that I directed him to collect all the rifles off the saddles, all the handguns, and bring them in and dump them on the floor. Jacobbsen had brought along a fine telescopic rifle. I exchanged that for the shotgun, threw back the bolt to make sure a shell was chambered, and then directed Wall out the door. I pointed toward a cedar tree about fifty yards away. "Go over there and break off a big branch. Then come back here." When he'd done that, I said, "Now, you see that set of hoofprints and sign leading off toward the hills? Well, I want you to walk backward and use that branch to wipe out all traces for about two or three hundred yards. I'm going to sit here on the porch with Mr. Jacobbsen's telescopic rifle and watch you. When you get far enough away that you think you've got a chance to break and run, why, you go right ahead and try. Might be a little risk in it, though. I'm a pretty good shot."

He said earnestly, "I ain't gonna try nothin', Mr. Williams. I was ag'in' this from the first."

I said dryly, "Nice to hear, now."

"Didn't I try and warn you? Didn't I steer you right about that creek? Didn't I do everythin' a man could under the conditions?"

I shrugged. He was more than a little right. I said, "Just do it. Time is getting short."

What was getting short was my strength.

When Wall came back, I swapped back for the shotgun and then had the cowhand go and lay facedown against the floor. I knelt down by Jacobbsen. "I got a witness now. Did you kill the woman? Did you kill Mary Mae Hawkins?"

He just lay there panting, his eyes half closed.

"You thirsty yet? You want some water?" I said.

It took him an effort to get the word out, but he finally managed. "Yeees."

I stood up. "Then pretty soon you're going to know how I felt."

He whispered, "Williams, let me go. I'll give you anything. Anything."

"Oh, I'm going to let you go. When I turn you over to the authorities. The real authorities. But I want you to have a little taste of what I had before I do." I turned. "Wall! Get up and drag him into that back room. Move!"

When Wall had him just inside the root cellar, I directed him to stand back. Then I pulled up Jacobbsen's neck thong and tied it off. He made little grunting sounds. "I'm making it a little worse than it was on me," I said, "but I ain't got the leisure of time like you had. I advise you not to struggle. You'll strangle if you do."

After that I ordered Wall out into the other room. Then I took the big plank and barred the door.

We went outside and I mounted up. I told Wall to get astride his own horse and take Arty's on lead. I raised the shotgun at him. "You ride in front. Be assured that if there's any trouble, you'll be the first to go down. We're going to town and you'd better behave."

About thirty minutes into the ride Wall said, "He's crazy isn't he, Mr. Williams?"

I was feeling very tired and weak. "I guess so, Wall. I can't imagine a man acting like that if he wasn't. Though I've just done it."

"But you was just paying him back."

Now that it was almost over, I could feel the pain all through my body. "I don't know, Wall. Right now I just don't know anything. Except I didn't ask for this, and the law wouldn't help me. I had to do it the only way I could think of."

"Think he'll live out the night?"

"Oh, yes. I'm going back to see to that."

There was a pause and then Wall said, "In case you're interested, and I don't reckon you'll believe it, but I was trying to get away when Arty come for me. I can't say I was going for help for you, but I was just trying to get clear of the whole mess. I was even leaving a half month's wages behind. You never took no notice, but they wasn't no gun in my holster. Arty had it."

"No, I didn't notice."

"Well, for what it's worth, it's the truth."

"Just ride," I said. I was feeling about half faint. I'd been running on fear and desperation and adrenaline for close on to twenty-four hours. Now, with the loss of blood, it was all starting to catch up with me. I could feel myself reeling in the saddle, unable to stay with the horse's gait.

Not far out of town, I was aware that Wall had dropped back and was riding alongside me, supporting me upright in the saddle. He took the shotgun out of my hand and put it in my saddle boot. I let him.

We tied up in front of the hotel and he helped me across the lobby with a strong arm under my elbow. As we mounted the stairs, I said, "Why didn't you show me you had no gun in your holster?"

With a small smile he replied, "Pardon me, Mr. Williams, but right at that moment I figured the less I said and did the better. When a man's got a double-barreled shotgun trained on yore belly, you do what he says and you do it quick and quiet."

"A worthwhile attitude," I said.

When we burst through the door, Ben and Hays were sitting at the table looking considerably worried. They jumped to their feet the moment we came through the door. Ben said, "Justa, good God! Where have you been?"

I was making for my bed. "Let me get sat down," I said, "before I fall down." I eased myself down and then lay back. Dick Wall lingered in the background while Hays and Ben damn near peppered me with more questions than Jacobbsen had fired shot at me. I held up my hand. "Listen, I need some things, and then I'll tell you all about it. Ben, you've got to go and find me some boots. Get a big size. At least a twelve. If the stores are closed, make somebody open up. And order me a big steak from downstairs on your way up. Biggest they got. Hays, you go hunt up the doctor. If the sonofabitch is out of town, get over to the apothecary and bring him and all the salves and stuff like iodine and witch hazel and hydrogen peroxide he's got. And tell him to bring a pair of tweezers. But try and get that doctor first."

Ben jerked a thumb backward at Wall. "What's he doing here? Who is he?"

Hays said, "He's a Treetops rider. Dick Wall is his name."

Ben suddenly whirled on him. "By God—"

"Take it easy, Ben," I said. "He's a convert. One of us now. Like Hays."

Hays made a noise somewhere between a grunt and a growl and said a little stiffly, "I believe I was here first."

"Oh, Lordy. Yes, Ray, you were here first. And it'll never be forgotten. Now you two get going. Ben, I forgot. Tell them to send me up a bath. Hot."

Ben was looking at my clothes like he'd just noticed them. "Where'd you get them duds? And those boots? Just where in—"

"Go! I'll tell you later."

When they had left, Wall handed me the bottle of whiskey and a glass. He said, "You better get that shirt off while you can."

"Yeah. I been dreading that. Let me get a good drink of this whiskey down and I'll give it a try. You might have to help me."

We started with the boots. That was a chore that nearly brought tears to my eyes. I was stiffening up very rapidly. After that we got my jeans off, which wasn't too difficult, as short as they were. I figured I must have made a sight coming into town in short pants and English riding boots.

Then it was time for the shirt. I turned sideways on the bed so Wall could help me get first one arm and then the other out of the sleeves. After that he started peeling it slowly off my back. It seemed to be stuck to my skin in a hundred places, and each place was agony as shirt separated from wound.

Wall said, "It's starting to bleed again."

"Good," I replied. "That helps to cleanse it."

He whistled as he got the shirt all the way off. "Boy, he shore shot the shit outer yore back, between that and them whip cuts. Hell, I've cooked beefsteak wasn't hurt this bad."

I poured out another drink of whiskey and then handed him the bottle. "You not having any?"

"Hadn't been asked. An' I wadn't exactly shore what my position was around here. Am I a prisoner?"

I shook my head. "Naw, I reckon not. I don't hold anything against you. Except you owe me fifty bucks."

He looked a little down at that. "I done spent it," he said. "Or most of it. See, I tend to drink when I get real nervous, and most of us been mighty nervous lately, what with one thang an' another. But I did try to get the information. I just wadn't in the know."

"Don't worry. I'll take it out of your wages."

"Am I drawin' wages?"

"Yeah. Fifty a month and found."

"Damn," he said. "That's a pretty good deal."

"Now go stable the horses around back and hurry them up with that bath."

I was soaking the pain out of my battered body in the hot water and eating a steak when Ben and Hays got back with the doctor. They'd had to ride two miles out of town to fetch him from where some silly woman had gone into hysterical labor and had had her baby a month in advance. I was feeling better from the whiskey and the soak, but I wasn't looking forward to the doctor's work. He was a friendly, neat little man in gray tweed who seemed detached and above the questionable activities that went on in Bandera. But when I stepped out of the bath and walked over to the bed to lay facedown, the sight he saw brought a sharp exclamation. He said, "Here! Heavens!"

But Ben let out a positive howl. "My God, Justa, what's been done to you! You ought to see your back! Good God!"

"Ben, just hold it in for a time. I think what the doctor is fixing to do is going to occupy my full attention."

The doctor sat down on the edge of the bed by my side and opened his bag. "I'm afraid you're right."

Hays said, "Look at the soles of his feet. Look like they been ground up for sausage."

The doctor said, "First thing is to get these pellets out. I'm going to start up at the top and work down. Also looks like you've been whipped. Is that right?"

"Yeeeesss . . ." I said. I strung the word out, gripping the pillow to my head because he'd started digging out the first shot. It apparently was pretty deep because it seemed to take him an uncommon time.

"Ah," he said. "Here it is. Odd size. Bigger than bird shot, but not quite as big as buckshot."

Sweat was starting out on my forehead. "It was fired out of a long-barreled, rifled English fowling piece. Very accurate up to a hundred yards."

"Hmmmm," the doctor said with what I took to be clinical interest. "Very effective. Make you bleed but don't kill you. Not all at once, I should say."

"Yeeessss . . ." I said again. He'd started on the second one.

It took the doctor the better part of an hour to get all the pellets out. By the end of the time I was soaked with sweat and had almost bit a fold of the blanket in two. There were eighteen pellets in my back, two in my buttocks, and one each in my arm and my leg. Each wound had bled copiously. The doctor said, as he put away his surgical instruments, "Now, I'm going to wash this with a mild solution of carbolic acid to sterilize and cleanse the wounds. Then I'm going to treat each with iodine, and lastly, I'm going to lay on a good coating of an unguent to keep out infection. Then I'll bandage."

All of that, especially the iodine, was a lot easier said than endured. Toward the end I said faintly, "God, I think the damage is easier on a body than the treatment."

He said, "Mr. Williams, you've absorbed an astonishing

amount of punishment to still be up and about. Would you mind telling me who did this to you?"

"Doc, right now I've got to keep that to myself. But don't worry, he won't be doing it to anyone else."

"He's deceased, I take it."

"Not yet."

After that the doctor treated my feet, mostly with iodine and thick salve. His pronouncement was that I had lost a lot of blood, should stay in bed for several days, and eat as much red meat as possible to regain my strength. I thanked him, Ben paid him, and then I set about getting dressed. My upper body was still so stiff and sore that I had to be helped into a shirt, but I knew that would pass. I put on clean jeans and then three pairs of socks. They just made a fit with the extra-large boots Ben had brought.

They wouldn't wait any longer. I barely got sat down at the table and got a cigar lit before Ben said, with finality in his voice, "Well?"

I told them the whole story, leaving out very few details. It had come dark outside, but we still had some time. The further I got into the story, the madder Ben got. By the time I got to the whipping, he was nearly ready to burst. He just kept getting progressively more angry as I made my way down the creek and then fought my way through the little finger ridges to evade Jacobbsen. At the incident of the first shot he jumped out of his chair and said, "By God, that does it! I'm gonna burn that man's balls off with a branding iron. Let's go."

It took awhile to get him settled down, but by the time I'd finished relating the extent of the matter, he was looking delighted. He said, "And you left the cocksucker bound up like a slaughtered pig exactly where they held you?"

I nodded. "Yes. We're going back out there tonight."

Wall said, "Cap'n, if—"

"His name ain't captain," Hays said. "It's boss to you."

I gave Hays a look. "What, Wall?"

"If you're worried any of those Treetops riders will come looking for Jacobbsen, and I figure that's why you had me sweep out that sign, you can forget it. We had orders to stick close to headquarters and take care of your brothers or anybody else that come along inquiring about you. But that ain't the main reason ain't nobody going to go looking. Ain't nobody left except cowhands who don't want to get mixed up in it nohow. You've kilt nearly all the gunmen Jacobbsen had hired. That one this afternoon, Arty, was about the last hard case left on the place."

"That's not the only reason we're going." I looked at Ben. "When is Tom due back?"

"Sometime tomorrow. We had a telegram."

I stood up, stretching and bending. I was still very stiff. "Hays, go down and order us all up a steak. I think I better eat another one." Then to Ben, "I'm truly grateful that you and Hays didn't try and come to my rescue. You'd have gotten us all killed. I'm just glad you had sense enough not to ride straight into the enemy camp."

Ben just looked down at his hands and didn't say anything. But Hays, with one hand on the doorknob, said, "We was fixin' to. Ben said as soon as it got good and dark we'd—"

"Shut up, Hays!" said Ben. "Just shut up and go down to the restaurant."

I looked down at Ben, grinning. "So that was the way of it."

He looked up at me defiantly. "Well, at least I didn't let myself get roped into no ambush with my tongue hangin' out over a piece of split tail. Like some people I could mention."

I said, "Ben, you've got an extra revolver. Give it to Wall. Somebody took his away from him."

He frowned and looked at the rider. "You sure you can trust him?"

"I've already put him on the payroll. Now give him the revolver."

He said to Wall, "Are you with us?"

"Yes sir." He'd been looking a little hangdog at Ben's attitude, but he brightened when he spoke to him.

"All right," I said. "I want you to stay here in this room tonight. Don't go out. When our lawyer gets here tomorrow, I want you to bring him out to Treetops in the afternoon. Have you got that?"

"Yes, sir."

Ben handed him the revolver. "It's loaded," he said.

Wall gave him an innocent look. "I've handled that kind before."

Ben looked sour. "Another smart-mouth. Just like Hays."

CHAPTER
13

We slept a couple of hours and then rode out a little before midnight. I was still riding Jacobbsen's horse. I didn't care much for the man personally, but I had no quarrel with his choice of horseflesh.

We had provisioned ourselves, persuading the reluctant hotel cook to open up the kitchen and make us a quantity of beef sandwiches. We also had along enough whiskey and ammunition to stand a pretty good siege. The doctor had given me a small bottle of laudanum to be taken in case the pain became too severe, but other than stiffness and discomfort, I felt surprisingly well.

The moon was well on the wane, and we came cautiously up to the line camp in the darkness. I sent Hays forward on foot to scout around, but he came back shortly to report that there were no fresh tracks or any sign of visitors. We rode on up to the cabin and tied the horses on the side away from the direction of Treetops headquarters. The door was as I'd left it. I shoved it open, revolver in hand. The room was empty. While the others were bringing in the provisions and the rifles, I lit a lantern. I didn't care if the light could be seen or not.

By its light I could see that the back-room door was still

barred. Ben and Hays came in and deposited their loads on the table. Ben said, "Where is he?"

I jerked my thumb toward the door. "In there."

Ben had never been in the cabin before. He said, "Was it in there they kept you?"

"Part of the time. When they weren't bringing me out here to beat the hell out of me." Then, seeing Hays's face, I said, "Not they. Bull. And Lonnie."

Hays said, looking at the floor, "Gawd, that was an awful time."

I put my head to the door of the back room and listened. For a second I couldn't hear anything. Then there came the slightest sound of a sort of gurgling moan. I said to Ben, "Draw your revolver and stand ready. I want to make sure we've just got the one customer in the guest room."

I flipped off the heavy plank and stepped back. Nothing happened. I reached out and swung the door open. It was still quiet. Finally I stepped into the entrance and lifted the lantern. Jacobbsen lay where I'd left him. With an obvious effort he turned his head slightly to the side so he could see me. Drool and a little blood were hanging from his lips. "Williams . . ." he said, the word barely able to clear his mouth, "for God's sake . . ."

Ben whistled. "Boy, you do have him hog-tied. I bet that sonofabitch is hurting. How long's he been tied like that, six or seven hours?"

Hays looked on and didn't say anything.

"You thirsty, Jacobbsen?" I asked. "Want some water?"

He made a barely perceptible nod of his head. "Please . . ."

"I bet you do." I shut the door and put the bar back in place.

Hays said, "What are you going to do, boss?"

I went over to the table and picked up a bottle. "Do? Why, I'm going to have a drink of whiskey."

"No, I mean—" He stopped.

"Ray, you go outside and take the first watch. Stay on the porch and stay back against the wall. There's a chair out there I noticed. Don't go to sleep."

"Yes, sir," he said.

I took the bottle of whiskey and sat down on the floor by the keyhole so that Jacobbsen could hear me. "How you getting on in there, Jake? Anything you need? There's some old cans of tomatoes in the corner, but they might be out of your reach."

I could just hear a low, guttural murmuring.

"That's a damn good shotgun you've got, Jake," I said. "I killed your man Arty with it this afternoon. The way I understand it is you're just about out of outlaws. So I wouldn't look for anyone to come riding to the rescue. Of course, it wouldn't do you any good anyway. They'd just be rescuing a corpse."

"Did he admit doing the murder?" Ben asked.

I called through the keyhole. "Hey, Jake, my brother wants to know if you raped and murdered Mary Mae. How about it? Which story you want to tell this time?"

There was a low moan.

I laughed. "Hell, Ben, he'll tell you whatever you want to hear. Right now. After I broke a couple of his ribs he was willing to swear that he was an Eskimo."

Ben sat down facing me. His young face was troubled. He said, "Justa, what are we doing here? Why don't we just take him back to town and hold him for Tom's return?"

"Oh, I ain't taking him back to town. That wouldn't do any good. Besides, he gave me an entertainment and let me take the principal part. I'm going to give him one too."

"But what are we doing now?"

I took a drink of whiskey and gave him a hard look. "I don't know what you're doing, but I'm sitting here enjoying the hell out of this. If I wasn't afraid I'd kill him, I'd smash his face up a little for him."

Ben looked down. "Justa, this ain't like you."

"No? Then I'd like for you to have spent a couple of days behind that door in that black pit and see what you'd be like." I took another drink. "Besides that, what was that I heard back in the hotel? That you were going to burn his balls off with a branding iron?"

He got up. I saw him grimace before he turned away. "I guess you're right. I guess you got it coming. I can't blame you. But I think the sonofabitch is honestly insane. I don't think he's in his right mind."

"Meaning?"

"Meaning nothing."

"Meaning if I'm doing the same thing to him he did to me, I must be crazy too?"

"No. You know I didn't mean that. I just mean it ain't right to torment the bastard if he's out of his mind."

"If all I'm doing is tormenting him, then I'm falling far short of my goal," I said. "I'm surprised at you, Ben. Let me give you a horsewhipping and then run you over about ten miles of mountains in your bare feet, peppering you with shot every so often, and see what you learn about hate. You'd be surprised at how good you can get at it. How many times am I supposed to let the bastard try to kill me?"

He was busy at the table. "I knew you were hard, Justa. I've always known that. Norris and I have understood that you had to be hard, that you saved the family on a number of occasions. We're proud of you. It's just that—"

"Just what?"

He shook his head. "I just never knew how really hard you were."

"You want me to cut him loose? Is that it?"

He said uncomfortably, "I think he's strangling to death. That rawhide around his neck. He can't keep his head up forever."

"I'm testing his character," I said.

Ben sat down at the table and opened a fresh bottle of whiskey and took a small drink. Eerie shadows danced around the cabin from the flickering light of the lantern. I got up and threw the plank off the door and opened it. Jacobbsen's head was sagging more and more. I could see that the thong was beginning to cut into his neck. "I bet it's mighty uncomfortable breathing with them broken ribs, eh, Jake?" I said. "You don't mind if I call you Jake, do you, Mr. Jacobbsen?"

Ben said, "I'll go relieve Hays. He's maybe hungry."

I started to stop him because I knew why he wanted out of the cabin. But I let him go.

I heard him and Hays talking outside for a moment, and then

Ray came in and went to the table. He didn't glance in at Jacobbsen or look at me. I said, "What's the matter, Hays? I thought you'd jump at the chance to see Dag Jacobbsen groveling on the floor."

He was unwrapping a sandwich and didn't look up.

"Well?"

He mumbled something.

"What?"

"I said I din't care for it, boss."

"You worried about Jacobbsen too? Like Ben?"

"No, sir," he said. "I don't care if the sonofabitch rots in a bonfire."

"Then what is it? Come look at the bastard."

He said in a low voice, "It ain't him."

"What?"

"It ain't him, boss."

"Aw, shit!" I said violently. "You two sonsofbitches! You make me sick. Now I got to live up to the picture you've painted of me. Well, fuck the both of you." I went over to the table and grabbed up that same stubby little knife that Jacobbsen had given me and went into the little room and cut the thong that ran to his neck. His head fell to the floor. He made a sigh and began to gulp for air. Next I cut the line that bound his feet to his hands. His legs straightened and fell to the floor with a thump. He sighed again. I looked around the doorsill at Hays. "How's that? Satisfied? Or you want me to cut him completely loose?"

He was eating a sandwich. He wiped his mouth. "Boss, I never said a word."

"You cocksucker. You and that brother of mine! I ought to fire you and whip the shit out of him. How about if I cut him loose and give him a gun? Will that suit you?"

Hays said softly, "Boss, you knowed it wasn't right what you were doing. You'd of done it anyway, cut them thongs. We just speeded you up a little."

"Don't come that talk on me, Ray. You sanctimonious bastard."

"I don't know what that word means, boss. But if it means you couldn't never stoop as low as Jacobbsen, then I reckon it fits you. I know you got a lot to get back at him for. Don't forget, I was here when it started. He ought to have left you alone, but he didn't. Now I reckon he's learning a pretty bitter lesson. I know he'd of never showed you no mercy. Which is all the more reason I think you ought to show him some."

I sat down in a chair. "Hays, I hired you for a cowhand. Not a philosopher. Now eat your sandwich and shut up."

"What are we going to do with Jacobbsen?"

"*We* ain't going to do anything. As far as what *I'm* going to do, it's exactly what I've promised all along."

The night wore on. Jacobbsen seemed to be sleeping, which didn't serve my purposes at all. If he was asleep, he couldn't hurt. I wanted him to hurt. It was my last chance to pay him back, even if in small part, for all the pain he'd caused me. I reckoned that the hours he'd laid there hog-tied hadn't hurt him any worse than the hour I'd spent under the doctor's scalpel and tweezers. It made me angry to think how lightly I was letting him off.

Lightly in one sense. The physical-pain part. I had no intention of letting him off lightly where it would really hurt.

Just before dawn I got angry at myself and went in and gave him some water. I don't know how much he was able to swallow, but it was a damn sight more than I'd been given. I just got the pitcher, knelt down, and turned his head up as far as I could and poured it in his mouth. He gasped a little, licked his lips, and then let his head fall back down. It seemed to hurt him to breathe. I said, "Well, Jake, ready to confess to the murder yet? Better start practicing. You're going to get to do it in front of witnesses pretty soon."

Ben was standing in the doorway. "He did it, then?"

I pushed past him. "Ask him yourself. He won't talk to me. I think he's mad at me for some reason."

Ben laughed. "Well, fuck him if he can't take a little joke."

He and Hays both had been stepping around very lightly, trying to make up to me for having passed disapproving judgment on my treatment of Jacobbsen. Ben had even tried to mimic what Hays had said: that he hadn't been worried about Jacobbsen—it had just hurt him to see me being like that.

I told him that now I'd found out he was of such a pious

nature, he could expect to see himself bundled off to church every Sunday. Without fail. "And don't think I'm kidding. You *will* go."

He looked at me, a little alarmed. "You can't make me do that."

"Don't you bet on it. I got all kinds of ways to make you do what I say. You wait until we get home. You'll find out."

"Aw, Justa," he said, "you're kidding."

"Am I?" I said grimly. "Hide and watch. Maybe it'll give you pause next time you go to passing judgment on me."

Dawn came and Ben and Hays began to walk restlessly around the cabin. Ben said, "Well?"

"Well, what?"

"It's daylight."

"You're right. Go take the horses some water."

Hays said, "What are we going to do, boss?"

I said, "You're going out on that porch and watch in the direction of Treetops headquarters. I'm going to sit here and eat a sandwich and drink about a gallon of water."

When I finished eating, I thought it was about time to let a little circulation start coming back into Jacobbsen's legs. He was facing a long walk. I went in and cut the thongs loose. He was awake and staring up at me. With an effort he said, "What are you going to do?"

"Chase you over the mountains," I said.

"Water. Can I have some water?"

"Hell, I gave you some before, but all you did was let it run out of your mouth. Can't be wasting water."

But I did get the pitcher and pull him up into a sitting position and hold him up while he drank. When I let him go, he fell over on his side. He let out a shriek when his chest hit the floor. I said, "Those broken ribs are hell, ain't they? Better get up and walk around a little bit. We'll be moving soon."

I shut the door and barred it.

About half an hour later Hays came in from outside. "Rider coming, boss."

Jacobbsen's telescopic rifle was laying in the pile of guns where Wall had dumped them the day before. I took it and sighted out the little casement window, picking up a horseman a half mile away and headed our way. He was loping along, looking around in all directions. I said to Hays, "I'm going to shoot that fellow's horse. Then you go out and catch him and bring him here."

Hays said, "Let me see who it is." He looked through the telescope for a minute and then laughed. He said, "Hell, that's just old Billy Parkins. He won't be any trouble. No use shooting his horse. I'll go fetch him."

"You sure? Don't get yourself shot."

"I won't get near enough for him to hit me. Besides, he's going to ride right up here anyway."

I watched the rider through the telescope. About a hundred yards away he pulled up and stopped. Then I saw Hays come into view. He pulled up beside the man, talked for a moment, and then they both rode toward the cabin. I came out on the porch as they came up. The rider was a man getting along in years, but with the weather-beaten marks of an oldtime cowhand all over him.

Hays stepped down from his horse and said, "Boss, this is Billy Parkins. He's all right."

I said, "Mr. Parkins, I want you to take a message back to Treetops. I've got Jacobbsen and I'll be bringing him to the ranch about three hours from now. I want every hand on that ranch assembled in the yard. That open space to the south of the ranch house. Just in front of the corral Jacobbsen whipped me in. Will you take that message back?"

He shrugged and spit tobacco juice on the ground. "Shore. Ain't no skin offen my nose."

"What are you doing out this morning?" I asked.

"Jus' lookin'. Got curious. Wondered if the bastard had kilt you."

I said, "I want you to make it clear to every man that he is to do nothing. I'll come in with a shotgun right at the back of Jacobbsen's head. Anybody tries anything, I'll blow his head off. Understood?"

Parkins spat again. "You can blow it off right now for all I kere." He pointed with his chin. "You got him in there?"

"That's right."

He sat there a moment more, studying me. Finally he

nodded to Hays and turned and rode off. Hays said, "Ol' Billy don't give a shit. But he'da been mad as hell if you'd shot his horse. That's out of his own string. Ain't a Treetop's animal."

I watched the old cowboy riding off. "Hays, why does a man like that work for somebody like Jacobbsen?"

"Wages, boss. Wages. These are poor times for cowhands and a man will look the other way many a time if the wages are good."

I just shook my head. "Let's go inside. We got to start getting our guest ready for the entertainment."

I went in and let Jacobbsen out of the room. I had to help him to his feet. I told him to walk around and get the circulation going in his legs, but he claimed he couldn't. Only when I offered to give him a couple of licks in the ribs did he make an effort, hobbling and stumbling around the room. He said that he couldn't put any weight on the foot I'd hit him on.

Ben and Hays stood watching him. Jacobbsen was still clad only in his silk drawers. They were long and white but now stained with a little blood and a lot of dirt off the floor. He asked for his pants, but I told him they'd gone to Bandera and wouldn't be back for some time. As he started to get a little of his strength back I could see the beginnings of that insane hate coming back in his eye. He didn't say much, but I knew he was thinking plenty.

After he'd walked enough, I cut his wrists loose and sat him down at the table and put a beef sandwich in front of him and the pitcher of water. He grabbed at the water but took his time with the sandwich, wincing every time he tried to chew. I expect I'd gotten in some pretty good licks on his face. He was bruised up enough, though not as bad as I'd been.

I said, "You better eat, Jacobbsen. You're going to need your strength. Today is your day for the entertainment."

He looked up at me with savage hatred in his eyes. "Williams, you will pay for this. You're a low cur. You'll regret the day you ever come to my country. I'm going to have you torn limb from limb, you lowbred mongrel."

Before I could reply, Ben came up. He put his hands on the table and leaned toward Jacobbsen. "Listen, cocksucker," he said. "I am a man of quick temper but soon got over. I ain't good at hating. But I believe I despise you more than any man I've ever seen. I'd like to take my fists and beat you till there was no blood in you. I'd like to pound you into the ground. You've nearly killed me and both my brothers. You've been crueler to Justa than I thought it was possible for one man to be to another. You've corrupted everything you've touched. You've raped and murdered a woman. You've held a town in fear and ruined the law. You're going to hang, but that's too good for you. I'd like to lay you over a bed of hot coals and give you an early taste of where you're headed."

I had never heard my brother speak with such controlled vehemence. He was a great one for sudden, passionate outbursts, but not for the kind of level, determined lashing he'd just given Jacobbsen. I said mildly, "Why, Ben, what happened to all of the sympathy of last night? That doesn't sound like the compassionate young man who was practically begging me for mercy for the indicted and indicating I was as crazy as he was."

Hays said, "That was because he looked different laying there hog-tied. We forgot. Now he's up and we can see him clearly again. For my part I wish you'd of let him choke to death."

"Well, I'm damned!" I said. "And here I've been feeling guilty ever since ya'll showed me the error of my ways." I looked at Ben. "But that still don't get you off from going to church when we get home. You can bet your last paycheck on that and I mean *that* literally."

"Aw, Justa," he said.

About ten in the morning we took Jacobbsen outside. I put the lariat around his neck, jerked it tight, and then mounted my horse. Ben and Hays swung up. I took a dally of the rope around my saddle horn, putting Jacobbsen on short lead, and said, "Let's go."

The first step caught Jacobbsen off-guard, and the pull of the rope jerked him over on his hands and knees. I kept going, walking my horse at a steady gait. I looked back. He'd grabbed the rope with both hands to keep himself from being choked to death and was trying to scramble to his feet. I never slowed. As far as I was concerned, he could be drug on his belly the three or four miles to the ranch headquarters. I heard Hays laughing and I looked back. Jacobbsen had gotten to his feet and was trying to walk as fast as the horse, but the slide along the ground had ripped a hole in his underwear so that his private parts were exposed.

He panted, "Williams, I can't do it. I can't breathe! You've broken my ribs."

"Then you better save what breath you have." I gave the rope a jerk. "C'mon."

But after an hour we had made so little progress that it appeared we wouldn't get to Treetops before afternoon. Jacobbsen was limping badly and falling every few steps. I had no doubt the falls, with his broken ribs, caused him plenty of agony. At first I'd been willing to just pull him along the ground, but it wasn't doing much good other than taking most of the skin off his front. He was almost too weak to hold the rope with his hands to keep from being strangled to death. I stopped and looked at him in disgust, laying in the dust and rocks. I said, "Jacobbsen, you are as weak as runny shit. I thought you were supposed to be such a big, strong *empire* builder. Hell, you lay there like a worn-out pussy."

He was struggling for breath so hard, he couldn't answer.

I had his shotgun in my saddle boot. "How about if I put you about a hundred yards in front and take this shotgun of yours and dust your ass every once in a while? Reckon that would keep you moving?"

Hays said, "Hell, boss, whyn't you just drag him by the neck until he is dead, dead, dead. Save the state the trouble of hangin' him."

I sighed. "Hays, take him up behind you. We'll never get there at this rate."

Hays rebelled. "Beggin' your pardon, boss, but I'd rather walk than have that scum-suckin' pig on the same horse as me."

"I can't blame you. Well, get off and help him on your horse and then get on behind Ben. It ain't but a couple more miles. I don't want the reception committee to get anxious."

Ben said, "Justa, what the hell we going to Treetops for? We ought to be taking him to San Antonio."

"Treetops is where it started, Treetops is where it's going to end. Hays, how many men you reckon are still there?"

"Not many, from what Billy Parkins said. He said a good number have left since you kilt Arty. Maybe ten or eleven."

I looked over at Jacobbsen. He was just slumped over the saddle horn. Hays had tied the reins and was leading the horse. "Well, Jake, don't seem like your men are too loyal."

He didn't say anything.

Ben said persistently, "You still haven't said what we're going to do at Treetops."

"Finish the job," I said.

We rode in silence and finally passed through the big, ornate portico. Gradually the mansion rose out of the hard-rock prairie. A quarter of a mile from the house, I made Jacobbsen get down. I wanted to complete his humiliation by letting his men and his family see him coming home like a whipped dog on a leash. He was practically naked by now, the rough ground having shredded not only his skin but also most of his underwear.

I said, "Hold your head high, Jacobbsen. You're about to make your triumphal entry, bearing your spoils of war."

Hays laughed. But Jacobbsen gave me a murderous look. Even as beat down as he was, he was still a dangerous man. Hatred and madness can make anyone that way.

As we got nearer the house I could see that Billy Parkins had delivered the message and that the men were where they were supposed to be. Then, as we got within a hundred yards, I spotted three figures on the west porch of the mansion. It was Torrey and Marriah and an older woman with dull blond hair who I took to be Mrs. Jacobbsen. We rode slowly forward. The men were grouped just at the back edge of the yard, watching us silently. At about fifty yards I stopped and pulled the shotgun out of the boot. Then I unwound the rope from the saddle horn and dismounted. I looked around. I'd already given Hays and Ben their orders. They'd drawn their rifles and dismounted, keeping their horses between them and the Treetops hands. I came up behind Jacobbsen and put the shotgun at the back of his head. I cocked both hammers. "Move," I said. He stumbled forward.

Out of the corner of my eye I could see the three figures on the porch walking parallel with us. I pulled backward on the rope and stopped Jacobbsen. "Torrey!" I yelled. "Get out here. Get out here in front where I can see you."

I waited until he'd descended the steps from the porch. He was wearing a maroon-colored jacket and gray pants. He was carrying a book. While I watched, he walked over to a stone wall and sat down. He opened his book; I couldn't tell if he were reading or not. I was very much aware of Marriah, now standing at the head of the porch steps, just ten or fifteen yards off to my right. At the quick glance I'd had at her she seemed to be wearing the yellow frock I'd first seen her in.

I walked Jacobbsen forward until we were only some ten yards from the men. I said, "I want every man to walk forward and drop his guns on the ground. Right here. Right in front of Jacobbsen. *Every* gun. Rifle *or* revolver. You try anything and I'll blow Jacobbsen's head off."

They didn't move. I jabbed Jacobbsen with the barrels of the shotgun. "Tell 'em, big Jake. Tell them!"

He said, "I'll give ten thousand dollars to whoever kills this man." He tried to shout it, but it came out a hoarse croak. I gave him a hard jab with the shotgun. "Tell 'em."

The men stared silently back. No one was moving. Then one of them laughed and said, "Look at that. His dick's hangin' out." A few more laughed. Then, one by one, they began coming forward. They put their revolvers down carefully in the dust a yard or two in front of Jacobbsen. A few had rifles, and they brought these also. I glanced over at Ben and Hays. They were behind their horses, holding their rifles leveled over their saddles.

"Now, I've come here to get one thing straight," I said. "From the day I rode into this country I have been treated like an animal. I've been beaten, imprisoned, shot at, whipped, starved, and falsely accused of a murder I did not commit. Worse, this man"—and I shook Jacobbsen with my free hand—"has told me I'd go to the gallows for that murder that I didn't commit because several of you would swear false witness against me. Now, right now, I want to hear any of you say that they ever saw me near Mary Mae Hawkins, or anywhere near her place. Speak up! Say it to my face!"

They stared back at me.

I rapped Jacobbsen smartly across the top of the head with the shotgun. "Which ones, Jacobbsen? Which ones?"

He said hoarsely, "I'll give ten—"

I rapped him again. "I want to know who is going to bear false witness against me. Step forward, damn you, or I'll blow his fucking head off!"

Suddenly a man yelled, "Go ahead. We don't give a damn."

And then another said, "Was none of us going to testify ag'in' you. It was Bull and Cully and Arty. And one more. But they be dead."

"Do you all swear to that?" I asked.

There was a murmured chorus of assent. I looked at them carefully. "Do you know who killed the woman?"

A man in front spit and said, "It was Jacobbsen. We've knowed that all along. None of us wants trouble over him."

I looked at them a long moment more. Then I slowly reached out and took the rope from around Jacobbsen's neck. I shoved him forward a step or two. I let out a long breath. It was finally, agonizingly, painfully over. I said, "Look at all the guns on the ground. Why don't you go for one? Here's your chance to show all your men what a real hero you are. They're right there at your feet. Grab one. Grab one, you shit-eater, so I can blow you straight to your preordained destination."

I could see him looking down. Staring at the guns, so tantalizingly close. It amused me. Even he wasn't that crazy. Not with a man standing behind him with both barrels of a shotgun on full cock. But I wanted him to be teased by the thought of just how close he could be to taking a shot at me. Shooting me. Winning. Smashing me instead of being smashed the way I'd just done to him.

I heard a voice, very close. "Justa?" I glanced quickly to my right. It was Marriah. She'd come quietly off the porch and crossed the few yards between us. Now she stood there, her right arm extended, her hand holding a derringer that was pointed straight at my breast. She said, "Let him go, Justa."

I was so shocked, I turned my face full to look at her. "Are you crazy? Put that gun down!"

"I can't let you kill my father," she said.

"I'm not going—"

I never finished. There was a yell from Ben and I swiveled my head back to the left just in time to see Jacobbsen grab up a revolver and whirl. I swept the shotgun around, falling backward as I did, and fired both barrels at him. There was a shot from his gun before mine. The bullet passed through the space I would have been standing in. It went on and hit Marriah.

We had got her in the house and a doctor had been sent for. Jacobbsen had been laid out in one of the back bedrooms. The blasts from the shotgun had nearly cut him in two. We were sitting in the big parlor with the shattered chandelier. Every so often I'd hear a low wail from somewhere back in the house. Tom Hudspeth had arrived not too long after the shooting. Ironically, he'd finally managed to bring the marshal down from San Antonio with him. Now he and I sat talking quietly. The marshal was outside interviewing the men. Ben and Hays and Wall had gone with him.

Tom said, "Well, it's over, Justa. A shame it had to happen in the first place. Be a few details to clear up, but that's all."

"Yeah," I said. I stood up. "I'm going back to town. I'm kind of weak and tired."

"You should be. I got a look at your back when the Marshal examined it. I can't believe one human being would do that to another."

"Yeah," I said.

I rode slowly back to town and took my horse and put him up at the livery stable. Then I walked across to Davis Mercantile. I needed some new boots to replace the outsize ones Ben had bought me. My feet would be healing up in a couple of days. Besides, I wanted to have a quiet talk with Mr. Morris Davis. Maybe I could get him to change his mind about serving me.

CHAPTER
14

At last it was finally and fully over with, at least it was finally
and fully over with for Dag Jacobbsen. He'd spent his last
drunk night in his castle, shooting out chandeliers and drib-
bling brandy down his silk shirts and thinking up demented
cruelties like some feudal lord who loved to hurt people just
because he could. I had never understood the man. I don't
think anyone else could either. Just to say he was mean or crazy
or sadistic wasn't enough. Maybe he had had, as Marriah had
suggested, something growing inside his head that drove him
to the god-awful extremes he seemed pushed to. I could find no
trace of goodness about him, except that he had fathered
Marriah, and after her flinging down on me with that derringer,
I wasn't so sure about her. Strangely, though, I was sorry that
I had killed him. I'd never wanted to do that. I'd only wanted
him to experience what he'd put me through. I'd wanted to hurt
him; hurt him bad and let him know what it felt like to really
suffer. Maybe that would have pierced that insanity of his and
brought him to some understanding of just how sick he was.
But then Marriah had shown up with her little popgun and my
choices had gotten damn limited in an awful hurry. But it
hadn't really mattered. I'd planned to humiliate him in front of
his men, but he'd already handled that chore for me. Without

exception I don't think there was a man on his ranch who didn't despise him. He'd tried to buy their fear and loyalty and respect with money, but all his wages had bought him had been their contempt for the insane sucker he was. In the days that had passed since his death, it seemed that every last one of them had made their way to either Ben or me, to ask if we might now have work for them down on the Half-Moon. We'd turned them all down. To us, with the exception of Hays and Dick Wall, they were like cattle who'd been exposed to Mexican tick fever; the symptoms might not yet have appeared, but the sickness was sure enough there. And we didn't plan to import any of Jacobbsen's particular brand of tick fever to our part of the country.

But even though Jacobbsen was dead, there were still a few good many ragged edges that needed trimming up, and our presence was required. Naturally, all charges had been dropped against me. Judge Hummil and Sheriff Rose couldn't work their mouths fast enough to accuse the other of being the main instigator and wrongdoer of all the corruption. Since it couldn't be conclusively proven that Dag Jacobbsen had killed Mary Mae Hawkins, the court, with the assistance of the U.S. Marshal's office, had returned a verdict that she was "murdered by person or persons unknown."

But, as one man in the saloon had said, "Ever'body and his dog knows that damn Dag Jacobbsen done it. The low-life sonofabitch."

And another had said, "We should have run that bastard out of this country the day after he set foot in it."

I'd just smiled. It was amazing how rapidly public opinion could change.

In spite of their finger pointing, it appeared that both Rose and Hummil were in for a pretty hot time. On information received from the Marshal's office, the federal district court in San Antonio had decided to undertake an investigation of both the circuit court and the Bandera County Sheriff's office. Little by little Jacobbsen's tendrils were being sought out and uprooted. But it was said that both the sheriff and the judge were making plans to leave town.

Norris was back. On the second day after Jacobbsen's death

I'd been standing out in front of the hotel staring across at Davis Mercantile. Morris Davis was in there, hating me and no doubt trying to think of some way to get out of the slipknot I had him by around the balls. What he didn't know was that I was fixing to pull that knot tighter. I'd been smiling to myself at the thought when the stage pulled in and a travel-weary, anxious-looking Norris had got off. At first a bolt of fear ran through me, and I thought there might be trouble at home. Something the matter with Dad. But that had been quickly cleared up. It seemed that Tom Hudspeth, before hotfooting it for Treetops, had, in his wisdom, decided that Norris's presence was required. Maybe for an extra gun, maybe as a witness, maybe just to give me advice. Whatever the case, he'd fired off a telegram just before taking to horse, advising Norris to get there as fast as he could. No other explanation. Consequently, Norris arrived in a considerable state of agitation and worry. After we compared notes we jointly made plans to separate Tom Hudspeth from his mind, but the lawyer innocently explained that he hadn't known the circumstances when he'd been told by Wall to get out to Treetops. He knew it was some sort of showdown, but he didn't know the outcome and he thought it was wisest to summon all the help he could.

So we let him off with nothing but the price of supper and drinks for the whole crowd. Secretly, though, I was glad that Norris had been in at the finish, even though he'd had a fright and a hard trip. It seemed only fitting that we should finish as a family.

Besides, there was some unfinished business with the Jacobbsen estate where his fine, meticulous mind would be a definite asset. When I explained it to him, he took to the task with the air of a man at home in his own arena. We worked late on it that night, along with Tom Hudspeth, Norris relishing every itemized detail. There was, however, one particular that I kept back from both Norris and Tom. It really didn't have anything to do with them and it was something I'd planned to keep to myself if I could. Aside from the bill we were preparing for the Jacobbsen estate, I had a paper that was going to transfer one very small part of Jacobbsen's holdings to me. On the sly I'd had a young attorney in town draw up the paper.

He'd been flattered and anxious to do the work for me, and made more pliable to silence by the sizable fee I paid him. It wasn't anything I was ashamed of, it was just something that was best kept secret.

Next day Norris and Tom and I rode out to Treetops. We'd had word that Marriah was out of danger, and I hoped to see her while we were there. Jacobbsen had been buried the day before. It was said that no one but his wife had been there.

I hated to intrude at such a time, but we'd been in Bandera far too long and I wanted Norris there to conclude this final piece of business before I sent him and Ben home. As soon as the various bodies of law were through with me, I was finally going on to San Antonio to buy those blooded cattle, which had been my destination in the first place. God, it seemed like half a year had passed since I'd been roped out of the saddle and flung in that root cellar, so much had happened. In actuality, it hadn't been quite a month. It was hard to believe that so many lives could be changed in such a short while. And so drastically.

We saw Mrs. Jacobbsen and Torrey in her husband's old office. She looked awkward sitting in her husband's chair. I could see where she had once been pretty; now she was just an overweight, middle-aged woman, tired before her time and borne down by grief and strife that she still didn't understand should have come to her.

I told her that we were sorry to be coming to her on business matters so soon after the burial but that we'd had no choice. It sounded very odd to be making consoling noises to the widow of a man you'd just killed. Norris said, "I know this is uncomfortable for you, Mrs. Jacobbsen, and we should like to make it as easy as possible." He glanced at Torrey when he said it, including him, although Torrey didn't look like he much gave a damn either way. He had a glass of something in his hand and was staring away from us.

Norris said, "The fact is, our family has suffered considerable loss at your late husband's hand. We don't hold you accountable for the pain and suffering he caused my brother here, nor the mental anguish he caused our family. But we do hold his estate accountable for the real and significant monies and property that we've lost as a result of your late husband's actions. And since you are his widow, it is right and proper that you be the one we come to seeking redress for our losses. And we'd like to do it as easily and with as much civility as possible. There has been far too much violence and anger already." He took a paper out of his pocket and unfolded it. It was the list that he and Tom and I had worked on. He handed it to her; she took it but didn't look at it right away, just sort of stared over the top, as if she were thinking about something else.

The paper itemized, at what Tom called excessive detail, all our losses. It began with the theft of my horse, saddle, bridle, and other rigging; my rifle, handgun, saddle blanket, and the various oddments I'd had in my pockets, such as a knife, cigars, the two hundred dollars in my wallet, and even my loose change. It listed the cost of train tickets for Ben and Norris, stagecoach fares, the cost of the horses they'd had to purchase in San Antonio, the cost of a new pistol and rifle and clothes and boots and other accoutrements I'd been forced to buy. It listed the cost of our meals and lodgings; it took in the doctor's several bills and certain medicines I'd had to buy. It itemized the extra ammunition we'd been forced to buy. It noted the second horse and the second pair of boots that had been taken from me, along with another hat and a shirt. It encompassed not only my lost time from the ranch, but also that of Ben and Norris. It noted the extra wages I'd had to pay Hays and Wall. Lastly it took into account Tom Hudspeth's bill for $3,500. I'd thought that was too low, but he'd said it was his regular fee for such affairs, especially if he didn't get shot.

The final amount came to $11,235. Even though she still hadn't glanced at the paper, Norris said, "Now, that final figure is assuming the bank is paying interest on the money we had to put up for Justa's bond. If they're not, we'll have to charge for that, too, since it was your husband's actions that directly caused the need for the bail. You'll notice we haven't added anything for whiskey even though it's my considered opinion that a great deal more was drunk than would have been under ordinary circumstances. But we'll let that go."

She finally looked dully down at the list, her mouth working

as she read the words and the figures. You would have
expected Torrey, because he was so close, to have leaned over
and taken an interest. But he just kept on with his drink and his
interest in the wall behind us.

After a long time she said, "I can't pay this. I don't have any
money. My husband . . ."

I said, "Mrs. Jacobbsen, we already know you can write
checks on several of your husband's corporations. You can
pay." I pointed. "I also know there is quite a lot of gold in that
safe. Somebody around here ought to be able to open it."

For the first time she looked at me. Before she'd just sort of
been taking us in as a group. Now she looked directly at me.
She said, "You think I should pay you? You killed my
husband. You shot my daughter."

I said, "Your husband shot your daughter. While they were
both trying to kill me. You were there, you saw it. So did
Torrey. If you can blame me for killing Dag Jacobbsen, then
you're as mad as he was. Now, are you going to pay?"

Hudspeth said, "Mrs. Jacobbsen, as a lawyer, I advise you
to pay. Mr. Williams here is clearly the wronged individual.
The Williams family is not asking for this money as money.
They want it because they are the kind of people who believe
in squaring accounts. If you don't pay them now, I can assure
you that they'll bring suit in district court in San Antonio and
will more than likely collect punitive damages in the amount of
three times as much."

Torrey suddenly said, "Pay them, Mother! For God's sake,
let's be done with this whole sorry affair. Don't go on trying to
protect that evil man."

I looked over at him. "Torrey, you ought to get away from
here as soon as you can. Go somewhere with your sister and
start over."

"I am," he said. "I'm glad he's dead, the bastard!"

His mother said, "Torrey!" but she didn't seem to put much
heart in it. I wondered if she, too, wasn't secretly glad he was
dead. Lord, the misery he must have dealt her! I said, "Mrs.
Jacobbsen, I've brought your husband's horse and guns back.
But I'm afraid you'll have to come to town with us to write that

check. I want to be sure it clears. And then there's the matter of the interest on the bond."

"Town," she said. Her eyes got a distant look. "I haven't been to town in so long."

Norris said, "Torrey, would you go see about getting your mother's carriage hitched up? Maybe you'll want to go along too."

"Why don't you all go attend to that?" I said. "I need a few moments alone with Mrs. Jacobbsen."

Norris and Tom looked at me uncomprehendingly, but when I didn't say any more, they just shrugged and shepherded Torrey out of the room. When we were alone, I took out the legal paper I'd had the young lawyer draw up for me. I spread it out on the desk in front of Mrs. Jacobbsen. "As you can see, this paper transfers and assigns to me all rights and interests that Dag Jacobbsen held in Davis Mercantile. Namely, a controlling interest. I want you to sign this paper, giving me that controlling interest."

She stared at it uncomprehendingly. "I didn't know we owned Davis Mercantile. What about Morris Davis? Such a nice man. Did he sell to Dag?"

I picked up a steel pen, dipped it in ink, and held it out to her. "Just sign, Mrs. Jacobbsen. It's a long story."

She looked up at me. "But if we owned it, why did we have to pay?"

"I don't know about that," I said. "Your husband had his own reasons for what he did about the mercantile. Now, will you please sign?"

"What will you pay me?"

The question surprised the hell out of me. Here was this bereaved widow, beat down and downtrodden, just back from her husband's funeral, and suddenly she wanted to dicker about an insignificant item that wasn't a grain of sand to the size of the estate she was inheriting. I figured she wasn't herself or, hell, maybe as a woman the idea of owning part of a mercantile where they sold cloth goods and bonnets and such just appealed to her. But I said, rather sharply, "I won't pay you a cent. I don't want this for myself, and I can't allow it to stay in Jacobbsen's estate. I'm not going to explain it to you except to say I'm trying to keep peace in a town that doesn't really deserve it. But that's neither here nor there. Now sign it."

She said, "Torrey should see. He should know about this."

I put some warmth in my voice. "No, he shouldn't. This matter has to be kept private. You are to sign, and then you are never to mention it again. Is that clear?"

"What if I won't?"

I had not anticipated this unexpected resistance. I said, "Mrs. Jacobbsen, investigations are still going on. The United States Marshals are here. There's going to be a great deal of trouble for more people than you think. Now, in front of no less than fifteen witnesses your daughter pointed a pistol at me and announced she was going to kill me. Would have, in fact, if your husband hadn't shot her. How would you like me to go to those marshals and bring charges against Marriah?"

She stared at me, horrified. "You wouldn't do that. You love Marriah. All the men love Marriah."

"I don't love Marriah, and she did threaten to kill me."

"She was protecting her father."

"Her father was going for a gun. Hell, lady, you were there. You saw it. So did fifteen other people. Sign that paper right now or I swear I'll bring charges against her."

I guess she could see in my eyes that I meant it, because she took the pen and signed in a shaky, quavering hand. "And you understand that you are to keep quiet about this," I said. "But it won't matter either way. I'm not going to record this transaction until I get to San Antonio and nobody is going to care anyway." I put the paper in my pocket. It was really going to delight Morris Davis that I was his partner and boss.

I was going in to see Marriah before I left. But I ran into Norris as I was passing through the big main room. He was standing, staring up at the ruined chandelier. I said, "What do you suppose Dad would think of all this if he could see it close up, firsthand? Jacobbsen?"

He just shook his head and said, "He might come a lot closer to comprehending it than you or I. He's seen a lot of country and a lot of history in his time. I don't think Jacobbsen would have come as a surprise."

The shot had taken Marriah in the side. It hadn't hit anything vital, but she was going to be laid up for several weeks. I said, "Well, a Jacobbsen to the end."

She looked away from me. "I couldn't just let you kill him."

Even though she was weak and pale, she was as beautiful as ever.

"I wasn't going to kill him. I didn't want to kill him. You forced that. I wanted him to live with nothing. I said I was going to smash him, not kill him. Hell, I thought you understood me. Killing him would have been doing him a favor."

"I know," she said.

"Why'd you force the issue, Marriah? Why'd you make me kill him?"

She turned her face away from me. After a long moment she answered, "Because."

"Because you thought it would be better if he were dead?"

She looked very pale. "Perhaps."

"For your mother? For you? For Torrey?"

"Perhaps. This is so tiring. Would you mind if we didn't talk about it anymore?"

I shrugged. "I don't mind—if you'll answer me one question. Would you have shot me?"

The best smile she could manage in her weakened condition flitted across her face. She said, "Me shoot you? How could I have shot a man like you? A will-o'-the-wisp. A shadow."

"You didn't have to call out. Just shot. Without a word."

A trace of sadness came across her face. "He looked so humiliated. I wanted him to have a little dignity at the last."

"So you arranged for him to have a chance so I'd shoot him."

"If that's what you'd like to believe."

I just shook my head at her. "You really were his daughter right down to the last."

She put up her hand and I took it and gave it a gentle squeeze. "It was nothing against you," she said.

"I know. I don't guess I'll ever see you again."

She smiled that same weak smile. "You never know. I'm very determined. You're not a man a woman easily forgets." She tried a weak laugh. "Gallantry is so difficult to find these days in a swain." She stopped and looked at me for a long moment. "Do you hate me? Because of my father?"

I thought about it for a moment. Then I said, "I don't know that *hate* is the right word. When I was ambushed and brought back here, I thought you had sold me out. I was angry, but mainly at myself. I was *disappointed* in you. Of course, when I found out it wasn't your fault after all, I was still angry at myself because I'd made myself vulnerable by wanting you so bad, but I wasn't disappointed in you anymore. Then when you tried to shoot me . . ." I half smiled. "No, I didn't hate you. But if things hadn't fallen out the way they did, no matter what you *say* you were trying to do, I might have had to shoot you. And you wouldn't have just got any little pop in the side either."

She looked at me calmly. "I don't believe you could have shot me."

I made a little noise. "You don't know me very well, Marriah. Just now your mother was giving me some trouble about compensating us for what we've lost on this little adventure. When she balked, I told her I was prepared to swear out charges against you for attempted murder." I gave her a level look. "I would have too."

She smiled. "Ah, Justa . . . in another time, another place, things could have been different. So good. So wonderful."

"Yes," I said.

"I meant those nights in the carriage."

"So did I."

"You'll be going home now?"

"Pretty soon."

"I suppose you'll be glad."

"Oh, yes." I was still holding her hand. I gave it another gentle squeeze. "Good luck to you, Marriah."

"And you, Justa. Don't think too hard of me."

I kissed her hand and then laid it back down on the bed beside her. I stood up. "Good-bye, Marriah."

It had come time for Ben and Norris to go home. I had a few incidentals to clean up that would take a day or two, and then

I was off for San Antonio to buy that breeding stock that had been waiting so long for me. I was sending Dick Wall back with them to work on the Half-Moon, but Hays and Tom Hudspeth would stay with me. Hays to assist me in San Antonio and Tom to help with the last few legal matters.

Since the Jacobbsen estate had, in effect, bought the horses we'd had to buy, we'd returned them to the Treetops ranch and Ben and Norris were taking the stage. We all stood out in the street, waiting while the driver got a fresh team in harness. Their luggage was already loaded and there wasn't much left to do except say good-bye. Hays was lording it over Dick Wall in view of his seniority (about two weeks) and telling him he'd better look sharp because he, Hays, would be along plenty soon enough and he didn't want to see any of that sloppy cowboying that Wall had been observed doing at the Treetops. We were out in front of the hotel and I could see Morris Davis glaring at the bunch of us through the front window of his store. As soon as we'd finished our business with Mrs. Jacobbsen and Torrey, I'd gone over and shown him the paper and told him very clearly my intentions. He hadn't been pleased, but then they were better intentions than Jacobbsen had had, so you'd of thought he'd of shown a little gratitude. But not Mr. Morris Davis. It didn't really make me a damn. I had him by the balls and there wasn't a damn thing he could do. He could wiggle, but he couldn't get loose. All he could do was hate me, an ability he seemed to possess in abundance. I watched him idly through the glass, wondering what went on in the whole family's minds. They were hell for going to church; too bad they didn't bring a little of whatever they went in there to get back out with them.

The driver was having trouble getting his off-wheeler strapped up in harness. I walked around to the far side of the coach, leaving Norris and Tom and Ben talking, to see if I could lend a hand. Just as I stepped around the end of the coach, I heard Ben suddenly yell, "Justa! Look out!"

It confused me for a second, costing me that precious instant that can sometimes mean the difference between life or death. I thought it had something to do with the stagecoach team. Certainly I wasn't expecting a threat from any other direction

in Bandera. I half turned back toward Ben and his group, and
then I saw him. It was Alvin Davis. He had come bursting out
of the mercantile and was running straight at me, shouting. He
had a double-barreled 12-gauge shotgun to his shoulder. In a
tableau that played out like slow motion, I could see that the
hammers were cocked. His finger was inside the trigger guard.
I made a desperate attempt to throw myself to one side and
draw my revolver at the same time. Alvin was still screaming;
I could dimly make out the words while I tried to clear my
revolver and bring it to bear. But even as I was trying, I could
see that I was going to be too late.

Then there came a sudden *boom!* and Alvin Davis quit
running. He quit running and flipped over backward, a dark red
stain rapidly coloring his white shirt. The shotgun fell harm-
lessly into the dust of the street.

I looked to my right. Ben was standing there, his revolver
still out, a thin trail of smoke still rising from the barrel. He
looked stupefied. He turned slowly to me. "What—what the
hell was that all about? Justa, he was trying to kill you. He was
gonna kill you."

"Yes," I said. I stared at the poor, frail figure on the ground,
made even frailer now that the life had gone out of him. It
made me feel very sad.

Ben said, "But why? Why? Why would he want to kill
you?"

I didn't have time to answer him. It was way too involved.
I understood, but it would take a lot of explaining before
anyone else could. Meanwhile a crowd was starting to gather,
and Morris Davis had come out of the mercantile and was
bending over his son. It could all be gone into later, but right
then I wanted Ben and Norris gone before a downpour of other
details came up to keep us from home and business. There was
no question of the right of what Ben had done. A U.S. Marshal
had even been there to see it happen. All I wanted now was for
them to get aboard the coach and get the hell gone.

I said, taking them both by the arm, "Load up. The driver is
waiting. I'll explain it all when I get home."

"But . . ." Ben said, holding back.

Fortunately Norris could see the point in what I was trying

to do. He took Ben by the other side and pulled him along. Together we got them both in the coach. Ben stuck his head out the window. "But what about the shooting? Don't I have to—"

The driver was in his box, the reins in his hands. He said, "Shootin' or not, I got me a schedule an' I intend on keepin' it."

"Then go," I said.

He slapped the reins down on his team and they bolted from town in a cloud of dust. I turned to face the crowd that was staring at me and where the coach had been. They looked bewildered. So was Tom Hudspeth. He said, "Justa, what just happened?"

I shook my head. "Not now," I said. "Let's me and you and the Marshal get the last of my testimony finished so I can get the hell out of this crazy town." I thought to myself, My God, what next? One minute you think it's finally finished and the next thing you know, it's something else.

I went off by myself that night, avoiding company. I didn't want to talk to anyone, especially about what had just happened with Alvin Davis, and I didn't want anyone talking to me. Especially asking questions.

We rushed through the balance of our legal business the next morning, and by eleven o'clock we'd packed what little gear we had, settled our bill at the hotel, and were waiting for the stage. We just sat around in the cool lobby, not saying much. I'd sent Hays for a bottle of whiskey for the trip to San Antonio, and every once in a while we'd have a pull at that. The only thing Tom Hudspeth said was, "I'm glad this business is finally over."

I didn't say anything. We were still in Bandera.

Two hours later we were rattling along the road, our gear on top of the coach, with ten miles between us and that town. In two more hours we'd be in San Antonio and I'd find out how tough the traders were I was going to have to deal with. We'd passed the bottle back and forth several times when Tom said, "Well, the hell of it is—no matter what the official verdict says—the hell of it is that it was clear from the first that Dag Jacobbsen killed the girl. It's just too damned bad you had to get caught in the middle. But at least you're not out any money." He chuckled. "I will say I never saw a man under the charges you were facing so concerned about being reimbursed for what he was out of pocket. Down to the last damn penny. Even taking that ninety dollars off Gibson, the one you'd given the money to furnish you information. Forget the charges. You wanted your money."

I yawned. I was still so stiff and sore that I wasn't sleeping good. I said, "Wasn't *my* money. It was my family's money and I'm responsible. Besides, Jacobbsen wasn't going to get away with anything."

Tom said, "Well, he didn't. And he damn sure paid for killing the girl."

I said, "Jacobbsen didn't kill that girl."

Tom and Hays were riding on the seat opposite me. We had the stage to ourselves. Hudspeth was smoking a cigar. He took it out of his mouth and said, "What? Are you telling me Dag Jacobbsen didn't kill Mary Mae Hawkins?"

"That's correct." Hays was staring at me. "Close your mouth, Hays, before you collect a fly."

Tom said, "Then who? Torrey?"

I laughed. "Torrey? Hell, no. Not even close. Somebody you'd never think of."

"Well, who then, dammit?"

I said, "Alvin Davis."

They both stared at me for a moment. Then Hays said, "That ribbon clerk? I don't believe it."

"Neither do I," Tom said.

I nodded. "It's true, nevertheless. In fact, I knew better than a week before, even before Jacobbsen sent those riders into town to ambush me in the stables."

"But if you knew . . ." Tom said. He left the question hanging in the air.

"I told you, Tom. I told you it was Jacobbsen I wanted. Not the murderer. If it turned out to be one and the same, then fine and dandy. I went looking for the murderer for two reasons. One, I didn't like being under indictment, but mainly because I felt it would force Jacobbsen to act if he thought I was getting close to the truth. It did, but I played the fool and got taken unawares."

"What makes you think it was Alvin Davis?"

I yawned again. "Well, for one thing, he confessed it to me. I don't remember the exact day, but it was near two weeks ago. Time has taken to running together here lately."

Hays said, "Is that why he tried to kill you? Because you knew?"

I laughed. "Naw. He'd of had plenty of chances for that before yesterday. Was it yesterday? Yeah, I guess it was. No, he tried to kill me because I'd killed Jacobbsen."

That made them both look at each other and then back at me. Hays said, "Say what?"

I said, "That and the fact that his daddy had probably just told him I'd taken Jacobbsen's place as the majority owner of Davis Mercantile."

Tom gave his head a little shake. He said, "Justa, I hope you can appreciate that I'm not understanding a word of what you're saying. I think you've just said that Alvin tried to kill you because you'd killed Jacobbsen, plus the fact that you'd replaced Jacobbsen as the majority owner of that store. As your lawyer, why are these revelations coming as such a surprise to me?"

I had to smile at that. Tom and Norris favored each other when it came to their sense of humor. Maybe it was something that was caused by reading a lot of books. I said, "Well, I really hadn't meant to mention any of it. But then Alvin went and pulled that stunt and got himself killed and now it doesn't seem to matter anymore. But before I had things kind of worked out, and it wouldn't have helped matters to have spread around what I knew."

Hays said, "Boss, are you going to tell us why Alvin wanted to kill you for killin' Jacobbsen, or do I have to bust?"

I sighed. I was physically worn out and tired of the whole mess, and wanted to forget about it. At least for the time being. But I knew they wouldn't let me rest until I'd blocked out the biggest part of it for them. I said, "All right, I'll tell you some of it. But what you have to do is try and understand Alvin Davis and his mother and his daddy, and that hellfire-and-brimstone church he belonged to, or ain't none of it going to make any sense."

Hays said, with a knowing air, "I allus thought he was a strange one."

Tom said, "Funny you never mentioned that to me. And I quizzed you about every soul in town."

I ignored them. "Alvin was wound as tight as the E string on a cheap guitar. I noticed it the first time I ever met him, when I was in jail. If you didn't look close, you'd of thought here was just a nice, normal town boy who was making some extra money as a deputy. But I looked close. Along about then I was looking close at everybody in that town, and Alvin interested me. He was so wound up, he just quivered. Besides that, I got to wondering why he'd want to be a deputy. Bandera didn't need a deputy. They barely needed a sheriff. But Alvin needed to be a deputy because it gave him a chance to preach to the evildoers. And them a captive audience, so to speak. I've heard he'd keep some poor old drunk locked up so he could read him the Bible when the drunk was about to die for a drink. Alvin converted a lot of those drunks that way. Hell, it would have converted me if I'd needed a drink bad enough."

I stopped and lit a cigar.

Tom made a waving motion with his hand. "All right, all right, we've got the picture. He was a religious zealot. How does that transpose to murder and attempted murder?"

When my cigar was going, I said, "You still haven't got the picture. *Zealot* is just a word. Alvin was a man and he was way on beyond zealot. The first time I tried to talk to him about Mary Mae Hawkins, he blew up in my face and practically said she had got what she had coming. That she was a harlot, a floozy, entertained men. Now that's pretty strong talk about a young woman who's just been murdered, saying she had it coming. Especially to the man who is accused of doing it."

"Is that when you got on to him?"

I shook my head. "No. It was a number of things. Remember that receipt for the load of supplies that had been billed to Grummet that we found at the Hawkins house? Alvin dropped that the day he killed her. He'd deliberately taken the delivery that day to Grummet's so he'd be near her house and nothing would be thought of it. You'll be a little surprised at the purpose of his visit."

Tom said, "Why, to rape and murder her."

I shook my head. "No. He didn't think he'd have to rape her. He thought she'd be willing. He was that naïve. And he certainly never expected to kill her. That was an accident. Or an incident that happened in the heat of the moment. He went there to kill Jacobbsen." I paused. "With his dick."

After a second Hays slapped his leg and looked out the window. "Aw, shit!" he said. "He's just pulling our leg. He ain't gonna tell us nothin'."

"I told you, you had to understand Alvin. That was probably the most confused young man I've ever seen. That's one of the reasons I had sympathy for him and was going to do what I was going to do. In a way you could say he was as crazy as Jacobbsen, but he wasn't. He was misguided. He was so pumped full of that Old Testament hell and damnation and a lot of that other bullshit his parents and that church were cramming down him that he just couldn't handle it. Gentlemen, that boy thought he had a mission." I leaned toward them. "A mission. Believe it or not, when he confessed to me about what had happened to Mary Mae Hawkins, he told me about his mission. It was to rid the world of evil. And to him Dag Jacobbsen was the most evil man in the world. He was the devil incarnate. He knew because he'd heard his mother say it often enough. Before Jacobbsen came, there were no whores over at the Lantern Saloon, there were practically no saloons, there were no toughs in town walking the sidewalks like they were decent citizens, there was no cussing, there was no card playing. And everybody went to church. They didn't have enough money to do anything else. As far as the Davis family was concerned, the devil himself might as well have set up shop up there at Treetops. Of course, that didn't keep them from enjoying the extra trade that Jacobbsen brought in. That was only right and was probably what kept him from just suddenly going up in flames one day."

Hays said, "An' you mean he was gonna try and kill Jacobbsen? That boy? He'd of been cut down before he could have got within a hunnert yards."

"He knew that," I said. I was about halfway beginning to enjoy myself, watching their faces try to follow the crooked path that had taken me so long to work out. "He didn't want to shoot him. He wanted to pay him off in kind. And Mary Mae as well. He knew Jacobbsen was fucking Mary because he'd slipped out there many a night and spied on them through the window. He told me so himself, told me how it just made his skin crawl to see that animal lust, said he could just see the fires of hell burning in them."

Hays said, "I bet he had it in his hand while he was a-watchin'."

"You'll remember I sent Ben around to check and see if he went with any of the local girls," I said. "When Ben said no, I knew I had me a real religious fanatic on my hands. Now, I've known some religious fanatics in my time, and without exception every one of them has had to have a release in some form. Alcohol or women. Sometimes both. That's when I went up to see the girls over at the Lantern. I found out that Alvin was a regular customer but a kind of strange one. I started out offering twenty dollars to get them to talk about him, but it ended up costing more to get the whole story. They were kind of ashamed. It seemed Alvin preached to them first. Then they had to repent for their sins. Down on their knees. Then they had to swear to live better. Then he fucked whichever one he thought needed the most help."

Tom was shaking his head slowly. "My God," he said. "Who'd of thought it. Then what?"

"Then young Alvin catches himself a dose of the clap. Or he thinks he does. Anyway, he's got the drips. He goes around to the doctor, but the doctor can't be sure. As you know—or maybe you don't, Tom—you can strain yourself lifting heavy loads and get the drips same as the clap.

"But that ain't the point. The point is that Alvin thinks he's got the clap and he comes up with this plan. He's going to go out and fuck Mary Mae and she'll get it. Then Jacobbsen will come along and fuck her and he'll get it and then they'll both die."

Tom said, "Die?"

I leaned forward. "Alvin believed that the clap was *fatal*. He expected to die, too, but at least he'd be taking two of the devil's helpers with him."

Tom shook his head again. "That poor guy. Poor, misguided, ignorant bastard. Sounds like his parents are the ones ought to have been shot. And he told you all this?"

I snapped my fingers. "Just like that. He had so much pent up in him, he couldn't wait to bust. I walked him down to the church and got him in there and confronted him with what I knew, and he let fly. Left him crying his eyes out. Besides that, he was sick at heart because he'd found out he didn't have the clap."

"Was he sorry about killing the Hawkins woman?"

The coach hit a bump and I had to wait while we swayed back and forth. "He's not real clear about that. Or he wasn't. I keep forgetting he's dead. He's not even sure how he killed her. He remembers having her down on the daybed, and she was struggling, and then, while he was trying to get his pants down, she broke free and ran. He picked up a stick of stove wood and fetched her a lick and knocked her down and then brought her back to the bed. He can't remember if she was struggling after that. He knows he had his hands around her neck, but he can't remember which time."

"Did he rape her?"

"He says he didn't. Not that it matters. He remembers sort of coming to and noticing she'd gotten real still. After that he said he just got out of there as fast as he could."

Hays said, kind of plaintively, "But you still ain't told us why he wanted to kill you."

I smiled. I could see from Tom's face that he knew. I said, "Tell him, Tom."

The lawyer said to Hays, "Didn't you hear what he was screaming when he ran at Justa with that shotgun?"

Hays looked blank. "Don't know for sure. Somethin' about a sword, but I didn't see no sword."

"He was yelling at me that he was the Sword of Jehovah. Understand?"

"Naw."

Tom said, "He was the sword, Alvin. It was his duty—no, his right—to kill Jacobbsen because he was the Sword of Jehovah. And Justa had done him out of that—I won't call it Christian—duty, and Justa had to pay for it."

Hays's mouth fell open. "I swan," he said. "That boy was more than a little mixed up."

"I think his daddy triggered it," I said. "I think he told Alvin that I had replaced Jacobbsen as the real owner of the store. Maybe even told him I'd been whoring with Marriah. That I was probably as sinful as Jacobbsen. I could never prove it, but I halfway believe he sent Alvin out there to kill me."

Tom asked, "I wonder where Jacobbsen got that majority share of the store. Did Davis get in financial trouble and have to go to him for a loan?"

I smiled. "No. Jacobbsen knew that Alvin had killed Mary. He didn't give a shit about that, but it just gave him another little game of meanness to play. So he went to Davis and made him give him the controlling interest in the store. In return Jacobbsen would find another sucker, in this case me, to confess to the crime."

Hays said, "What in hell did Jacobbsen need with that puny little store?"

"He didn't. As much money as Jacobbsen had, it was about like adding another drop of water to the Colorado River. But he loved power, he loved to push people around. Just more meanness, another person he could make lick his boots."

"Yeah, but what I don't understand is what you wanted with that interest," Tom said.

I smiled slightly. "Maybe for the same reason. Maybe meanness. By the way, it was him took that shot at me. The one who hit my saddle horn. I got that out of him when I was getting a lot of other stuff out of him and he saw the game was up and I was holding the cards. He wanted me out of that country, and bad. He knew I was getting close to the truth and, worse, I was stirring Jacobbsen up. But I wanted that controlling interest for several reasons, and only one of them was meanness, you'll be glad to know."

"What?"

I looked out the window. "I made a deal with Davis. He was to send Alvin away, completely away from all the influences of that town and that church and himself and his wife. I didn't care where they sent him, so long as it was far away and under different conditions."

"And he agreed to that?"

Through the open window I could see that it was beginning to green up. We were leaving the hard-rock country and the terrain was beginning to gentle down and soften up and look more hospitable. "Oh, yes. You see, Mr. Morris Davis made an awful lot of noise about what a good churchgoer he was and how he sung the loudest in Sunday school and seen to the welfare of his soul and the souls of others whether they needed it or not. But I knew where his real god was. And it wasn't in that church. It was in his cash register. He said his prayers over his account books and done his psalm singing every time that delivery wagon of his went out with a load of goods. Oh, yes, he agreed. I made it simple for him. So long as he sent Alvin away and neither he nor his wife put any more strain on him, then I was going to leave his store alone. But if he didn't, and he understood I'd be watching from afar, I was going to step in and own me a mercantile."

"You mean, he put his store before his son?"

"Didn't I tell you I think he sent Alvin out there to shoot me? Or at least put the idea in his head? Wouldn't have taken much."

"I see," Tom said. He puffed on his cigar. "And if Alvin hadn't rushed you, and Ben hadn't shot him dead, you were just going to leave town? Just like that? Without a word? Leave a murderer on the loose?"

"Didn't I just tell you I'd made arrangements for Alvin to go away?"

"But he'd still have been a murderer."

I leaned back and yawned. "Tom, I ain't in social work. And I don't give a damn what gets loose in that particular town. They can kill each other for all I care. Let's just get us that part straight before I say I don't think that boy was a killer. Mary Mae Hawkins was an accident, just a bad piece of luck for both parties. As for that attempt at me . . . Didn't you see him with that shotgun? He could have cut me down from the boardwalk. Hell, he could have never left the store, just shot me through the door. I was standing there with my back to him. He couldn't have missed. But what does he do? He comes charging out into the middle of the street yelling his fool head off. Making enough noise to rouse the dead. And all that with you and Ben and Norris and Hays and Wall and a U.S. Marshal standing right there. All armed, all excellent with guns. Except you. And one exceptional, Ben. Not even counting me. And I think I'd of had time to fire the way he kept coming and not shooting. Figure he wasn't very smart, but you'd have had to be awful dumb to come charging at a man with a shotgun in your hands, screaming threats, and him with friends all around. Don't you reckon he had some idea what was going to happen?"

"You think he did it on purpose? Some sort of punishment? Some form of atonement?"

I tried to get more comfortable on the seat, but my sore back just couldn't find a spot. We still had half an hour to go, and I badly wanted a short nap. "Well, I'll tell you, Mr. Hudspeth," I said. "I ain't a authority on religious fanatics and I don't claim to know what their minds get up to. What's more, unless I am personally affected, which I'm not anymore, I don't give a damn. I will leave it to the learned counsel to mull over and figure out." I tried to arrange myself on the seat. "Now, I have told ya'll everything I know to tell you." I managed to get part of me laid down on the seat. "So ring the bell. School is out. I am going to try and get some sleep."

Hays said, "Boss, they's a pillow up there on the overhang. You want me to fetch it down for you so's you'll have something to rest your head on?"

I opened one eye. "Hays, don't try sucking up to me. It won't do you a damn bit of good. I ain't taking back but one of your fines, and that one only because you taught my brother to cheat at cards. And when we get to the Half-Moon, I am going to work your ass off."

He looked a little anxious. "But I'm supposed to be working for Ben."

"Suppose again. I'm not letting you two work together. I know what kind of work would come out. Couple of monkeys would do more."

Tom said, "Might as well give up, Ray. He's a hard man."

Which reminded me of something I'd been meaning to mention to the lawyer ever since we'd left Bandera. It wasn't ordinary of me to overlook such matters. I supposed it was fatigue. I said, "Tom, I want to square accounts with Morris Davis. When we get to San Antonio, I'm going to give you that instrument applying to the mercantile. You've already got my power of attorney. I want you to run Davis out of business. Appoint a manager to go down there and take over. I don't care how you do it, just get it done."

He sort of raised his eyebrows. "Isn't Davis pretty small game for you, Justa?"

I raised up on an elbow. "He tried to fuck with me, didn't he? Didn't he mean me harm?"

Tom said, "Well, yes, I suppose he did. In several ways. Took a shot at you certainly."

"But he mainly didn't follow our agreement about Alvin. He was supposed to send him away. But not to the graveyard. And especially not out to kill me."

Tom shrugged. "If you say so. Seems like a lot of powder and shot for a small bug."

"Listen, Tom . . . I want you to understand something. You may work for us again. My family believes in playing just as straight as we can with everybody. If we make a mistake, we'll square accounts if it breaks us. If you make a mistake against us, we'll still square accounts if it breaks us. That applies to all customers, big or small. We keep a strict ledger."

Tom nodded slowly. "All right. It'll be done. I think I'm just now starting to understand some things about you and your brothers."

"And my father," I said. My eyes were starting to close. I said, "Wake me up when we get to San Antonio. Hays, we've got some hard dealing to do there, and you better act a hell of a lot smarter than I've seen in the past."

Just before I slipped off, I heard Tom say, "I think I'll stay on his good side. How about you?"

I didn't hear what Hays said. I was finally starting to unwind and I could feel a good sleep creeping up on me, the kind of sleep it didn't seem like I'd had in years.

ABOUT THE AUTHOR

Giles Tippette is a Texan by birth and by choice. He has earned his living as a writer since 1966. Prior to that he was a venture pilot, a mercenary, a diamond courier, and a bucking event rodeo cowboy. In addition to his books, he has written over 500 articles for such magazines as *Time*, *Newsweek*, *Sports Illustrated*, *Esquire*, and *Texas Monthly*. He presently lives in San Angelo, Texas.